P9-BZI-411

This novel, like all my work, is first dedicated to the Almighty . . . and to all those good, hardworking souls out there who labor so hard for justice, try to do the right thing, and who hold the line no matter what others around them do, or how they profit.

In that regard, this novel is also dedicated to my dad, who passed in September 2004 . . . ya did good—thanks for the indelible community service legacy and for being such a wonderful father! You, Mom, and all my aunties and grand-parents are now angels on my shoulder. Bless you all for the love that never wavered.

BLIND TRUST

BLIND TRUST

LESLIE ESDAILE BANKS

Kensington Publishing Corp.
http://www.kensingtonbooks.com

DAFINA BOOKS are published by

Kensington Publishing Corp.
850 Third Avenue
New York, NY 10022

Copyright © 2005 by Leslie Esdaile Banks

All rights reserved. No part of this book may be reproduced in any form or by any means without the prior written consent of the Publisher, excepting brief quotes used in reviews.

If you purchased this book without a cover, you should be aware that this book is stolen property. It was reported as "unsold and destroyed" to the Publisher and neither the Author nor the Publisher has received any payment for this "stripped book."

All Kensington Titles, Imprints, and Distributed Lines are available at special quantity discounts for bulk purchases for sales promotions, premiums, fund-raising, educational or institutional use. Special book excerpts or customized printings can also be created to fit specific needs. For details, write or phone the office of the Kensington special sales manager: Kensington Publishing Corp., 850 Third Avenue, New York, NY 10022, attn. Special Sales Department, Phone: 1-800-221-2647.

Dafina and the Dafina logo Reg. U.S. Pat. & TM Off.

ISBN-13: 978-0-7582-0736-4
ISBN-10: 0-7582-0736-0

First trade paperback printing: September 2005
First mass market printing: February 2009

10 9 8 7 6 5 4 3 2 1

Printed in the United States of America

Acknowledgments

I would like to acknowledge as always, my agent, Manie Barron, my editor, Karen Thomas, the Kensington staff, fan club president, Zulma Gonzalez, as well as Patricia Peterson . . . a group of individuals who are friends and family, who are always there, always so supportive, and who simply inspire just because of who they are.

My family, husband and children, are also in that number—people who always love me, no matter how crazy I am or act, but support every endeavor, suffer through my muse binges and pizza dinners over protracted periods of time, but still hug me at the end of the day. *Thank you!*

Chapter
1

Grand Cayman Island . . .
Present day, after the storms . . .

He hadn't called. She hadn't asked him to come. Detective James Carter hadn't even sent a postcard or birthday card. Her birthday was in November, his was in April, and neither had made contact. But hadn't that been the way she'd wanted it? Almost one full calendar year had passed. The lies she'd told herself had worn thin. She'd stopped checking the mail and running for the telephone months ago. She'd survived a miscarriage alone, while he'd apparently dealt with a miscarriage of justice by himself.

It seemed they both quietly understood that they had to do what they had to do. Everything in her life had been decimated. Her parents were dead. His parents were dead. She'd lost the baby to an early miscarriage. Although she'd survived, layers of her life had splintered and peeled away like the wood from her villa. Her faith . . . What was that these days? It seemed like the good died young and those who were evil lingered indefinitely to do more injustice—unless helped to a timely demise. None of it was fair. None of it was right. But it was what it was . . . and there wasn't a soul on the planet who could understand the depth of her losses, or who she could fully share the pain with, not without revealing too much. Laura had to take care of Laura.

With everything else that had been washed away, why wouldn't what she'd briefly shared with James Carter have been as well? They hadn't been together long enough to cement anything between them. Then again, had they been together for years, the cracks and fissures in any old mortar they might have shared would have surely given way.

Her island home was now mere rubble after a category five hurricane. Vengeance also apparently gave as good as she got. There was no sanctuary from any of it.

"Miss Caldwell," her manservant said, "please consider coming back, once all of this is behind us. It will take at least six to eight months, they're saying, before all of this is sorted out." He looked around in despair at what had been a palatial villa. "But we should get you to the airport soon. The roads are still questionable, at best." His wife simply sighed and walked away with tears in her eyes.

Laura nodded toward the graying couple, not really looking in their direction. Yes, Mr. And Mrs. Melville understood, just like she also intimately understood the emotions that underscored loss. Things should have been different, but they weren't. What was supposed to just be a tropical storm had become something so much worse.

James should have seen this place before it was destroyed. They should have had breathless nights here, his thick, six foot five, chocolate frame enveloping hers . . . their child sleeping peacefully in her crib. But their relationship never stood a chance and she'd never carried his child to term. Just like the devastating storm, the loss had been an act of God. She remembered James's eyes, though. A year away from him couldn't erase that.

All of it crowded into her soul so quickly that she couldn't speak as she picked her way around the perimeter of what had been her villa, knowing true disaster would never be fully behind her. The past was a specter, it was a living and violently haunting thing. Just like they named hurricanes, old deeds also had enough velocity and force to shatter and take lives. Perhaps those things seemingly past needed to be given a name, too. But it was probably best that no one did.

Splinters of pink wood lay strewn along the sparkling white sand . . . like flesh of the house torn away from the frame, bones. It was all gone. The sun had the nerve to be out strutting her stuff, stunning in the aftermath. Laura wondered if that was how she'd appeared to others when she'd shown up at the funeral in a designer ensemble, her black hat elegantly tipped to the side with a dramatic veil. Flossing, like the sun, without censure or shame . . . a contributor to a murder, much in the same way the sun's warm air masses had collided with a cold front to create a force of nature to be reckoned with.

What did Senator Scott do in the aftermath of his niece's death? Did he walk around in a daze, wondering about all his past deeds that led up to the shamble of his life? Although she wasn't a direct contributor, Laura had to admit that she'd provided the heat in the system, and Monica Price was dead. *That*, she'd take to her grave.

Turquoise blue waters lapped against the beach, returning sodden deck furniture with its attention. Ruins were washing up on the shore. Laura wondered as she stared down at the waterlogged personal effects, what battered part of her life might one day wash up on a beautiful coast?

Shards of stained glass mingled with coral, seaweed, and downed silver thatch palm branches on what had once been her front steps. Dead birds, that had once been gorgeous jewel-green hued parrots, were ugly, bloated, sand covered, and gray. Like her furniture, the birds were hardly recog-

nizable as they lay in nature's open morgue beside dead
shellfish and injured turtles that had simply become part of
the sewage now taking up the center of the road. No power,
water only in sporadic, rationed quantities, fuel was almost
nonexistent.

Yes, it was time to go back to Philly.

A full year, almost, and not a call from her. She'd dropped
off the face of the earth, just like she'd promised she would.

But despite the court cases, the grand jury indictments,
and trials that he and his partner, Steve, had to endure testimony at as cops . . . and despite knowing in his soul that she
was as guilty as sin, he couldn't get Laura Caldwell out of
his mind. Tall, cinnamon-skinned, curvaceous, crazy . . . with
short, dark, velvety hair and legs that could stop traffic on
Broad Street. Unforgettable. Dangerous as hell. Sexy enough
to make a man reconsider his badge. Lethal.

James held the twisted hunks of metal in his fist. The moment the funeral director had quietly summoned him from
the hospital, he knew what the melted fragments were—the
cell phones she'd used to set up and take down a family empire. Being a detective had its advantages. Favors were always
being curried. The good senator had obviously forewarned
his man to give anything to the cop who could be trusted.

The irony was profound; the senator worried that an old
Blackberry or Palm Pilot stashed in a cremation-destined coffin
by Monica's friend, Laura, might indict him—but Laura had
hidden evidence that would have taken them both down
and cleared the Price-Scott family name.

That was the problem with double-dealing. Sometimes
you played yourself. This time, unwittingly, the senator had
given away the keys to his kingdom. He now owed a morti-
cian. The senator probably thought he also owed a cop, big
time. Maybe he did. It might buy Laura more amnesty, if the

good senator thought she was protecting his family interests to the very end. In any event, it was an excellent marker to have out there in the streets to call in one day. The woman had brass balls.

James rubbed his tender thigh that still ached in certain weather. He still walked with a slight limp. The cycles of bullshit never ceased. Where was his woman, and who was she with?

He leaned against the stern rail of the cruise ship and waited, allowing the sharp fall breeze to cut at his face. Raw winds took up residence in the old gunshot wound in his thigh, making the muscles begin to knot. Over forty wasn't no joke. But she wore it well . . . last time he saw her, at forty-four, Laura Caldwell was drop dead fine. He'd always envisioned taking a cruise with her, versus a cruise to nowhere to simply cover her tracks. But he had to let the past go while in international waters . . . just like it was time to let Laura go. It was over. She hadn't called for him. Hadn't remembered the hot nights that were still burned into his skull forever. James opened his hand and watched the charred remains of her many lies fall from his palm and disappear beneath the churning water's dark surface.

Maybe it was better that way.

Laura put the key into the front door of her Pennsylvania Avenue home in Philadelphia and turned off the alarm as she crossed the threshold. There were no suitcases to set down. Her handbag was the only weight on her shoulder—that and her conscience. It was so quiet that her shallow breaths echoed throughout the immaculately kept space.

She glanced around. The maid had been diligent. Nothing seemed out of place, except her. This wasn't home, it was a place to crash and burn. She'd never owned a real home; everything in her name was simply real estate.

Weary beyond imagination, she moved throughout the sand-colored environment. Her mind still had the beach within it; salt water and surf still stung her nose. The fall was beautiful back East, the colors profound. But there was no sun like Caribbean sun, no water so blue on the planet. No ebony sculpted body like James's. Yet, paradise had ousted her. Cosmic justice.

Johnny Walker Black was calling her name. James used to drink that, she remembered, as she dropped her barrel Coach purse on the crescent shaped secretary and hung up her Burberry raincoat. A lot of things were calling her name. She hadn't been in a man's arms in a year. Hadn't really laughed, except when her sisters and her cousin, Najira, came to visit. But that was different. There were things they couldn't discuss, things that they couldn't comprehend through a mere glance. Suddenly, being within her own space felt hollow.

He nursed a Grand Marnier from the observation deck, wondering why he'd chosen her old drink instead of his. Nostalgia had him in a headlock. He saluted the wide-open sea with his brandy snifter. Good riddance to a bad woman. A Scorpio woman could be poison. She'd been trouble since the day he'd laid eyes on her, worse from the moment he'd put his hands on her. Now what was he going to do?

Going back to life on the force was out of the question. Early retirement, then what? Now that the trials were over, Steve had suggested that they open a PI agency, but hunting for criminals, even for way better pay, had lost its appeal. Although he and that crazy, roughneck white boy would make one helluva team. Still. The thing with Laura had been a mission. She'd helped him solve his father's murder, and put the past behind him. Justice got served, even though it wasn't legal. James raised his glass to the sky; may the dead rest in peace. Mission accomplished. Anything else was just something to do. Just like jumping on this ship was something to do, all the amenities of being here felt like something critical was missing. Laura.

She stared at the telephone, willing it to ring and then laughed out loud at her own insanity, snatched it, and punched in the number she knew by heart.

His hip vibrated and he let out a long, annoyed breath. But when he stared at the number, his thumb hit the receive button so fast that he almost disconnected the call.

"Hey," her voice said, coming through the line like a silk noose.

He pressed the phone closer to his ear and shut his eyes—instantly hung. "Where you been at, girl?"

"Home . . . Detective. Why?"

"So now I'm just 'Detective' again?"

She laughed. He was slightly pissed. Where had she been and why hadn't she called?

"No, James, you're more than that." She chuckled. "Why so testy, though? 'Hello, baby,' would've been nicer."

"Ain't heard from you in a long time. A man might have a few questions."

"And I haven't heard from you . . . in, like, a year, James."

He could hear a tinge of annoyance in her voice that was comforting.

"Lotta trials. A lot of things had to be made neat."

She smiled and closed her eyes. Of course, that made sense. Wise move. "Yeah. True. On both ends."

"Cool."

Silence rippled between them.

"You busy?" she asked carefully.

He could tell she was listening to his environment, as

though sensing his whereabouts. He liked that. "I'll have to get back to you in a few days."

"Oh," she murmured. "So, it's like that, now. I understand."

He stared at the horizon. She'd never understand, just like he'd never tell her that he hadn't been with anybody while waiting for her call like a fool. He didn't want to know if she hadn't. That would fuck him up worse than he already was now. "You hear, but you don't hear," he said, his tone distant.

She hesitated. "What don't I hear, James?"

"That I'm somewhere that won't allow me to get back tonight."

She chuckled. "Tell her I said—"

"Her name is *Sea Farer's Mist,* and she's about as long as a football field—"

"What! *You* took a cruise and didn't come see me? Why?"

Laughter filled his ear and coated his insides with her warmth. He took a sip of his drink and winced. "Yeah, I took a cruise, alone. All right? And the ship just crossed into international waters about an hour ago."

A long silence numbed the line.

"I had to put some *heavy* things to rest. Hear me?"

Another long pause greeted him, and he could hear her swallow.

"Thank you for the belated birthday present." She stirred the liquor in her short rocks glass with her finger. The lack of calls and correspondence made so much sense. James was a practical man; that was one of the things she loved most about him. His mind.

"Don't mention it," he finally murmured. How did a man forget a Scorpio woman? Especially when the nature of their relationship needed to remain off all radar. "What are you drinking?"

"Johnny Walker. Black. For old times' sake."

He smiled.

"I said thank you," she said, her tone growing gentler.

"Yeah," he said quietly, thinking of how to catch a plane the moment he hit landfall. "You can do that later."

"Was on my agenda anyway, baby."

Donald Haines drove slowly as he came off the Schuylkill Expressway and tried to remember which way to turn to access the Girard Avenue Bridge. From there he'd have to make a left, or was it a right, to go by the park to meet his friend, Mr. Akhan. Good thing he'd allowed extra time in case he got lost. But the very fact that he had to mentally struggle at the directions he should have known in his sleep, told him all he needed to know. It was time to end the game.

Finally bringing his silver-gray Mercedes to a rest at the curb, he remembered how Akhan liked things done. Neat. He would get out, walk to a bench, sit quietly and wait for his aged, fatigue-wearing comrade, who often donned African robes and sandals under his ragged combat gear. Akhan would pass him with a nod to signal that they might walk a bit together and talk where there were no walls with ears. Then they would sit like two obscure old men on the benches. One from the Main Line, one from North Philadelphia, one an Anglo aristocrat, the other a dignified black activist . . . and they would see eye to eye, before returning to their very private, powerful lives.

A shudder ran through Donald Haines as he smoothed the velvet lapels on his herringbone tweed chesterfield, grabbed a large manila envelope off the passenger's seat, and got out of his sedan. Brisk winds cut through the warmth of his coat. It was raw outside, just like his nerves had become.

He found a bench quickly and sat down, glancing over his shoulder. What if it was the wrong park, or the wrong day? Mild panic began to seize his breath and it made him stand and glance around with added purpose, his motions jerky as perspiration began to cover his skin. Hot tears of frustration rose to his eyes, blurring the dangerous-looking images around him. Shadows of humanity seemed to be everywhere. The park had predators, drug addicts and dealers, all lying in wait for an unarmed white stranger from a neighborhood far from here.

As a thick-bodied man approached, bearing a face he didn't recognize, Donald clutched his manila envelope tighter. He had a right to be in a public park. "Get back," he said through his teeth. "Get away from me."

"Old friend," Akhan said, his tone soothing. "Let us sit today and watch the birds. A stroll may be too taxing."

Donald Haines relaxed as his mind grappled with the dark image before him. The man's face was vaguely familiar. Ruddy skin, wise old eyes. His bald head shielded beneath a crocheted knit cap. A bright orange dashiki peeking out from under a weathered, military green army jacket. Brown corduroy pants that ended at dingy white socks and sandals. He let his breath out in relief. "Mr. Akhan. You came."

Akhan nodded and sat first, peering up at Donald Haines. His once steel blue eyes seemed clouded by fear. His normally immaculate, barbered blond hair was out of place, as though someone had been chasing him. Although he wore an expensive coat, he still had the appearance of being slightly disheveled. "Why wouldn't I?"

"I don't know . . . one can never be sure how things will turn out." Donald Haines glanced around and then sat slowly beside Akhan.

"We go way back, you and I," Akhan said calmly, trying to stem the alarm coursing through him. Haines didn't look well. "The hour of the call, the sound of your voice, I knew it was important."

Nodding quickly, Donald Haines thrust the manila envelope toward Akhan. "I changed this right after Laura left town—so it should hold up."

Akhan accepted the package but studied his ally's face. "Talk to me, Donald. We are too old to play cat and mouse."

Haines leaned in and then shut his eyes. "I'm losing my mind," he whispered and then sat back and studied the sky.

Neither man spoke as Donald collected his emotions and tucked them away. Akhan was a patient man, always had been.

"Alzheimer's, is what they're saying," Donald Haines finally murmured. "For a man with as many secrets as I have . . . I cannot start babbling, or begin speaking to the wrong person at the wrong time. Cancer I could have accepted—but not this." He balled his fists tightly and then opened his hands slowly as he stared at them. "My medical records are in there as well . . . should I say something incriminating, it can be chalked up to the insane ranting of an old man with a diagnosed condition. You might need to have that as a defense one day. My will is in there, too, with a notarized alteration to it that was done long before I became less than myself. Guard these records well, my friend."

Akhan nodded as he addressed the brilliant blue fall sky. "Ashe," he said quietly. "Ashe."

"I have too much personal dignity to be held hostage in my own home by a wife who despises me, or be sequestered to a bedroom, drooling on myself, with a fucking day nurse to wipe my face and my ass." Haines spun on Akhan, holding his line of vision with rage glittering in his eyes. "After all you and I have been through, this final indignity cannot be!"

Akhan nodded and closed his eyes. "And you have come for a last favor."

"Between friends."

Akhan nodded. "Between friends." He looked down at the manila envelope. "I would have done it for free, you know. We have history."

"Yes, and because we have history, I want you to be sure that everyone who is supposed to get what they deserve, does."

Again, neither man spoke as the far off sounds of street traffic filled the void.

"They will be hiring a nurse?" Akhan asked quietly, not looking at Haines.

"Yes. Soon I won't be allowed to go out alone or drive, and my telephones at home are already compromised." Haines looked toward the tree line. "Please make sure she's skilled so I don't choke to death on my own vomit."

"It will be quiet and in your sleep," Akhan said, standing slowly. "You are owed that much."

"Thank you," Haines whispered as he stood. "But . . . I don't suppose we could just walk one last time, you and I? I will miss our collusion as we strolled." He gazed up at the sky and then at the dilapidated mansions that rimmed the park. "There just wasn't enough time to fix all the wrongs."

"No," Akhan said, as they began to stroll. "We fixed so much and then had to tear down so much . . ."

Donald Haines let out a long, weary breath. "That's why I had to concede to the gaming industry coming to this state. It's the cycle of political life—you itch, I scratch, then vice versa." He searched the sky for words as sentences began to elude him. "It was out of my hands," Haines said with another weary sigh. "For a hundred twenty-five million in city program funds routed the way I wanted, I had to give the state level a pint of blood."

Akhan clasped his hands behind his back as they continued their lazy stroll across what had become park badlands. "Legislators are allowed to enter into blind trusts . . . one percent personal equity in each of fourteen slot charters, which means they could own up to fourteen percent at any one time without having to ever make the public aware of their interests. They don't have to show a paper trail on any lobbyist forms; only the blind trust has to be named."

Haines chuckled, but the sound was laced with pain. "See, my friend. I was already becoming senile, then. Insane."

"Crazy like a fox," Akhan said with a knowing smile. "Oh, no, Donald, I am sure you had a plan."

When Donald Haines didn't answer, but only smiled in return, Akhan pressed his point. But the tone of his voice was not accusatory, just a bland statement of fact. "The casino industry will descend upon the region like vultures, and will also bring the rest of their more unsavory businesses and colleagues with them." He stopped walking and looked at Haines hard. "Donald, they made you give up more than a pint. Under any circumstances, that is not like you to get cheated."

"For a man who has run out of time to use his mind . . . where his influence is dwindling and health failing as his son begins to realign his assets, I decided to offer them my head on a silver platter rather than lovely Laura's. It was only a pint," he said with a sad smile. "I'm already dying and can do without the transfusion of more assets. Let it rest."

They began walking again. For a long time neither man spoke.

"I had to allow my Italian friends to bring their casino interests here," Haines said casually after a while. "I owed them for the Paxton situation, even though I paid in cash— we know that cash is merely the down payment. Until a favor is bestowed, a solid one, it doesn't count. Besides, who will ever keep my busy little bee, Elizabeth, from unraveling all our good work?"

"Ashe," Akhan said deep in thought. "Your wife could be very . . . It could get complicated."

"If I begin talking in my sleep or begin to forget how much she hates me?" Haines nodded. "Yes. Now you really understand. So rather than also have her sudden, yet timely, demise on my soul when I die, why don't we simply take my piece off the board. I'm only sparing her for my son's sake. That's the least I can do for him after she ruined him." He stopped walking and held Akhan's shoulder. "The king is finally down, even though the queen is still alive. But it was a good game. Checkmate."

"It was a good game, indeed," Akhan said, placing a firm hand on Haines's shoulder to match his stance. "And I shall miss our walks."

Donald Haines nodded, and then glanced around. New tears suddenly rose to his eyes and then burned away. "Show me to my car, old friend. I cannot remember where I've parked it."

She heard a heavy motor enter her street, stop, and back up. Laura quickly got up from the sofa, closed her cream silk robe and tied it hard, and then walked to the front bay window. She stared out at a vehicle that she didn't recognize. Frozen, she watched the black Sequoia with tinted windows pull into her driveway. She immediately cut the lights and moved toward the closet to retrieve her father's peacekeeper from the hatbox perched high on the top shelf. At five A.M. this wasn't a pop call from friends and family, it was most likely a hit. If so, she had an old .357 Magnum to address it.

She slid against the wall and glimpsed out of the window without moving the butter hued sheer curtains, and then smiled.

Chapter
2

He watched the garage door slowly open and smiled as he turned off the engine, then got out of his SUV. She was standing deep within the darkened space, clutching the front of her silk robe closed and holding a gun down at her side. Just like old times. Her svelte form stole his attention away from the weapon. He loved how the cold morning air created goose bumps on her forearms and made her nipples stand up under the thin fabric. Her smile was a magnet. He gave her a brief nod of recognition and was rewarded by her low, sexy chuckle as she shook her head.

For a moment, all she could do was stare at him. The man looked too good in an olive turtleneck and black bomber jacket, casual black slacks pressed to military precision, cuff dropped just so over his leather slip-on shoes. James had grown a beard . . . a neat, trimmed covering of shadow over his jaw that connected to a new thin mustache. He'd ditched his department issued Crown Victoria for a new truck. What else about him had changed?

"You want some coffee?" she finally asked, finding her voice.

He smiled wider. "Isn't this how it all got started before?"

"Possibly. But you could have rung the doorbell to give me fair warning."

He motioned toward the gun with his chin. "The last time I rang your doorbell, I got shot."

She laughed. "Then I take it coffee is out?"

He stepped inside the garage as she hit the button to close the door behind them. "You got anything a little stronger in here?"

"I might have something you like in here." She turned and walked away, going deeper into the garage and up the basement stairs.

Understatement. He watched the muscles in her firm ass knead beneath her robe. "Should I have parked around the corner, like old times?"

"No. I don't think anybody is looking for me these days," she said over her shoulder without glancing back at him, but with mirth clear in her voice. "Why? You worried?"

He didn't answer as she paced through the house toward the dining room. He was too awed by the view of her from behind. A year was a long time, and his memory was coming back quickly as an ache in his groin. He watched her lay the gun on the table and then move to the small glass bar, fill a short rocks tumbler, and hand it to him with a smile. He accepted the glass, but set it down carefully without taking a sip.

"I missed you," he said quietly. And then touched her face.

She closed her eyes and turned her mouth into the cup of his palm. "I missed you, too," she murmured, sending her warm breath against his hand.

That was all he needed to hear. Where she'd been and what she'd been doing was irrelevant at the moment. He lowered his mouth to hers as he stepped in closer, sealing off the slight space that had been between them. The intended slow kiss became an instant tongue battle. She felt so good in his arms, and her body molded against his as though they'd been sheered from the same piece of skin. Her cool fingers slid under his jacket and up his back, producing a shiver that made him hold her tighter, kiss her deeper, and then need to break from her mouth to keep himself from passing out.

The hundred questions that he'd nursed for a year fled his brain as her low murmur chased them away. The swell of her behind under his hands eclipsed speculation. Her soft skin was a hallucinogen. Yeah, she was guilty, but so what. She was his.

Her body moved like a pulse against him, warming every extremity, making him pull off his jacket and drop it to the floor as the room temperature steadily rose. Her touch traced his back, then his ass, and shot up his spine like liquid heat to find his shoulders. He pulled in her scent, her pendulous breasts pressed against his torso. A year was way too long; the dining room table was only steps away. Her hand went to his chest as he began to lift her.

"I missed you, too," she said, tearing her mouth from his. "But I'm trying to be practical."

He nodded, pulled the knot out of her robe sash and made it fall to her feet, then found the curve of her neck. "I am practical," he whispered hard against her throat as his hands covered her breasts. "Practically out of my mind."

He watched her lean into his palms and grimace, and then cup his behind and extract his wallet from his back pocket. She held it in her fist, nearly crushing the contents as he picked her up and slid her across the table, spilling his drink. A loaded gun was close to his temple; a Lenox bowl, imperiled.

"Tell me you brought more than your driver's license."

He closed his eyes and answered her on a deep exhale. "Yeah. You'd said thank you, remember?"

She thrust her tongue into his ear and whispered, "Yes . . ."

Dark amber liquor fused with ivory lace and mahogany. Her clean washed scent became one with Johnny Walker Black and sex. The sound of her nightgown rustling to the floor blended with shoes thudding in a collision with Oriental carpet-covered wood, heavy clothes and his belt dropping, a sweater being shorn away, the rip of foil as her voice ripped the ceiling. Blinding entry staggered breath. Lenox danced toward the edge of certain calamity. Damn, he'd missed this woman.

No lights, daybreak only cast gray, moving shadows against the dining room's bone walls and art, creating living frescoes. A rocks glass finally rolled the length of the table, dropped, and shattered when it fell. Acapella memories. Sound lit a dead house. A bowl wobbled and tried to survive. Chippendale groaned as it was christened. Damn, she'd missed this man.

Her calves found anchor around thick, muscular thighs, and then followed the high natural curve of hardworking sinew to clamp the dip in his spine. One hand held a steel cabled bicep too large to fully grasp, the other, the edge of furniture that could tip at any moment. Baritone questions pummeled her ear, her senses, her womb, sending pleasure through her stroke by stroke.

"Oh, God, baby, where have you been?"

How could she answer that when she couldn't even think!

"Promise me you ain't goin' nowhere like that again."

She nodded, kept her eyes shut tight, and allowed tears to stream down the sides of her face as her answer.

"Don't you know how I feel about you, woman?"

A sharp inhale that produced a windpipe gasp was all she could offer as the first convulsion hit her.

A year . . . three hundred and sixty-five days and nights of waiting for her call, waiting for *this*, waiting for her to resurface, all of it ricocheted through his back, snap-jerked his spine, opened his lungs, made her skull vulnerable to high glossed wood, emptied his scrotum, shot through him, and ended in a molten latex barrier. She caught her Lenox bowl before it hit the floor and made him laugh as he dropped.

"Happy birthday," he said through staggered breaths, sweat rolling down the bridge of his nose onto her breasts.

"Had I known you were saving up my present all year . . ."

They both chuckled as he rolled over and stared up at her chandelier. "I'm sorry I had to save it that long to deliver it."

She snuggled against him and petted his abdomen, and then let her fingers follow the new bearded line of his jaw. "So am I," she said quietly, her voice tender. "I'll even break my old rules and make you breakfast. I just have to pick up a few things at the store. The fridge is bare. I just got home last night."

He closed his eyes and covered her hand. "No. Don't leave to go anywhere, right now. Let's do this all morning till the local joints open, and then order a coupla cheese steaks."

She laughed and leaned over and kissed him. "All right."

He traced her jaw with his finger and looked into her eyes, his mood shifting to become stone serious. "When I say I missed you, I meant more than just this."

All mirth left her. "I know. So did I."

"This is *real* trifling, James," she said, laughing as he took another huge, sloppy bite of his cheese steak in bed. Ketchup and onions slid out the back into the paper wrapping, along with a slurry of grease and cheese and peppers. "Look at the sheets!"

He shrugged, considered the stained white silk, chuckled low in his throat, and leaned into to her. "No, this is real *primal*," he said, sucking her chin and sending a shudder through her. He licked a trail down her windpipe, planted a kiss in the hollow of her throat and nuzzled her cleavage, and then looked up at her with a grin. "I'll buy you new sheets and a new rocks glass, cool? But, seriously, aside from a few lost household items, I'm such an easy man to satisfy. Feed me, hook a brother up," he said with a wink, kissing her exposed nipple, "and let me watch the game on Sunday afternoons and Monday nights . . . what's not to love?"

She laughed and pushed him away as he dangled a clear onion over her breast like he'd drop it on her. The waning sunlight kissed his back reddish orange, and she knew for all the playful banter, he was asking her questions and testing her out to see if it was safe to ask what he really wanted to know.

"You should have picked up another box while you were out, at the rate you've gone primal," she said, snuggling down into the sheets and taking a small bite of her sandwich.

He nodded as he filled his mouth with a hunk of meat and cheese, and then scooped up some of what had fallen out of the back of his sandwich with his fingers and dropped it into his mouth. "Uh-huh," he mumbled while chewing. "Wish I didn't have to, though."

She didn't say a word.

He stopped chewing for a moment and looked at her, and then went back to his cheese steak.

"I remember, you know."

She nodded.

"That one time."

"Uhmmm-hmmm." She took a sip of her soda and set it down carefully again on the nightstand.

"Was awesome."

"Yup."

He laughed. "Okay, okay . . . you can't blame a brother for trying, especially on a full stomach."

She relaxed. "James, it's just that I can't play like that."

He stopped chewing. It was something in the tone of her voice. "What, you don't trust me?"

She tilted her head to the side and just stared at him. In this day and age, trust didn't have shit to do with it. Pullease. A woman could be married for years and still come up burning. Sisters in their seventies were coming down with the dread disease, all because their husbands had stepped out with a young girl—*once*.

Laura slowly reached for her soda again, but kept a steady glare on James. When could anybody just give in and be natural without their lives hanging in the balance between lies and honor? It was crazy. So she studied this man who sat in bed wanting to know, with her arms folded and her best sister-girl scowl to back him up. But trusting where he'd been wasn't her first concern, getting pregnant again was. She'd already passed the first AIDS test she'd taken on Grand Cayman, once she'd learned she was pregnant.

"We could both go take a test, and then, maybe use something else?" He waited, watching her reaction. The fact that she smiled, even though sadly, made him feel better.

She touched his face. Blind trust, is what he offered, and it was such a rare gift that she'd try her best not to squander it. "Yeah . . . maybe we can do something like that one day." She watched every muscle in his shoulders relax. It was a half-assed commitment, but all she could offer at the moment.

"If it's me and you," he said quietly, setting down his sandwich, "you know there's not gonna be nobody else."

She nodded and closed her eyes. He was getting ready to launch into a commitment type conversation. She could feel it like she knew her name. She didn't want to talk about what had happened on Grand Cayman. He didn't need to know about the lost baby, because then he'd want to try again— and her heart couldn't take it. And then there'd be the whole question of marriage; it was in James Carter's nature to want that level of closure. She couldn't deal with that right now, either. So, she said the only thing that she could to satisfy him at the moment, said the only thing that could deflect further inquiry. "While I was away, there was nobody else. As long as it's me and you, it's me and you."

She felt him move in to kiss her, and she accepted his salty, pungent kiss with loving care. Greasy paper crinkled beside her, the scent of onions and peppers wafted up from it. Cold cheese fries on bedside tables begged to be nuked. Sodas were going flat in their bottles. This man had messed around and fallen in love and wanted normalcy. She loved him, but what was normal?

"Listen," he said, his eyes holding hers captive, searching her face for answers. "I know we're no spring chickens, have a lot of water under the bridge . . . there are things I probably will never know about you, but . . ." He stopped and quietly sat back in bed. "Like, I know it's too late for the traditional thing—kids, a dog, a house." He closed his eyes and laughed at himself. "My career is all up in the air, money might get jacked."

She seized upon the only thing she could talk about with him right now. "What happened down at the department?"

"Me and Steve retired, simple as that," he said, with his head leaned back against the headboard and his eyes still closed. "Might go into a PI business together, because I can't see myself teaching at a college and dealing with a bunch of bright-eyed, bushy-tailed eager beaver students." He opened his eyes and stared at her. "I'm no author, so a book, like you suggested, is out of the question. Half of what I could say about my father's murder and life on the force doesn't need to be in print, anyway. Justice was already served. Case closed. And I don't want to revisit it."

Laura picked at her cold cheese fries and took a swig of soda, and then carefully folded up her remaining half of cheese steak in the soiled paper as she set it on the side table. She watched James fold up the small bite that was left from his sandwich, and stash it on the table next to him, and then sling his arm over his forehead.

"I've been thinking about this a lot," he finally said, looking out the window as he spoke. "When you and I got together, we were both on a mission. We did what we had to do. We won. Now what?" He looked at her and dropped his arm, as though hoping for answers. "So, you disappear for a year while things cool off, I do the trial circuit and tie up all the legal loose ends. Now what, Laura? You have a thriving fund-raiser business to go back to, all you have to do is give your cousin Najira the word, and you step right back into life as it had been. Me . . . I can't go back to police work as usual. Neither can my buddy, Steve. I don't have the drive for it anymore. Maybe I'll open up a restaurant, or some crazy, boring shit like that. Who knows?"

She came in close to him and placed her hand in the center of his chest and stared at him. "I can't do the grants and the political fund-raisers anymore, James. I don't care about any of it anymore, either. I know what you mean—it feels very weird, strange, as though there's no ambition left in me, and that scares me to death." She sat back and wrapped the sheets around her to cover her breasts. "Once it was done, I thought I could outrun the hollow in my soul."

He nodded and sat forward. "Yeah, girl . . . I hear you. It's like, what do you do after you've won the heavyweight championship, or gotten the gold medal? We're too young to retire, to old to do all the other rites of passage shit that generally keeps people busy." He looked at her hard, but it wasn't an accusatory glare, just one filled by deep thought. "I can't be a kept man, Laura, you know that. So, if I globe trot with you for a little while, I'd have to pay my own way. But it still comes back to: *and then what?*" He let his breath out hard. "You ain't trying to marry some brother without a clear direction, no more than I'm trying to get married without having one."

Her shoulders lowered two inches from sheer relief. He'd said it; she didn't have to. They both understood. She could drop her mental guard for now. She'd ask him exactly what he'd tossed in international waters later—much later. Right now he was still in love and loving her. His hand traced a slow smolder against her thigh. She studied his honest expression, and the way his jaw was set hard and resolute, but not against her, just against the vagaries of life.

"Right," he said, calmly, no anger in his tone when she'd taken too long to respond to his statement about possible marriage. "We both know each other that well, and that's half the attraction. From the door, we've been real with each other. You know I love you. I figure you love me. We've been there for each other. Became friends. In bed, it's fantastic. But we need to figure out what we're gonna do with the rest of our lives—together, as well as separately."

"Yes, we do," she said, licking a bit of dripped cheese off his dark chocolate hued chest. She closed her eyes as the flavor of him mingled with the hint of cheese steak saturated cheese. "But we won't figure it out this afternoon in bed. Not while in a primal state of mind."

He laughed as she kept licking a trail lower down to his belly. "Ohhh . . . definitely . . . won't be figuring out anything much now."

"Right," she whispered in a hiss beneath his navel, allowing her tongue to explore the rim of it.

"Later . . . this week, can we figure out a new birth control method, though?" His eyes slid closed. "Latex is killing me."

She laughed and drew him into her mouth. James Carter hadn't been anywhere he wasn't supposed to be. The deep, hitched groan he released told her that much. Just like the instant shudder the burn of wetness she'd sheathed him with told all. This man had already been inside her, and her blood had passed rigorous tests. Her tongue found every groove and vein of his member to explain her position. His back arched in reply, and his fingers became tangled in her hair, as though confused. He wanted commitment, and this was as close to it as she could offer. Marriage was out of the question, but if he was clean and she was clean, then she could grant him pleasure instead.

He moved with her. Each time she drew back, his hips tried to find her. She could taste him becoming saltier, each hard pull pearling more fluid in his thickened shaft as she gripped it tightly at the base. Sweeping her tongue over his sac, and up the underside of his length, she planted a kiss on the tip and suckled the head, circling just that swollen area with her tongue until his breathing and thrusts became frenzied.

Seeing him hovering on the verge did something to her, though. No matter what had gone down before, she wanted him inside her. Rhythm method was insane, but it wasn't a dangerous time of the month. She felt his air thrusts in her bud, and it became a peristaltic ache that traveled up her canal and made her squeeze her legs together tighter. Mild contractions made her sphincter twitch. Her nipples stung so badly that she released him and covered both breasts with her hands. Yes, he was right. Latex was a barrier.

He pushed himself up to sit, leaned against the headboard. "I should put something on, now," he said, his breathing ragged as he watched her thumbs roll back and forth over the tiny coffee colored pebbles at the tips of her breasts. Nearly hypnotized by the sight of her doing that, he knew not to chance skin-on-skin contact. He was three strokes from cuming, she had to know that. He reached out to grab the box of condoms and hit cheese steak wrapper instead.

But she hadn't moved away from him to allow him to do what he had to do. He had to touch her, and he pulled her to him hard to replace her thumbs with his mouth.

She released a sound so low and sensual that it immediately made his fingers seek her bud. The link between her voice, his motions, the feel of her wetness, the way she moved against his fingers, the texture of her nipples against his tongue, it was a blur of sensation so profound that it stole his breath. They needed to finish this now and stop courting disaster. He reached for the box blindly, and knocked over his soda.

"I mean . . . if you . . . baby, listen."

She'd heard him when he shut his eyes. She'd heard him as she'd straddled his lap. Yeah . . . she'd heard him as he groaned real low and deep and held her tight, as her body sheathed his. Yes, she'd heard him say something about Jesus through his teeth. Oh, yeah. She'd heard her man in more ways than one, and all it took was a few real, hard, driven to the backboard, knock the air out of his lungs strokes till she heard him real good. Till her name became one with the Almighty, till James became more than his name—but a chant. Till all the things that they couldn't say to each other got replaced by pleasure tears. Till the losses got drowned out by mattress springs and the steady smack of wet skin against skin. Yes, she'd heard that moment-of-truth-breath-hitch two seconds before orgasm, and pulled up in time to let him hot-release against her belly without shame.

His fists slowly opened to fingers that trembled against the nape of her neck and at the dip of her spine. His breaths came in short, steam bursts against her throat. His face was wet from a combination of sweat and tears. She gently raked his close-cropped hair with her fingers in a soothing lullaby. Yes, she loved him, but it was so hard to say that. He kissed her shoulder and pulled her against him more closely, ensuring that no cold air came between them, almost as though shielding his spent seed from it, too. Her shudders abated slowly, mild pleasure spasms still rippled mini-tremors through her. His stomach tensed and released in slowly waning contractions. Commitment from a Scorpio woman was not to be questioned or challenged.

"Damn . . . Laura," he murmured and leaned his head back, staring at the ceiling, breathing hard. "Blind trust."

Chapter
3

Donald Haines sat in the driveway of his Radnor home, staring out at the matured line of maple trees and hundred year old oaks, knowing that the ancient Tudor, which had offered protective residence to generations of Haineses, would soon become his tomb.

Resigned, he got out of his Mercedes and walked up the expansive front steps, glancing around at how the leaves now littered his manicured lawn. So be it. Like all the rest of the rot that had been created, Elizabeth would have to cope with it after he was gone. Perhaps she'd won the game by outliving him, but it would be a hollow victory. There was some small measure of satisfaction in that.

As he entered his house, he could hear her moving around within it. The help had probably gone for the day, but he knew the distinctive sound of Elizabeth's footfalls coming from above. Her pace was frantic, as though she were always rushing to go somewhere when she was supposedly at home. His wife created and lived in a constant state of unrest. Now even the cut lilies she always kept in vases about the house wore on him.

"I was worried sick about you, Donald," she said, her voice strident enough to make him cringe.

He simply stared at her, wondering how or when this beautiful woman had become a shrew. Her chignon was perfect, her figure still close to the hourglass it had been when they'd married. Her skin was like refined, flawless porcelain, save a few well-deserved worry lines and age spots, but skilled surgeons and Botox treatments had erased all else. Under any other circumstances, he might have found her attractive. Long ago, she'd been ravishing, and had given him a son. But after years of passive-aggressive struggle, she was anything to him but that.

"I do still have a life," he said evenly, taking off his coat and carefully hanging it in the foyer closet. He didn't bother to look at her as he walked through the house toward his study, the only sanctuary he'd been able to claim within their war zone.

She followed him, her steps across the hardwood floors angry, filled with purpose, and then disappeared onto plush Turkish textures.

"You've been forgetting things, Donald. You could have gotten lost out there!"

He poured a brandy and considered the dark liquor in his glass. "And how would that be such a bad thing, dearest?"

She found the vodka and vermouth and made a sloppy martini. "It is not like I don't worry, you know. You shouldn't be drinking brandy, either. You're a diabetic."

"Please, Elizabeth," he said with a weary sigh, sitting down with effort on the burgundy leather sofa that faced a dead fireplace. "It would make your life simpler, in the long run, if something happened to me quickly. Wouldn't it?"

She leaned against his wide mahogany desk and glanced around at the leather-bound law books within the built-in walnut shelving and twirled her drink to mix the two liquors together. "We have not been friends or lovers for a long time, but I do care what has become of my husband. Is that so wrong?"

He sipped his drink wishing that he could cause the fireplace to start without having to get up and attend it. "Your husband. Now that's an interesting turn of phrase."

"Donald, stop it," she said calmly. "We have a lot at stake together, no matter what issues we've had."

He nodded. "Always the practical one. I respect that."

"At least you respect something about me," she said in a lethal tone, sipping her drink and swallowing hard. "I should be thankful for that."

He lifted his glass to her. "I respected you as a good mother. I respected you as my wife—you bore the title and burden well. And I have always respected you as a worthy adversary."

"Touché," she said with less venom. "And I, you."

"There we have it. A mild truce."

She stared at him.

"We know what's going to happen, love. Soon I won't know my own name."

She took another sip of her drink and gazed into the clear fluid. "I really think you should have a nurse while I'm out, or if I have to go places."

"I agree," he said, resigned. "I won't fight you on that any longer."

She looked up and their eyes met.

"No," he said quietly. "I won't fight you this time. All the fight has gone out of me. And there was, for what it's worth, a time when I truly loved you."

"And I you," she said just above a whisper. "I will miss your challenges."

He raised his glass again and downed his brandy. "One last request . . . simply for dignity's sake?"

She looked at him with a poker expression, neither agreeing nor resisting, just listening to his tender offer.

"Let me pick my own nurse . . . and do not interfere with the swiftness of my demise."

She set her glass down very precisely on the edge of his desk, but didn't speak.

"As always, I've taken good care of you and our son, despite some of my other marital lapses. But it's best this way. No need for you to suffer. You're still a beautiful woman, Elizabeth, with many good years left. The money will be solid, as always."

Elizabeth wrapped her arms around herself and nodded. "You were many things, Donald, but I could never take chivalry away from you."

He stood and placed his crystal glass down on the coffee table and slowly crossed the room toward her. "If I could have gone back and done it differently . . ."

She placed two fingers on his lips and her eyes filled. She smiled a gentle smile, the one he remembered from so long ago. "Then where would that have left us, darling? Neither of us would be who we are."

"You'll allow my choice, then?" He touched her cheek, studying the years of combat within her pale blue irises.

"It is done, final wish granted."

"Thank you."

The smell of coffee pulled her from the bed like a zombie in a trance. The room was still littered with cheese steak wrappers, spilled sodas, and Styrofoam cartons with stale cheese fries congealed with cold grease. The sheets were in a tangle. Her hair was practically standing on top of her head. She remembered her robe was cast off in the dining room, her nightgown lost somewhere along the way to the bedroom on the stairs. Her bed linens were ruined, her dining room tablecloth probably was also. Laura laughed and paced to the bathroom. What a night.

Hurrying toward the smell of java salvation, she quickly washed up, threw on a jewel blue caftan, and made her way to the kitchen. James was standing in the middle of the floor in his boxers, a wide grin on his face, and a cup of black coffee extended.

"The dead come back to life," he said, handing her a mug of coffee.

Laura chuckled and accepted the mug, closed her eyes, and allowed the steam to wash over her face and enter her nose. "Oh . . . yeah . . ."

He laughed and opened her refrigerator and stared into the empty space. "You didn't lie, girl. There's *nothing* in here. It looks like you just plugged it in off the showroom floor. Dag!"

"I was gone *a year*, James. If you find anything in there, trust me, it's lethal."

"Point well taken. I-HOP, Denny's, a good diner, you call it, because I have got to get a grub on."

She went to the breakfast nook and sat slowly. Her legs felt like rubber; she had friction burns lacerating her crotch. Her back was stiff and every muscle in her body felt like she'd been in a prizefight for a day and a half. "I need a real shower—alone, and some clean clothes, and some danged Vaseline."

He slurped his coffee, chuckling low in his throat, looking pleased. "Good."

She laughed out loud. "Good?"

"Yeah. Good. *Real good.*"

When she tried to stand with effort, his brilliant smile flashed wider.

"Oh, yeah. That's what a brother is talking about. Take your time in the shower. I've got all day."

She wasn't sure if it was the fact that he was so chipper, and she was so beat that was making her peevish, or if the complete invasion of her personal space was wearing on her.

But it might have helped her ego a bit if he'd been the one that had woken up in the morning needing a physical therapist. Laura smiled and took her coffee upstairs without further comment.

Maybe she could get used to this.

She watched the man put away an entire stack of pancakes, three scrambled eggs, what seemed like a half slab of bacon, orange juice, coffee, hash browns, and a few pieces of toast, and then he'd asked if she wanted all her sausage. Then he'd burped, rubbed his stomach, and closed his eyes for a moment, and suggested they go back to his place. Laura simply stared at the man.

"You know," she said, half laughing, "at some point, I do have to show up on radar . . . call some family, reconnect with my life."

"Yeah," he said wistfully. "But, damn, I wish I had a cigarette."

They both laughed.

"You're avoiding the inevitable, James."

"I know. I know. Just wanted to forgo having to make about fifty phone calls myself." He picked up his coffee and looked out of the Roxboro Diner window. "I need to call Steve and tell him something soon."

"He lives around here, right?"

James nodded. "Used to be up in the northeast, but moved down here when he and his wife split."

Laura nodded and sipped her coffee slowly. "Why don't I catch a cab, that way you don't have to run me all the way back to the art museum area."

"Be serious," he said, seeming offended. "Ain't nothin' but a run."

"I know," she countered. "But I think his idea has merit. You two would be good together."

He smiled. "You pushing me off on Steve so I'll get out of your hair for a little while?"

She smiled. "Until the chafing heals."

Again they both laughed.

"It's a bright sunny day, and I can find my way back home. Might even go into the office. I know Najira has a lot for me to catch up on. I'll place a few calls—"

"By land line, I hope."

Their eyes met.

"I'm sworn off of cell phones."

He sipped his coffee with care. "Good. Then I won't have any heavy issues to drop off anymore."

She offered him a slight nod, one both filled with deep appreciation for the task well done, and for not digging into the sore subject. "Never again."

"I guess you can handle a cab all by yourself, then."

They smiled over their cups.

"Did I properly express my gratitude?" she murmured.

"Over and over again, baby."

"You and Steve have a good meeting of the minds. Maybe we'll catch up later tonight to watch a movie—platonically."

He chuckled and set down his cup. "You really think this is a solid idea?"

She nodded. "If you only take on high-end clients, and build upon your current notoriety. Right now, after the trials, you two are hot property. That's a rare opportunity and won't last."

"So, you've been working out our business plan in your head, huh? I like that."

She chuckled and pushed her plate away from her. "I hear everything you tell me, and most of what you don't tell me."

He wound his SUV down Ridge Avenue, hung a right, and hit the steep hill that ended in parkland and tiny row houses in gingerbread configurations of narrow streets that almost seemed to be bike paths. Parking was out of the question on a weekend, just as it was most days during the week. But as soon as he spotted Steve's silver Durango, he knew it was a simple cell call to get his boy out of the house.

He sat double parked in the center of the street, hit Steve's digits, and yelled, "Yo!" into the receiver. Steve opened the door in his sweats and a T-shirt, laughing.

"Two minutes, man, and we're out."

"Cool," James hollered out of the window and then found his smooth jazz station.

Within minutes, Steve had his keys and pulled on his Eagles jacket, and was rounding James's car.

"So, I have to blast you out of hiding?"

Steve jumped into the SUV and pounded James's fist.

"Me?" Steve said, astonished. "I didn't go underground, you did."

"Beer?"

"Absolutely."

"Name the hole."

"Just drive."

Laura had called and was back in town after a year? Akhan set his telephone down slowly and stared out the window, preparing to leave his North Philly row house to head to the park for the second time in as many days. The universe was truly efficient, and yet also a very unsettling thing.

It was clear from her tone that she hadn't informed Najira that she was home. At this juncture, knowing how Laura operated, that could mean everything or nothing at all.

He put on his faded army jacket with care and found his keys. This might be a very interesting day indeed.

* * *

True to form, her uncle was waiting on a park bench where they always met. Theirs was still an act of righteous paranoia—she would stroll by an old man feeding the birds and finally sit. She would address him as Brother Akhan, no familiarity allowed until it was safe. It was rarely safe. Telephone lines were potential taps and traps. Walls had ears. One was potentially never alone. Big brother was always presumed to be watching.

The concept gave her pause as she thought about the time spent with James. Hell, if they got that on tape, they'd really have something to talk about for years! But, her first order of business when she'd arrived home, and right after taking off her coat, had been to sweep the entire house for electronic devices, and to disengage the ones she'd installed secretly herself.

She pulled her black Jag into a parking space across from the park, hopped out, and straightened her ivory cable knit sweater over her jeans, depressed the alarm lock, and hoisted her bag more securely on her shoulder. She approached the older man with care, but just couldn't erase the smile on her face. She'd missed him, and he had missed her. It was in their eyes.

"You look like the cat that ate the canary," Steve said, putting a fistful of peanuts into his mouth and then slurping his brew.

James laughed and sipped his beer slowly. "Naw, man, I've just finally come to some conclusions—and maybe you're right. We should do this thing."

"Yeah, okay, if you say so," Steve said with a wide grin. "But if you ask me, and my detective senses are rarely wrong, you look like a man who just got laid."

"C'mon, man, stop playing," James said, trying not to

smile too broadly as he took a healthy swig of his beer. "Your ass is always so suspicious. Why can't it be that I've finally warmed up to the concept?"

"Because you've been a miserable sonofabitch for a year, and now you're buzzing past my house like Mary Sunshine. Uh-uh. Talk to me, brother."

James laughed so hard that he had to wipe his eyes. He glimpsed his buddy who sat there unmoved, his brown eyes defiant and amused as he raked his fingers through a dirty-blond crew cut. "Steve Sullivan, you are a suspicious man."

"Last I checked, being suspicious is what people are gonna pay us for. You feeling all right?" Steve laughed and ordered another round. "So, is she back in town?"

James polished off his beer and slid his mug toward the bartender. "Figured the Eagles are gonna kick ass this year with T.O. on the squad. All McNabb needed was a little backup."

"Oh, shit," Steve said, looking at the overhead bar television. "You've gone metaphoric on me, so I take that as a yes."

"Everything's cool, man." He *would not* allow Steve to ruin his good mood.

"Like hell. Last time—"

"Yeah, yeah," James said, unable to keep from chuckling. "We both got shot."

Steve laughed. "Why do you always go for the dangerous types?"

"It's a sickness. Now can we talk about the business?"

Steve sighed. "Need an office, some phone lines, business cards, a license, furniture, fax and computer, and some well-placed phone calls to let the right people know we've hung a shingle, then we're in business, brother."

"Sounds like a one week proposition," James said, clinking his beer mug against Steve's. "Everything you talked about is done in a one-day deal—a quick trip to Staples or Office Depot. Partnership paperwork, a bank account, and whatever, isn't rocket science, if you've got a good attorney."

Steve nodded with a grin. "I'm sure we can dig up a favor or two off the barrister's circuit, and get a license through Harrisburg with the quickness."

"I'm liking how you think," James said, "but the key is location, location, location."

Steve ruffled his crew cut and sat back. "Depends on who you want as clients."

"That's where I was going." James took a slow sip of beer. "You wanna be chasing roughnecks, gangbangers, and cheating spouses for a coupla hundred bucks with the likelihood of getting shot?"

"I feel you," Steve said, leaning forward to circle his drink with both hands and stare down into it. "Why not go discreetly Main Line? Even if it is a botched marriage job, or a criminal fraud case, with civil overtones—the money is way sweeter, and the likelihood of getting popped is way lower."

"We're getting old, my friend. Alleys and drug holes ain't my thing no more."

"No lie. And, if we play this proper," Steve said, "ten years and out. Retire, yet again, at fifty-five or so, and maybe really write that book." He smiled and raised his mug. "Might get on Oprah, if she's still in the business, or can go do one of those cop shows—but from the studio as the hosts, not the streets busting narc jobs and nutcases."

James nodded and let his breath out slowly in relief. Steve was cool. Asked hard questions, but was all right when you didn't answer them. "That's what I'm talkin' 'bout," he said. "Main Liners don't like Center City, and the badlands, even though the rent is cheap, is out. Chestnut Hill is too close to where they live and where people they know might see them coming and going."

"Then do it here in a discreet, second floor walk-up," Steve said. "On the nicer side of Roxboro, otherwise known as Manyunk."

She walked past her uncle, affectionately known to all community leaders as Brother Akhan, and waited for his greeting without glancing over her shoulder. It was their way.

"Hotep," he finally said.

Laura turned slowly and smiled. "Good afternoon, brother."

"Help me feed the birds?" Akhan held out some stale bread that the pigeons and sparrows were already engaged in fighting over on the ground.

"Sure. Why not?" Laura moved to the bench, sat, and accepted a piece of broken bread with affection. "It's been a while since I've done this."

"Yes, and seems too long."

They both sat in companionable silence, watching the birds squabble and feast, each bird angrily dodging squirrels that raced through their ranks. The wind swirled the leaves in a spiral; a force of nature. Laura watched wildlife interrupt the multicolored dance.

"That's what's begun to happen," Akhan said, pointing to the struggling huddle of fowls that bumped and pecked each other for province over the crumbs.

"I'm surprised it took this long," Laura murmured, and then cast a piece of crust into the fray.

"It was a large loaf, but consumed quickly, even though it was cast to the masses with the best of intentions."

"They were starving for too long," Laura said with a sigh of defeat. "It's getting cold out, winter's coming early, and panic has begun to set in."

Akhan nodded. "You took from a very dangerous table, and shared. That is to be commended. But the whole system is broken, sweetheart. This will feed a belly for a few days . . .

that is what I was trying to tell you before. Alas, some things one cannot be told but must see on their own."

"I know." Laura twisted stale crust off the loaf and flung it to the teeming huddle on the ground. "But I had to do it, just once. Plus, it was a matter of principle."

"Ashe," he murmured, his wise old eyes staring at nothing on the horizon as he absently handed her another piece of bread. "It's gone beyond the city level. It's at the state level, now."

"I know," she said quietly, lost in her own thoughts. "I stayed connected to the news online while I was away. The gaming commission is . . ." Laura sighed. "It is what it is."

"Leave that matter be."

"You do not have to tell me twice," she muttered, truly meaning it. "I've been worried about you."

"Good, then all is well." He smiled. "I've been worried about you, too. But now that I've laid eyes on you, all is set aright."

Again, silence and the sounds of traffic and birds feeding filled the verbal void between them. Yes, seeing him made all the difference in the world. They shared that quiet comfort as greedily as the birds and squirrels consumed the bread at their feet. Knowing that he'd survived the storms that had swept so much away was a ten-pound weight off her conscience. But her uncle didn't have to worry about her doing anything so risky or foolish now. To avenge her father's death and her mother's subsequent suicide was one thing; to go around jacking with Italian casino owners on some altruistic mission was something else. James's father's murderer and her father's had been dealt with. Her conscience was clear, except that Monica Price had been blown away by her own husband. Children had been orphaned. It was partly her fault, but not totally, she reasoned. The marriage had been a lie; domestic violence and adultery had filled it. Her heat in the system had simply exploded it. Perhaps she'd beaten herself up about the whole fiasco long enough. It was time to move on.

It was just that it was October, and people had Halloween decorations up, and children filled the streets running home with art class projects flapping in the swirling winds. She'd seen them while in the cab and while on the drive over from her house . . . and she couldn't help but wonder, who would hang up Monica's children's refrigerator art? Who would make their costumes and take them out for a night of trick or treat? Then would come Thanksgiving—damn an election. That was adult chaos, what about the kids? And then came the worst holiday of all to be parentless—Christmas. Laura briefly shut her eyes. That's what she couldn't shake.

A year of running away from it couldn't make it right in her soul, never would. There wouldn't be enough community service, checks, or donations to bring back the dead. A woman had been caught in the crossfire in an affair. Monica Price had been busted, practically exposed with her pants down and her husband's best friend's contempt, which led to her husband's eyes blazing . . . yeah, but Monica was *still* some child's mother. Two little kids, in fact.

Laura sighed and was glad that her uncle didn't face her to inquire with his eyes, or speak. She remembered being a child who had lost a father and mother. There were some voids that could never be filled, and she hated that she'd been anywhere near creating one for any child. The harsh reality reminded her that she needed to call her sisters, again, and check on her nieces and nephews.

"Let it go, Laura," her uncle finally said, his comment seeming to come from out of the blue. "An old warrior has also cast in his hand."

For the first time since they'd shared the bench, she turned to look directly at her uncle. It took him a moment to give her his complete line of vision, but when he did, his eyes were pained.

"What's happened to Donald?" she murmured, clasping the stale bread so hard that it nearly became dough in her moist palm.

"Alzheimer's."

Laura looked away. "How long does he have?"

"Years, since his body is strong."

Again she stared at her uncle. "That is not what I'm asking. Did he ask you for a favor?"

Her uncle looked away and began feeding the disgruntled birds again. "He deserves his dignity, Laura."

Tears suddenly filled her eyes and she blinked them back, picking off very small sections of bread to fling at the ground hard. "Yes. He most certainly does."

Chapter
4

Deeply disturbed by what she'd heard, Laura drove to her office in silence, taking the scenic East River route just to look at the leaves. Golden orange fall colored her path. Sunlight hit the ground in dazzling shards as it bounced off the river. Ornate boathouse architecture that had been the province of Ivy Leaguers for years held its dignity against the coming winter. But nothing could eclipse what her uncle had said: Donald Haines had Alzheimer's.

She didn't want smooth jazz to accompany her on the ride through Center City to the historic district where her Bourse Building office was housed. Silence was in order. A moment of silence, save Saturday afternoon traffic, was a gesture of private respect for an old friend, mentor, sometimes adversary, and once brilliant mind.

Everything was changing, much like the leaves, peeling away, fluttering to the ground, so fragile that all that was needed was a good storm to bring it all down.

Snaking her way through shopper gridlock, she finally made it to the mouth of the parking lot and entered what had always been her sanctuary—her business location. But she was forced to smile and release a resigned sigh when her re-served spot was taken. Najira's candy red, custom-fitted Lexus was sitting in what had always been the CEO spot, her cousin's vanity tag signature as unmistakable as the garish vehicle: *Najira*. Laura laughed and found a regular, unreserved spot.

Perhaps this was the beginning of life to come, she mused, as she pulled into a vacant parking space and shut off her engine. Anonymity had its benefits.

She depressed the alarm lock on her black Jag and headed for the elevators, no longer in a rush. The year away and events that had unraveled had taught her to pace herself. It was a new habit that would take some getting used to, but life had a way of dealing harsh lessons if you didn't get the message the first time around.

Laura crossed the marble expanse and passed the eclectic assortment of vendors who had taken up residence to sell their wares in the lobby. She needed to get up to her suite of offices and just see it all again for herself. Her cousin was working on a Saturday. Never in a hundred years would she have dreamed it possible.

Once the second set of elevators let her out into the hall-way of her floor, Laura stood for a moment staring at the brass plate marquis of Rainmaker's, Inc. So much had gone into building the firm. But so much of the engine driving that process had been revenge; her aunt, grandmother, and even her mother's old adage, *you can show 'em better than you can tell 'em*. Laura had, yet something was missing. A sense of purpose now.

Quickly crossing the floor, she opened her door with the key she still had on her. It was so hauntingly quiet that she stood in the outer lobby for a moment just staring. Nothing seemed to have changed, even though she knew everything had. The appointments were still the understated elegance of deep walnut grains and mahogany with Oriental carpets and taste-ful African and African American art. Her plants were still living, but then, she'd paid good money for a plant service to keep them that way. Still, she felt like a stranger within what used to be her world.

She moved past the stack of mail in what was Najira's in-box and opened her office door. Her cousin's head jerked up as though startled, and in seconds Najira was on her feet with a wide smile.

"Girl! You scared the life out of me!" Najira rounded Laura's desk and rushed forward to embrace her. "When'd you get home?"

"You looked good back there behind my old desk," Laura said, squeezing her cousin hard and laughing as they held each other out to get a full look at one another.

"Learned from the best," Najira said, laughing and appraising Laura with a gentle gaze. "The islands seem like they've done you right."

"They did," Laura said, hugging Najira to her again quickly before letting her go. "But look at you . . ." she added, honestly stunned at the transformation. "I'm loving what I'm seeing. Wow."

Her cousin had given up the hip hop gear and was wearing a long, camel-colored suede duster and slacks, cashmere sweater of the same hue, and butter soft, natural brown Prada flats. Najira's rust-toned locks were swept up off her neck with tortoiseshell sticks; cowry shells and amber graced her ears, and her makeup was the merest hint of bronzes that brought out her beautiful walnut colored skin and wide eyes rimmed in charcoal. Laura could only gape at what had once been the wild child in the family, who had been doing her twenties by burning the candle at both ends. But, today, on a Saturday—steeped in work, no less— her baby cousin looked like a real CEO.

Najira just smiled and started to go get Laura some coffee, inadvertently falling back into their old routine.

"Hold it," Laura said, elbowing Najira away from the

coffeemaker on the small end table by the picture window. "Have a seat, Madam President. You're in here working, I just popped by to check you out in your new digs."

Najira laughed, but seemed suddenly unsure.

"Go ahead, and sit down, girl. We have a lot of catching up to do." Laura retrieved Najira's cup from her desk, and watched Najira take the seat in front of the desk, instead of behind it. Old patterns died hard, but Najira had earned the right to sit in her old chair.

"As you were, soldier," Laura said with a grin. "You ain't giving me back my old job on a Saturday afternoon, just like that."

They both laughed and settled into the new routine; Najira taking Laura's old seat and a cup of java to go with it while Laura sat in the leatherbound chair facing her old desk.

"You've got so much yang with you, girl, I don't even know where to begin," Najira said, smiling harder as she sipped her coffee. "My first round of questions is about the hurricane, how you got through all of that, scared all the family to death. Your sisters called me twice a day until we heard from you. Staff was tripping, too. Everybody had the news on in here listening to The Weather Channel. Then I wanna know how long you've been in Philly. I know you didn't just fly in today, and since I didn't hear from you earlier, I can only assume you had to handle your bizness—not that that's *my* bizness, but I know the bizness was male. You call James?"

Again they both laughed as Laura offered her cousin a shocked expression.

"I survived the storm in a shelter in the hotel district. And, James is fine. I got back late Thursday night."

"Dayum. I guess James *is* fine," Najira said, laughing harder. "Since Thursday, and a sistah couldn't pick up the telephone to call family? Uhmph, uhmph, umph. Well, ya look happy, so I won't talk bad about you—even though I'm jealous."

"Pullease. You've always got something going on, 'Jira."
Laura chuckled as she took a deep sip of her coffee, simply
enjoying the familiar banter that she'd so dearly missed.

"No, gurl. It *has* been a while." Najira shook her head, set
down her mug, and motioned with her hands to the desk.
"Now I understand why you didn't have a lot of time to play.
Dag, lady. For real. The pile of work is endless, not that I'm
complaining, because the money is righteous—thank you.
But with the campaigns, a November presidential election
happening, grantees scramblin' to be in the right fund-raising
position, and managing the grass roots programs that got the
monies after everything went down last year . . . I'm out all
night working the wine and cheese circuit, doing lunches,
breakfasts, dinners, and still gotta keep the paper straight
and check behind the grant and proposal writers."

Laura lifted her mug and saluted Najira. "It's great to be
the queen, ain't it?" Then she laughed.

"I don't know how you did it for all those years," Najira
said, losing some of the mirth in her tone.

"Be careful what you pray for, then, kiddo, because you
just might get it." Laura forced a smile and took another
steady sip of her coffee, watching Najira over the top of her
mug as she did so.

"I gained a lot of respect for what you had going on, sis.
You made it all look so easy . . . but, I'll be damned, it ain't
no joke."

"The three week hiatus down in the Caymans with Na-
dine, Lavern, and their crazy brood helped a little, didn't it?"
Laura held her cousin's gaze, as well as her breath. She wasn't
ready to come back here yet, and could only pray that Najira
wanted to stay a little longer. Hope was eroding as she carefully studied her cousin's eyes.

Najira smiled, but it wasn't as fluorescent as it had been
earlier. "Yeah, it did," she finally admitted, and then picked up
her coffee. "That was good. We all needed to get together."

She stared at Laura. "Mrs. Melville told me what happened, that you were physically all right, but made me promise not to say anything about it to you until you came home," she added gently. "You okay?"

Laura nodded, stood, and went to the window. She didn't want to talk about losing the baby. That was history. She hadn't even been pregnant that long. Her eyes scanned the majestic skyline of the city on a nearly cloudless, blue October day as she brought her mug beneath her nose to cradle in her hands for warmth. The steam from the cup felt good.

"Did you tell James?"

"No," Laura said quietly, her back still toward Najira. "What would be the point?"

She could see Najira shrug in the reflection of the window.

"Because he cares about you, I think. The brother might have wanted to know what you went through."

Laura's eyes stayed on the horizon, her voice suddenly so quiet that even she almost couldn't hear it. "'Jira, I missed my prime doing this," she said, referring to the business. "I missed that time of kids, and family, and building that kind of life. I was on a mission when I was your age. In fact, I was on Wall Street, then. I amassed a fortune the way some people drop kids. James was the same way, just in a different profession. He was on a mission, too, and the time for the family thing also passed him by. I know he cares, that's why I'm not going there. Why rub salt in the wound and make him know what almost could have been?"

She turned and looked at her cousin. "Almost is worse than never, trust me."

Najira nodded and stood. "I never thought I'd have a chance to do this," she said, her voice so tender that Laura had to look away. "Almost being the one in charge was hard. I kept dreaming about what it would be like." She came close to Laura and placed her hand on her arm. "But, girl, you got this. I suspect motherhood is the same way. Not all it's cracked up to be . . . the whole all-that-glitters-ain't-gold reality."

They both laughed softly as Najira railed on.

"Buncha little banshees that want this and that . . . Bey Bey's kids in your face. No, girl, stay an auntie. I might do the same. Then when they grow up, they're dragging baby mommas and baby daddys home, their little monsters, plus bleeding you for money to get them out of whatever mess they've got into. Nah, sis. You have always made wise decisions. Unnecessary drama. Men don't understand."

"No, they don't," Laura said with a sad smile, her tone not one of pure conviction, but she deeply appreciated her cousin's attempt to cast away the sore subject.

"So, when you coming back?" Najira asked, walking away from Laura and beginning to clear off her desk.

For a moment, Laura didn't answer and just watched her cousin pack away folders with resignation. She was drawn back to the window deep in thought. In all honesty, she didn't have an immediate response.

What had once been a burning desire to improve her net worth and to "show 'em" was gone. Laura glanced around the trappings of success, knowing in her soul she couldn't go back to that hollow existence. She'd won. The 'round the way girl who had pulled herself up by her bootstraps had bested them. She'd already set up every dirty local politician and entrepreneur who had had his or her hands sullied by her family's demise. Payback had been a bitch. The old guard black bourgeoisie in the city had gone down hard.

Cell phones had transferred monies. James had ditched the evidence over international waters. Being well placed to know where the accounts were buried when it was time to do the embezzlements from their program coffers into their personal bank accounts to set them up made it a cakewalk white collar job . . . smooth criminal. They took the fall; she was still standing. Things got a little out of hand and a guilty brother shot his adulterous wife. Okay, unfortunate collateral damage. However, like an alchemist, she'd turned twelve point five million of their money into a hundred twenty-five mil strategically directed toward her choice of programs that really helped the community. It was all good. But now what? Problem was, one of her best allies, Donald Haines, was losing his mind.

"I don't know," Laura finally murmured. She forced another smile and turned to look at Najira. What did she want to be when she grew up? Who knew? Besides, how did one re-ignite passion for something they'd outgrown? Over the years, she'd already traveled everywhere she'd wanted to go, left no island or world wonder unseen. Had been with enough men to make her parents do back flips in their graves. Had tested the limits of the law, and then shattered it. Had given back to the community, albeit in a very creative way. And had millions stashed in Swiss and off-shore accounts that would last her a lifetime or two. Her family was well taken care of; her cousin was blooming under the new career path and increased income.

In that regard, bringing closure, she understood James's dilemma well. How did one get it up for something that you'd already seen and done to death? No wonder he didn't want to remain a cop. Right now she felt like she was drifting, coasting, but there was no forward thrust or rocket fuel driving her like old times.

"Maybe I'm having a midlife crisis?"

Again they both laughed, but the tone of Najira's voice was muted and knowing; Laura's sounded strained.

"Maybe," Najira said, setting down the folder she'd been holding. "You're allowed for a little while. I've got your back, though."

Laura nodded. "Always have. Thank you."

"Not a problem, girl. You know that. We family."

* * *

A sense of purpose filled him as he pulled up in front of his duplex in the 6900 block of Ardleigh Street, remembering home, remembering his parents, thinking of how so much had changed since they'd all lived as one. The quiet street still had echoes in his mind. Laughter and tears.

It only took a little while to check the property, speak to his second floor tenants, shower and change into something that could carry him through till Sunday. Hopefulness threaded through him as he packed an overnight bag—just in case Laura was down for more company. Then, before the walls and any sense of loneliness closed in on him, he was out.

Cruising the streets, he made a few calls. Steve was right; it was time to let some well-heeled people know they were going into PI work. It was time to handle his business. Time to get into a new game. Two months of being retired was jangling his nerves. He'd never had long stretches with nothing to do. Vacation wasn't his thing, unless he could do that with the right person, and she hadn't been around. He and Steve could agree on that, at least: being on vacation in the islands and sipping a pina colada with a fine woman you wanted to be with was one thing, being home all day hanging at loose ends was something totally different. It was just like listening to jazz . . . needed someone to go with the mellow mood that it set. He didn't know how people just hung on the corners all day, or sat in front of the TV; it made him crazy.

This new venture was gonna be good for his head, though, even if it might initially dredge his pockets with the basic start-up cash required. But it was possibly the new energy he needed.

James turned up Wadsworth and then made his way to Mt. Airy Avenue, crossing over to Stenton, his eyes roving the scene, his ears drinking in the chaos of life in the city. 'Round the way was all the way live. Pipers were trying to hawk stolen

DVDs, socks, whatever they'd scored at the gas station while a brother tried to pump his gas. An argument in front of the Chinese food joint had a sister fussing, her head bobbing. Thuggish-looking teenagers stood in menacing huddles making patrons of the local fried chicken joint nervous. A fast food franchise manager almost got in trouble while catching a smoke out back, eyeing a hoochie-fied sister pushing a stroller when her man drove up.

Yeah. The streets were live, there was much to do, and if you turned a corner, you could be in a quiet residential zone, then two blocks later, in the badlands. Such was life in Philly, but it kept a brother on his toes.

James continued winding his way over to Walnut Lane, then to Johnson Street, and after a while got lost in the driving. Fall colors danced across his windshield, just like his thoughts raced. He needed a haven from thinking too hard, or from the glaring stimuli of the 'hood. Cresheim Valley Road was one of those oases. Row houses were nonexistent. Original, mature foliage graced wide lawns. Houses sat back from curving blacktop. Street parking was ticketed. People parked in driveways as long as airport landing strips. Had things been different, maybe Laura would have liked to live up here in one of those.

James slowed his car as he saw an impressive Victorian that only needed a little work. He almost laughed out loud thinking of the price tag the property probably carried. But if she wanted it, he knew he'd find a way to make enough PI collars to buy it for her. Stupid. What was he doing out looking for real estate, when girlfriend would barely commit to seeing him on a regular basis?

By the same token, it could be something new, a potential joint venture. He depressed the accelerator. Creating something new with her would be awesome. She had a business head that worked like a steel trap. He knew the law and was a damned good sleuth. Truth be told, so was she. Excitement coursed through him, but he jettisoned the idea as he turned onto Germantown Avenue and headed back toward the city away from Chestnut Hill.

First of all, Laura had a business and something to go back to. He didn't. This was some new crazy shit that he and Steve were scheming to do, which could go belly-up in a bad economy. Second of all, Steve would have a canary if he even broached the subject of working with Laura, assuming that she'd be so insane as to give the concept a chance. Clearly, he was getting way ahead of himself. Being without her for a year was making him irrational—or maybe having been with her a few hours ago was making him that. Either way, it didn't make sense.

Yet, he wanted to share his news with her. Of all the people in the world, it made a difference what she thought. All his family was gone. Steve was already clued in and would be his partner, but there was a difference between associates and friends . . . Laura and Steve were like family.

And he didn't want to drop this on her in some upscale joint. He wanted to bring her to where he hung out, around his environment, where he felt comfortable . . . around places that had drawn him to her initially. Soul food.

He chuckled quietly and reached for his cell phone on the hands-free unit and hit speed dial. He'd fallen for this woman as she ate fried chicken at Miss Tootsie's in a knockout designer get-up, sipping pineapple iced tea, and with the smell of candied yams gracing their table.

"Yo, whatcha doing?"

She laughed into the receiver and filled his SUV with her sultry voice. "Cruising downtown, about to go home. Why?"

"It's Saturday night," he said, smiling as he turned onto Lincoln Drive and headed in her direction.

"Do tell?"

He laughed. "Wanna go to Champagnes—up on Cheltenham Ave, get some fried fish, listen to some oldies, dance in the upstairs section, and laugh?"

"For real!"

He laughed harder and drove a little faster.

"You'll go?"

"Yeah! Shooooot, brother, pullease."

He watched her eat fried shrimp like it was a delicacy, and got an erection when greens juice dribbled down her chin. She had this sexy way of sticking her fork into her macaroni and cheese, twirling it slightly and dragging strings of cheese up out of the hot dish. Then she chased it all with a neat swig of beer. Candied yams had lost their appeal as he watched her and listened to Sade followed by Barry White.

"James, seriously," she said, leaning back in the black and gold upholstered booth, rubbing her stomach. "All we do is eat like dogs when we're together. I'm gonna need to work out hard now."

He smiled, sipped his brew, and pushed his plate away. "That can be arranged."

She shook her head and chuckled.

"I was talking about dancing."

She laughed and looked away. "Do tell? So was I."

"Yeah, okay."

She feigned shock and made him smile wider. He loved playing with her. But he loved even more that she'd listened to his business idea with a serious gaze, had knitted her gorgeous eyebrows, nodded and heard him out. Had offered some pointers on people they might want to call, and had said the concept was fabulous.

All the waiting and thinking as he'd driven to her place to pick her up had been worth it. He hadn't even waited until they got back up the way to tell her, had just spilled his guts in his Sequoia. And she hadn't laughed, or said it was risky, or anything like that. No negative vibes. Her eyes had lit up and the first words out of her mouth had been, "Oh, James, that's fabulous." It was the *Oh, James,* that was replaying itself in his mind now, with background music and a full stomach in a very old hangout. The woman had practically breathed the words. Right now he didn't even feel like dancing.

"You want dessert?" he asked, instead.

"No, but I'll buy ya an after dinner drink upstairs," she said, grinning.

"Only if you promise we'll dance a little bit." He had to stop looking at her to let things cool off. He glanced around the small establishment wondering how long he'd be able to fake it.

"No problem, brother," she said, leaning back farther into the cushioned booth, looking full and sated, her smile warm and her eyes half closed. "A little Grand Marnier would do me lovely right now."

He hailed the waitress for the check without even looking at the young sister. "You want it down here, or upstairs?"

Laura sighed. "Upstairs is just fine. I can wait."

"Cool." His line of vision sought the waitress again with more urgency. Damn, the sister was slow. Cash was the only option. If girlfriend took half as long to come back to the table with his credit card as she did to put down the check, he might have to round the bar and put the digits into the machine himself. "You ready?" he asked Laura, once the girl had taken the plastic money tray.

"I'm so ready, it doesn't make sense."

When she smiled and walked ahead of him, he knew she'd been messing with him. "Oh, okay. So, it's like that."

"I don't know what you're talking about," she said, her

smile lighting up the room. "I'm trying to go get my groove back upstairs. I haven't been out dancing in I don't know when."

He followed her, glad that she hadn't quoted a time frame that would have given him pause. It was hard not to wonder who might have approached her during her year away. In the islands, too? All those brothers . . . He banished the thought. It was stupid. She was with him. Whatever had happened, the only concern was the here and now where she was playing with him, enjoying herself, and he needed to squash any bullshit in his mind. Yet, as she passed the upstairs bouncer, who gave her a light once-over of appreciation, and they entered the multi-bar second floor dance area, he watched every man in the house glimpse her—even if just from the corner of their eyes.

No doubt about it, Laura was that kind of drop dead gorgeous that would make a man lift his head from his drink, no matter if he was with someone else. It was a gesture of respect, reflex, when seeing a sister who wasn't run-of-the-mill. A few brothers nodded at him and then shook their heads, the unspoken message being, *dayum, man, I see you.* Cool.

"About that Grand Marnier," he said, threading his arm around her waist as he ushered her toward the bar.

"Yeah, but they're playing vintage Phyllis Hyman, though. One dance, then we head for the bar?"

How was he supposed to argue with that? He took her short leather jacket and folded it over his arm as he reversed direction and led her toward the dance floor. There were no tables available, and he wasn't about to hang her butter on a hook where the jacket could walk. But he loved the fact that she filled his arms like they were in an upscale ballroom, no resistance, no fuss about not having seats or a place to safely stash their coats. She just shoved her purse higher on her shoulder and got it out of the way and laid her head against him. Immediate warmth radiated from her. Soft mohair filled his palms, making them ache to run down the leather back-side of her pants. Her breaths were slow, steady, rhythmic like the music. This woman needed to be in an environment that matched her . . . even though she could hang in whatever one he exposed her to.

"I was thinking," he murmured against her temple as he led her in a slow drag. "You wanna escape and run up to Chadds Ford for a couple of days? Wine country, a bed and breakfast, just the two of us? Maybe the Poconos, or something?"

She slid her hand down his chest and pressed her pelvis against his a little closer. "Yeah, or something."

He swallowed hard. "You still want that drink after this song?"

"You got Grand Marnier at your place?"

He closed his eyes briefly and let out his breath slowly. "Yeah. I do."

"Then no sense throwing good money after bad."

Somehow, whenever he was with Laura, all his best-laid plans went awry. His place was just a man's den, a place where he stopped, dropped, and then rolled. It was not set up for company tonight, and his bed wasn't even made. But she had a way of making him forget all that against the inside of his front door. He hadn't even turned on the lights, much less been able to cut on the music, or maybe kick a few things out of her way. But her body pressed against his, his back was against the door, her mouth tasting like dinner and her sweetness plus a mint . . . candied yams, flavored greens, mac and cheese, battered shrimp . . . Lawd, he'd straighten up the place tomorrow.

Newspapers were all over the sofa. Dishes were in the sink. He shuddered to think of what condition he'd left the bathroom in . . . had he known she was coming . . . but damn she felt so good pressing against him, her velvet hair in his hands, her mouth devouring his, her soft caresses stroking fire through his groin. He'd worry about amenities and shit, later. Right now there was one imperative: find a suitable place to put girlfriend down on her back.

She could feel his mind racing, knew this hadn't been planned. What the hell did she care about some newspapers on the sofa? If it didn't bother him, she couldn't care less.

Street lamps pushed filtered amber light through the windows and offered enough luminance to allow her to see his eyes. She touched his brows with the pad of her thumbs. James had magnificent eyes. Her thumbs traced his cheeks, then over his smooth, soft beard until they found his mouth.

"I love your mouth," she whispered, tracing his full bottom lip till it quivered.

Her comment seemed to make his expression become more intense before he kissed her.

"Let me share it with you, then," he whispered against the lobe of her ear, drawing it into his mouth and producing a small shiver within her as he led her to the sofa.

Oddly, she felt at home, like this was a place that had been waiting for her without pretense. There was also something about the way he slowly undressed her right in the darkened living room. No other woman was going to walk in the door. This was his sanctuary, and he'd finally brought her here. She sat down, allowing him to again lead their dance, watching him strip away his clothes, mesmerized by the way his body was sculpted, even though she'd just seen it earlier that day.

Yeah . . . there was something about watching this man slowly peel off layers in the semi-darkness before her, anticipation building as shadows played across his broad shoulders, chest, and rippled torso. His eyes became eclipsed when he shifted position, now only a large, dark form looming over her, seeming at times menacing, intense, but then surprising her by planting a deep, wet, sensual kiss against her skin.

James created small patches of fire where his mouth torched her, and then icy air rushed in to briefly quell it the moment his warm kiss went away. It was maddening, his slow unraveling of her senses—she wanted to rush him, but didn't. She knew better than that . . . the man knew what he was doing, she just wasn't sure her sanity would hold up under the strain.

His hands stroked her hips as he looked up from her belly, and then spoke against it. "You want that drink now, or later?"

It took her a moment to answer him. "Later."

"Cool," he murmured along a thin trail of hair he'd found beneath her navel, and then opened her on a deep exhale that nearly made her sit up.

Oh, yes, this man knew what he was doing . . . was not to be rushed, or messed with. He'd invited her home, brought her to his private haven, and knew his way around it, just like he knew her body inside out . . . sipped her like a fine aperitif, a thick, pungent cognac to be savored slow and steady. Made her need more air than seemed available in the room. Had first filled her mind with hope and his excitement, then filled her belly with deep fried down home, now opened her to fill her with his tongue, his lush mouth working in harmony with the music that was still in her spine, his lips and a moist suckle that lifted her in an arch.

It was the rhythm, his timing, the slowness that made her peel her damp buttocks, thighs, and back up off the dark leather toward him. But he wasn't trying to dance with her, yet. Not until sofa springs were groaning a higher octave than she, her own tones going deep, low, needing more than his sugar battered tongue lacing Southern Comfort pulses. Perhaps not till she begged him.

"James, please . . ." Her voice was a ragged murmur. What the hell was pride, when it stood in the way of results?

"You want that drink now?" he whispered hard against the inside of her thigh.

"Later," she whispered, shutting her eyes tight.

When he blanketed her, the shudder ran through each vertebra. "Just checking," he whispered, his voice now raw, and then he entered her as slowly as he'd kissed her.

Her breathing hitched, got caught up in her windpipe and was lost. But a deep thrust found it hiding behind her voice. Two hundred plus muscular pounds kept her from rushing him, kept her following his lead. Plush leather swallowed her back, gave in to his demands. Tears wet her lashes. Her only defense was her breathing, the tone in it, of it, her hands running the length of his spine, clutching his buttocks, urging him without words to give up the slow torture.

But James Carter was a very stubborn man under normal circumstances. His deep inhales thundered in and out of his chest, labored but controlled, and let her know that only Jesus could help her or make this man relent in his quest to drive her crazy.

She wasn't sure if she'd said just that one name, or put it in some haphazard sentence with James's, but it did something to him . . . had sent a spasm through him, had shifted his gear, picked up his tempo, his breathing, and made him throw back his head.

No lie, *Oh, Jesus* . . . this woman felt beyond good, was divine, was making him forget to do what he was gonna do, take his time. When she'd said that, it had messed him up, had made him lose some measure of control. Now he could feel everything pressing hard, down, immediate . . . wet, satin, tight, making his eyes roll to the back of his skull. Causing him to grip her under her bare ass with his arm, her shoulder a brace, get leverage into sinking leather, put a hump in his back, take his focus off the word steady, meet her wild thrusts, her voice a razor to reason. Oh, shit, baby, no lie, sweet Jesus . . . don't stop, girl, this is how we got messed up before. One breath, same octave. One rhythm, shared dance. One shudder, splintering many. One holla, long—agonized till it was over. Oh, shit, it was good.

His face was burning. Sweat rolled down his nose, stung his eyes, and made him simply have to close them. His pulse thudded in his ears. Her breathing was just as ragged. Her forehead felt damp against his. This was crazy.

"You want that drink now?" she sputtered.

He nodded and then collapsed on her. "Yeah, later."

Chapter
5

Terrible storms made the house groan. Winds shattered her deck sliding glass doors and made the ocean lap at the threshold. An eerie male voice called her name in a repeated, long, hollow sounding echo.

Laura awoke in a cold sweat. A heavy weight trapped her body. Panic swept through her for a second until she became oriented again. Right. James. The body covering her was James. She wasn't at home, or in the islands. She was at his place.

Gingerly extricating herself from his hold, she slipped off the sofa and went deeper into his apartment, blindly in search of the bathroom. Feeling for doors and peeking into semi-dark spaces, she finally found it and flipped on the light once safely inside with the door closed behind her.

What the hell was on her mind? James had just brought tears of pleasure to her eyes and now she was feeling haunted. Nude save her jewelry and watch, she glanced at the time. She'd only been asleep for maybe forty-five minutes. And why would she have Donald Haines so firmly implanted in her brain at a moment like this?

Laura turned on the faucet slowly, and allowed a thin trickle of cool water to hit the porcelain bowl and then splashed her face with it. The hair on the back of her neck was practically standing on end. Think, think, *think*, she told herself harshly as she tried to steady her breathing.

She knew she had to get to Haines, see him, communicate with him, and see his condition for herself. That had to be it—her gut telling her to connect with her old friend before it was too late . . . before Brother Akhan got to him and granted his final favor.

In the morning, it would be Sunday. Game day. She could tell James the truth with a bit of omission. James didn't need to be anywhere near this. He didn't understand hard choices at this level. She had to go home and change, and pack, if they were going to make a quick couple's getaway. Then perhaps he'd want to watch football while she did her minor errands. After that, they could go. It sounded plausible. Was a reasonable thing, she reassured herself, as she became more steady and stared at her reflection in the mirror.

But what if the voice was that of Michael Paxton Jr., a man who'd lost his life in the revenge equation? She'd set him up. James had shot him. Only circumstances and a badge had put it to rest in court. Or what if it had been Darien Price, a man who'd blown his own brains out after being set up lovely? There were many ghosts, and enough disturbed, restless spirits to haunt her for the remainder of her life.

With shaking hands, she brought a towel up to her face and blotted it dry, dispensing with formality and not worrying whether or not it was fresh. One thing for sure was, she had to get out of there. Suddenly being with a man who had a conscience made her claustrophobic.

Moving like a thief in the dark, she picked her way back to James's side, and found her underwear and bra. She froze when he stirred and rolled over, but then continued dressing when she heard him resume snoring.

Madness. This was complete madness.

When he moved again, she was holding her sweater midair.

"Hey, baby . . . what's the matter?" James said in a groggy voice.

"I was cold, that's all. Go back to sleep."

He slung his forearm over his eyes. "Lemme go in the bedroom and do something with the bed. It's all messed up, and I know you ain't comfortable."

"I'm all right," she said, feeling suddenly trapped into spending the night. "In fact, tomorrow's Sunday, and I know you probably have plans to go watch the game with the boys."

He sat up and rubbed his palms down his face, and then slung his legs over the side of the sofa. "I'll get it cleaned up, baby. I'm sorry, I wasn't expecting company . . . my bachelor's pad doubles as a pigsty, but I do have clean sheets and towels in the closet."

What could she say as he stood, stretched, and pecked her mouth as he passed her? There was no way out.

By the time the sun hit the horizon, she was ready to jump out of her skin. She peered at James and began to ease out of his bed. The man was still sound asleep, but already had a morning erection. If he was still so inclined upon waking, that was at least an hour, then chill time, then breakfast, and it might be near noon before she could extricate herself to get to Haines.

But how would she get past Donald's gestapo, his wife? Ever since she'd brought down Elizabeth's boy toy, Michael Paxton Jr., the reception had been icy, at best. Paxton had told Elizabeth most, but not all—just enough to make her a very dangerous person to have once crossed. Laura gazed out the window.

Common sense told her that the woman probably didn't

do church, but this was an election year, and there had to be major breakfasts going on, events, something that Miz Liz had to attend for the sake of propriety. The son, Donald Jr., never graced the house unless Mommy dearest was there to protect him from Papa—that much Haines had intimated over drinks . . . So, unless a nurse was already on site, or the man-servant of the house was more loyally wedded to the Mrs. than the Mister, a slight opportunity to approach Haines existed. But she'd have to roll up on him, go to him within his house, instead of on neutral ground.

"You roaming the floors again, girl?"

Laura started and spun to meet James's question with a smile. "I always wake up at sunrise," she said as calmly as possible.

He peered down at the tent his body made in the sheets and grinned. "So do I."

Under any other circumstances, she would have been flattered and turned on. But her nerves were rubbed so raw that she didn't even walk toward him for a moment. Bad move. He'd immediately sensed her hesitation. It had only been a beat, but James saw it.

"Everything all right?" His smile was gone, his brows were knit, his erection was fading.

She drew a dramatic breath and made herself laugh. "No, everything is not all right," she said, shaking her head and waving her hand at him. "I'm scared of you."

For a moment, he didn't answer, and then burst out laughing.

She let out her breath.

"James, when I woke you up last night, you were just gonna change the sheets and get me a clean towel. Two hours later, you wore my ass out. I finally get to sleep, and am still sore—and I sneak out of bed to get my head together, and I peep over my shoulder, and you've got a tent in the sheets? Get away from me!"

"Aw, baby," he said, his smile one of total trust, "you tired? Can't hang?"

She laughed and moved away when he stood and began to cross the room. "What time is the game on?"

He grabbed for her and she dodged him. "Not till one o'clock—but how you gonna pawn me off on the Eagles?"

She did the only thing that was expedient, allowed herself to melt into his embrace. "Promise me you'll let me go home, wash, and get some clothes while you and Steve do your caveman thing?"

"Yeah, I promise," he said in a husky tone against her throat. "But that's hours from now."

Laura tried not to run as soon as she got out of the car. Instead, she leaned over, gave James a long, tender kiss in full public display to ease any further concerns he might have, and stood inside the front door waving like a sailor's wife until he drove off. The moment his SUV rounded the corner, she was a blur of motion.

Dashing up the stairs, she peeled away clothes, flung them at the hamper, and made it into the shower. In and out, was the mission. Blue-gray suede walking suit, gun-metal gray silk tank, black mules, changed purse—black Coach, silver accessories, makeup to be done in the car—hair, finger combed. Overnight bag stuffed with jeans, slacks, sweaters, and a couple of good teddies, courtesy Victoria's Secret. Spritz on her favorite fragrance, Red, and drop it in the bag, too. A standing cosmetics case loaded into her arsenal. Down the steps, grab keys, set alarm. Gone.

She dialed Donald Haines's number as her car peeled out of the garage. A silent murmur crossed her lips as she prayed for him to be home. A manservant answered the telephone— God was good. Donald got on, not sounding wholly himself, but had enough clarity to know whom she was once she told him her full name twice.

Sunday was being kind. Traffic was headed toward the new stadium; she was going in the opposite direction toward the Main Line. Elizabeth wasn't home. Good riddance. The butler seemed cool. Fine. Her mentor sounded like his voice would crack with emotion, once he was sure it was her. Heaven help them.

Laura took Lancaster Avenue until it became Route 30, not chancing the expressway with a big game in town. That's all she'd need, to get hemmed in by some stupid accident, and then have rubbernecks slow progress.

"You bought two *season tickets*, man?" James said, standing in the middle of the street in front of Steve's house. "When!"

"Brother," Steve said laughing, "it was part of the divorce settlement. She got the house, the dog, and all the rest of my shit—but the judge had mercy when it came to my heart." He kissed his tickets, locked the door, and ran down the steps. "All you've gotta do is drive, so I don't lose my parking spot." He motioned toward the ragtag assortment of folding metal and plastic chairs neighbors had left in abandoned curbside spaces as territory markers and approached James's Sequoia. Then he dangled the tickets in front of James and made him laugh. "Wanna go to the prom with me—or do you have another date? I tried calling you all night, but obviously you had other things on your mind. Lucky you got me before I'd found another partner."

James glanced at his watch. He hadn't factored in the length of the game, plus traffic, post-game beers. "Nah, I'm down with the program, man."

Steve laughed. "Yeah, all right. But you had to check your

watch, is what I noticed. Her first weekend back, and you're already in the doghouse."

James put his arm out his driver's-side window and pounded Steve's fist. "A man has to do what a man has to do—so if I'ma get in trouble, then, hey, might as well make the time fit the crime."

They both laughed as Steve rounded the hood and piled into James's vehicle. The day would be shot, Laura would be pissed . . . but, hey, this was football season.

She stood outside the massive Tudor and waited. The doorbell nearly gonged when it sounded and the echo reverberated through her bones. An elderly, genteel man appeared at the door with a smile, in his Sunday relaxed uniform—a dark burgundy Alligator sweater, white button down shirt beneath it that matched the color of his hair, and a pair of gray wool slacks with penny loafers. He greeted Laura with a warm smile, and offered to take her coat. She gracefully declined, wanting to keep her suit jacket with her, in case she needed to leave quickly.

Laura watched his thin, gaunt frame disappear into the bowels of the house as she stood in the exquisitely furnished parlor, quietly inspecting the turn-of-the-century Victorian motif. Glistening walnut surrounded her. Nothing was out of place. Anxiety bubbled within her and made her clasp her hands tightly in her lap.

Everything was coordinated to the point of unnerving, from the heavy velvet drapes in muted, Ivy League hues, to the camel-back sofa ensconced in watermarked ivory satin, that partnered the high-backed Queen Anne chairs, and Chippendale curio cabinet and secretary. Ivory Lenox vases stood on the mantel. Thick Turkish rugs protected the floor that gave way to slate before the massive fireplace that was whistle clean and seemingly never used. A Virginia sugar chest sat in the corner adjacent the claw-footed, oval coffee table that shone so that one could see their reflection in the dark cherry wood. Hunting landscapes in oil with pedigree hounds, pheasants, and horses graced the walls in huge, gold leaf frames. Crown molding in eighteen-foot ceilings sat recessed to an ornate, Austrian crystal chandelier. Beveled leaded glass made sunlight enter the windows in controlled prisms. A Tiffany lamp added hue and diversity to the light.

It felt like a museum, smelled like a museum, or more like a well-preserved tomb. Power lived here. *Old wealth . . .* from generations of landed money. Elizabeth's cold touch exuded from the very walls and the furnishings like claws. Laura drew a shaky breath filled with inexplicable rage; that bitch would die in this house before she let Haines disinherit her from a penny. What had happened to Donald to allow himself to be backed into a corner like this?

Laura stood when she heard two sets of footfalls. As expected, the manservant came into the room first, quickly followed by her old friend. But the sight of Donald Haines wore on her. His always-immaculate hair was slightly disheveled and he had a scruffy five o'clock shadow that had formed in silver gray stubble along his jaw. His eyes held a slightly erratic quality, much like his tall, lanky gait. He had on an old Yale sweatshirt and a pair of corduroy pants that needed mending. When she discreetly looked down, she noticed he didn't have on shoes or slippers, just gray sports socks.

"No introductions required, Harold. Laura is my dear friend from long ago," Donald Haines said. "Thank you."

Donald beamed at Laura, and without another word dismissed his manservant, as well as the very concerned expression Harold wore. Laura forced a smile and went to Donald to touch his arm with affection.

"How have you been, my friend?" she asked carefully, studying Donald's eyes.

"Trapped in my own home, but making Elizabeth rue every day that I have left." He chuckled and motioned around the room with his hands as he bent toward Laura to whisper in her ear. "But we should be very circumspect when speaking ill of her. The walls have ears."

"Sir, should you need anything, just let me know." Harold hovered by the door, seeming unsure if it was safe to leave Donald to his own devices with a guest in the house.

Haines nodded without turning. "Laura, let us stroll in the garden, shall we?"

The manservant hesitated at the archway of the parlor. "Might I bring your coat and a pair of loafers, sir?"

Donald Haines looked down at his socks and chuckled. "Yes, Harold. That would be wise."

"It just don't get any better than this," Steve said, stuffing a hot dog with sauerkraut, mustard, relish, and onions in his mouth with one hand, and slurping an oversize beer after that from the other. "You missed the real action last night, though."

James had his eyes fastened on the field as he slurped his beer. "Not necessarily," he said with a grin. "But what happened last night that a brother should know about?"

"Got our first client," Steve said proudly, leaning forward so the contents of his sloppy dog would fall on the ground instead of his lap.

"Very cool."

"Very upscale," Steve corrected.

"Mo' betta."

"Yep," Steve said, polishing off his hot dog with a belch. "Last night was definitely couples' night."

"Cute. What's the job?"

"Lovely life partners—you remember 'em. Alan and Don."

James glanced away from the field to Steve's profile, and

then sent his line of vision back to the game. Suddenly the roar of the crowd and commentators sounded far away. Hell, yeah, he remembered Alan Moyer, Esquire, and knew of his partner, Donald Haines Jr. But what would bring them to Steve?

Steve simply nodded. "Later, man. Never mix business with pleasure. Let's watch the game."

The overcast sky weighed heavily on her as she strolled past sprawling echinacea, alliums, and a lush profusion of hardy border plants. The air was more than brisk; it was raw like her nerves. She watched Donald Haines carefully as he meandered about, finally found a white, decorative wrought iron bench near an elderly maple, and sat down heavily.

"You're wondering why I'm dressed like this. I know you are. Tell me," he said in a conspiratorial tone, mischief twinkling in his wandering blue eyes. He leaned in close enough to her that she could smell brandy on his breath. "They're the only pieces I've hidden that I can wash myself. Besides, it makes her crazy when I dress this way."

He sat back, triumphant. Laura didn't know what to say. A deep sadness made it difficult to breathe, much less witness.

"All my suits and normal clothes could have been compromised. She'll bug my boxers, I know it."

Laura didn't say a word. He'd gone mad. Was delusional . . . paranoid, and that was a very dangerous thing. But he seemed to sense her alarm and simply patted her hand as he grasped it between his cold, aged palms.

"Don't worry. I have it all worked out," Donald said, lifting his chin. "You see, she thinks she can wait me out, can learn all my secrets and find out what I've been up to all these years to unravel everything I've built. But that's why it pays to have friends in every profession."

Laura squeezed his hands tightly within her own, understanding his reference to her uncle. "I know you and Akhan go way back . . . to places I'll probably never understand," she said, halting between statements. "But—"

"Oh, Laura . . . dear Laura. Don't worry. Mr. Akhan and I are very good friends and we understand each other. Murder brings men across boundaries, and forms bonds one can never fathom."

Laura sat very, very still as Donald Haines's gaze roved the grounds of the back lawn.

"You see, dear child, he helped me years ago, because I helped him. We had a common enemy, and once I realized that Akhan hated the man as much as I did . . . and he was in my employ—we became close. He did me a favor, I was able to do him a favor, and such became the forging of our bond." He looked at Laura tenderly. "He is a man of his word, something so rare these days."

She didn't want to hear it, but could guess without it being said. All roads went back to the sordid details of Donald Haines falling in love with a black judge's wife, Colette Paxton. A wife so treacherous that she would sleep with Haines just to get her husband, Michael Paxton Sr., positioned for greatness. Two men used, but not innocent by a long shot. Elizabeth Haines was a player, too, turning a blind eye to Donald's sideline ventures as long as the money kept flowing while she locked up other areas of the city funding sources on the foundation fronts. Dear Elizabeth had dangled bait, too.

Laura could barely breathe, it was so sick to revisit. A judge's best friend, J. D. Price II, the city's managing director, duped by the judge, who sleeps with his wife, Juanita Price. Decades of drama, leaving paternity in question with two sons, both warring with each other, and only one knowing the real reason why.

Her family, always in service roles, was in position to see it all . . . a cheating judge who'd killed his wife and then had to be eliminated. The same judge who had his hands in the demise of his best friend—the managing director, who had ordered Laura's father's media assassination, and had contributed directly to James's father's murder by way of his sick son, Paxton Jr.

To the bitter end, like Haines said. It was all about generational wrongs that she and James had righted and addressed. Now all Donald Haines wanted was the last laugh. After orchestrating a hundred twenty-five million in grant monies distributed by her order to go to chosen grass roots programs, her uncle's service debt had been paid in full. Akhan and Haines were finally squared. Therefore, so was she.

Laura shut her eyes. She knew her uncle well enough to know that he had a part in avenging his own brother's death.

Donald Haines simply nodded and let out a sigh. "I may be a bit dottery and a tad senile, but do I strike you as someone who would go quietly into the good night?"

"No," Laura murmured as she squeezed Donald Haines's hand again to say good-bye. "Not at all."

"She thinks that she'll be able to co-opt my assets by taking power of attorney over me when I finally waste away. But I've beaten her at her own game. I've asked for a favor." He sighed and dropped Laura's hands to stretch and close his coat more tightly around his body. "I'd redone my will before the diagnosis. I haven't left that bitch a dime, and have only left my very disappointing son enough to let him know just how much he has broken my heart. The rest I've left to foundations that will carry on my work, with specific programs mentioned as recipients. This is why my friend must act quickly, before she ever suspects." He smiled a serene, faraway smile, and then looked at Laura. "If I say anything inappropriate that could harm anyone I love, darling . . . I gave my friend my doctor's diagnosis—my medical files, just in case."

"Just in case . . ." Laura murmured, her gaze holding Haines's in a deadlock.

"I've given you a double edged sword. My will, trust me, will be hotly contested and may be in probate for years. So, if it gets ugly, and certain people want to open old wounds and implicate you in anything from the past, you have my medical files to demonstrate clearly that I was out of my mind."

He smiled and touched her cheek when she failed to breathe, and then sent his gaze toward the line of trees beyond the stream. "Medical records normally have to be released by the family in a court battle. They're confidential. But I've given your family express instructions to stay abreast of my condition—therefore I gave you access to them." His gentle gaze hardened slightly. "Find a good attorney, one more ruthless than my son, and all will be well, if there's a problem. I had Alzheimer's. Anything I may have said about you or Mr. Akhan was the paranoid delusions of a sick old man. The will was redone the moment you left the city, a full year before I started having episodes and was diagnosed— so she can't necessarily use that to scrabble for more than I'm leaving her."

A current of nervous electricity ran down Laura's spine and produced an undetectable shiver within her. What was unfolding was becoming so ominous that she was sure she didn't want to know any more, but was transfixed.

"Donald, to me, you appear fine. Your mind is not failing. Maybe—"

"Don't be sentimental, Laura." He cut her off with a gentle wave of his hand and a smile. "I've watched this beast consume brilliant minds almost overnight. Some linger for years in a semi-life of drugged stupor. That's when they get you—your enemies. I swore on my family name that if I ever came down with this dread disease, I would act swiftly with authority." He chuckled and winked at her. "I've even gone to another doctor, recently, trying to best this thing, but his diagnosis may be like all the others. Laura, you know I must be in control to the bitter end."

When she nodded, he relaxed.

"You see, men with as many assets as I've amassed, cannot take the old, chivalrous way out. Insurance companies do not like suicide. One cannot fall on one's sword and avoid financial catastrophe. It makes them quibble about properly settling estates. Skillful assassination, ordered like a neat martini, gently shaken and never stirred so it doesn't bruise, is the only option for a man like me. Plus, there are other people near me who are already nervous about what I might tell as I become feeble. They won't be gentle. Everything must be tidy before they see me nearing my worst."

He stretched his long legs before him and bobbed his feet up and down like a child with a dangerous secret. "They might invade my home and make it look like a robbery, or something so crass as to attempt arson with me in it and damage such splendor. That would make me turn in my grave. But done my way, I will drift off and be gone, not a piece of Lenox disturbed, and all so beautifully choreographed that Elizabeth will lose her mind once she learns that it will become a gallery for intercultural women's art."

Donald Haines laughed a crazed laugh and leaned in close to Laura again. "The house. Think of the majesty of that. Colette should have been in this home; not Elizabeth . . . but such was the era. So, I'm giving away Elizabeth's pride and joy, just like she took my son and ruined him. It's my last act of defiance. The house," he whispered gleefully, "*that* will *certainly* kill her!"

"Look, like I told you when we were in the Linc, I knew where you probably were last night, so I didn't keep calling.

But it was beautiful," Steve said. "Just like that freakin' game—awesome."

James listened to the post-game highlights on WIP Radio with one ear while they sat in bumper-to-bumper Lincoln Center stadium traffic and he let his partner talk.

"Ten grand, do you hear me, man! I was hyped about the game when you rolled up, didn't want to get you all in a suspicious mood like you are now," Steve said laughing, "but it was sweet."

"Okay," James said, his tone distant and even as he kept his eyes on the cars in front of him. "Donald Haines Jr. calls you back after you tell them we're hanging our shingle. You meet his pretty ass in Rittenhouse Square Park, where he hands you twenty-five hundred."

"What, are you deaf? And he's bringing the other twenty-five on Monday as our fifty percent down retainer. We do some snooping, tell him if anybody is about to whack the old man, and we get five more."

"I don't like it," James muttered. "That's too easy."

"Oh, man, gimme a break. Whyduya always have to go looking for problems?" Steve chuckled and snatched off his Eagles emblem baseball cap, then raked his fingers through his hair. "I know, I know, it's our job to be suspicious—but ten grand fast is also ten grand."

"Ten grand fucked up and dead ain't worth the paper it's printed on, though. Feel me?"

Steve sighed. "Listen, Junior is worried that his father is going senile. He knows that the casino boys sweat him to influence the vote to allow gaming into the state. That happened, the games are coming to town. He's just scared that they might think the old man will dribble and tell, and he wants to be sure that his mother is safe in the house, because the guys from the casinos play rough when threatened."

James took his eyes off the traffic and looked at Steve hard. "They do, man. You and I both know that. Where there's smoke, there's also fire. We also know, from your boy Mike Caluzo, that Haines was already well known by them, they did favors back and forth of all sorts, everything from construction and real estate deals to whatever—and Haines had a connection to a judge's wife that got iced. Now, from where I sit," he added, his line of vision going back to the traffic, "either Junior has serious Spidey senses, and he and his life partner are getting nervous like they did before—or the kid overheard something and is running scared." He glanced back at Steve. "Think about it. Why didn't he just go to the police? Haines Jr. and Alan Moyer are both high flying attorneys who can pull favors from here to Bucks County."

"Point taken," Steve said with less mirth. He rubbed his chest and let out a deep belch that smelled like sour pork, beer, and kraut. "But you're blowing my game high, man. Remind me to bring Pepto Bismol with me when I take you on a date. Damn, you are fucking with my digestive system."

"I'm being real so nobody fucks with either one of us. Remember the plan, live long enough to retire twice and go sailing in the Caribbean?" James inched his car forward. Half of him was glad he'd gone to the game with Steve to get this info today instead of tomorrow, the other half of him wished that he was still blissfully ignorant until he got back from a few days' mental respite with Laura. Damn. All that was on hold, now. He needed to be on top of his game.

"Maybe the reason they came to us instead of the authorities is 'cause they know that we know all the players, and ins and outs . . . after all, Alan Moyer was the one who came to us and spilled his guts when Philly's elite was going down the crapper. Moyer probably told his lover, Junior, that we were cool. Nobody ever heard shit from us about their angle. But since the department has leaks, and I'm sure Junior doesn't want any media on this—nothing to link his father's name and legacy to any Italian jobs . . . especially if the old man is about to kick the bucket," Steve said in a weary tone as he sat back in his seat, "odds are that old man Haines has a house of cards, a lot of pending deals and assets still in transition for after this election. If I was the son, I'd want everybody to be real cool and real comfortable so as not to screw up my inheritance—such as their relationship is—already on shaky ground."

James rubbed his jaw and reluctantly nodded. "Yeah, all right, Sullivan. Just be alert and stay on your toes. It might be a quick surveillance job, doing a little probing to make sure there's no hit on the street on Haines, and a report back with some pictures, if necessary. That would be the hopeful thing. But my gut is telling me that ten grand for a week of digging, plus expenses—agreed to in cash without blinking, means the shit is about to hit the fan."

Chapter
6

Laura Caldwell was all up inside his head. He had to set up the business this week; there was no way around it. They'd landed their first client. It was a potentially dangerous job. He couldn't tell her about Donald Haines Jr. Not with a possible link to the casino boys and the new legislation that had just gone down. That would open the past up and cut her to the bone. He knew his woman well. Laura would get in it, start digging or try to protect her old mentor, if she thought he was at risk. Worse, she might get herself implicated in what should be left off shore. He'd done as much as he could do to protect her and keep her out of prison. Then again, if he started digging, he was half afraid of what else he might find.

James took the long way to Laura's house. Rather than hit Ridge Avenue to the expressway from Steve's, he went down Main Street in Manyunk toward the winding drive. A furniture store caught his eye across from Channel 48's small studios and tower. The access to the expressway was perfect; access from the Main Line was appropriate. There was vacant loft space above it and adequate parking on the street.

The location discreet. He'd tell Steve about it Monday. Right now, he had to figure out what to say to Laura.

She heard his car pull up, but took her time to go to the door. He took his time getting out of the vehicle. Something was wrong. Either James Carter was dead drunk after a game, or he was wrapping his mind around an excuse to not go away. She hoped it was the latter. She had things to do.

Laura watched him methodically exit his car and walk up the front steps. She opened the door before he rang the bell. Worry was all over his face.

"How was the game, baby?"

He forced a smile. "We won."

"Good," she said, making her voice sound upbeat. "You hungry?"

He shook his head. "Ate a lot of junk at the game, but if you are, we can go find some grub."

He wasn't hungry? Oh, yeah, something was really wrong. She closed the door behind him and began walking through the house toward the kitchen.

"Listen, baby," he said slowly, as he followed her through the house. "Something came up."

She nodded and relief wafted through her. "Not a problem. We can do this some other time."

He turned her around to face him in the archway between the kitchen and the hallway. "It's not like that. Me and Steve are starting this new venture . . . we got our first client, and it's a job that can't wait."

"I've been in business for myself long enough to appreciate that," she said with a gentle smile, really meaning it, but also really curious. "Who's the client?"

She'd expected him to smile, but he didn't. His expression became tight and closed. She stared into his eyes. She knew this Aries man well. Something very serious had just hit the fan.

"I know," she said when he took too long to answer her. "I forgot. Client confidentiality. Got a lot of those myself."

He relaxed a bit and stroked her cheek. "I'll make this up to you, I promise."

She kissed the center of his palm. "You do what you have to do. I'm not going anywhere."

He pulled her into an embrace and nuzzled her neck. "Damn, Laura . . . I'm so sorry, baby. You have no idea how much I'd rather get away with you than deal with this job right now. But . . ."

"But you have to get your business up and running. Some opportunities can't wait."

"Yeah," he murmured and let his breath out hard. "They can't."

"I'm a big girl and can take care of myself. I've got plenty to do that I haven't addressed while I was away."

He nodded and allowed his hands to splay against her back. "You ain't mad?"

She shook her head no. She kissed the underside of his chin. "Later."

"Yeah. Later," he said quietly. "I need to go home and pull my shit together for tomorrow."

"All right," she whispered, and then put a little distance between their bodies. "Just be careful, whatever you do."

He kissed her long and slow and then gently wrested himself away from her hold. There was no way in the world that he would allow her to come within a hundred yards of what this job might turn out to be. He wanted her safe and whole and as far away from any potential muck splatter as possible. She'd gotten away from the first debacle by the nonexistent hair on her chin. Smooth. He just wanted to make sure she'd keep it that way.

She touched his face. "James, you look so worried that you're starting to worry me."

He forced another smile and kissed her quickly. "I'm just conflicted, is all. Hate that we have to wait and put off our getaway . . . hate having to leave you tonight. Was very prepared to continue to catch up after missing you for a year."

She smiled, and it wasn't forced. The lie was a sweet one.

He leased the loft; Steve got the money from Haines's son. The license application had been filed. The skids to get it through Harrisburg quickly had been greased. They opened up the joint account and hit the spy-ware store. By noon, they had furniture en route, business cards in their pockets, and computers loaded into the back of James's SUV. By two P.M., they had registered their business, had partnership papers drawn, and a friend of a friend attorney filed their fictitious name: Carter and Sullivan, Private Investigators.

Laura donned her best Ann Taylor navy blue suit, set off by a strand of pearls and a red silk blouse. It was about motion. Time to get back in the game. She placed a call that she'd dreaded for more than a year. It was time to talk to Senator Scott.

If she were lucky, he'd be in Philly, and not Washington or Harrisburg, on the campaign trail and able to squeeze her in for a brief chat. It was imperative that she look into his eyes, face-to-face. She needed to get a sense of what he knew thus far, how tied he was to the new gaming charters, and how much he knew of Haines's failing health. Predators had to be assessed. If people were coming for a weakened Haines, her uncle might be in jeopardy, too. James's worried expression was enough to let her know, his new job was tied to an old one. Business, done the way it had all gone down, was never finished.

She steadied herself, called the Scott family home. When Senator Scott's voice filled the receiver, she brightened her voice and took on a corporate tone.

"Senator," Laura said calmly, her voice lilting as though she were a long lost family friend. "It's Laura. How are you? How has your family been?"

"Ah . . . Laura," he said, sounding truly engaged by her. "So happy to hear your voice. Are you well?"

"Yes, sir. And you?"

"As well as can be expected. This is a hectic time of the year, but we are coping."

She paused. "Yes, I know it must be difficult these days."

"It is," he said, hesitating. "So, you're back in the city?"

"Indeed." Again she paused, choosing her words with care. "I'm sure you're rather busy, but I was wondering how your calendar looked?"

"I can always make time for a cup of coffee with you, my dear."

"Thank you," she said quickly enough to let him know that it needed to be today, if he could manage it.

"I have to be in Harrisburg by ten," he said, reading between her lines.

"Will City Line Avenue work for you?"

"The Adam's Mark, so I can get on the road, works perfectly. Give me an hour."

"Eight A.M., it is."

The call disconnected almost as abruptly as it had started. She glanced at her watch and grabbed her purse. There was much work to do and very little time.

She arrived at the hotel before the senator, and she waited impatiently for him to come through the restaurant doors. Gray sunlight filtered into the atrium above her, plants sitting like quiet witnesses to the business meetings taking place at scattered tables. She stood when she saw him. Not much had changed, it seemed.

He was still expertly coiffed, his blue suit hanging with razor precision above his wingtip Florsheims, his monogrammed white cuffs peeking an elegant inch beneath his jacket sleeves—white handkerchief showing a quarter inch from his breast pocket, paisley tie coordinated with the French blue of his shirt. A dap old cat, Laura mused, as he opened one button on his suit, smiled a full capped, white dashing smile, pecked her cheek in familiar welcome and sat down across from her.

She stared at the ruddy brown face that was framed by silver hair. "It's been a long time."

He smiled and hailed the waitress for coffee. "Too long, Laura. So, tell me, what's on your mind?"

She smiled. He was in no mood to dance before coffee. "While I was away, it seems the landscape has changed. I wanted to be sure I didn't step on any land mines as I reinserted myself into the equation."

He smiled and waited for the server to leave their table. "Then I'm so glad you came home to me, first. That tells me everything."

She sipped her coffee slowly, hedging her bets. "Among the personal tragedies, there were severe financial losses," she said with a well-timed sigh. It was important to keep him believing that her motives were aligned with his old guard families, and that any changes had been the result of the trials and media—which she had nothing to do with.

He nodded and let his breath out hard. "Very unfortunate losses, all the way around. However, water seeks it's own level. New tides have washed positive developments ashore."

Laura nodded, but didn't smile. So they were going to play games this morning. The senator was back to speak-

ing in code. "Yes, I'm just glad our old friends are still
our old friends."

Senator Scott brought his coffee cup to his lips and stared
at Laura over a sip. "Have you seen Donald lately?"

She set her cup down very calmly. "Why? Is there something wrong?" Skillfully evading the question, she let her
question linger with her knitted brows.

The senator let his breath out slowly. "He is still a friend,
Laura, but there are concerns."

She simply cocked her eyebrow to ask the question that
was making her heart pound in her ears.

"Word is, he is not well."

Bingo. No wonder Haines was freaked out. She covered
her heart with her hand and leaned forward. "Cancer?" she
asked in a near whisper.

"Worse, for a man like him," the senator said with perfect
diction.

Again she cocked her eyebrow with a slight tilt of her
head to convey that she didn't understand.

The senator stared down into his cup as he set it precisely
in his saucer. "His mind."

"Oh, God . . ." she whispered. "Are you sure?"

The senator declined comment, but skillfully changed the
subject. "He was most instrumental in trying to staunch the
hemorrhages that plagued the family. But there are many
things that we hope he takes to his grave."

She simply stared at him, and then forced herself to nod.
"The charters prove, though, that he is still thinking clearly."

"And that should buy him some time." The senator glanced
at his watch and then pushed his cup away. "This is a very
hard business."

"Yes. I understand," she said quietly.

He stared at her, his gaze softening. "That is what we've
always admired about you most, Laura. You always under-

stand." He smiled and motioned for the check. "Have you ever considered running for political office?"

She chuckled. "Never. I've got too many skeletons buried in my closet."

He chuckled with her. "Like that has ever stopped any of us."

Laura watched the driver collect Senator Scott from the valet circle in front of the hotel. She had embraced a man who was still oblivious to her involvement with bringing down his empire. The shudder that ran through her was from more than the raw October air. They already knew Haines was weakened, had already begun to make decisions. . . . Who had hired James to do what?

Donald Haines Jr. had given them access to the carriage house. His mother and the butler had been distracted while they set up surveillance equipment in it, and wired the house. They were dressed as alarm installers, and an old male nurse had passed them on a shift change. Steve glanced over his shoulder at him. The old man nodded at James, ever so discreetly, and then at Steve, but kept moving into the house.

Brother Akhan? Laura's family?

A bad feeling entered James's bones, sunk down to the marrow and lived there with him for the rest of the day.

"You thinking what I'm thinking?" Steve asked as they climbed back into the rented white truck.

"I'm trying not to think about it," James said, his nerves shattered. The hopeful thought was that old man Akhan had been called in to bodyguard an old comrade. He didn't know how far they'd gone back, but word from his buddies on the force was that Haines and Akhan had been spotted with Laura at Monica Price's funeral. A year was a long time to have things weigh on his mind . . . a long time to resist digging on his own. He knew her family, now, and her links—even though she'd never disclosed them. Before he said anything to Haines's son, he needed to know for sure. Problem was, he couldn't ask Laura. If he did that, then she would definitely get in it. Or, his worst fears might be answered that she was a part of what Donald Jr. feared might go down.

He tested the video reception as they pulled off before the manservant on an errand and the wife returned home. It was time to have a casual conversation with some people who knew some people.

Laura set the phone down with frustration. Where was Akhan? She already knew the answer. But if the sharks were circling, he had to be made aware. A hit could claim more than one target. He'd be collateral damage if he was over there, or worse, a perfect alibi.

She raked her fingers through her hair and headed toward her uncle's home, panic driving her.

They parked on Atlantic Avenue and began walking. AC was as cold as hell with the heavy winds coming off the ocean and skirting past the boardwalk. James looked down the desolate streets. Casinos loomed against the neighborhoods, having swallowed up all that he'd remembered as a child. Homes had been demolished to make way for glitz and glamour. Small merchants squeezed out, the diving horses at the Steel Pier a thing of the past. A hot dog now cost damned near five bucks. He shoved his hands deeper into his pockets.

"You up for this?" Steve asked, glancing at James over his shoulder.

"Yeah, man. We do this by the numbers."

Steve nodded. "We're freelancers, just checking out a worried client's concerns."

"This time, we put it all on black," James said, as they approached the back door of a local hoagie shop and he punched a number into his cell phone.

Steve shifted from foot to foot in the back alley with James, the vermin in the Dumpsters making him shake his head. "I shoulda asked him for more."

James didn't respond, but spoke into the cell with single syllable bursts. "Yeah. A cigarette. Out back. Right about now."

After five long minutes, a large, burly brother opened the back door hauling trash, and he walked past Steve and James, let the screen slam, and slung the refuse into a Dumpster. He pulled out a pack of Marlboro reds from beneath his rolled-up white T-shirt sleeve, and tapped the pack with his lighter, extracting a butt that instantly went into his mouth.

"Thought you was coming alone," he said to James, eyeing Steve. He wiped the sweat from his palms down his grease-stained apron, and adjusted his black fishnet hair bonnet.

"He's cool," James said with a nod in his partner's direction, keeping his gaze steady on the man who was a head taller than him and resembled a thick tree trunk. "Coupla questions, then we're out." He pulled out an envelope and handed it to his old informant as the brother lit his cigarette and dragged hard.

"Heard y'all wasn't po-po no mo'."

"Word travels fast," James said evenly.

"That can change a lot of things."

Both men stared at each other.

"Could be good," James said with a shrug. "Could be bad.

But believe that we're still in the loop—and have friends everywhere, feel me?"

The burly chef nodded and took a hard drag, expelling a puff of smoke in Steve's direction. "Tell your boy to take a walk. I don't double date."

Steve nodded and took out a pack of smokes, fired one up and calmly began walking to the end of the alley.

"Your break is almost over," James said, nodding toward the envelope. "Wanna dance?"

"Everybody's in a holding pattern," his contact said, glancing over his shoulder. "They're waiting to see how bad he is before anything rough goes down. He's been cool. Did the right thing. People not feelin' the job, but know if he starts looking sloppy, it's the only way."

James nodded. The brother instinctively flipped open his cigarette pack for James. He took one of the butts, leaned into the lighter, and came away on a deep inhale. "How much time?"

"Maybe a few weeks, months. It all depends on how long he's out of sight, how jittery people get."

"The law of the jungle is fucked up."

Both men nodded.

"Ain't it?"

James took another long drag; the nicotine rushed through his system, giving him a buzz. "How they coming for him?"

"Smooth."

James's eyes narrowed on his contact. "Isn't that always the way? How?"

"My break is over," the brother said with a sly smile.

"Yeah, it is." James crushed out his cigarette under his heel. "But doesn't a man who's done so much for so many get a break—get to go out in a very cool way?"

The brother nodded as he walked back toward the screen door. "Yeah. No women, no kids, no house fires, and lately, he hasn't been driving."

* * *

He drove with Steve in silence back up the Atlantic City Expressway toward Philadelphia. Akhan was in the house. Something was gonna go down smooth, but soon. Laura's people were possibly involved or in the way. Either scenario was problematic.

By asking the questions, he and Steve had probably sped up the hands of time. There was information to give Haines Jr. A hit was imminent. His father had outlived his usefulness on the planet. But until he knew Akhan's angle, he wasn't ready to drop that info on the son.

He glanced at his partner, struggling with the conflict over whether or not to tell him that the elderly male nurse that had entered the house was related to Laura by blood.

"We've only got equipment on the periphery," Steve finally said, taking a drag from his cigarette and blowing the smoke out the window as it slowly lowered. "We can see who comes and goes. Will know if anybody is lurking in the bushes. But I don't like the fact that we can't see what's going on inside."

James nodded. He needed a cigarette. Cold turkey for over a year wasn't working right now.

Steve tapped the back of his pack, absently knowing. "This is why we don't live long in this profession. Fucks with your nerves."

"Truth," James said, accepting Steve's half-smoked butt to draw a light from it. He inhaled slowly and let the smoke out through his nose.

"Like good sex, ain't it?" Steve said with a smirk. "The new nurse."

James took another drag and flicked an ember out the partially opened window. "Yeah. A possibility."

"Talk to me," Steve said. "You ain't mentioned him all day since we seen 'im."

"Yeah," James said, his tone sullen. "That's 'cause I know him."

Steve turned in his seat, the over-the-shoulder belt harnesses straining. "You know that's a fucked-up way to let your partner get fucked up."

James took another drag from his cigarette and nodded. "My bad."

"My bad?" Steve flicked his cigarette out of the window.

"All right, man, listen . . . it's involved. He could be trying to protect old man Haines, since they seem to go way back."

"How fucking far back?" Steve shouted. "You and I both know that when they come for you, while you're in favor, they send a friend!"

James briefly shut his eyes and then stared at the road. "I know, man."

"Then what's the fucking problem? We call Junior, make sure we get the guy's picture—hope like hell he's just in place tonight to scope out opportunities and won't act for a few days, and let the old man's son address that shit with the authorities. Our damned job is done."

James flung his half-smoked butt out the window and lowered both with the automatic buttons to allow cold air to sweep the vehicle clean of the foul air. "Right. My bad."

For a long while, neither man spoke. Steve sat back in his seat seeming so furious that his face had flushed red. Taillights confronted James like warning beacons as he drove, his mind a million miles from the road.

"What's the connection?" Steve finally said, his voice even, his gaze deadly.

James didn't answer him for a moment. "To who?"

"C'mon, man. Do not jack with my head. *We're partners.*" Steve punched the dashboard. "The only thing that can ever come between partners is a woman—even money won't mess shit up like that." He shook his head and stared out the window. "And you ain't never been the one to take a side deal." He leaned back and closed his eyes. "If we know a man is about to be hit, and we sleep this, we're involved. We ain't even got our license yet, and could go down hard by turning a blind eye. So stop protecting her and cover your own ass. If she's in this bullshit, then this time, you've gotta let her go. Or, you'd better pray that her family did this solo, and she doesn't know. Who's the nurse?"

James kept his vision trained on the white lines that whizzed by them. "Her uncle."

Chapter
7

It was a quiet little tavern, neatly tucked away in Ardmore. A few scattered drinkers, men escaping God only knew what, hovered over their drinks—but dressed well. James kept his gaze roving, his thoughts within himself. His partner sat stone-faced, looking at the late evening news blaring from a screen far across the room.

"Listen," James finally said, nursing his drink. "I've got a bad feeling about this all the way around."

Steve sipped his beer and remained mute.

"Before we go spilling our guts to Junior, I want you to run a few scenarios through your brain."

Steve kept his eyes on the television.

"Yeah. All right. It was fucked up that I didn't mention the affiliation. But what if we're being set up?" James stared at his partner.

Steve stared at him.

"Yeah. That's right." James took another sip and set his glass down with care. "Been thinking. There's no love lost between the old Don, literally, and his son. The wife is in the same camp with the son. You and I have seen a lot of twisted shit with these families."

"You're blind," Steve muttered. "Fucking compromised beyond the point of reason."

James took the charge stoically. "Maybe. Maybe not. What if we're wrong?"

"How?" Steve said, his tone a low rumble as he polished off his beer.

"We'd be giving a young, hotshot attorney an alibi, if he and Mom were about to ice the old man." James waited and allowed what he'd said to sink into his furious partner's brain. "Sure, we confirmed a hit on the streets, but who's to say they weren't the ones that ordered the job?"

For the first time since they'd gone at it in the car, Steve's expression mellowed.

"Yeah," James pressed. "I've got a thing for Laura. But how about the fact that her uncle helped Haines orchestrate bringing down Paxton—the wife's lover? What if the son found out his mom was screwing his old buddy and now enemy? Wouldn't that be enough to make him want to rush the hands of time to get his inheritance faster, to be out from under his mother's financial control? Remember what his lover said, 'Donny would commit suicide if he ever found out about his mother.'"

James sipped his drink and sent his line of vision toward the television. "A lot of questions still have my personal jury out. What if that old man, Akhan, is over there to watch his boy's back, like old times, and the wife and son know a hit is about to go down? So, mysteriously, we get called in on a price-is-no-object job. Then we come back and say that there is word on the street confirming their hunches that a hit, in fact, is about to go down. They walk clean, an old man goes to jail, and as far as I can tell from all that plant and equipment and assets they've got over there, the only folks who walk with a fortune is the wife and son who we just gave the green light."

Steve rubbed his chin and stared down into his empty beer mug. "We mighta just got played, partner."

"Like I said. Maybe. Maybe not."

Steve stared up at him. "When Donny boy comes in here, how you wanna work this?" He let his breath out hard. "Damn. It's always the soft, quiet ones you've gotta watch out for."

James nodded. "Now we're on the same page, man. Look, when he comes in here, we tell him that we went to the casino district, got the word that there were concerns, but nothing was imminent. Give me twenty-four hours to pull Laura's family out of there, and while I'm doing that, you make the call and tell Donny that you got new info that something was gonna go down. At least, this way, they'll have to find another fall guy—not Laura's people."

"Cool," Steve said, and pounded James's fist.

They looked up simultaneously as they saw the bar door open. A slight, nervous-looking blond male entered the establishment, wearing a Bill Blass black trench and clutching his briefcase. He immediately spotted James and Steve and slowly approached their table in the back of the room. He glanced around, sat down with care, and set his briefcase on the floor beside him.

"Buy you a beer," Steve said.

Donald Haines Jr. shook his head and hailed the barmaid. "I'll have a Chardonnay. Thank you."

James raised his rocks glass to signal for another Johnny Walker. Steve glanced at James to let him lead the dance.

"We went down to AC," James said quietly, after the drinks were provided. "We did a sweep of the house, and all appears to be in order there. Got surveillance on lock. But your folks have a lot of activity to keep an eye on. Maid ser-

vice, landscape service . . . suffice to say, there's a lot of move-
ment around them that makes the job harder."

Donald leaned forward and fidgeted with his glass.
"Money is no object, but I hope you aren't gouging me." He
looked at Steve and then James hard.

"I'm just telling you the scope of the job. Did anybody
ask you for more money?" James shook his head as Donald
looked away.

"No," Donald said quietly. "I didn't mean to offend. It's
just that this whole business is very difficult."

"Whatever," James muttered. "Like I said, we did some
digging and wanted to give you an update on AC."

"What happened down there?" Donald's eyes held a fer-
vent quality between eagerness and fear.

"Had a conversation," Steve said, and took a swig of
beer. "An informative one."

James nodded, making Donald's attention ricochet from
one partner to the other. "There are people who are concerned, but not ready to move. They said no women and children, and no crazy shit like fires. Your father was respected
and did some recent favors that have kept people cool."

"So, that's it?" Donald sipped his wine and set it down
with shaking hands.

"For the moment. It's only been twenty-four hours."
James glared up from his drink at Haines, and then glanced
at Steve. "Seems he has asked an old friend to come by and
attend him in the evenings, when he's most concerned something could go down. Your father had enough presence of
mind to do that."

"Oh," Donald said, seeming shocked. "So, you think this
new nurse he has checks out . . . is legitimate?"

"We're gonna run a background check on him tomorrow,
just as a safety precaution," Steve hedged, his gaze laser on
James. "But this guy didn't come up on radar from the casino
circuit. Feel me?"

Donald nodded, his expression containing a mixture of what seemed to be both relief and disappointment that was hard to read. "I just want to be assured that my mother is safe while home, too."

"We got that part when we accepted the job," James said evenly.

Donald looked at him, his gaze narrowing at James's tone. "Is that so wrong?"

"No," James said coolly. "Our goal is to make sure they're both safe and the property is protected. That's what you want us to do, right?"

It seemed as though Donald checked himself, tucked away his momentary anger, and had become the nervous victim again. "Yes . . . by all means," he said, his gaze going toward Steve's for support. "That's all I want. Thank you."

James nodded and tipped his drink in Donald's direction when he stood. Steve sipped his brew and watched the play go down from a spectator's position.

"I . . . I have to go," Donald stammered. "You will call me, correct, if there are any new developments?"

Both men nodded.

"I don't like it," Steve said, as James pulled up to his block. "Dude didn't seem relieved enough."

James nodded. "Now you see what I was talking about?"

Steve jumped out of his car with a nod. "Yeah, partner. Owe you an apology."

Najira walked across the Bourse parking garage, her cell phone pressed to her ear. Fund-raisers, dinners, call backs, everything was a blur, and at almost eleven o'clock at night, she was still at it. How did Laura cope without losing her mind? She'd only been able to spend a few quick minutes with her dad that morning, and now she better understood why Laura was so absent from family functions and hated fall-by visits.

She clicked off the one call when it ended, adjusted her stack of folders in her arm, the load too heavy to completely fit into her briefcase, and then called another client. She just wanted to get into her car, go home, and fall down.

Everything was out of control. She sighed as she realized that she'd dropped an envelope. Her call reception was breaking up. She mumbled a curse under her breath as she walked away from her car toward the section of the lot closest to the street, searching for a signal on the path that she'd doubled back on to get the envelope. She kept talking, walking, engrossed as she depressed her car alarm while fetching the stray envelope.

In an instant, the world gave out from under her. Blown to the concrete ground, she hit the hard surface with a thud, glass and metal flying like shrapnel. Instinct made her cover her head. Gaseous fumes billowed around her, eclipsing light, entering her lungs, her ears deafened, car alarms sounding like muffled hysteria. She had to get up or die.

Limping, gagging, half running, half falling, she blindly moved forward with survival instinct as her guide. Her hands hit a wall, scrabbled at an exit door, and her feet propelled her down three flights and into the street. Tears blurred her vision, her knees felt like claws had torn the flesh from them. She couldn't get enough air into her lungs. She vomited, but kept running, far away from the billowing smoke. Sirens were coming from all directions, people shrieked and dashed through the street, another explosion sounded. Cars swerved to move for emergency vehicles. She had to get home. She simply had to get home.

* * *

Laura stood in the middle of her living room floor, welded to it as she listened to her cousin's hiccupping cries. Then she became motion itself, moving through her house oblivious to weather, the need for ID, anything but her car keys— she had to get to 'Jira.

"You should eat," Akhan said, motioning toward the untouched tray near Donald Haines's bedside.

"Why is everyone so concerned that I eat? I'm no child," Haines scoffed, issuing a weary sigh. "Harold feeds me well, like the calf being fattened for the slaughter. If you must know, I've had roasted quail and wild rice with a garnish of asparagus for a late lunch . . . but have lost my stomach for any of it. I'm so tired and this rich food just seems to run right through me, anyway."

"Have you taken your insulin yet?" Akhan stared at his charge with concern.

"My friend," Donald Haines Sr. said, smiling at Akhan as they sat across from each other in his master bedroom, not answering his question. He lifted the silver domed cover to his uneaten dinner plate with a shaky hand and sniffed the broiled salmon, red potatoes and squash with disdain, and then re-covered the meal. He closed his eyes and leaned back against the high-back, burgundy leather wing chair and sighed, tightening the belt on his ragged, plaid flannel robe. The tea beside him had grown cool, and wasn't what he wanted to sip on, either. "Why prolong this dance?"

Akhan shook his head and rubbed his chin. "Because I'm not convinced."

Donald sighed. "I like things of the past, too. Take this robe, for instance. It's warm, worn in, and is comfortable, unlike the silk smoking jacket that Elizabeth would prefer I wear." He chuckled softly, and opened his eyes to stare at

Akhan as he futilely tried to rub away the indigestion gurgling in his stomach. "Getting sentimental in your old age, are we?"

"No," Akhan said quietly. "I'm a patient man who observes."

Donald Haines rubbed his chin. "You intrigue me, my friend. Tell me a story."

"Have you noticed that you only lapse when you have a bit of brandy?"

Donald Haines's expression went from shock to quiet rage. "No. I hadn't."

"That is why you keep your friends close, and your enemies closer." Akhan dug into his nursing bag. "I brought you some brandy without the seal broken. Shall we have a sip for old time's sake?"

"Yes," Haines said, standing with great effort and going over to Akhan to put a hand on his shoulder. He leaned down and spoke very softly into his ear as he studied the bottle, wincing at the mild headache that became worse as he bent to whisper. "Perhaps you should give me a brandy and then go home, old friend. If what we both suspect has happened, you are in grave danger."

"And how would that be the way of old warriors, or friends?" Akhan said with a sly smile, pulling out a gleaming Smith and Wesson to lie on his lap. He watched Haines move to the small in-room bar hidden within his bedroom armoire. "If you are indeed ill, I shall grant you a favor. But if you're not . . ."

Haines nodded, poured a drink from the new bottle after breaking the seal, and handed a brandy snifter to Akhan. "Thank you."

She wasn't home. Wasn't answering her cell phone. All the lights were on in the house. Her message machine picked up on the land line. Yeah, she might be pissed, but this also wasn't Laura's style. If she had beef with him, she'd let him know it. James waited across the street, determined.

It was now or never. She had to pull Akhan out of there.

Najira was standing on the corner of Fifth and Spring Garden when Laura nearly pulled up on the curb. Her eyes were wild, her clothes dirty, her knees bleeding, her makeup smudged by relentless tears. Laura didn't even get out, just leaned over, opened the door, and grabbed her cousin to her once Najira climbed into her car, then swerved away from the mayhem unfolding blocks away.

Driving with one hand, she rubbed Najira's back with the other. It was a hit, a botched one, but undoubtedly a message for Akhan. Laura knew it in her soul. Najira's car was too identifiable. The strike wasn't aimed at her. Anyone on the circuit knew her black Jag. She shuddered.

"I just want to go to Dad's house," Najira said, her teeth chattering as she spoke, shock and trauma sending waves of shivers through her.

"Uh-uh," Laura said. "Too dangerous for both of you."

"What the fuck is going on!" Najira shrieked. "I thought this shit was over!"

Laura pulled into a parking space along the curb, stopped the car, and gathered Najira into her arms, petting her back. "When was the last time you visited your father?"

"This morning before he went to work. He got a new free-lance—"

"Where is he working tonight?"

Laura held Najira away from her hard. She knew the answer before Najira said it, but her filleted nervous system needed confirmation. "Tell me!"

"Somewhere up on the Main Line, and—"

"Oh, God!" Laura banged her hands on the steering wheel

and then leaned forward and took deep breaths through her nose. Out of reflex, she reached for her cell phone, only to realize she'd left it in the house. Her gaze went to street corners, searching for a pay phone that looked operable, to no avail. "Do you have your phone on you?"

Najira blinked twice and wrapped her arms around herself. "It was blown out of my hands when I fell."

Laura nodded. Rage made it hard for her to breathe. "I'm glad you're alive, kiddo. They're setting up your father to take a fall. This was a message, if he figured it out."

Najira covered her face with her hands and breathed deeply into them. "What was Daddy gonna do?"

"Do an old friend a final favor." Laura swallowed hard. The last thing she'd ever banked on was getting her younger cousin into the nasty details of the power game. "But it was something they were going to do, anyway. Do you understand?"

"No!" Najira suddenly shouted. "I don't understand any of this shit!" Her eyes were wild, her hair was, too, snot was running down her nose and she wiped it away with the back of her hand.

"An old friend wanted your father to grant him a last wish—to die in dignity. But someone else obviously already had that friend targeted. Now your father is over at a VIPs house about to do something that other people can walk away clean from. They'll pin it on him, if there's any scuttlebutt in the press about the old man dying from shaky means. Your car was to warn your father to take the weight, or you would later. Now do you understand?" She looked at her cousin hard to make sure the information entered her synapses. "If they'd wanted you dead, you would be. Most people hit their car alarms from at least ten feet back, and you walked away from the blast. Next time they'll rig it to your fuel line and not your door lock."

Najira began rocking with her arms wrapped tightly around

her waist. "I was on the phone talking to a client," she murmured, her voice distant and way too calm. "An envelope fell, and I doubled back to pick it up and to get a better signal, because the deeper I walked into the garage, the more static came on the line. There but for the grace of God . . . I was maybe twenty-five feet or more from the car when I hit the alarm to unlock it. The blast happened, I fell, and I ran . . . then as I was running I heard another bigger explosion."

"The second blast was your fuel line igniting. Probably wasn't supposed to happen, but who knows how fast they had to do the install? Fuck 'em." Laura kept her gaze out the window. "I need to get to a telephone to call James so he can tell me how you should play this at the hospital, and then you'll need a good lawyer."

"I'm not going to the hospital!" Najira screamed. "I'm not in this and I'm not talking to the police. I'm not a suspect! I'm out, Laura!"

"Your father is about to take the fall for a mercy killing, when a hit has already been arranged!"

Laura snatched the front of her cousin's suit and held it tightly in her fist. "You *are* going to the hospital, you *are* going to fully cooperate with the police. You *are* going to act like what you are right now, a goddamned deer caught in the headlights. *I'm* gonna tell them that your father, my uncle, was over there as a favor to protect his old friend, who *knew* something was about to go down—that's why he was there posing as a male nurse! As security. You don't know any of that, which will keep you as far away from it as possible. I'll draw the fire in my direction, if you listen to me. The blast that rocked your car was to scare your dad off, is the logical deduction the cops will make with well-planted suggestions from me. You hear?"

She released Najira's jacket when two big tears rose in her eyes and fell, but she waited for her cousin to nod before she pressed on. "Pull yourself together and *think*. Your father can't go to prison at his age—how long do you think he'll last in the joint, if he makes it that far, huh? Don't you realize that he could have an untimely accident there, too?"

"We have to find him, Laura," Najira whispered. "He said he had to go play nursemaid to an ailing client." She stared at Laura. "Dad isn't a nurse, has no license to . . ." She swallowed hard and looked out the window. "I thought he meant he was going to clean up and do butler type work, like he did back in the day when he first came to Philly. I thought he needed money, but was too proud to ask—that's why I went to see him. I didn't know . . . honest to God, I didn't."

"Then keep to your story, because he *is* going to clean up," Laura whispered, and pulled out of the parking space. "That's the problem."

"You walk into the emergency room, looking disoriented, and tell them you were in a horrible accident," Laura said calmly. "Do not speak to any reporters, if any are there. You wait for me." She stared at Najira until she nodded. "I'll call James from a pay phone, and get his take on how to play this. You remain too in-shock to talk, even if the police show up. Just cry and cover your face until we get to you. Tell them at the hospital that you were so freaked out that you just kept walking toward Center City medical facilities."

Panic made Laura's hands shake as she stroked Najira's hair. She leaned forward, kissed her cousin, and then pulled her into a gentle embrace. "It'll be all right, sweetie," she whispered against Najira's temple. "I never wanted you anywhere near this shit, that's why I would never tell you things . . . just like your dad wouldn't tell either of us a lot of things. But I'm not letting any of our inner circle take the weight."

Najira tearfully nodded and clutched the back of Laura's suit in tight fists, bitter sobs jerking her body as she finally let go. Then Najira leaned back in the seat for a moment, sucked in a deep breath, and got out of the car two blocks away from her destination.

Laura blinked back tears as she pulled away from the curb on South Street, and took the back way through South Philly to wind her way over to Twenty-second and back to Spring Garden to get to her house. This was over the top. She would put a bullet in the bastard's head who did this for sure. Her cousin . . . her little cousin? The shit was foul and it was on, and Akhan was *not* taking the weight.

She didn't even bother to pull into the garage. She left her car parked crooked on the driveway cement, ran up the front steps, and barreled through the door. All she needed was her purse, her cell phone, and . . .

Laura became very, very still as she slowly glanced around and witnessed the destruction inside her home. The small secretary by the closet was overturned, her purse on the floor, contents strewn about on it. Slowly, quietly, she picked up her purse, and shoved the contents back in. All the lights were still blazing in the house. Her cell phone was on, as though someone had been going through the calls she'd received that day. As she backed toward the door, she spied the dining room. Breakfront drawers were cast on the floor, the large secretary was open and mail and contents littered the floor. The living room was in shambles. But it was not vandalism. Someone had been searching for something, had been looking for papers, as CDs, technology, art, and even the credit cards and money from her purse had been left. She was out.

She backed down the front steps, pivoted, and dashed for the car. She hadn't even locked the front door. How they got in was moot. If someone came in after that, who gave a damn? The people who'd been searching her place were more dangerous than a common druggie or thief.

Her car peeled away from the driveway, and she headed for James's house, fumbling with the phone as she blew through several red lights.

* * *

James sat quietly with the phone pressed to his ear. Laura and Steve's old buddy, Luis, from the squad, told him information that made him nauseous. He turned his SUV around in the middle of the street, making a crazy hairpin U-turn, and headed back toward Steve's.

Steve was on the front steps waiting for him when he got there, strapped. Without a word, he circled James's vehicle and got in.

"Akhan didn't do it," James said through his teeth.

Steve nodded and kept his eyes forward. "Smothering an old friend in his sleep ain't in the code."

"No, it ain't." James could feel the muscle in his jaw tense. "Forensics is over there now. We had our surveillance gear set up, and might be able to pull in a few old markers."

"Where's Akhan?"

James let his breath out hard. "Lankenau Hospital in custody. A head wound and shot in the shoulder. The boys are saying he fell in the struggle, Haines got the gun and tried to defend himself, shot Akhan, point blank—but through a section of his shoulder where it just passed through, and didn't kill him. Then Haines must have fallen and that's when Akhan was able to smother him to do the hit."

"That's complete bullshit," Steve muttered, letting out his breath hard.

"Right. That's also why I told Luis to discreetly check out any insulin in the house, the food on trays for Haines, glasses he might have used, even his toothpaste. I told 'em to sweep the whole fucking place." James kept his gaze hardened on the road. "They knew Akhan was in there, I'll put good money down on a bet that there's suddenly other incriminating evidence in the house that would link someone fronting as a nurse. Food, medicine, all that shit is tainted—trust me."

Steve nodded but looked at James. "Yeah, but here's the thing I can't figure out. If they knew Akhan was in there—even if the wife and son suspected he was protecting Haines, and it was only a matter of a short time before he'd slip up and accidentally give the old man something that could quietly kill him, what gives on the breaking and entry, hardball, smother job?"

"That's just the thing," James muttered. "I don't know."

Chapter
8

When James's cell went to voice mail again, Laura almost slammed her phone against the dashboard in frustration. She hit his number again and waited; this time it rang twice.

His hip vibrated as he and Steve got out of the car. The second he saw the number, he motioned to Steve. "Hold up. It's Laura."

He and Steve leaned against the SUV, watching the police cars swarm the front driveway of the Haines mansion.

"Can't talk now, baby. In the middle of—"

"Come home now! It's an emergency," Laura shouted, cutting him off.

"What's wrong?" His nerves coiled around his spine threatening to snap it.

"Najira is in the hospital. Someone rigged her car and it blew in the Bourse garage. She's okay, but shaken. My house was ransacked."

James stared at the police cars and morgue vans, and then

at Steve as news vans entered the once quiet street. "Where are you now? Haines is dead."

Laura slowed her car to a dead stop at the end of James's block under a huge oak tree before turning into Ardleigh, and then pulled over into a parking space, cut her lights, and simply stared down the street at his house. "What happened?"

"He was smothered by a bed pillow."

Her hand slowly went to her mouth.

"Akhan was with him."

Laura briefly closed her eyes.

"We need to talk," she finally said. "Where is Akhan?"

"At Lankenau. He took a bullet to the shoulder."

"Oh, my God," she whispered. "James—"

"Don't go back to the house," James said. "Wait for me over at mine. Don't go to either hospital. The police have your uncle in custody, and will be all over your cousin. Understand?"

Laura nodded, but couldn't speak.

"Good. Sit tight. I'm on my way. I'll leave Steve up here to fish around. Meanwhile, you raise the best attorney you can."

Again, Laura nodded, but no words would immediately form in her mouth. Haines was dead. Her uncle was shot. Her cousin was implicated and had nearly been blown away. Her home had been violated. The sound of her man's voice was unsure.

"Akhan didn't do this," Laura said, her tone firm and professionally distant. "Not his style, not his way, and he had no motive."

"I know," James said, flatly, his voice quiet. "We need to talk."

"All right, then . . ." she said, about to end the call, but then froze.

"Laura, talk to me."

The open line between them crackled with static.

"Your upstairs tenants don't have a key to your apartment, do they?"

James hesitated. "Hell, no." He added in a very tense murmur, "Stay down and get a tag on any car that pulls away. But stay out of sight."

She nodded. "Done."

Laura watched a silver BMW's lights go on as a tall figure in a black bomber jacket calmly strode down the front steps of James's duplex. The man flicked a smoldering cigarette butt away from him, shook his head in the direction of the sedan with blackened windows, and walked across the street toward it. He glanced up and down the street, and then got into the vehicle. It careened away, and she scooted down farther in her seat, and then peeped up just as it rounded the corner, getting only a partial tag number.

Jersey plates. The last four digits burned into her brain. White male, approximately six feet tall, bulky build. Dark brown hair. Smoker. Fine leather shoes. Black slacks, not jeans. Cocky strut. She'd remember every detail until James got there. She'd remain crouched in the front seat, until James got there . . . no, she wouldn't.

Laura dug in her purse, found an old shopping receipt, eased herself out of her Jag, and nervously peered around. The bastard had tossed a butt. The ground was dry. It should still be smoldering. That would give her a brand. That would give James and Steve forensic evidence. They'd fucked up and her timing was good.

She casually strolled down the street, just in case the BMW came back. She kept her gaze sweeping the ground, then over her shoulder, and toward miscellaneous traffic that passed by—each car making her freeze, her heart pound faster, until she was on James's front steps. That's where she found it, still smoking.

* * *

"You say what?" Steve whispered, raking his hair till it stood up on end. "No. This wasn't Akhan's handiwork. He wouldn't pop his own daughter—for what? Then ransack his niece's joint? Doesn't add or gel."

James nodded as he backed out of the end of the block. "See if Luis will give you a courtesy pass on some additional info. The captain might also be cool, since we did good last year."

Steve nodded. "Yeah, man, I'll catch a cab home."

"No," James warned. "Laura said somebody just strolled in and out of mine. You call me; I'll tell you where to meet us in the streets. Right now, everything is hot."

Steve nodded and reached for his hip. "Hold on, partner. Got incoming." He glanced at the display. "Donny boy."

James waited while every nerve within him finally frayed and snapped. But he remained silent, picking up his partner's end of the conversation.

"Hey," Steve said hotly, but kept his voice low. "We still don't know if—" Steve walked in an agitated circle, his gaze darting between James and the activity way down the street. "Oh, so you're gonna just stiff us for the other five, all because—" Steve shook his head. "No, that *wasn't* part of the deal!"

Steve flipped his phone shut and got into James's car. "Whatever," he muttered and then slapped the dashboard. "Sonofa*bitch!*"

"He said, what, man?" James stared at his partner.

"Asshole said that he was paying us to protect his father, we'd slept the job and allowed a perp to waltz right into his mother's home. Said she was at the Ritz Carlton in Center City at a political fund-raiser when she got the call from the police, and took to her bed with a Valium up in her suite. So, basically, fuck us, and if we try to get him to pay the balance, he'll sue us for fraud."

Steve's chest heaved from short, angry breaths. James simply nodded.

"And you expected a different response?" James rubbed his palms over his face. "Lemme go get Laura, we'll go find a place to convene. See what else Luis can put us down with. Now ain't the time to get amped."

"Yeah, fine," Steve said, pointing at James as he got out the car. "But, see, now it's personal. I don't like getting jerked off by some wimp little bitch, and we need to pursue this just to hang his ass."

Again, James just nodded. "Agreed."

Laura slammed her cell phone shut. Oh, so it was like that. The good senator wasn't returning calls. Voice mail could kiss her ass.

She turned the variables over and over in her mind, making them worry beads. It was unlikely, but not impossible, that someone had followed her to the park when she'd met with her uncle. Not. No one knew she was back in town yet. But someone had to be watching Haines's house the day she'd visited—that was Sunday. James and Steve get this new client, the same day. Not a coincidence. She meets with Senator Scott on Monday morning, and he tells her people are concerned about Haines's mental condition, and his potential to spill the beans on all his little deals. Najira is over at her dad's house; 'round about the same time, or at least shortly after Laura leaves from her meeting with Scott. Meanwhile, her uncle goes over to Haines's house to do the favor. But this shit was sloppy—Akhan was anything but that.

Her head jerked up as she heard a car come down the

street, slow down, and then stop. James's Sequoia made her let her breath out fast and nearly jump out of her Jag, but she remained still and allowed him to approach her. His gaze went to the house, then to her, and his expression told her to stay put. She watched him pull a gun from his shoulder holster and mount the steps. That's when true terror set in.

When he didn't immediately come back out, she turned on her engine, although she didn't turn on her lights. She maneuvered her sedan so that it could quickly exit the parking space on a moment's notice. She only began breathing normally when she saw James come down the steps, offer her a nod to follow him, and then jump back into his car.

Instantly, her cell phone rang, and she knew it was him.

"You were right. They jimmied the back entrance, got in like experts through the garage, came up through the basement, took the door frame out, and were in my apartment. They went through my closets and drawers, looking for something, and were out."

"Where are we going?" she said, keeping her eyes on his SUV taillights.

"Denny's on City Line," James said. "It's bright, visible from the street, open all night. I'll hit ya back. Gotta let Steve know."

She nodded and cut the call, knowing that James could see her in his rearview mirror.

They took a small booth. She asked the waitress for a cup of coffee and a piece of Saran Wrap. James watched her practically without blinking. She ignored him as she carefully produced a half smoked cigarette butt from her purse that had been folded into an old receipt.

"An early birthday present," she said. "Dumb bastard tossed it as he left your place."

James accepted the gift for what it was—a treasure—as Laura gave him the full description of all she'd seen.

"Casino boys," James said. "The clothes, the car, pro job on the break-ins. Odds are your place was hit the same way for the same reasons, and same people looking for something they didn't find."

Laura leaned in, her eyes searching James's face. "But what are they after? They've already set Akhan up."

"You tell me, Laura," James said evenly, as he folded away the cigarette butt.

"What's *that* supposed to mean?"

He stared at her. "If there has ever been a time for you to give it to me straight, no chaser, baby, it's now." He leaned forward and dropped his voice. "I'm not playing, Laura. What the fuck are you into and how deep?"

She glowered at him and sipped her coffee with precision. "Nothing, James." This time it was the truth. The only aspect of this entire nightmare that she'd omitted to disclose was the fact that Akhan had agreed to grant Haines a death wish. But beyond that, there was nothing else. The fact that James implied otherwise, grated her.

"I'm going to say this one time, and one time only—then we squash it." He leveled his gaze at her and spoke very slowly to make sure she heard every word. "I want to know all of it, from the beginning. I want to know who might have an old score to settle. I want to know where the bodies are buried and where the skeletons lie near you. I know your uncle didn't do this hit, but that's *all* I am pretty sure of, right about through here. Yank with me, Laura, and I will burn you and leave your ass flapping in the breeze—because I'm not going to jail, not ditching any more evidence, and refuse to get caught up in bullshit that I had nothing to do with. We clear?"

"Very," she said between her teeth as she set her coffee cup down very slowly and folded her arms over her chest.

"Good." He picked up his mug and took a deep sip from it.

"Follow the damned money, James," she said, her voice a lethal whisper. "Isn't that what this is always about?"

"Talk to me." He would not be moved by her rage.

"You've got a number of people who have perfect financial motive. A vicious wife and pampered son who couldn't stand that old man." She swallowed hard, thinking of how Donald Haines Sr. must have struggled for his last breaths. Her friend wasn't supposed to die like that and have his life become a media travesty. "You have those in power, like the good Senator Scott . . . punk bastard like the rest of the lot, who could stand to substantially gain from new casino charters and the building construction contracts that might go with them, just like the casino boys would gain exponentially from both—so long as Haines didn't blab about how that was already rigged, the contracts already decided. Akhan knew it was about to go down, and owed Haines for all the dollars he'd swung in the direction of programs he'd been unsuccessfully trying to get funded for years. So, my uncle literally took a bullet and put his body on the line, a favor for a favor. Case closed."

She sat back and sent her hot gaze out the window.

"Then why are people going after his daughter, you, and now in my apartment, and possibly Steve's?"

She shrugged and spoke to him without looking at him. "Maybe they wanted Akhan to step off and stand down from his bodyguard role. Or maybe they thought I might have been able to influence a feeble-minded old man Haines into breaking off a chunk of the charters that were originally supposed to go to them. They clearly came into my house looking for paperwork of some sort, because there was nothing stolen that I could see from first glance. Or maybe it was both—telling Akhan to back off so they could do Haines, and then keep his mouth shut and take the weight no matter how the cops spun the case . . . and to be sure I didn't get anything I wasn't entitled to that could pare down their victory pot."

What she said sounded plausible, but something still nagged at his gut. It was an indefinable presence of a dark cloud that he couldn't seem to shake.

"All right, I'll buy that, for now. But how do I factor in?"

She narrowed her gaze on him. "You'll *buy* that for now? Since when did I go back to being a suspect and no longer your woman?" Her tense question made him look away. "No, 'Baby, I'm glad you weren't hurt'? No, 'Sweetheart, I know you must be losing your mind because your family has been traumatized'? Just some shit about what I might have done to kick all this off? Fuck you, James. I thought you retired from the force, or did you and Steve go back on tonight?"

He was almost ready to smoke the evidence butt in his pocket. Yeah, he'd deserved that, but instinct was still roiling inside him. "My bad," he said, abandoning his cup to rub his palms over his face.

She folded her arms tighter across her chest and sent her gaze out the window again.

"I'm sorry," he muttered.

"I'm not," she said between her teeth. "At least I know where we stand."

"Laura, don't go there. I'm sorry. We've been down this road before, and—"

"Should have never had to go down it again," she whispered, fast and hard, leaning in and cutting off his awkward apology. "Like I said, James. Fuck. You."

If it weren't for his buddy Steve walking up the steps outside the window, he wouldn't have known what else to say to her. Everything she'd run down made so much sense, but why was his gut still gurgling like a piece of the puzzle was missing?

"Yo," Steve said quietly as he slid into the booth. "Everything cool?" He glanced at Laura and then James to be sure it was safe to talk openly in front of her.

"Yeah. It's cool," James said, hailing the waitress for more coffee. "Laura put a lot of pieces in place." He kept his eyes on Steve but hoped that would be enough to assuage her offended ego. If everything was on the up-and-up and like she'd said, then damned straight, she had a right to be pissed.

Steve nodded and sighed, but hesitated until the waitress had filled all coffee mugs and left their table before speaking.

"I traded some info with Luis for a little courtesy," Steve said, leaning into the group. "Told him that Haines's son, Donny, had contracted us just before everything went down, and didn't seem very relieved when we told him about the word we got down in AC."

"Donald Haines Jr. was your client?" Laura asked, breathing the question in a gasp.

"I thought you said everything was cool," Steve said, sitting back and glaring at James, confused.

"It is," James said, letting his breath out hard. "We just hadn't talked that deeply into the subject yet when you came in. Go 'head, man. Finish what you gotta say." He gave Laura a warning glance not to start, or dissect the omission now in front of Steve. He slightly relaxed when she sat back and studied her coffee mug. He could tell her poker exterior was only that, the façade of a true game-player—cool.

"But I told him the unedited version," Steve said, pressing on with caution. "That the hit was imminent, but people were in a holding pattern. That's the thing that doesn't make sense, unless your contact was wrong?" He looked at James.

"This hit was sloppy, very public, and they had said it would go down smooth."

"It probably would have, unless somebody got real nervous."

Steve slurped his coffee and glanced at Laura and then James. "The only person who seemed nervous after we met and said there was nothing to worry about was Donny boy."

"You gentlemen ever consider that he might have placed a call to get it done ASAP, once he was sure my uncle was in the house? Then he could just as politely slip back into a fund-raiser event with his mother on his arm at the Ritz Carlton. Perfect alibi, full view of the public eye, even though we all are pretty sure he wouldn't have put the pillow over his father's face. But he was involved. I can feel it." Laura set her cup down hard and kept her gaze on the dark liquid within it.

"Still," Steve said, "I don't see the casino boys jumping like that for some punk son and crazy wife. The Haineses have money, but not *that* much money, to open a can of worms around their very new and fragile casino charters worth long-term billions. They wouldn't want that much light shed on 'em at this juncture."

James motioned toward Laura with his chin. "She told me about how her cousin's car was rigged. Again, not totally on-point. Set to blow to shake her up, and then accidentally hits the fuel tank several minutes later. The casino boys are all pro. This wasn't."

"What about freelancers?" Laura stared at both men as they held their cups midair and then set them down very carefully on the table. "Listen," she said, leaning in and rubbing the soreness from the back of her neck. "We know Don Jr. and his mother didn't give a rat's ass about Haines. They're in line for a lot of dough, now. We also know that casino boys have been sniffing, but haven't necessarily acted—just by the profile of how all this went down. But there's a third element, another party involved. I know it's always financially motivated, so we need to understand what's in Haines's will." She sat back, allowed her gaze to travel to the window deep in thought for a moment. "It was something he said to me about how it would kill Elizabeth."

"When were you out there?" James said in a tone so low that it made both Steve and Laura go still.

She leaned into him, two inches from his face. "Sunday during the game. Why?" Then she sat back and glared at him.

Steve raked his hair and pushed his coffee mug away. "Shit . . . well, so now we know." He shook his head. "All cards, I hope, are on the table, and from this point, it looks like we're all in this together."

James simply looked out the window, too deep in thought to speak.

"I say we need to rattle some cages," Laura murmured over her mug. "They don't know what we know. They are obviously looking for something they think we have. Take me to AC to the gaming tables with you and let me drop a few coins and a few smiles . . . make it look like the three of us—"

"No," James said, his hands flat on the table as he monitored the volume of his voice. "No."

"Then, you two need to come with me to a few political fund-raiser events, since the good senator isn't responding to my calls," Laura continued, ignoring James. "We've got a son and wife in one slice of the pie; casino industry players in another, and dirty politicians in a third—and an old man's life gone, with my uncle's hanging in the balance . . . plus my cousin afraid to drive, go to work, or even enter her own apartment. Meanwhile, I've gotta get a good lawyer and figure out how to put both of them into protective custody or somewhere safe, until we get to the bottom of this."

"Laura—"

"I, for one, am willing to put it all on red," she said, her finger pointed at James. "This ain't about what you want, what you think; last time I checked, your family wasn't at risk—mine is."

"Tomorrow, the boys from forensics should have something," Steve said with a sly smile. "They were real glad a little birdie dropped a tip in their ears about the car bomb link, too. Makes their paperwork easier."

"I could call Donny's cell," Laura said with a smile. "Act like I want to set up a meeting to follow up on the conversation I had with his father. That should ruffle his pretty feathers, because I'm sure, no matter what he and his mother planned, they did not want this thing to get large and ugly and public. That's how I *know* there's a third party involved. If they did anything directly, they would have waited until after the elections only a few weeks away, most likely."

"Laura, all of this is pure conjecture," James said, shaking his head no as he spoke.

"What good police or detective work begins with more than that, brother?" Steve said, his smile widening.

"Yeah, and maybe the butler did it," James muttered, seething.

"I like how the lady thinks. Donny will be real twisted in a knot, especially after the call I just had with him. Bastard stiffed us, Laura, can you believe it?" Steve folded his arms over his barrel chest that was puffed up with indignation.

"Yes," she said, chuckling, "the rich ones are always the cheapest ones you have to watch. They'll stiff you in a minute and feel entitled to." She let her breath out in relief when Steve smiled. Good. She'd been admitted to the game, even if James was salty that she had been. "I just want to get another plausible name other than my uncle's. Najira doesn't know anything, was never involved, and was just in the wrong place at the right time."

"That's the other issue," James said, hailing the waitress for a check. "Everybody's house has been broken in to. What're we gonna do now? Sleep on the office furniture and floors like one big happy PI family?"

Laura grinned. "Yes, James. I also have a gun. Why not?"

Chapter
9

Time had become the enemy. Between waiting for her attorney, Andrea McPherson, to show up at the hospital to protect Najira, and for the police to walk through each property to make sure they were safe and then file break-in reports for her, James, and Steve, the powers that be may as well have shoved bamboo shoots beneath her fingernails.

Too edgy from the adrenaline riddling her system, there was no way to heed Andrea's advice to sit down, be still, and remain calm. In her mind, they still had to get all the way across town to Lankenau Hospital to her uncle's bedside. Laura mentally willed the man not to die, especially not before his daughter, Najira, got to lay eyes on him.

Laura's head jerked up as Andrea began to speak after nervously glancing around the hospital cafeteria table. It was as though she'd been in another world, a self-prescribed place of exile, listening without comprehending while her brain continued to grapple with the facts. James, Steve, and Najira saw her cool exterior. God knew better. Laura picked at the plastic lid on her coffee while her weary attorney laid out the facts.

"You are a victim," Andrea said, her tone low and even as she addressed Najira. "You are the man's daughter, have a legitimate profession, and have never had a run-in with the law. We will get you to his bedside, and if I have to wake up the DA at his home tonight, consider it done."

Najira nodded and swallowed hard. Laura looked up at the woman who would represent her cousin. Andrea was clearly *the one*, the right woman for the job—even came out at one A.M. full face makeup, hair beat to the nines, wearing a nice pair of casual charcoal slacks and a cashmere cardigan plus penny loafers at no-o'clock in the freakin' morning.

Andrea turned her attention to Laura. "We've worked together for years," she said, her tone tense. "You're more than my client, you're a friend. But I have to tell you, this one is going to present challenges."

"I know," Laura said quietly. "Put it on my tab." She smiled at Andrea, who didn't smile back, but only glanced at James and Steve.

"I can't represent them, if I handle your cousin and your uncle. In fact, we need to split up these cases."

Laura nodded; James and Steve bristled.

"Listen, number one," James said, keeping his voice to a low murmur, "I don't need Laura to pay our bills. Number two, we've also been victimized. Somebody broke into our homes and—"

"Mr. Carter, no offense," Andrea said, folding her hands on the white linoleum and leveling her gaze at James, "but, you cannot have an ambulance chaser from off a UHF television advertisement do this. I have other attorney friends who will do me a favor and they start at $250 per hour—those are the junior levels. Are we clear? So, if Laura is willing to pick up the tab, then my first bit of advice is that you and your partner stow your male egos."

"Have them invoice me," Laura said coolly, "for work

done for the firm, not legal fees for any of these cases, if this gets sticky."

Andrea nodded as Laura raked her fingers through her hair.

"Wait," Steve argued, backing up James. "I don't see where we even need an attorney."

"The ink isn't even dried on your license, Steve," Laura hissed as she lowered her voice. "You don't think Haines Jr. will sue you for a botched security and snoop job? Just out of protocol, he'll have your ass in a civil case that will financially neuter both of you."

When the color drained from Steve's face and James pushed back from the table slowly, Andrea nodded and leaned back in her chair and closed her eyes. Najira was hugging herself and rocking. The obvious strain was beginning to tell on all of them. Laura had decimated the plastic top of her coffee cup, turning it into confetti on the table.

"Just as a precaution," Andrea finally said. "I'll rally the right people for the job and put them in a holding pattern in case it gets ugly—but I know how Donny works. Ruthless bastard, and you gentlemen failed on the job. Expect papers from him served soon." She opened her eyes and again sought Laura's for confirmation. "You might be able to save this lady a few bucks if you can call in some of your own markers and get info on exactly what happened, to help clear yourselves of any negligence, though."

"Split up the team, each from a different firm," Laura said, riffling her fingers through her hair. "Put a good business liability man on their business, cover my uncle with the best in the criminal case, and you stand by Najira—send me the bill."

"And, what about you?" Andrea shot back.

"I'll be fine."

The two women stared at each other.

"Nothing doing," Andrea finally said. "You met with Haines the day before he died, and the police will need a statement from you soon, not to mention, you may even be called in by either side as a witness. Therefore, I run this up the flagpole to get my mentor on this one—you got that? Courtesy."

Laura smiled. "Jim Ziegler charges more than Johnny Cochran. Isn't that overkill for my minor role in all of this?"

Andrea chuckled. "And when has that ever been a problem for you?"

"The man is allowed to have an attorney present, and next of kin—you. We'll both go in for a bit, and then you go to the safe house with Laura and the others. I'll escort you back to the hospital in the morning with your uncle's attorney of record." Andrea placed her hand on Najira's shoulder and waited for her to nod, and then glanced around at the others.

"He'll be groggy and may not wake up completely from the anesthesia. While the wound wasn't fatal, he is an older man, and the shot was fired at him point blank," the doctor warned. "Only a few minutes in there, understood? No questions—just to see him."

Najira clasped Laura and Andrea's hands. "I just want to see him."

Laura stood with her eyes fixed on the direction of ICU until she saw Najira and Andrea return through the double doors. Najira's face held a mixture of relief and sadness. Andrea's normally even walnut complexion was ashen. Her neatly coifed twists had come out of the barrette in sections, as though she'd been raking her fingers through it.

"How is he?" Laura murmured, and hugged Najira. But

her gaze eclipsed James and Steve when they stood, and remained steadily on Andrea's expression.

"I think he's gonna make it," Najira said on a thick swallow. "God is good."

Andrea hadn't said a word. The officers that flanked ICU watched her like a hawk. "Can you all call in a protective custody marker?" she asked in a casual manner, glancing at Steve and James.

"Done," James said quietly.

"Let your boys sweep your offices before any of you go there," Andrea replied. "I think I need one more cup of coffee before we all call it a night. Shall we?"

All eyes went to Laura, who simply nodded.

According to Andrea, the conversation was brief, but very specific. Akhan was roused for a moment, mumbled something about a will with Laura in it, and protecting the papers. Then he drifted off again. Najira had been warned not to breathe it. James and Steve were left at the table, while Laura stood in a quiet huddle with Andrea.

The attorney's eyes blazed as she stared at Laura hard. "Girl, do *not* fuck around and lie to me," she whispered. "You lie to them," she said through her teeth, motioning with her head toward James, Steve, and Najira. "You lie to the media. Together, we can lie to the world. But you come clean with me. *Always*. For something this potentially damning, *I* am your Alpha and Omega."

"So, what was all that about after we went to Lankenau to see Akhan?" James asked, flinging his overnight bag on the first chair that would catch it. No one said a word. Each person simply dropped their rush-packed suitcases on new office furniture and took a neutral position in the room.

Laura walked the perimeter of the white-walled open loft space that James and Steve had sectioned off with cubicle dividers. She didn't want to discuss it with them, any more than she wanted to discuss it with Andrea. Donald had mentioned a will, as had her uncle, but she had no idea she'd been named in it. *That was a problem.*

Instead, she focused her weary mind on immediate logistics. There was an adequate bathroom, open storage space in one room in the back and another that had a sofa, but had yet to be turned into a private office. The joint needed some plants, but as body tired as she was at the moment, the fact that there was wall-to-wall carpet in those rooms worked just fine. The fellas had even gotten a couple of computers. Good.

"Do you hear me talking to you?" James said more loudly.

"Yes. I did. But I don't feel like dealing with money right now." She let the comment linger, hoping that he'd assume she was referring to the payment arrangements she'd absorb for all their legal bills, not possible big bucks in a will. She didn't want to lie to James, but now was not the time for true confessions, especially when she hadn't a clue what she was up against. She peered out the window, for once glad to see the thin blue line of police protection in plain view.

James stared at her slack-jawed. Steve sat down heavily on what would one day be a receptionist's desk. Najira tore off her coat and flung her purse on the floor.

"Laura," James said one syllable at a time, crossing the room like a slow-moving storm. "Tonight, you talk to me. Stop—"

"Playing!" Najira shrieked. "Just stop fucking playing, Laura!" Her eyes were bloodshot and crazed as she swung her arms wildly. "Stop all the secrets! My father is lying in a hospital bed near dead with tubes and machines hooked to his body, and that dear man could go to jail—at least with family, you need to stop all the secrets!" Bitter tears streamed down Najira's face and she sputtered her complaint through mucus that garbled her voice. "I've had enough! James, *I know*, has had enough! That poor brother hasn't even got a clue." She whirled on James before Laura could move. "Start with what happened in the islands, and then I'll know you're for real."

James's eyes went from being frozen on Najira then toward Steve for a moment, and then held Laura as he resumed his slow stroll across the room to stand before Laura. "Begin at the beginning," he said in a near whisper. "Like your cousin said. No games. Stop playing."

It was a split-second decision; tell what could be told, what no longer mattered, versus get into something that could capsize everyone's lives.

"All right," Laura said evenly. "Since I'm now a liar, and a game-player, instead of someone trying to protect those I love." She glanced at her cousin, but couldn't stare at her, not sure if she was more enraged or hurt that Najira had betrayed her confidence like she had. "Something deeply private. A profound loss occurred while I was on Grand Cayman . . . which is why I stayed as long as I did."

James's intense glare cut her, but the razor's edge was the fact that he glanced at Najira for confirmation that the truth had indeed been told.

"What profound loss, Laura?" James waited as the question dangled. "How much was it? A million, ten million?"

"Priceless," Laura whispered, her glare now burning shame into her cousin's conscience.

"Laura, I'm sorry," Najira finally said, coming to stand between Laura and James to attempt to end the stalemate. "It was just that—"

"You didn't trust me, either," Laura said, her tone icy enough to make each word snap.

"We're all tired, everybody has been—"

"Stay out of it, Steve," Laura warned. "You're an innocent bystander, so far."

Laura turned away from her cousin, and didn't even glance at James. There were no words.

"How much did you put on the line, gamble with, and lose, Laura?" James shouted at her retreating form.

"It wasn't *money*," Najira shouted back, awkwardly attempting to shield her cousin's shredded dignity. "I shouldn't have gone there about the baby. I was just so—"

"Baby?" James's question was quiet thunder.

Laura stopped walking but didn't turn around. Najira stood paralyzed with her hands over her mouth. Steve backed up.

"Now do you see why I've kept certain things to myself?" Laura murmured. "It's dangerous to have vital information in the minds of those who cannot handle it under duress." She began walking again, but a rough tug on her arm stopped and spun her. James had to have crossed the room in two long strides. She thrust her chin up, willing tears away.

"What baby?" He'd asked the question in such a low, threatening octave that fury made her ears ring.

"Ours. I miscarried." She stared at him without blinking.

"Miscarried it, or abort—"

Her slap made spit fly out of his mouth. From some pent up place deep within the recesses of her being, her open hands became fists, and with every ounce of muscle in her she became an unstoppable whirlwind of punches, slaps, kicks, bites, using clutched fingers to grab at James's shirt, ignoring his defensive arms to protect his face, Steve's attempts to pull her back, Najira getting slapped as much as James when she'd foolishly entered the fray. Breathing hard, tears streaming, she caught Steve in the jaw and felt the blow send pain through her knuckles and her wrist. But she didn't care. She'd kick James Carter's ass this early morning. Abortion? Abortion? A year of nursing that wound, trying to disconnect her hopes and dreams from what had been a cruel reality, and this black SOB had said *what?*

"It wasn't money! There's not enough money in the world

for what that meant to me!" Laura hollered, her cool gone, her mind splintered, and her spirit ready to die. "Fuck you! I wanted it more than my next breath, but I'll kill your ass or die trying!"

"Let her go!" James hollered to Steve and Najira.

They gave James a spurious glance, but when he rushed them to get to Laura, Steve pushed Laura behind him and Najira grabbed James's swing arm.

"No man, you can't hit her."

"Hit her, and I go down to the po-po outside," Najira said, eyeing James, unsure.

"Let her go," James said again, less fury in his voice. Hot tears rose to his eyes as Laura began to sob.

"You stay away from me," Laura shouted, her eyes wild as hiccupping sobs became broken by her angry words. She pointed at James who kept coming toward her anyway. "You've accused me—so that's what you think? Is *that* what you think!"

James just shook his head, took several more slaps, and pulled Laura into his arms. "Oh, God . . . why didn't you tell me?" He rubbed her back and rested his forehead on her shoulder. He took in several shaky breaths, refusing to cry. She'd been pregnant. In all that time, he hadn't been there . . .

It was something in the tone of his voice, the way James couldn't seem to steady his breathing . . . the way it hitched in his throat and hot-coated her shoulder, damp, that made her finally stop struggling against his hold and just cry.

Yes, it had been horrible. Yes, she'd wished he'd been there, but knew that that was impossible—just as it was impossible to explain that she might be in a will, destined to inherit a significant sum of money from a man who her uncle may or may not have killed. Intent was everything; outcomes were circumstantial . . . The finer points of truth were always omitted from the courts. Just like no one would ever believe, if she explained, how she'd masterminded the takedown of Philadelphia's black elite, but that she'd never meant for Monica Price to die. As she held this man, now rubbing his back through his torn sweater, willing him not to sob, she knew that there'd be no way to explain how convoluted this had all become. Akhan had gone over to Haines's to do a hit, but not a hit—a favor.

"Laura, I'm so sorry," Najira whispered.

Laura didn't answer her, but kept her face buried in James's chest. "I have to lie down," she murmured, "before I fall down."

James nodded. Steve raced into the next room to put a green garbage bag filled with blankets and pillows on the sofa in the private office.

For four hours, she slept like a dead woman. James had curled around her and wouldn't let her go. In the distance of her mind, she heard the front door sound and knew Najira's footsteps. A light tap at the door made her sit up.

"The boys brought some coffee and donuts," Najira said, cracking the door open slightly, and then quickly shutting it behind her.

Pure nausea at the thought of ingesting anything made Laura untangle herself from James's hold and stand. He was on his feet instantly, weaved a bit, looked at her bleary eyed, and then walked away to find Steve.

Truthfully, at this point, she didn't care. She saw Steve sprawled out in a makeshift bed of two chairs pulled together, and Najira had obviously been given the sofa up front. Whatever.

"Hey," Najira said, brandishing the bag of food and motioning toward the desk that had four cups of coffee on it. "You okay?"

Steve roused with a grunt and slowly stood as James selected a random cup and handed it to Laura. She just stared at it and walked away, folding her arms around herself.

"Listen up," Laura said, her voice monotone, holding no emotion. "Haines gave some papers to Akhan. That's what Andrea and I were discussing. May be a will, or he might have been delusional coming out of surgery and anesthesia. But one thing for sure, whatever he gave my uncle, other people were also looking for those papers—hence the break-ins." Her gaze stayed on the horizon as she spoke quietly but with authority. "It's daylight, we have a lot of work to do, and anything that went down last night is irrelevant." Laura waited. "We split up and do what we do best. You guys find out whatever you can about the crime scene, I'm going to have a discussion with a few people in high places. Najira, you go to the hospital and stay with your father . . . tell him I love him."

Behind her she could hear plastic lids being taken off Styrofoam cups and packs of sugar being ripped. This morning she was very glad that there were no more arguments to be had.

Luis glanced around the Roxboro Diner four ways before speaking. "You never heard this from me, and after this, I can't give you any more," he told Steve and James, and then looked around nervously again. "Forensics has been working on this all night, on account of the fact that Haines is a serious VIP. Dig?"

"Appreciate it, man," James muttered, wiping his face with his hands.

Adrenaline and caffeine battled with fatigue as Steve slumped over a cup of java and issued Luis a sideline glance. Apparently too weary to speak, Steve just raised his cup a fraction of an inch from the booth table.

"Found all kinds of shit in there," Luis whispered, leaning into the small huddle. "Poor bastard's tea was laced with a glycoside called covallatoxin, otherwise known as, Lily of the Valley."

"What, dude?" Steve whispered. "I don't follow."

"Shit, man, neither did we at first, till the boys ran it down."

Luis's nervous gaze went from James to Steve and back again. "You know all them flowers in vases around the house?" He waited until the memory registered in the two ex-cops' expressions. "Come to find out, that shit is a deadly poison, yo. Even the water from the cut flowers can kill you. Reaction time is immediate—irritability, nausea, vomiting, headache, hallucinations, slowed heartbeat and then heart failure."

"The wife had flowers all over the house," James said quietly. "And all the symptoms you mentioned would seem pretty normal for an old man who would soon go to bed and die in his sleep."

"Yeah, but unless you can prove that she was the one who fixed him the tea, then, hey," Steve muttered.

"Besides, old Haines was smothered by a pillow. Wasn't enough Lily of the Valley in his bloodstream to kill him, just a trace from hours earlier." Luis glanced around nervously again and dropped his voice to a tense whisper. "Ain't nobody trying to fuck with, or dig up, no spurious shit on the Haines family—you got that? Unless it's real tight, don't even bring that bull my way. I've got a family and a career, and ain't ready to go down without a pension."

"Okay, so the old dude took a sip of tea and didn't drink a whole cup earlier that day—fact remains, somebody laced his cup," James said, his gaze narrowed on Luis.

"I hear you," Luis said, letting his breath out hard. "We wouldn't have even looked for anything in his food, if you all hadn't given us the heads up—so I owe ya. But somebody on the scene who meant to do him in one way or another could have had a plan B, or that could've been plan A . . . the old man didn't drink his tea, or whatever, and then they decided to go the traditional nursing home route and smother his ass." Luis shook his head. "Looks bad for the nurse, man. I gotta tell ya."

"Yeah," James said, and slurped his coffee with disinterest. "I know. But I still ain't convinced." He ignored his partner's worried glance.

"Face it," Luis pressed on, but keeping his voice low. "The nurse had probably also laced his food."

"What was under the silver dome, man?" Steve said, blowing his breath out hard. "Rat poison, or some shit?"

"No," Luis said, again glancing around the diner. "Wasn't nothin' under the dome. The dinner plate was clean as a whistle. But in his stomach there was residue of hemlock."

"Oh, get the fuck out of here," James said, becoming exasperated.

"Seriously," Luis said, beginning to talk with his hands. "Hours before dude got smothered, he had roasted quail, wild rice and vegetables and whatever for a late lunch, given the digestion rate. The forensics experts said that sometimes wild quail eat hemlock seeds—but they're immune to it. Shit originally came from Britain, but grows here now, especially near farmhouses on the East Coast. So, whoever prepared lunch could even get out of it because—"

"It would either be the butcher's fault, or the fault of whomever he buys from—a business would take the fall, not an individual, because I'm sure the establishment that services the Haineses gets their meat from some chi chi place up in Chestnut Hill, and the people who fixed the food had to know not to also eat it. But somebody could have asked for a special one-person catered delivery." James stared at Steve. "A nurse's job ain't to cook, if there's a butler on staff, right?"

"And we know who's in the meat packing, meat providin'

business, right? A caterer is also an easy way to get a bad plate onto somebody's table, real smooth-like." Steve set his cup down without even looking at it.

Luis nodded and sipped his coffee slowly. "But dig it— this poison takes several hours to work. Has the symptoms of fatigue, muscle weakness, weak pulse, then paralysis until the lungs just stop working, but the bitch is, your mind stays clear until the end . . ."

"Everything that an old man with dementia might have, except the clear mind," James said, leaning in and looking at his partner.

"Bingo. And ingested before the nurse got there," Steve said, glancing between James and Luis. "Scratch the nurse."

"The old man had a lot running through his system, high blood pressure medication, insulin, and mematine HCI— Namenda, along with the poison."

"Namenda?" James sat back. "Talk to me."

"For dementia. It's a relatively new drug, came out in late 2003. Makes sense, since he'd been diagnosed with Alzheimer's, and Haines would have access to the best," Luis said, standing and then sitting down again quickly to make his point before he left them. "When we shook down the house, the wife told us to look in her vanity where she stashed his pills. Said her husband was getting so out of control with the dementia that she was afraid he'd overdose or something, wanting to take his own medicine and forgetting how many pills he'd already had. But he was so stubborn and didn't want her to dispense it for him—like old folks get when sick—that, he wouldn't take the medicine prescribed by his doctor. The only way she could get it into him was to slip it into his brandy."

Luis shook his head. "What was that word she'd used to describe him . . . oh, yeah, *obstreperous*, whatever that means. But you get the picture. Girlfriend was living a quiet, dignified nightmare with him. My grandmother went through that shit, and Liz Haines just gave the Alzheimer's Fund a hundred Gs. Have a heart. Let her grieve in peace."

"Call me suspicious, but I'm having a problem with all of this," James muttered. "The man has had three potentially deadly substances added to his food." He ticked the charges off on his fingers as he stared at Luis. "One, supposedly prescribed by the doctor, but nowhere in the room with the nurse—who I would imagine should have been told about *all* his medications by Mrs. Haines when he came on for the job. Number two, the man has hemlock in his gizzard, by way of gourmet wild quail—which you say produces paralysis after hours that it takes to set in. But he ate lunch, and may have even had some Lily of the Valley laced tea . . . served before the nurse came on shift. Then, you find the smoking gun, literally and figuratively—a cup of tea on his tray deadly enough to take him out for sure, plus, you just said that Lily of the Valley creates a state of mania."

"Yo, a good lawyer could make the circumstantial case that with all this shit in Haines's system, he wigged, went for the nurse, or ransacked his bag. If it were my ass in the sling, I'd claim I had the gun on me because I travel through the badlands at night to get to my job—the old dude found it, shot me, and in trying to keep him from killing me in his demented state, I tried to subdue him with a pillow so as not to break his bones or to make him fall, or whatnot—but then not realizing he couldn't breathe." Steve shrugged. "The poisons would be my freakin' alibi. Your boys at the morgue need to be sure a pillow suffocated him, and not the hemlock paralyzing his lungs so he couldn't breathe, regardless of a pillow in his face."

This time when Luis stood, it was with finality of motion. "Look, do what you can with this, but everybody downtown is ready to pin it on the old dude who got shot. Makes the paperwork easier, closes things up tidy, and keeps a very powerful family in a real nice neighborhood off our asses, feel me?"

James and Steve nodded.

"Yeah, I feel you. Can't have the neighbors thinking there's a killer still on the loose."

"Hey," Luis said, leaving James and Steve with the tab. "I don't make the rules of the game, I just play it."

Chapter
10

There was no way in the world she was sitting around, waiting on an escort. She had things to do. It wasn't even about a hospital vigil. Her nerves couldn't take it. Either fate would be good to her uncle, or it wouldn't. Those people still in good stead with heaven could pray for him—she respected that. However, she'd do her part by making sure the man lived to see another day, if he ever recovered. Long time ago, her grandmother had told her: faith without works is dead.

Tucking the pain that she had visited the night before deep within her, Laura allowed it to propel her into forward motion. Never again would she revisit that shit that had gone down with James and Najira. She didn't have time to dwell on personal drama.

Laura hailed the police squad car outside of James and Steve's office loft and began walking. No cab in sight, Najira at the hospital and out of her hair, and James and Steve gone wherever, as much as she hated to deal with it, SEPTA was still an option.

She walked down Main Street until she was standing at a

crowded bus stop at the bottom of the hill on Ridge Avenue. Absently, she glanced at the political buttons people wore as well as the pre-election posters flanking the road and the stores that stretched into a nearby mall. Already, vans and trucks were pulling into the Restaurant Supply Store that marked the beginning of the entry to Manyunk. Despite news to the contrary, commerce was still alive in America. Some people had, some people didn't. Yeah, the slogan said it all— Vote or Die. It was time for her and Senator Scott to have a private chat.

The wait for a bus that would take her over the express-way to a place where she could jump out and catch a cab was almost as outrageous as the entire situation she'd been hurled into. But she waited, and coped, and got on the crowded pub-lic transport, her focus singular: to get home, get her real clothes, her car, and a gun.

Laura put the key into her front door without fear. If someone was laying for her, so be it. But she played the odds. Chances were they wanted information more than they wanted her dead. The ransack made that obvious. The real person at risk was Akhan.

She made quick work of jumping through the shower, collecting her makeup, several outfits and coordinating ac-cessories and shoes. The places she had to go required that she look the part and play the role. Donning a moss green cutaway wool jacket that stopped at the knee a fraction of an inch above its matching skirt, she found her lizard-skin pumps and emerald earrings to go with her pearls and approved her choice. Laura spritzed on some Red and dropped it into her bag. She didn't care what Steve and James had said about leaving the weapon. The Magnum went into her barrel Coach purse, her sable got slung over her arm, and her best designer gear went into a suit bag along with a couple of evening gowns. Her laptop and Blackberry were coming along, as well. Screw a couple of hastily packed sweaters, jeans, a toothbrush and some deodorant. Laura Caldwell had work to do.

Although angry, she wasn't crazy. Instead of opening the garage from inside the house, she grabbed the door opener with care, stood in the driveway, and depressed the automatic button. When it didn't blow, she rushed to the trunk and thrust her luggage into it, and then checked and double-checked the undercarriage, brake lines, the engine, and the entire vehicle a few times before trusting to commit her body to it. Then she was out.

Laura idled her engine in the valet parking line outside the Marriott Convention Center while staring at her electronic calendar. Like she always told Najira, even if you don't attend, having standing tickets to everything going on in the city was a way to play the game. Republican or Democrat, notwithstanding, one had to know what was going on in all circles, stay sharp, and keep one's eyes on the bouncing political ball.

Chances were great that Liz Haines would be in hiding, so would her son, as would only be appropriate since Donald's body was still warm. But Senator Scott had to make an appearance here, if only a brief one—which would be enough time for her to send a silent message by her presence. This hit was sloppy. She was not afraid.

Playing the hunch through to the end, she entered the hotel lobby that stretched from Arch to Market Streets, her gaze roving the glass and chrome bar area first before turning to go up the escalators to the banquet rooms. There would be enough VIPs in the house to make a splash at the Chamber of Commerce event, even if the senator didn't show. The real question was, which way to work it?

As she went up each level, people watching the entire

time, her strategy began to gel. Someone was looking for papers. Someone was afraid of what they could contain. There was obviously a will stashed somewhere that named her as a significant beneficiary—or else all this bullshit wouldn't have gone down. But if they knew what was in it, naming her as a serious heir, then why hadn't they eliminated her first? Unless . . . Laura smiled. They didn't know.

Producing her ID, she smiled at the reception table workers. Her name was immediately located amongst the heavy contributors list, and she was granted entry. At eleven o'clock, the room was already filling. Media was there, and she spotted her buddy Rick right away. He smiled from across the room, inching his short, pudgy frame through the circles of tables toward her, heavy camera in tow.

She breezed past small clusters of people whom she knew from her former life, regaling them with stories of the hurricane that had swept the Caribbean and the southeastern part of the country. Whatever. It was all a well-orchestrated performance. She told them what they wanted to hear in perfect sound bites; yes, she was back. No, she wouldn't miss this political race if her life depended on it. But she kept moving, stayed aloof, and watched Rick from the corner of her eye until she could unobtrusively get next to him.

Rick kissed her on the cheek as they came into contact. She'd missed his slightly damp hugs and round, flushed cherub face, just as much as she missed the mischief that always twinkled in his small, brown irises.

"Hey, lady," he said with a bright smile. "You're a sight for sore eyes. Just up and leave a guy without a trace, and I thought you loved me."

"You know I love you, Rick," she said, chuckling as she pecked his cheek again. "You're doing good?"

"Yeah, working like a demon."

They both laughed.

"So, what else is new?"

He cocked his head to the side and raised an eyebrow. "Was hoping you'd tell me."

Laura laughed. "Don't I always?"

He nodded and moved in closer to her. "That you do, love—which is why you're always my favorite girl."

They exchanged a knowing glance and then Rick looked away as he spoke to her.

"So, uh . . . what's your take on this whole Haines thing?"

She touched his shoulder. "Like before, as soon as I know, I'll feed it to you first. Okay?"

He nodded, gave her a wink, and sighed. "I'll take that to the bank."

"Like cold, hard cash."

He stared at her, shifting from foot to foot as excitement overtook him. "God, I missed you."

"Same here," she said in a delicious whisper. "But I need to go to work."

"Anybody I can help you get next to today?"

Laura smiled and shook her head as she strolled away from Rick. "Baby, you know I always work alone."

Najira clasped her father's hand, her eyes riveted to his form, her mind locked in silent prayer. She watched his chest move up and down slowly, each breath representing another second of life within him. If God took him from her, there would be no recovery. Whatever she'd done wrong in life, she vowed to make amends for . . . if he would just be all right.

"Daddy," she whispered, "when you get better, we're gonna go to the park like you always do. We'll spend more time together, me and you. I know I've been running around, busy, and haven't visited as much as I should . . . but I love you. Please get better."

Tears made it nearly impossible to make out his frail form

in the bed. This was the man who'd always stood for something, always carried the family wisdom and stories—even her brother couldn't be here for him now, an ex-felon disallowed seeing his father at death's door. Something very serious was broken in the system. Najira gently laid her head against her father's stomach and willed herself not to sob. They had righted the wrongs of the past, had fallen those who had originally attacked their family, but the price now seemed too high.

A soft squeeze of her hand made Najira's head jerk up. She looked at her father's face. He hadn't opened his eyes, but she could tell he knew she was there. That's all that mattered; that he was aware that he hadn't been abandoned to possibly die alone.

"I want to go where there are trees and flowers," Akhan murmured hoarsely. "New flowers."

"Don't try to talk, Daddy," Najira whispered, stroking his bald scalp as fresh tears rolled down her cheeks.

"Next to my brother," her father croaked. "Go see about that very soon," he whispered. "Promise me."

"Shhh," she told him, swallowing hard. "We're talking about getting you home, not about burying you."

He shook his head slowly. "Go to Northwood and look at the flowers for me. Take Laura. She understands about these things."

"All right. All right," Najira said, as he seemed to become agitated. "I promise," she told him, saying anything at this point just to keep him relaxed.

"God, baby," he murmured, drifting off again. "I'm so tired."

"Knew it before we got here," Steve said with disgust as he cruised down the street past Akhan's house. "Crawling with our boys."

James nodded. "How much you wanna bet that the joint was ransacked, first?"

Steve nodded as they exited the narrow North Philadelphia street and headed back toward Huntington Park. "Think the locals will talk?"

"Not to the cops," James muttered. "But info is always on sale for a brother from around the way."

"Say no more, partner. Drop me off to go get my ride. I'll work South Philly, you work North Philly, and hopefully, we'll live to meet up in the middle somewhere."

Laura tried not to bristle when Senator Scott took the dais but didn't so much as offer her an acknowledging glance. Fine. So be it. That was how the game was played. Distance was a survival requirement, this close to voting day.

Scanning the room for a conduit, she saw several of Donald Haines's old cronies from the Micholi Foundation. *That* would send a message that she was still in the inner loop. Edging her way toward the huddle of grim-faced men, she simply touched their arms, kept her expression somber and let out a well-timed sigh that was no act.

They nodded, said nothing in particular, but their nonverbal message spoke volumes—as did their gentle, politically correct pecks on her cheek. Then she left them, glanced up at the senator who had his eyes fastened on her. Yeah. *Now,* let's talk.

He was still glad-handing after a particularly boring lunch. But she noticed that he hadn't hustled out of the event, as would be the norm. He meandered near her, saying goodbyes and offering platitudes, offering her the opportunity to come up to him for a few public seconds.

Laura pasted on a sad but respectable smile, and extended her hand toward him. "I wish you the best," she said, her tone even.

"Thank you," he said calmly, his attention diverting in multiple directions as others fought for his attention, too.

"I'm ready to make a substantial contribution after what I've heard," she casually offered.

He smiled, but not too widely. "Thank you, Ms. Caldwell. Our campaign appreciates your generosity."

She smiled, but it was a tight one. "I have the papers and will see to it very soon."

He hesitated, but for just a fraction of a second. He was good—damned good . . . but so was she. Laura nodded and moved away from him so that the media could eat him alive.

James took up residence on a bar stool at the far end of the corner joint at 17th and Diamond. Noon wasn't too early for it to be half filled with straggling barflies. He slid a fifty across the dingy wood and nodded to the poorly stocked shelves within the dark space. "Jack. Black."

"You want change?" the bartender asked.

"No," James said, holding the bartender's suspicious gaze. "Just a little conversation to go with the hefty tip."

"Depends on what you're itching for. Might not be able to scratch it with a fifty."

"Just wanna know if anybody went into old man Akhan's before *the man* got there."

"Yeah," the bartender said, moving his burly form behind the bar and cleaning out a rocks glass with a dirty rag. "But you don't want none-a that."

James stared down at the smeared glass that now contained amber liquid as the bartender slid it toward him. The only people that nobody in North Philly wanted any parts of were those that the so-called badlands didn't offend—the casino boys. James studied his options, downed the drink, hoping the alcohol content would kill any bacteria. "Cool," he said and stood.

* * *

Mike Caluzo looked up from his lunch as Steve entered the small Port Richman hideaway. Steve nodded at the white-haired bartender, who gave him a warm salute as he passed.

"How come you always come around here when I'm eating?" Caluzo said, abandoning his roast beef sandwich to give Steve a familiar embrace.

Steve laughed. "Because that's how I know how to find you."

"You gonna eat, or just wanna beer while you talk?" Caluzo picked up his sandwich again and took a huge bite from it.

"How about just the beer?"

Caluzo dropped his sandwich and mumbled, "Oh, so it's that serious?" He chuckled and shook his head. "Fifty bucks I can guess what it is."

"You win," Steve said, waiting on the beer that was already being filled from the tap. He glanced around at the checkered red and white plastic cloth–covered tables.

"Shame what happened," Caluzo said, sheepishly.

"Yeah . . . a man that old should die peacefully in his sleep."

Caluzo didn't glance up from his paper plate, but simply nodded. "I know whatcha mean. That was the plan. But, hey, life throws curve balls all the time."

"For old time's sake, wanna tell me who set the ball in motion?"

Caluzo belched and looked up with a smile. "That's what we wanna know. Even for old time's sake, can't help ya."

"You interested, if I should stumble upon some info?"

Mike Caluzo smiled and folded his hands over his rotund belly. Steve watched Caluzo's sweat suit stretch to accommodate the girth of the man who was his age, but looked ten years older.

"Now, you're fucking with me, right?"

"No," Steve said, his expression suddenly stone serious.

"Well, well, well . . . ya just never know what politics and business make for strange bedfellows, duya?" Caluzo sighed. "It ain't in my authority to cut you in, but for the right info, I could introduce you to some people."

"Not necessary. I'm just trying to understand a few things that're keeping me up at night."

Caluzo motioned toward the greasy remains from his lunch. "A man should eat right, ya know. Should have somebody who can cook old world style, prepare his food and have it delivered to his family, single portion—so as nothing goes to waste." Caluzo stared at Steve without blinking. "*Capice?* Sulli, you know there're plenty good caterers in the city who work the Main Line. It's a good business. Profitable. Very smooth operation."

"Who placed the order?" Steve waited, as Caluzo slurped his beer.

"I dunno, but we wasn't in no rush."

"That'll cost you ten Hail Mary's," Steve said, accepting his beer as he stood with a smile. He downed his brew as his old friend from high school laughed. "Thanks."

"Got it," James said into his cell phone, and pulled away from the curb in front of Laura's house.

That crazy woman had gone back in, according to the tip the patrol car had dropped on him. Steve had just confirmed what his gut had already told him: that the food job was the casino boys' initial intent, but they hadn't followed through. The key was to find out who'd placed the catering order. Still, there was no way to prove foul play, even if they could say the wife, the son, or the butler had placed the fatal order. To everyone except those in the know, it would appear that the Haines family ordered a specialty lunch, as is commonly done, and the meat so happened to be tragically tainted by a stupid, free range gourmet quail that simply ate the wrong thing. Most likely, even the business couldn't be criminally charged for the so-called accident, and any civil charges would be up to the Haines family to pursue—a doubtful outcome, at best, since the man died from being smothered.

Yet, three very important questions lingered: who tainted the tea; who actually put the pillow over old man Haines's face, if Akhan didn't; and what were the casino boys looking for in everybody's house?

More than that, however, what was Laura up to on a solo mission? The question deeply disturbed him.

By the time he'd met up with Steve in the underground lot at the Constitution Center, his nerves were fried. If Laura was out and about refusing to answer her cell phone, that meant only one thing—trouble.

"You drive, partner," Steve said, closing the door to his truck with a thud. "We go get Najira and hold tight back at the office. She's gotta surface sooner or later."

James kept his eyes forward as Steve depressed his remote alarm and climbed into his SUV. "'Jira ain't heard from her, either."

Steve stared at him. "You think she's crazy enough to go to AC without us?"

James put his vehicle in reverse. "Yeah. Laura Caldwell is out of her mind."

"No, I'm not staying here," Najira said, her voice escalating and bouncing off the office walls. "I know how she thinks, and she's like a rat with her back against the wall right now, totally ready to do something off the hook to make a statement."

Steve glanced at James, but spoke to Najira. "Listen, based on what we just ran down to you—which direction you think she'll go? Main Line to find Haines's secluded wife, or AC?"

"I'd put my money on AC, since your surveillance videos didn't show nothing. Ain't that what your boy said?" Najira's gaze darted between both men.

"Fact," Steve muttered, worry making his neck stiff as he slowly paced. "Maid service came in and was out. Caterers dropped off lunch at the door, and were out. The wife left before lunch even arrived and was seen at an event. The butler ain't talking to nobody but his attorney. Nobody could've been in there at the time the pillow went over Haines's face, sadly, darlin', but your dad. So, any idea where she might show up—there're, like, twenty hotel casinos down there, and we're not even sure which one to start at. It could take all night, and we'd still miss her."

James sat in front of the computer, unconvinced. He kept running the duplicate tape back, stopping it and searching for something he wasn't sure of—but very glad that they'd given up the on-site videos to the police without a hassle. It was real cool of Luis not to mention the direct stream to their systems, but he knew their inside man wasn't exactly trying to be all that diligent.

He got up from the desk and rubbed his face with both hands. "We start by finding out which casino block got the construction contract." James let his breath out hard and stared at the tube again. "If I know Laura at all, she'd say, follow the money."

Najira edged to the tube and stared at it with James. "I could go on-line and pull up old newspaper clippings. She showed me how to do that, and I could search for slot machines, gaming charters, to see which ones are slated to build first. If I know her, too, she'd waltz in there and put it all on red."

When Najira received no resistance, she sat down where James had been, staring at the people frozen in pause motion on the screen. "James, clear me out of this so I can surf on-line."

He came to her side and took the tape off pause to click out of the program.

"Hold it," Najira said, stopping him before he could exit the streaming video. "Four maids went in, three came out."

They all stared at each other.

"That's what fatigue will do for you," James said quietly. "Make you miss shit that's right in front of your eyes."

Steve came over to the computer as James slowly wound back to the section Najira had indicated. "I'll be damned," Steve murmured.

James looked up. "The boys downtown oughta see this."

She crossed her legs neatly at the blackjack table, allowing her sable coat to fall off her shoulders and expose the skimpy black halter she was wearing beneath it. She glanced at the older Asian man at her left, and the nervous-looking European businessman at her right. Then she coolly pushed ten thousand dollars in chips forward. The dealer looked at her, the expressions beside her paled.

"Ma'am, this isn't roulette. You sure you want to do this all in one hand? Maybe baccarat might be a better game for you."

She smiled at the blackjack dealer, and tipped her chin toward the hidden cameras that she knew had followed her ever since she'd gone to the cashier for a huge sum in chips. "Tell the boys upstairs that Laura came to play." She picked up her chips calmly and dropped them in her purse. "I might be at the wrong table. So, I'll be over at the bar while I figure out the best game to play."

She slid out of her high stool like she was made of silk,

sauntered over to the bar, and waited. She ordered a Grand Marnier straight up in a cordial glass, and sipped it very slowly. A tall male bouncer approached and leaned in close to her ear.

"Had we known a high roller like you was in the house, we would have invited you to the VIP lounge. Would you care for a tour before you place your bets?"

Laura nodded and followed the man wearing the stylish, loose constructed, black Armani suit, leaving her drink and a substantial tip.

Chapter
11

There were levels and degrees of bold; Laura smiled as she pushed her agenda over the top. What did it matter? she wondered. So much had happened, so many people she'd cared about had died or were in jeopardy . . . There was no point in turning around as one huge hulking form joined another behind her in the hallway as she passed through the opulent, glittering oasis around her.

This was over the top, she mused. Anything she could think of couldn't be half as ostentatious or bold a flaunting of money and power as what these boys were into. Ten thousand dollars on the table only got their attention because sisters usually don't roll like that at the Jersey shore. Had this been Vegas, it wouldn't have registered. As soon as they'd figured out that she wasn't a cop, drug dealer's known woman, sports-wife or mistress, she'd come up on their worry radar. Good.

The first man who had approached her smiled and opened a suite door. She nodded and remained civil—after all, the best and most ruthless business was conducted that way. He ushered her into a heavily mirrored room, replete with enough gold, white, and teal to make her gag. The revenge of Liberace, she thought, and smiled, without needing to force it.

"Welcome to our high rollers' suite," a well-dressed man in his late fifties said, looking her over. He extended his hand and warmly shook Laura's. "I'm Anthony Rapuzzio, head of security. My job is to make sure that all our VIP guests feel safe and comfortable while visiting us."

"Laura Caldwell," she said, dropping her coat with flourish, and allowing one of the suit-wearing bouncers to catch it. She understood the process, which is why she'd worn the revealing dress. She didn't even look over her shoulder as they discreetly patted down her sable. The boys had to feel comfortable that she wasn't wearing a wire. She handed her bag to Rapuzzio, and sighed. "Given how much I came here to play with, you'll understand why I packed the Magnum. I couldn't walk across the parking lot with a knot without a little heat."

"That won't be necessary," he said, inspecting her weapon with appreciation. "Haven't seen one of these in years."

"It's vintage. My father's."

Rapuzzio nodded. "May I offer you a drink? Some champagne as we tour?"

"Champagne would be lovely," Laura cooed, and took his extended elbow.

With a nod of his head, Rapuzzio dispatched one of the men who had trailed her into the room. He waved his arm as he spoke and walked deeper into the space.

"Here, on this side, you have a wonderful view of the water." Rapuzzio pivoted and moved her closer to the windows. "From here, the skyline—but please don't consider going to our competition."

Laura covered her heart with her hand. "Wouldn't dream of it. That's why I came to you, first."

They both offered each other a tense smile, the double

entendre implicit as he pointed out the big screen monitors on the far side of the room.

"You can see what's happening on the casino floors from here, or catch every sport on HDTV over there."

"Absolutely breathtaking," she said with enough sarcasm to let him know she was ready to get down to business, but didn't mean to offend.

"I would imagine a classy woman, such as yourself, might not be interested in the sports, but, uh . . . you do play games."

"Oh, yes," Laura said, unthreading her arm from his to go stare out the window. "I play well, too."

"Ah, then let us discuss which one brought you here."

Laura paused, allowing each fact to quickly roll around in her mind like a roulette ball. If they were searching for Haines's will, and had torn up her place looking for it, only two things would be of interest to the casino boys: the gaming charters and/or any control she might exert over construction contracts that were already supposed to be locked down. Since Haines couldn't get his hands on more than fourteen percent at one percent per new casino slated for Pennsylvania, and those wouldn't begin to be profitable for a few years, she hedged her bets on short-term money. Construction.

"Well," she said, taking her time as she studied the gray strands running through Rapuzzio's thick, dark brown hair. "I was hoping to have that conversation with another high roller—assuming one is available."

Rapuzzio smiled, but the line of it was tight. "Most of them are already on the floor at the tables. Games are in progress as we speak."

She nodded and let her breath out hard. "Guess I'll have to make a formal appointment with Joey Scapolini, then. I was hoping for a simple courtesy visit, though."

Rapuzzio remained very, very still. The men around him bristled.

"You do play high stakes, don't you."

She looked at him hard. "Is there any other way?"

"There's a lot of risk in that. Can be dangerous, especially for a woman."

"I'm insured," she snapped back, her voice losing some of its charm to match his threat.

"Shame what happened in Philly," he said, testing her.

"I'll miss the old man dearly. No one should have that happen to him."

Rapuzzio nodded. "Not at his level, after all the friends he made."

"I agree. Which is why I hate freelancers. Wanted to be sure no one else gets in the game they really can't play."

"I thoroughly agree," a voice to her right said as a door opened. A short, wiry man in his mid-forties walked out, his charcoal suit immaculate. "It's all right, Tony. This lady is a guest of our friend—even postmortem."

Laura quietly let out the breath she'd been holding as Anthony Rapuzzio stepped aside. She slowly moved forward, smiled, and extended her hand. "Mr. Scapolini, I am honored."

He took up her hand and swept the back of it with a soft kiss and allowed it to drop away. "C'mon, now—it's Joey. Mr. Scapolini was my father." He looked at Laura with deep appreciation that bordered on lewd. "I believe the lady asked for some champagne?"

Immediately three bouncers responded and headed toward the bar at once. Laura almost laughed, but didn't. Instead, she kept her eyes on the young heir of Scapolini Construction. Rapuzzio lit a cigarette—same brand, Dunhill, that had been on James's step.

"Come. Have a seat," he said in a weary tone, motioning for her to sit on the sofa.

Laura accepted the champagne flute and sipped it carefully, all the while watching the men who had surrounded her.

"So, you are one of Donald's favorites, I'm told," Scapolini said as he sat down with a grunt across from her in an over-stuffed chair. He didn't even have to ask for his drink to be poured, which was immediately produced by Rapuzzio.

"Was," Laura corrected in a reverent tone.

He nodded and lifted the sambucca shot. *"Salude."*

She followed suit and took a sip of champagne. "All the great ones are gone."

"Truth. God rest my father's soul." Joey Scapolini took another sip of his drink, winced, and then set it down with precision. "But to stay with the old traditions is respectful."

"I agree," Laura said, meaning it. "Problem is, not every-one has that respect. That concerns me."

He nodded and sat back, staring at her hard. "Do you have any idea who might be violating the old ways?"

"I might," Laura said, testing.

He sat forward, his brown eyes suddenly blazing. "The gaming tables are downstairs. Up here, we don't play."

"My apologies," she said, and set down her champagne with care. "You're right." She waited for him to sit back in his chair and for the others to show signs of relaxing again. But she needed a bluff, had to get as much out of them as she would give, so she tossed out a fisher card. "Donald left me very well off."

From her peripheral vision she watched the men glance at each other, although Scapolini's eyes never left hers. It was pure mathematics. Donald Haines had come to them long ago about a black woman . . . she was that, and a fair repre-sentation of what could have been a May-December tryst. Tonight, she'd play the role. Ambiguity was everything. They didn't know what was in the will any more than she did. But one thing for sure, they were looking for it to determine what Elizabeth and Donald Haines Jr. had access to, as well as any alliances that they may not have known about. All of it was a gamble. Laura put her money down on control of construction contracts, by way of a holding company—that's the only thing that could have put a wild hair up their asses.

"He was a generous man," Scapolini finally said. He gave Laura an appreciative gaze. "Any man could understand why."

She smiled and picked up her champagne flute. "His wife hates me." That was no lie.

Scapolini laughed, and the tension that had held the room hostage broke. "Let me repeat myself," he said, clinking the side of her glass with his. "Any man could understand why."

Laura returned the compliment with a demure nod. "But, Mr. Scapolini—"

"Joey," he corrected and then let her proceed, his eyes following the line of her legs.

"I'm a practical woman. I believe things should stay the way they were meant to be. I'm not into construction investment, and don't know a thing about it . . . so, whatever Donald left to me in that accord, I'd be happy to immediately divest."

They stared at each other for a moment; the bargain had been laid on the table, the stakes raised.

"You are a very smart woman, and I can see why you were Haines's favorite," Scapolini said, raking his hair with obvious relief and what Laura could only imagine to be astonishment.

She didn't care. The money wasn't worth it, and she didn't want to be in bed with any of them. All she wanted was a guarantee of protection for her family.

"Where I come from, greed and excess is a sin," she said after a well-timed pause, polishing off her champagne and setting the glass down hard. She waved Rapuzzio away as he leaned in to retrieve it to refill her glass. He nodded like a gentleman, and accepted her decline with grace.

"Let me dispense with excess, then." Laura leaned forward and threw out a wild card. "I can't prove it, but let me run this past you."

Again, the room went still, especially Joey Scapolini's eyes.

"I was being well taken care of," Laura said, drawing out the words for emphasis, and never losing eye contact with Scapolini. "I was patient, could wait, but someone couldn't. Donald warned me to be very careful with any documents he gave me—so I was. But the same night he died, someone broke into my home searching for them, as well as the homes of two of my friends—who just so happen to be detectives." She shrugged. "I had business to handle, and kept them on retainer, per Donald's orders. He was concerned that something might happen. Now, all of a sudden, the strangest people who always had time for me, don't."

"Really," Scapolini said, his eyes sliding to his henchmen and back to Laura. "Like who, for instance?"

"Like Senator Scott." She folded her arms over her chest.

"Very interesting," Joey Scapolini said and then stood to begin walking toward the window. He clasped his hands behind his back as he stared out at the dark horizon.

"My uncle was the nurse who took the bullet," Laura said, her eyes never leaving Scapolini's back. "He and Haines were friends for years, and my uncle never got greedy, never asked for much." She watched Scapolini shake his head and straighten his spine, sure that rage was wafting its way up one vertebra at a time. "Although I can't prove a thing, I do know this—if Liz and her son have anything to do with this, there won't be a way to prove it in court. Another issue is this: I'm quite sure they don't know that they've been totally disinherited."

Joey Scapolini turned slowly and stared at her. "What did you say?" he whispered.

Laura held her glass tightly enough to nearly make it shatter, forgetting for a moment that it was empty and she'd declined a refill. If she'd gambled wrong, she was a dead woman.

"Any interest Haines had in the construction investment holding company doesn't go to them. So, if they whacked him prematurely . . . All I can say is, they should have waited. If he was really losing touch with reality, then they should have allowed him to drift off mercifully in his sleep. Somebody was vastly overconfident."

Laura stood, wondering if her last comment was aimed more at her own antics than the very dangerous lot before her. But Joey Scapolini simply nodded and walked toward her, then shoved his hand in his pocket. She tried not to flinch and succeeded by a narrow margin, then let her breath out with dignified calm when he pulled out a business card instead of a revolver.

"Get me a pen, Tony," he ordered, and waited for Rapuzzio to hurry forward with the requested item. "Now, you listen to me, baby," Scapolini said, furiously scribbling as he jotted down a number. "This is my private cell. You call Joey, if there's any problem. *Capice?*"

Laura nodded and accepted the card.

She was armed with an access card to direct thunder and lightning. Pure power. Her foot depressed the accelerator as she bore down on the Atlantic City Expressway. She wasn't sure what she'd started, but she was pretty sure that *eyes* beyond the cops would keep her uncle safe while he was in the hospital—and maybe those same eyes might watch Najira, James, and Steve's back. Problem was, there was this small matter of paperwork that she'd never seen, couldn't lay her hands on, and she'd traded their temporary safety for what had to be a huge contract. *That was a problem*. But not tonight. Unless somebody found the will and could call her bluff.

Laura scrolled through the messages on her digital display as she drove. Her phone had been blowing up. All of the calls the same: James, Najira, Steve, James, Najira, Steve, her sisters—twice. Insane. Then, oddly, one from Senator Scott. She almost swerved off the road, and then pressed the telephone to her ear to retrieve his cryptic voice mail.

She listened to it carefully, replaying it three times. "Laura, it's me. Call me when you can." Okay . . . hmmm . . . Then she listened with impatience to the others, all the same theme: "Laura, call us. Come back to the office and don't do anything crazy."

"Yeah, yeah, yeah," she muttered and drove back to the office with frustration.

"I would feel better about this, if we talked to her, first," Steve said, his eyes on the road.

"Me, too," James muttered. He stared out at the mild traffic consuming the Atlantic City Expressway. Where the hell was she?

Laura sat behind the office loft, waved at the squad car and flipped open her cell. She hit the senator's number on speed dial and waited. Within two rings, he picked up.

"Ready to talk about that contribution?" she said, her tone upbeat without bothering to announce herself.

"Uh, yes," he said carefully. "Where are you now?"

She hesitated. "On the road."

"Traveling far? We could meet for a late coffee."

Laura smiled and put another card into play. "I've just

come back from Atlantic City . . . but could be on City Line Avenue in a half hour, if that works for you?"

The senator hesitated. "Or, if it's not too much trouble, I'd be happy to invite you here."

Laura smiled.

Najira rushed to the window as soon as she heard a car pull up. Her nerves were shot; there was so much to tell Laura. She waved at her cousin like a madwoman until Laura glanced up. She watched her cousin close her phone, step out of her car, and begin walking toward the building. Najira leaned against the wall and closed her eyes as the elevator motor engaged in the distance. Footfalls made her rush toward the door, but when the hall lights went out she froze.

Laura looked up at the same time the two officers in the squad car did.

"Get out of here," one of them shouted, waving her away as they jumped out of their car.

Their radios squawked as they called for backup and hurried in, weapons drawn. Laura eased into her vehicle, and immediately dialed Najira. Voice mail made her scream, but she could not leave the scene. James was the next immediate option, and she spoke to him in one unbroken sentence while the background chaos of ringing slot machines nearly drowned out his voice.

"I'm at the office, 'Jira is inside, the lights went out, the cops went in—I handled the casino problem, get home!"

Chapter
12

"Freeze!"

Najira hit the inner office light panel to shut them off and pointed Steve's extra Glock nine millimeter at the door. Heavy footfalls clattered down the hallway beyond it. Male voices bellowed, "Freeze!" What sounded like a scuffle ensued. A familiar voice repeatedly yelled, "Peace, man. Yo, peace!"

Najira instantly turned on the lights and flung open the door. "Stop! That's my brother!"

Confused officers looked up from their positions over the young man on the floor. Jamal Hewitt kept his hands on the back of his head and spoke to the carpet.

"Honest ta God, that's my sister."

"Ma'am, drop the weapon," one of the officers ordered. *"Now."*

"Yeah, yeah, my bad," Najira said quickly, stooping to gently place the nine millimeter on the floor. "I didn't know who was coming in here. Jamal, whatchu doing rolling up on me like that?" Once an officer had collected the weapon, Najira snatched her cell phone off her hip and speed dialed to get Laura, then rushed forward to help Jamal up.

Her brother grumbled as he stood, smoothed his FuBu sweat suit, and shook his head. "Damn, man. It didn't have to be all that."

"This man is family? Need to see some ID," an officer said.

"Laura," Najira hollered, ignoring the cops and hugging her brother with a cell phone plastered to her ear. "It's cool. It was Jamal."

Laura closed her eyes for a moment, and within moments, was out of her vehicle, inside the building, taking the stairs two at a time. When she barreled into the hallway, nervous police officers bristled and then relaxed.

"Y'all coulda told me about Dad!" Jamal shouted, shrugging out of Najira's hug.

"It's all right," Laura stated plainly, her gaze steady on the cops. She watched their expressions go from battle preparedness to confusion to something she really couldn't countenance—disdain.

Her family watched them, too, as they called in the order to stand down on their two-ways, gave them all a disparaging glance, and began to leave the premises. She hated that look, the one that quietly said, *you people*. It was the type of glare that had fueled her ambition and quietly launched her career. . . . It was the kind of look she'd seen all her life, the look that suggested that because of one's class or circumstances, or even sheer accident of birth, somehow your family didn't matter as much, your pain wasn't as real or visceral, your losses were to be expected. Laura was angry enough to spit, yet conflicted. The cops had done their job, true, but, still, that life-superiority assumption was in their eyes.

She advanced on her cousin so quickly that both Jamal and Najira stepped back. Part of her wanted to slap the taste out of his mouth for scaring her and Najira half to death; the other wanted to hug him close for being there, for not getting shot by the police, and for not being an assassin.

"Tell me why you are crazy enough to be skulking around in a building and cutting off the lights, when you know what just happened to your father and what might be going on?" Laura leveled her charge with her finger pointed at Jamal, her neck bobbing from a DNA pattern that could never be completely stamped out.

"I know you ain't arguing wit me, when y'all were the ones who couldn't call a brother and—"

"Jamal—shut—up!" Najira snapped, and went to stand by Laura. "You just got out and just got done a bid. So how we look like dragging you up into this shit, huh? We was trying to keep you as far away from all-a this as possible. That's why I wasn't answering no cell phone calls blowing up my line."

"That's right," Laura snapped, turning on her heels to go into the office. "We didn't call you because we didn't know how deep and far this could go."

"Yeah, but he's my father, too!" Jamal protested. "They wouldn't even let me see him in the hospital, so I came here . . . got word on the street this was where 'Jira and y'all might be holed up. I only hit the lights so if somebody was watching through the windows, 'Jira wouldn't be in the line of fire. Kiss my ass, bof of y'all."

Laura took in a deep breath through her nose as Jamal slammed the office door behind them. She counted to ten and then spoke more calmly to the furious young man before her. "All right, I'm sorry. That was good looking-out to hit the lights. But you coulda got shot."

"Word," Najira said, shaking her head. "Now Steve is

short one Glock 'cause the cops took it, and I only hope like hell he's got that thing registered."

"Get back to the part about what really happened to Dad." Jamal folded his arms over his chest and stared at his sister and his cousin.

"Sit down, J," Laura said with a weary sigh. "It's a long story and I don't have much time."

"Dude, you're breaking land speed records, and we do have to get there in one piece, ya know?" Steve warned, as James swerved off the nearest exit ramp and turned the car around to head back toward Philly. He glanced at James's speedometer. "Jersey state troopers don't play, either."

All James did was nod and accelerate.

"Well, god-*damned!*" Jamal said, shaking his head as he tried to absorb Laura and Najira's edited version of what had happened. His greased scalp glistened between the zigzag configuration of cornrows that graced his head while he paced back and forth as though still caged. "Now I understand why Pops tol' me to take that box up to Northwood. Damn . . ."

"Northwood?" Najira said, moving closer to Jamal, but looking back toward Laura.

Laura raised an eyebrow, her eyes steady on Jamal. "Northwood, as in cemetery?"

"Yeah," Jamal said, lowering his voice and moving into the group. He glanced around. "Yo, Pops gave me a box, tol' me to dig up his brother's grave—your pop's . . . shallow, but enough to cover a steel lock box with some papers in it. Did the job for him at night—'Jira, you know how Dad is with conspiracy theory, so I did what he asked, since the old man don't ask for much. He said to put fresh holiday flowers on there like someone had tidied it up for Thanksgiving, and whatnot. Truth be tol', I ain't think no more about it until all this shit hit the fan, 'specially since Pop's got shit hid all 'round the city since the sixties—who am I to argue?"

"Oh, Lawd," Najira whispered, covering her face with her hands. "When I went to see him, he said to go visit his brother's grave and to take Laura with me because she'd know what to do." Najira looked at Laura.

"Go get the box," Laura said and then moved toward the door. "Now, tonight, and bring it to me. I've gotta make a run." She looked at Jamal. "You might have saved your father's ass, and ours."

"Hold up," Najira said, putting both hands out. "Laura, what's in the dag-gone box?"

"I'm not sure, but I have a hunch." Laura hesitated. "Jamal, you got a key to it?"

Jamal shook his head no. Laura closed her eyes.

"Where are you going?" Najira asked, coming in close to Laura and holding her arm.

"To see somebody," Laura said evenly. "Don't worry about it."

She sat before the impressive Victorian that was quietly nestled behind mature West Mount Airy foliage. Its gorgeous three stories were subtly lit, security signs ever present against the perfectly manicured lawn. She wondered how long the senator would dawdle with small talk before the real conversation got launched . . . and then wondered how to play it. She'd just put a bull's-eye on his forehead, but he was a probable target.

Laura got out of her Jag and took her time strolling up the driveway to the front porch. Security lights instantly came on, sensing her motion. Before she'd even had a chance to ring the bell, old man Scott had opened the door.

"Good evening, Laura," he said, kissing her cheek as she entered his home.

She smiled and offered a noncommittal greeting in response, gazing at the tasteful antiquity surrounding her. "I know you must be exhausted after campaigning all day today."

He smiled and ushered her into the parlor. "I am, darling. Care for some tea?"

Laura sighed and shook her head no. A shot of Jack Daniel's would have been right on time; she didn't think she could stomach tea. "No, but thank you. Please have some, though. Don't stop your normal routine on my account."

"Then I'll have a brandy," he said with a smile, his voice warm and ebullient. "Can't I tempt you?"

Again, Laura shook her head no. This time he didn't press, but continued to saunter over to a Chippendale curio cabinet and extracted a crystal decanter along with a small brandy snifter. She watched him roam around, seeming relaxed in his own environment. Being on one's own turf was always the advantage. She studied his casual charm that was set off by his simple but expensive beige cardigan and camel hued wool slacks. She wondered how much of the dress down was real, and how much of it was for her benefit—a performance?

He opened a cigar box, smelled one, and extracted a clipper. "You don't mind, do you?"

"No, sir. You're home."

He sighed. "Indeed. I have to wait till the wife goes to bed to indulge my vices. She hates what it does to the drapes."

"You two have a lovely home," Laura mused, truly admiring what he'd built, although hating how.

"Hope to keep it that way," he said, not looking at her as he lit the end of his stogie and puffed with emphasis.

Ahhh . . . now let the games begin.

"That's how it should be," Laura remarked, not looking at him, but allowing her gaze to purposefully rove his home.

"I'm glad we see eye to eye, then." He paused, stared at the end of his cigar and sat down in an overstuffed chair adjacent to the sofa, motioning for Laura to also have a seat. "How was your visit to Atlantic City?"

"Tense," Laura said, allowing him to process the statement any way he chose.

"Is everything all right?"

She stared at him for a moment. He was holding his cigar suspended over the ashtray. "Yes and no," she finally said, and then watched him take another slow puff.

"Start with the no, then work back toward the yes. What's going on?"

"People are concerned that what happened to our mutual friend might not be as simplistic as originally appearing."

The senator cocked one eyebrow. "Oh?"

"Oh." Laura put down an ace and quietly waited.

"Well," the senator said with a weary sigh, "everyone is always anxious this time of year. I'm sure it will blow over, as unfortunate as it all was."

"I don't think so," Laura said firmly, looking the senator directly in the eyes. "Not this time."

After a stricken moment, he chuckled. "Laura, I've dealt with those boys a long time now, and they can be intimidating. But at the end of the day, they're good business people."

She nodded and offered him a deferential gaze. "I know. That's why I'm troubled. They seem to feel that some business is out of order, and *that* cannot be good."

Senator Scott flicked a heavy ash off the end of his cigar and looked at her for a long time. "What could make them think things were out of order?"

"You'll have to ask Elizabeth," Laura hedged. "It seems Haines updated his will without his wife's knowledge." She paused as he nervously tapped his stogie against the ashtray and took a long inhale from it. "She may not control his construction investment holding company, as she previously assumed. Now that his death happened so suddenly and criminally, the entire estate could go into a long, protracted probate process." She sighed and looked at her manicure. "As I said, sir, people are concerned."

He nodded and stood. "That is seriously disconcerting—isn't it?"

"Yes. It is," Laura said, standing.

"Do you have any idea who might be . . . ah . . . ?"

"No," she said crisply. "But the gentlemen I met with are very distressed at whomever helped our friend into an early retirement."

She watched his expression go from guarded to totally unreadable, and that's when her gut hunch was confirmed.

"I can understand your worry, then . . . given that your uncle is in custody." He'd allowed his voice to become fawning despair. "Oh, Laura, I do wish there was something I could do . . . whatever would make him do such a thing?"

"Oh, sir, please don't worry," she said, allowing her voice to also take on a tone of false depression. "They know my uncle didn't do it. In fact, they as much as told me that they knew he was over there as insurance for Donald. They asked me to allow the media and the courts to initially have their field day for now, but they are the relentless type, and are ready to do their own investigation." She smiled a sad smile as his complexion became ashen, and she went to him and touched his arm. "Everything will be set right in the long run."

He patted her hand with brisk enthusiasm. "Yes. Yes it shall. That's why I'm so glad we're very close and that you confided in me."

"Of course," she said, allowing her voice to drop to a subtle murmur. "I wouldn't have it any other way."

He walked her to the door, mute, his expression stricken,

and his cigar left burning in the ashtray. "You will call me . . . if there are any developments that I should be aware of?"

"Definitely," she said, pecking his weathered cheek. "And I still plan on a hefty contribution to the cause, as always."

He clasped her hands and squeezed them hard before opening the door for her to leave. "Laura, you might want to tell them to look into Donald's medical condition."

She simply stared at the man, and willed herself not to smile. Ahhh . . . yes . . . it was time to cover one's own ass. This was how it was always done. Survival of the fittest, no friends in the game. Elizabeth was now expendable.

"This may come as a shock, but Donald may not have been as sick as previously believed."

Laura kept her expression stoic and only offered the senator a nod. "I can tell them that," she said quietly. "It might better help direct their search."

He nodded emphatically. "She and his doctor were *friends* for *years*. You understand?"

"I do understand, and I'm not shocked."

The senator released her hands and closed his eyes, rubbing a smooth palm over his jaw. He spoke to Laura so closely and so quietly that she could smell the brandy and cigar on his breath mingle with his expensive cologne.

"His prescriptions for Namenda . . ." The senator looked at her hard. "I will never testify to this, if I ever hear it came from me, I'll deny every word, and then I'll—"

"Sir, I understand the implications," Laura whispered sharply as she went to his ear and placed a steadying hand on his shoulder. She waited until he relaxed. "Donald didn't have dementia from Alzheimer's, did he?"

Senator Scott shook his head, his gaze filled with dread. "Haldon made him think he did."

"This was her plan, then, to get him to—"

"We all got charter percentages," he hissed into her ear. "I was never involved in anything else. Everything was neat, there was no reason for this, except that bitch got greedy and wanted things to speed along in unnatural timeframes. She wanted his holding company so she could control us through her investment whims. If I breathed it, she had his medical records to prove he had this disease, then she'd cut me out of the gaming charters and whatever else she could."

Laura nodded, but only bought half the story. It made perfect sense that Elizabeth would want to control Donald's asset while he was in a false state of dementia brought on by a drug . . . but what didn't gel was, why she would have felt compelled to tell Senator Scott any of that?

However, she kept up the ruse, kissed Senator Scott again, and then hugged him in close. "I will be sure to inform those who have a need to know, so that they can do their investigation cleanly and very quietly—which is necessary for the future, and then I walk away from this." She held him away from her. "As should you."

Again, the senator offered her a nervous nod and let his breath out in relief. "I'm glad we had this talk."

"Yes, sir," she remarked without emotion. "So am I."

Steve and James walked into an empty office. Instinctively, both cased the joint twice before settling down. James went right for the computer that was still on, Steve went for the printer.

"Look at this shit," Steve whispered, riffling through Najira's research. "That sister is awesome."

James came in close to peer over his partner's shoulder. "Scapolini got the lion's share, just as we'd suspected. I hope like hell Laura wasn't crazy enough to go down there and jack with him." He walked away from Steve and raked his hair down to the scalp. "No wonder she was jumpy."

"Yeah, well, like the boys outside said, both her and Najira had every right to be a ball of nerves. Freakin' lights go out, and the damned brother rolls in here like a hit man—shit."

"That's my point," James said, his voice escalating with frustration. "Where is everybody's ass now! Once there was an all-clear, Laura should have called back." Fury roiled within him as he opened and closed his fists, trying to summon calm. "The whole ride over here, I was worried sick, then she'll sashay in the fucking door, I'll put money on it, talking about everything is fine."

"Look, 'Jira," Jamal said, shoving the steel lock box through the cemetery fence. "I think we should bust this thing open, find out what's in it, and then get word back to Pops. Might be all sorts of cash in here, or something."

"Boy, are you missing your mind?" Najira fussed. "If it's papers that Dad went to these lengths to hide, the only person who's gonna be able to figure out what to do with them is Laura."

"Yeah, yeah, aw'ight," Jamal said, grunting as he pulled himself over the high, wrought iron fence. He hit the ground with a sneaker-soft thud. "But, I did some digging, too. Soon as Pops sent me on this errand. Then, especially after I heard he'd gotten shot."

"Get in the car, Jamal," Najira said, her eyes darting five ways. "Tell me while you're driving."

When Steve's cell phone vibrated, he and James looked at each other.

"It's my boy Caluzo. Oh, shit. He never calls me."

James stood in the middle of the floor like a piece of stone as Steve picked up.

"Sulli," Caluzo said.

"Yeah," Steve replied.

"Just for the record, the caterer was ours, just like the order was—but we were on standby. Got it?"

"Yeah. So, who gave the order?"

"You sitting down?"

"No."

"You should be."

"Who was it?" Steve said, now walking in a circle.

"The fuckin' son."

Steve stared at James. "Donny?"

"Yep."

"You sure?"

"Look, you wanna stop offending a friend here? Had a little conversation with the butler, who is suddenly real open to conversation without his attorney, right through here. His punk ass wasn't involved—just set the food out like he was told, and reheated the tea the wife had left for her husband earlier that day."

"Right, right. I'm sorry. I owe ya a beer," Steve muttered.

"Yeah, I love you, too, motherfucker," Caluzo said, laughing. "Black maid service wasn't ours, though."

"Donny ordered 'em? Or the wife?" Steve held his breath.

"Naw. That's the problem. No money trail to people we know and normally use." Caluzo pulled away from the receiver, yelled something indecipherable to people in the background, and then came back on the line. "Look, Sulli, get me to an Eagles game soon. I gotta go—got things to handle other than your bullshit tonight. And next time you want info bad enough to send a chick waving ten grand down to Skinny Joey, you call me, first. Hear? Broad coulda came back to Philly in a body bag if she blinked wrong. Just my advice."

"I hear ya," Steve said, and clicked off the call. He looked at James with wide eyes and sat down slowly on the edge of the desk. "We do not move, we do not put another ball in play, until Laura Caldwell walks back into this office and gives it to us straight."

"Partner, the blood just drained from your face. Wanna tell me what just went down?" James leaned against a cubicle wall and kept his gaze in a tight line with Steve's.

Steve's voice dropped to a reverent whisper. "She went to Joey Scapolini, cut a deal, and my contact just spilled his guts on the phone."

Laura jerked her gaze away from the computer and narrowed it on James. "Listen, I don't have time to argue or go into any justification. I did what I had to do."

"Yeah, well, I'm tired of you doing what you have to do in a way that leaves bodies—okay, Laura? That was some dangerous shit and still could be," James bellowed and walked away from her, leaving Steve, Najira, and Jamal's heads pivoting between the verbal combatants.

"Just open the damned box," Laura yelled back, and pushed away from the desk, folding her arms.

"Easier said than done," Jamal muttered in a monotone voice, trying to stay out of the heated debate. "I ain't in it, but maybe we gotta find out where Pops has the key?"

Laura spun on Najira. "We do this by the numbers—like old times," she said, her voice so strained with frustration that it cracked. "You tell me *everything* Akhan said. I know how he drops hints, leaves clues, and speaks in—"

"What the fuck is this, 'like old times,' shit, Laura?" James railed. "This is exactly what I'm talking about! Either we're all in this together as a single unit, or we're not. The way I see it, there's no more one-on-one, because after you just went down there to see Scapolini by yourself, all of us need to be on high alert status—feel me?"

"Sheeit. That's what I'm talking about, too," Jamal said,

flopping on the couch. His hot gaze went first to Laura, then to Najira, before dismissing Steve, and finally settling on James for comrade support.

Laura raked her hair with her fingers and let her breath out hard in exasperation. "Okay. Fine." She rolled her eyes at James and Jamal, and then leaned forward and closed her eyes. "Najira. Take it from the top. Tell me what your father said."

Najira peered around nervously. "He said he wanted fresh flowers, or something."

Laura stood slowly, unfurling from the chair like a lion about to leap. "Close your eyes, and tell me word for word what the man said," she whispered through her teeth, her tone deadly. "Not, I think."

Najira swallowed hard, closed her eyes, and took two deep steadying breaths. "All right. All right. With so much bullshit going on, it's hard to get it word for word . . . but I'm pretty sure he said, 'I want to go where there are trees and flowers. New flowers. Next to my brother. Go see about that very soon. Take Laura. Go to Northwood and look at the flowers for me. She understands these things.' "

"Very good," Laura murmured and then sent her attention to Jamal as Najira opened her eyes. "Your dad told you to put the box on his brother's grave, correct?"

Jamal nodded. "Yeah, plus some holiday wreaths and whatnot."

"It's Indian summer, so did you notice anything out there blooming or new that was near or next to my father and mother's graves?" Laura waited, so did everyone else, barely breathing.

Jamal shrugged. "Look, I was out there on a mission, yo. Was doing what Pops tol' me to do, not stopping to smell no flowers."

"I know his house plants," Laura said quietly. "We need to go back out there tonight."

"Are you crazy?" Jamal shook his head.

"Naw, she ain't crazy," James said, rubbing his jaw and staring out the window.

"No, she's not," Steve added in, glancing at the box. "That's so old school that it would be the last place anybody looked—right in plain sight."

"Your father is a genius," Laura murmured, then she got up, grabbed her coat and purse, and held open the door.

Chapter 13

She should have put on something less revealing to be cast over a high wrought iron fence in the middle of North Philly during the dead of night, and was just glad that James had suggested she lose the sable coat before attempting the feat. Jamal reached to catch her on the inside as James and Steve hoisted her over the top. Najira held her shoes and the lock box, Steve stood with her petting his gun, while James scaled the fence to go with her and Jamal through the dark cemetery in search of fresh flowers and possibly a key.

Every ominous thought entered her mind as the cold ground stung her stocking feet before she put on her coat and shoes again and picked her way through the darkened landscape. Graves and headstones loomed in the shadows, street lamps cast an eerie yellowish haze over the hard earth. This was truly the wildest thing she'd ever done, and prayed it wasn't a sign of things to come.

But she knew the route to her parents' graves blindfolded. If there'd been less emotion charging the whole production, they might have thought to bring a flashlight, but planning was hard when one was making it up on the fly. She stopped short as Jamal slowed down.

"Over there," he whispered. "That's where I stashed the wreath and stuff Pop told me to buy."

Laura squinted in the darkness, and despite her irritation at James, his large, silent form beside her was comforting. She walked a little ways and then stooped to run her fingers across her parents' joint headstone. It had been so long since she'd come here, and the mourning would never be over. She glanced around, noting that flowers had been recently placed there, as well as on her Aunt Maude's grave.

"You put those down?" she whispered to Jamal.

He shook his head.

Laura advanced, wishing that daylight was on her side, but banished the thought. She'd work with whatever circumstances came her way. She allowed her fingers to rove over the hard granite surfaces and then the flowering plants, but stopped as she got to a waxy leaf. A house plant in the mix of flowers. She smiled.

Ever so carefully she touched the plant with reverence, almost laughing as she remembered her uncle's wilting libations plants that were always a tad yellow from being constantly overwatered. She poked into the pot that had been set only an inch deep in the dirt to keep it upright, allowing her fingers to sift the rich, moist earth that was new to the frosty night air. Couldn't have been there more than a few days, she thought, feeling granules of fertile soil work its way beneath her nails. Then she felt something hard and cold and almost screamed with joy.

Working more furiously, she extracted the metal from the dirt, stood, gave the others with her a nod, and began running. No one said a word; they were on her flank like they'd robbed a bank. Maybe they had. But all of them remained very still when they got to the gate. No Najira. No Steve.

* * *

"I may own a coupla casinos," Scapolini said, "but I'm not a gambling man." He stared at Steve and Najira and offered them a drink from his limousine bar. He smiled at Najira, who was still clutching the lock box to her chest. "Call you sister, or cousin, or whatever, and tell her we'd all just like to see the paperwork together, come to a meeting of the minds, and then, hopefully, everybody can go home happy."

Najira's gaze darted between Steve, Scapolini, and the henchman who held a gun against her ribs.

"Sulli—tell her not to play stupid. Caluzo says you're a good egg . . . you don't want no trouble, always keep your nose outta where it don't belong . . . your partner is cool with us, no beef. But tell that big, black asshole and the skinny kid with him, not to try to be heroes. It ain't worth it. Okay? I'm not trying to be out here all night with Tony and Rocco waiting around while they have to stash a body or two or four."

"Call her," Steve said in an even tone. "Laura knows what's in the papers, and had to keep them safe—so, do like Joey said. Cool?" He hesitated and waited for Scapolini to nod, sure that every syllable of what he'd just told Najira was being evaluated for fraud. "Be sure to tell her to tell Jim and Jamal to stand down." His gaze was so intense it was impossible not to understand. If Laura had bluffed and it was bullshit, they were dead. But, the call had to be made, or they were dead. Options were limited.

"See, now was that so hard?" Scapolini said with a sly grin as Najira slowly extracted her cell phone from her jacket pocket. "Heard yous guys were probably already looking to have a conversation with me tonight anyway."

* * *

Laura removed the phone from her ear very slowly and stared at James and Jamal. Gooseflesh stood up on her arms; the coat was no match against cold fear.

"They're around the corner parked in front of the funeral home . . . in Joey Scapolini's limo."

James's eyes said it all. Even in the dark they glittered with trapped fury. Jamal's shadowed anger felt like a thick cloak that slowly reached out from the trees to strangle her.

"I'm to walk across the street when the limo comes and get in. You two are to stay with Steve's Durango, and not move. Any change of plans, and Najira goes first, then Steve."

Nothing else needed to be said, or could be said, as the threesome stood together against the gate. Jamal was the first to move, expertly scaling it to assume the catch position, while James remained behind to shove Laura over the top. She waited at the curbside until they both got in Steve's car, and then crossed the street, feeling like a hooker as she stood on the barren sidewalk in a full-length sable, disheveled black dress, heels, a designer purse, and dirty hands clutching a key.

She observed her dangerously absurd condition as a black stretch limo rounded the corner of the desolate block, slowed down, and waited for her to cross the street. Her only thought, as the back door opened, was that a bullet in her head was one thing, but Najira and Steve didn't deserve this.

"Hey, Joey," she said brightly, and slid into the seat, offering her best performance.

"Hey, baby," he said, kissing her cheek as she settled her coat around her.

"Got what you were looking for, and I'm a woman of my word."

Curious glances shot through the vehicle.

"Jus' keeping you honest, *bella*," he said, his eyes roving over her body. "Never gamble with my own money."

Laura dangled the key in front of him and nodded to Najira with a shrug, ignoring Steve and Najira's stricken expressions. "Give him the box and let the man do the honors."

Anthony Rapuzzio pulled back his gun and put the safety on it. Tense shoulders dropped a few inches as Joey Scapolini accepted the box and the key with a smile and opened it. No one blinked or swallowed as he inserted the key and the tumbler shifted.

"Seems like we're golden," he said, lifting the heavy lid and grasping the papers.

Laura's heart pounded within her chest so hard that her ears were ringing. Small flickers of light danced within her eyes creating the bright floaters of stroke-level blood pressure. But on the outside, she was cool.

A few minutes seemed like a few hours as Joey's eyes scanned the documents and he put them back in the box and handed it to Laura.

"We're in business," Scapolini stated flatly, and then smiled. "We should have a drink. Name your poison."

Laura leaned forward and gave him a sexy smile. "After all this shit, Joey, don't play like that."

He laughed uproariously, causing his henchmen to follow suit. "Oh, yeah, I forgot. But, not in my limo—do you know what poisons do to bodily fluids?"

James let his breath out in small sips as the limo rounded the corner again and he watched it come to a stop, the door open, and his family get out. Jamal closed his eyes for a moment and wiped the sweat off his brow with the back of his forearm.

"No sudden moves, brother," James warned quietly. "Not even a sneeze until the limo pulls away and the tags are gone."

Jamal's head bobbed up and down in assent as the very

nervous triumvirate walked toward Steve's car. They both knew the deal. A car behind the limo could come out of any alley or street and finish the job, if the thing hadn't gone down right. If they turned the key in the ignition, it could blow right under them; it only took a minute to install a cell phone–activated piece of C-4 under the chassis. Or, this might have simply been a warning, with worse results to follow. Who knew? That was the point, they didn't.

Laura, Najira, and Steve piled into the backseat.

"It's okay. Drive," Laura said quietly, her voice shaky.

James glanced in the rearview mirror at Steve for confirmation, then they both jumped out of the car at the same time and swept it for an explosive.

Making eye contact as they got back in, the two ex-cops scanned the horizon for any traffic, and then started the engine. Laura had watched it all, so did Jamal and Najira—the extra measures weren't lost on a soul. James pulled off burning rubber, got to a light, and gunned through it, checking his mirrors the whole time.

"The office is out. What's in the box?"

"I don't know," Laura said quietly.

Everyone turned and craned their necks to look at her, even the driver.

"What?" rang out in unison, and then everyone began talking at once as James burned down North Broad Street doing sixty miles per hour.

"Oh, no, you didn't," Najira shrieked. "You was down there placing our asses on the line in a blind bet with *those* guys?"

Steve was furiously wiping rivulets of sweat off his forehead and temples. "Oh, shit, Laura . . . shit, baby, that's—"

"Crazy like a motherfucker," Jamal hollered. "Let me out now! Right the fuck here on Broad Street so I can take my broke, but alive, ass home! Aw, hell, no!"

"Open the box, talk to me fast, and keep me from pulling my gun on you myself, Laura," James shouted as he screeched to a stop to avoid thickening traffic by Temple University.

This time she didn't argue, but complied, almost dropping the key as she fiddled with the lock and got the box open again. The interior of Steve's car became so quiet that it felt like a tomb. Save for muffled outside traffic, she would have thought she was in a dream.

Using the quickly passing streetlights for illumination, not daring to turn on the interior lights, she scanned the documents, speed reading, as her jaw went slack.

"Oh, my God," she murmured, rereading the papers and clutching them to be sure she was seeing right.

The word "What!" from four very rattled sources ricocheted through the vehicle.

"He left a half percent to me and a half percent to James on fourteen gaming charters . . . oh, shit!"

"What's she talking about?" James shouted to Steve.

"Beats me," Steve said, leaning so close to Laura that he was almost in her lap.

"It means that we have a seven percent interest in a blind trust Haines set up—his entire share. That is not a good thing, if my uncle is implicated in his demise." She flung down part of the stack of papers and then picked up another. "But God is good, and I played that hunch right; I've got his investment in the holding company—not dear Liz, and believe me, as soon as the estate settles, Scapolini can have it—I don't care what it's worth."

James shook his head.

"Well, shit, cuz . . . hook a brother up," Jamal said, half teasing and really not.

"I am, that's why I'm not messing with those boys," Laura said, her tone firm. "This right here is a life insurance policy—which is why I'm sure Haines rigged it like he did.

But looky here, looky here," she said, shaking her head. "His medical records have advancing Alzheimer's, no prescription for Namenda listed, and Haines wasn't in the advancing stages of anything." Her gaze shot to Najira. "I want to know what that drug does to a man who doesn't need it."

"Dollars to donuts, it'll give him the symptoms of what it's supposed to cure," James said, reaching over the seat to pound Steve's fist.

Laura covered her mouth and shook her head. "That bitch . . ." She shut the box hard. "Oh, that's so rich, so very, very smart, though."

"Whassup?" Jamal said. "She poisoned him, so—"

"No," Laura said, her gaze going out the window as James slowed down and everyone listened. "Here's the perfect crime. Get your doctor, who you're in bed with, literally and businesswise, to give you a drug that will make your husband think he's going senile. But, then, you know how proud the man is, as his wife, and you know how many lovely secrets and dangerous liaisons he has out there in the streets . . . so you also know if you can really make him think he's slipping, he'll go out old school—by way of a favor from a friend."

"Aw, damn, Laura," Steve said, sitting back against the seat with a thud. "Make the man commit suicide via a very cleanly orchestrated hit by his own hand . . . that's some treacherous shit."

"Right," Laura said as Najira and Jamal gaped. "But something went wrong."

"Yeah," James said. "Think about it. Why would a woman, who already has a hit man in the house—ostensibly, your uncle . . . let's be real, and no offense, do the hit herself."

Najira looked out the window and Jamal hung his head.

"No offense taken, man," Jamal said quietly. "Since we being real."

"But Daddy wasn't doing those kinds of jobs anymore,"

Najira whispered. "And he only did those during the sixties and seventies, for the cause."

For a while, no one said a word, but kept their own quiet counsel.

"This is why . . ." Laura swallowed her words, but her eyes met James's in the rearview mirror. When he looked away, a silent understanding connected them. That was exactly why she didn't discuss the full details of everything with everybody. It wasn't just about secrecy, but allowing people to live, laugh, and to be able to sleep at night.

"That's why," she began again, this time with more conviction in her voice as she veered away from the path of chastising James, which would only confirm Najira's heartbreak, and went down another road, "I knew something was wrong."

She was almost sure she could see Najira letting out her breath in slow increments of relief.

"See, if Liz already thought she had her husband convinced he was losing his mind, and knew he'd probably go the traditional route to call in an old favor so that he could go peacefully in his sleep, then—"

"Yeah," Steve interrupted, picking up on her earlier trend of thought. "Why would she risk having his estate hotly contested, not to mention prison, to poison him and smother him?"

"Poison him?" Laura's gaze went to Steve and held him.

"That's why it's important to stay in communication with your team," James said through his teeth. "While you were out in places unknown, playing real dangerous games with real dangerous people, Laura, me and Steve were digging up information that could be pertinent to the case."

Even though James was pissing her off, he was also making her smile. So now they were a *team*, were they? When did *that* happen? And the brother must have been having a serious flashback, because this was hardly *a case*—it was about making sure everybody, including Uncle Akhan, got to live long enough to enjoy a significant chunk of change that just got dropped in their laps. Opting for diplomacy and team cohesiveness, she allowed his testy statement to pass while Steve filled her in.

"You know what this sounds like to me?" she said, after having heard out Steve's long, twisted chronology of events. "Multiple hits converging on a single target."

James pulled over and brought the vehicle to a stop by the curb across from the Doubletree Hotel. "The theory has merit, much as I hate to admit it under these circumstances." He glanced around at the group of weary travelers and then stared a Laura. "Fact one, we know the wife's angle—she gave the man Namenda and produced a false sense that he was losing his mind, and Akhan was supposed to finish the job. No offense. But it's all good, because he didn't."

"Fact two," Steve said, his eyes on James, "we know the mob had a standby hit plan, but from all indications, never moved on it. They said the son, Donny, called the hit in early. My hunch is that perhaps the right hand didn't know what the left hand was doing."

"Either that, or somebody got very anxious," James said, "and since the son made the call, then what made him anxious?"

"Two things," Laura said, leaning back into the seat and yawning. Now that the imminent danger had passed, she was so tired that she felt as though her bones were dissolving. "One. If Elizabeth Haines thought that the will stood as it originally did—created by his old law partner, Alan Moyer Sr., then there was no reason to be rash. Two. What if the son knew otherwise?" She opened the box again and peered at the documents. "The new docs were drawn up by Bernhardt, Driscoll, and Faust. Guess whose campaign they heavily contribute to every year?"

It frustrated her no end that they didn't get it. Laura let her breath out hard.

"Girl, how do you just know this type of shit off the top of your head? Does your brain ever rest?" Najira shook her head.

"I know, because for years it was my job to watch who was whose money source. To answer your second question, no. And, by the way, Senator Scott gave up the wife's angle; he and Donny are lawyers, and they travel the same circles— so to speak. The senator has a lot of *close* male friends in the legal community that his dear wife doesn't know about." Laura leaned forward as she snapped the lid shut.

She stared at the group, her gaze and logic holding them for ransom. "I know how this circuit operates. Jacob Bernhardt most likely never said a word about what was in the will. He wouldn't risk his license, reputation, or a suit. However, there is the thing called bragging rights, the wine and cheese circuit pissing contest. So, over a cigar with the senator, or by way of a little birdie who tells a friend of a friend what he or she heard at a party, whatever, I can hear Jacob now, saying, 'Oh, yes, Donald Haines is coming over to have his will redrafted . . . you know he wasn't happy with what was done with Moyer, so we're going to straighten things out.' Some variation on the theme."

Laura paused as much for dramatic emphasis as she did for the headache that was beginning to make her temples throb. "That's high level convo used to magnetically attract more money to the firm where old, respected money just took up new residence, not something just draped on lower rungs still scrambling to grasp the brass ring."

Blank stares greeted her and she closed her eyes. They had to understand, had to look alive and remain sharp, if they were going to keep Akhan and their own butts out of jail. All the media would have to do is get hold of this and then begin drawing popular conclusions—a jury wouldn't even be necessary. The only salvation was the fact that, the Haineses wouldn't exactly like having the new contents of the will disclosed yet if they knew about it or understood the extent of it. That was her wild card.

"Trust me," she added, pressing her point. "The senator knew a shift was coming down. So did Donny boy. We have the mob, the wife, the son, the senator, and even Haines himself, implicated. It's just a matter of who jumped first in the game of chicken."

"Shit," Steve said through a long whistle, "timing really *is* everything."

"Correct. And if Donny got word that his father was gonna change his will, timing had to move quickly, especially if Akhan was slow walking the situation." James rubbed his face with both palms and rested his head on the steering wheel.

"Remember how he acted when we told him that Akhan was probably in there to provide security, not harm his dad?"

James nodded, not even looking at Steve. "Dude freaked. Then, coincidentally, the same night, all hell breaks loose over at the Haines house."

"Right," Laura said, her gaze going to Najira and Jamal. "Your father didn't do this, and we're not letting him take the weight."

"So what now," Jamal said, his voice tight. "Pops can't go out like that. Neither can any of us."

"We get some damned rest," James said, glancing up at the hotel with desire. "A bed. A shower. A good night's sleep so we can think. By daylight, we go back to the office, while the squad cars cover our backs and change, and figure it out."

"We break them off and get them squabbling with each other," Laura said through another yawn. "We've satisfied the muscle tonight. No problems there, for the moment. They're pissed off that somebody unnecessarily did Haines—their very cooperative business partner. Now they've gotta groom someone else to take his place," she added, making little quotes around the word groom with her fingers. "That's why we give them their damned construction mess with no struggle—you do not want to be *groomed* by Joey Scapolini."

"Word," Najira said, shaking her head. "You already said a lil' somethin' somethin' to the senator, right?"

"You know I did. Gotta make the rounds." Laura looked at Steve and James. "You boys corner Donny . . . or maybe his live-in partner, and drop some wisdom on him, I'll give you the script as soon as I get a couple hours of sleep. I'll take Elizabeth. Jamal, you be on standby—may need a runner for anything that could go down."

"Just one question before we check in and pass out," James said, pulling away from the curb.

"Shoot," Laura said with a smile.

"How're we gonna get to Junior and the wife?"

Everyone looked at Laura as she chuckled and waved her hand. "Oh, pullease. That's easy. We deal with it at the funeral. He's a VIP, they have a so-called suspect in custody, they've been running facts about his philanthropic life across every local channel, and the department put a rush on forensics—which you haven't heard a word about in the media. The bereaved have to meet and greet the public, and we'll be there—along with Scapolini, and everybody else who has a vested interest in this affair."

"They definitely have to release the body for burial shortly." James sighed as he entered the underground parking garage.

"Laura, that's sorta sacrilegious, isn't it?" Najira's eyes were wide.

Steve shrugged. "We get our best leads at funerals, sis."

Jamal nodded. "Lotsa shit goes down in the pews, girl.

For real." He glanced at Najira. "Besides, it's them or us; our dad versus their shit. Ain't none of the folks we're about to do God-fearing, nohow."

"And Haines would do cartwheels and back flips in his grave if he thought I'd punk out on him just to stand on ceremony." Laura stared out the window, suddenly very morose as the reality of her old friend's loss slowly sank in. "I'll have Liz clutching her pearls and needing smelling salts, when I'm done with her."

Chapter
14

Dull, oppressive gray leaned against the windows, forming a blanket of gloom. Real sleep was impossible, and Laura had given that up hours ago. She peered at Najira who was fitfully battling unconscious demons, the poor girl's dreams obviously tormenting her even as she tried to get a few wasted hours of shut-eye.

Laura kissed her cousin's damp temple and crept between the two double beds, trying not to wake her. She went into the bathroom with the lock box and key, closed the door and turned on the light, and then sat down on the edge of the tub.

Her mind tumbled over the facts again and again, as her eyes carefully read every line of the thick complex matrix of documents. Elizabeth got virtually nothing. The house had been Haines's before he'd married her, and he'd cleaned out retirement funds, stock portfolios, money markets and IRAs, expertly moving his private investment monies from his businesses to holding companies everywhere. His son had only been left a measly hundred thou, which was peanuts in comparison to Donald Haines Sr.'s true net worth.

She closed the box with a sigh at the same time she

closed her eyes. What had Donald been thinking to name her in his new will? And *James*? Absurd. Why? That had to be a clue, something he'd peppered the documents with as a back door, a trap, should things have gone awry—which they did.

On the surface, there'd be no substantial way she could get Elizabeth to take the direct fall for her part in this travesty. Her affair with Donald's doctor was hearsay. The doctor's reputation was no doubt sterling, otherwise. A blunt case could be made that Donald wouldn't take his prescribed medicine because he was in denial, like so many dementia patients are. The man hadn't died of an overdose, and the medication was delivered into his bloodstream in the normal levels prescribed.

Laura exhaled hard, gripping the steel box. How to play this? Although the mob knew Donny Jr. had made the call to order the bad food, they certainly weren't going to testify to that. If anything, bringing light to that issue would be a death sentence for her and her ragtag band of detectives. Not an option. Plus, now that they knew she was the gatekeeper on the investment funds headed their way, they wanted the new will to be settled as quickly as possible—therefore, a long, protracted criminal investigation would only serve to piss them off. They'd allow her uncle to take the weight, help spur along any evidence that he'd poisoned the man, too, if that came out . . . which it probably wouldn't, courtesy of the Haines family, and selected other VIPs—since he'd died of asphyxiation.

But the tainted tea nagged her mind, as did the pillow over Donald Haines's face. If the butler was cleared by Steve's mob source, it still represented a missing element. Something wasn't firing correctly on all cylinders, and the senator's piece was still out there somewhere, although it was extremely doubtful that he'd gotten anywhere near the hit.

Her plan to rattle Elizabeth Haines at the funeral was unraveling quickly. What purpose would that serve, in reality, she wondered. It might make her feel better to make the bitch pass out in the pews, but beyond a little hateful personal satisfaction, it was losing its merit as a strategy. Unless . . .

Laura opened her eyes and stood. Elizabeth Haines and her son, most likely, had everything to gain if the will stayed as it had been before Donald changed it. *That* is what she needed to know. What did the before picture look like? Who had been wired to what? And who would have had access to that, when old man Haines was still using Alan Moyer Sr. as his attorney? She smiled, and slowly walked over to the sink, gently setting the lock box down on the closed toilet seat. She stared in the mirror, and then splashed her face with water and smeared toothpaste, courtesy of the Doubletree toiletries basket, on her finger and worked it into a lather, looking quite rabid as she did so.

This morning she needed to have a solo cup of coffee with James.

He wasn't asleep when his cell phone vibrated across the nightstand. Before he picked it up, he was pretty sure of whom it might be. He glanced at Steve and Jamal, who both slept like the dead. James spoke in a low grumble, and agreed to her terms—coffee across the street at the greasy spoon. Alone.

She sat in a narrow booth, watching the door. At that hour of the morning, with the sky weeping dirty rain, her hair finger-combed, wearing sable, spiked heels, and a skimpy black dress from the prior night, she definitely felt like a street-walker and was in good diner company. It amazed her how just a block up on Broad, everything was new and refurbished. But down the side corridors and alleys right off the main strip, Center City still had pockets that serviced the red light district and the blue collar Joes who couldn't afford lodging at the posh hotels that shadowed them.

A few late night party stragglers sat on the circular stools mounted to the floor, nursing hangovers with coffee and tomato juice. A few homeless men traded change for an egg and toast, their body funk mixing with the grubby grill offerings and fried sausages and bacon. An old lady sat alone and mumbled to herself. A few construction workers slept while waiting for their breakfast special platters. One glanced at her, gave her a once over lightly and patted his pockets with an apologetic look, as though he couldn't afford her at the moment. She scowled as he then closed his eyes, as if closing her image away with him in his slumber.

The joint, though unappealing, promised one thing: anonymity.

James spotted her before he even walked through the door. She stood out like a sore thumb behind the dingy window. She was sipping coffee like it was a wonder drug, but he had his concerns about the germs that were probably rimming every cup in the place.

"So, you wanted to talk," he said, his tone surly as he slid into the cracked yellow booth seat across from her.

"Yeah. I do," she said, her tone even and her voice noncommittal. "Coffee?"

"I'll pass."

"Whatever."

"Get to the point."

She let her breath out hard, and he didn't wave away the hefty waitress who waddled over, poured him a cup of coffee without asking him, and walked away.

"Shoot," he muttered, adding sugar to the brew he didn't want and knew was nasty.

"You're in the will—big time. Ever wonder how that happened?"

"Yeah," he said, looking at her hard. "Wanna clue me in?"

"That's the problem, James. It doesn't make sense, and I don't know why."

"You think I cut a side deal with Haines, or something?" He set his cup down hard, but kept his voice low and controlled.

"No," she said with disgust. "But I think it's a clue, a message. Something we're not up on."

He relaxed a bit, glad that some of this was also blindsiding her. It meant, to his way of thinking, that maybe she hadn't orchestrated the whole thing.

"Maybe," he finally grumbled, going back to the brew and wincing as the thick emulsion slid down his throat. "That's been bothering me since you told me."

"I didn't sleep well, either," she admitted. "I've been noodling this crap to death, and keep coming up with blanks."

He let his breath out hard, still feeling sleep deprived and groggy. "Next steps—any hot ideas?"

"We need to find out what was in it before Haines changed it."

He nodded. "That makes sense."

She offered him a hesitant smile. "Glad we're finally getting on the same page."

For a while they said nothing. He didn't commit to or deny Laura's assessment. The waitress hovered behind the counter, servicing others, but waiting for a sign that Laura and James would either eat, or leave. Business was business, and obviously the working girls added to the diner's trade, so she seemed versed enough in the ethics of clientele negotiations to wait until hailed.

James studied his cup like a man trying to read tea leaves. As awful as it was, the foul, dark brew within it was beginning to awaken his battered brain cells. Every fact from the current situation got placed next to all the scraps of evidence he'd gleaned from the huge debacle one year ago. His synapses began to slowly fire as he mentally worked the massive jigsaw puzzle in his mind.

Leaning on the wife would be futile. Leaning on Donald Haines Jr. would be, too. Messing with the mob any more than they already had, fatal. The senator would bluff and double talk his way out of a jam, too—and he was so far removed as a suspect that he'd be the hardest one to implicate. But, Laura had a point. The old will might produce a solid lead down this dead-end street.

"Last year," James said slowly, dropping his voice enough to force Laura to lean in, "Alan Moyer, Donny's *friend*, came down to the Round House and met with us and Cap, trying to get his client, Martin Ramsey, out of the take-down."

Laura nodded, remembering Martin Ramsey well. He was in the old guard families, was supposed to get a huge chunk of the now deceased Darien Price's program monies, but had spilled his guts to stay out of jail. Wise move. Of those she brought down, she was glad that Martin had escaped the media splatter . . . she liked him. All in all, he was just a good guy in bad company.

James took his time, rethreading the story to be sure he had it all straight before he spoke. "After Martin bled his heart out, his attorney, Alan Moyer Jr., asked him to leave. Shut the door with me, Steve, and Cap in there." His eyes held Laura's. "Dude said Mike Paxton, he, and Donald Jr. used to be friends. Seems that back in the day, Alan lifted Mike's fathers' will from his dad's files, while clerking for him—just as a lark. His then best friend, Michael Paxton Jr., wanted to know what he'd inherit, so, Alan copped the will for him."

Laura leaned closer. "Moyer's own son lifted restricted

docs from his own father's files while he was over at Moyer, Burrell, and Strauss?" She sat back. "That was more than a lark. Could've had them all disbarred, not to mention, have his father's clock cleaned in serious malpractice litigation."

James nodded and took a slow sip of coffee and then carefully set it down. "We know he did it, because he knew exactly what was in old man Paxton's will—which helped break the case."

He watched Laura's expression go from guarded to near elation. What frightened him was the fact that it was as though they were beginning to think alike.

"You don't even have to say it," James muttered. "You figure if Alan did a little sticky finger job for a friend, what might he have looked into for his lover?"

"I'll just be damned," Laura murmured.

"Won't we all." James sent his gaze out the window, watching a slow stream of traffic splash water up on the curb. The heat from the coffee mug felt good against his hands. "Figure me and Steve might be able to go have a brief chat with Alan, while he's not consoling Donny Jr. Might be able to allude that we need to know what's in the docs, because the casino boys are concerned that old man Haines may have died before his business was in order . . . and think Donny may have had a hand in it, despite what is or is not in the newspapers."

"Yup," Laura said, her gaze following James's out the smudged glass. "It'll kill two birds with one stone."

He stared at her. "How so?"

"One," she said, ticking off the possibilities on her fingers, "it will let him know that everyone isn't buying the neatly served explanation that Akhan did it—at least not the people who count. Two, it'll make him run home to Donny to tell him that there is, indeed, another will floating around out there . . . if you and Steve word it correctly, and make it look like a slip. But be sure they think Scapolini has it." She smiled. "Don't worry. They're not about to search his home for it."

"It makes sense, but I don't like it." Again, they were at a standoff.

"Just say that Scapolini wants to be sure that what was in there before jibes with what's in there now, and you're the hand-off. If they call Scapolini, which I doubt, saying they were told he had concerns—Scapolini will laugh and tell them that he did, but it's solved now . . . which will make them think a hit on them is imminent." She sat back in her chair. "If Donny and his mom are in it, you'll see motion, money moves, something to let us know who is *real* nervous—because anybody scrambling is going to be covering their tracks so the casino boys aren't pissed that somebody cut off their gravy train."

Laura leaned forward again, her gaze steady. "James, Donald Haines Sr. was worth more to them alive, than dead. If he lived another twenty years sweetening their deals, helping to shift plum real estate construction contracts their way, etcetera, they wouldn't have cared if the man lived to be a hundred—and they'll be crying harder than his widow at the funeral. For them, this was unnecessary, tragic, unnerving, and fucked up. The only reason they were on standby is because they'd observed or heard that Haines was losing touch with reality, and they were worried that in his growing dementia, the man might get a conscience and start talking about things that he needed to take to his grave. But, those guys are philosophical. Haines settled their business and his, didn't talk, died—unfortunately—but took everybody's secrets to hell with him . . . so, all is still right in their universe. On the big public day, they'll drop a rose on his casket and drink in his honor, and then keep rolling."

"That ambitious little prick will shit his pants," James said low in his throat. "I hear you, and you're probably right . . .

but what I can't fathom is how a son . . . *a son*, Laura, can just murder his father in cold blood." James shook his head, the nausea in his stomach coming to a crest with indigestion induced by bad coffee. "I've seen a lot of shit as a cop in my day, but some of it you just never get used to—no matter what."

"That's why I don't have any qualms about leaning on Liz Haines to let her know her darling baby boy has his ass in a sling, nor should you and Steve for dropping some heavy breathing in Alan Moyer Jr.'s ear."

The fact that Laura had a point wasn't making him feel better about the whole sordid affair. But it did cement his mission to not allow an innocent old man to go to jail.

"Listen," she said, stretching and pushing away her grimy cup. "How about if we get Najira and Jamal to dig around in the 'hood to see who might have been on that maid service team? We know somebody stayed in the house. That's the only way it could have gone down. Then she came out later. Was gone like a shot before the police got there. My uncle also has a nasty bump on his head, I'm told. I'm also gonna try to bluff my way past the butler to get a condolence call into Liz, even though I'm sure she's not formally taking telephone calls these days."

"Yeah. All right," James said, waving the waitress to them for the check. "Just tell 'em to be careful."

Although the logistics of getting out of the hotel, back into her vehicle, and changing into some comfortable slacks and flats was brutal, she was glad that some semblance of normalcy had been established. James and Steve had called off the squad cars. What was the point now? The hit had gone down, the casino boys had what they were looking for, and anyone else in the equation gained nothing by killing them at this point. All that would do would be to truly alert the authorities, which, at the moment, were okay with taking the simplistic way out by hanging Akhan.

She let her fingers do the walking as she dialed Haines's old house number. As expected, Harold answered the telephone. She could still hear how shaken he was, and it only took minutes to make him understand that she would not be deterred. A friend of Steve's, by way of Atlantic City, suggested that she have a private chat with Liz, and one Elizabeth Haines *would* see her when she rang the bell. When Laura rang the bell, she did.

"Oh, is Harold off for the day?" Laura asked with a dangerous smile as Elizabeth Haines flung open the door.

"He's not well," Elizabeth said through her teeth. "Do come in, before you make a spectacle on my front steps. We're all still grieving. Was this necessary?"

"Yes. It was," Laura said, ignoring her glare, and following Elizabeth into the house. "I'm sorry for your loss."

"Are you?" Elizabeth snapped, not inviting her beyond the foyer.

"What, no tea? No civilities? Elizabeth, I expected better of you."

Elizabeth's gaze narrowed to a slit, but she kept her voice low and even. "Donald may have tolerated you, but I don't have to any longer. What is it that is so urgent that you have my Harold taken ill and in near hysterics that I speak with you at a time like this?"

"People are worried about your son," Laura said without flinching. "I hope you are, too." She kept her tone civil despite Elizabeth's frostbite. "I'm only telling you this because Donald was a dear friend of mine, no matter what you may think of me."

"Who would someone of your ilk know that would be concerned about my Donny?"

Laura shook her head, but wasn't angry. That Liz had attacked her was a good thing—it showed overconfidence.

Rather than match venom with venom, Laura sighed and pressed her palm to her chest in sarcastic dismay. "Liz, why last year we were all such friends and getting on famously. Such a statement is so surprising and so uncharitable of you. What's changed, other than the fact that Mike got shot?"

"Get out of my house," Elizabeth said through her teeth. "The only reason I agreed to meet you was because Harold had insisted that it was urgent. But now I see that this is just an ugly attempt to upset me while I'm already overwrought. And after what you did to poor Michael. . . . Just get out. You don't know anyone of import who is concerned about my son." Elizabeth pointed toward the door.

Laura watched the woman and stared at her outstretched arm. So she was still salty about losing her young lover, Michael Paxton, huh? Guess her husband's doctor couldn't throw down like Mike could. Bastard should've written himself a script for Viagra, while he was at it. Oh, well . . .

Although Elizabeth was all pro, during her diatribe Laura noticed there was a crack in her arrogant armor. It began around the eyes and had entered her voice by a sliver.

"People in Atlantic City are *very* concerned," Laura stated flatly, and then folded her arms over her chest. "Like I said, I'm only telling you because Donald would have wanted me to."

"Why would *they* be concerned about Donny?" Elizabeth's expression held a hint of bewilderment. When Laura didn't immediately respond, she glanced around the foyer. "Maybe you should come in and have some tea, after all."

"Not on your life," Laura said with a smug smile. "That's what killed Donald in here. Thank you, just the same."

"Pardon me?" Elizabeth swallowed hard and began fondling her broach and then adjusted the pearls against her gray mohair sweater.

"In addition to Namenda mixed with brandy, it seems Donald consumed tea laced with Lily of the Valley—the water from the cut stems is deadly." Laura allowed her gaze to purposefully sweep into the parlor where the beautifully arranged vases sat idle. "And, of course . . . quail that had been spoon-fed hemlock didn't help him, either."

"That is absolute balderdash," Elizabeth whispered. "Donald, of course, had Namenda in his system. It was prescribed to him by his doctor, even though he was too stubborn to take it without a little assistance." She swept away from Laura and stood between the foyer and the parlor, her form blocking Laura's view to the vases. "And, anything else he might have consumed had to be done by that horrible man who was on the premises under false pretenses—surely people don't believe that *my son* would have had anything to do with something so deranged."

"I don't know what people believe," Laura said, going closer to the door for a theatrical exit. "All I came to tell you is that, they have heard the news reports, aren't buying a word of it, and got the leak from someone within the police department that forensics found other foreign deadly substances in Donald's bloodstream. That is making them question whether or not some crazy old nurse did it, versus it being an inside job by family and friends . . . so, they're questioning everyone, *closely*, who may have been at the house in the last few days before Donald expired. Which is why they visited me. Not pleasant. They visited Harold, too, and you can obviously see from his nervous condition that it wasn't a civil exchange. I'm assuming that they haven't made a house call to see you yet, but I'm sure the good doctor is on their list—as is your son."

Laura turned on her heels and opened the door.

"This is so highly out of order that I cannot believe I'm even sitting across from you," Alan Moyer said, glancing around the small tavern in Ardmore.

"We are having this conversation because Donny came to us to ask us to do a security job, which—"

"Which, you botched," Alan said, leaning into Steve and then sitting back to glare at James.

"We didn't stand a chance," James said in a low rumble, taking a sip of Jack Daniel's and wincing as it slid down his throat. He brought his face close to Alan Moyer's, enjoying how his dark brown eyes glittered with both fear and rage. "That's irrelevant. What's major is this," he said, setting his glass down with precision. "Donny came to us, then the man's father gets murdered within forty-eight hours. These people don't care about family issues; it's about protecting their investments. Problem is, some people think that Donny was the one who stood to lose a lot, given the new will that's in place and he could've upset their apple cart in the process. As long as Haines was alive, he was their cash cow. Now that he's dead, they want to be sure that they have as sizeable a section of his holdings as they did in the original will. They don't like fraud. Ironic, isn't it?"

Then James sat back, watching Alan's haughty disdain begin to dissolve. "They couldn't possibly think that Donny had anything to—"

"Yeah," James said, cutting him off. "They do."

"But that's absurd." Alan Moyer looked from Steve to James, as though his restless gaze was unsure of where it could safely land. "Donny wouldn't hurt a fly, much less commit his father's murder."

"They think it's an inside job, not the old nurse—on account of the poisons that the department is keeping a lid on—poisons that they found floating around in Haines's bloodstream. Plus, somebody had been slipping Haines Namenda in his brandy for months," Steve said with a spectator's shrug. "They've already had a long conversation with the butler and know, after he pissed himself, that he didn't do it. Once they talk to Elizabeth and her doctor, they're coming for Donny. Go figure."

They waited as Alan took a liberal sip of his martini, and watched the clear liquid in his stem glass ripple with the tremor that ran through his hand. "You said they needed to see the original will . . . because there's another one that they're comparing the new one to? That's all they want to clear Donny?" Alan's gaze ripped from Steve to James and back again. "I don't want them to go near Donny right now, or ever. He's in too fragile an emotional condition to ever deal with anything like this."

"We understand," Steve said, his voice soothing. "We're playing good cop, so those guys don't play bad cop. We came to you and haven't said a word to Donny . . . out of respect. If we can fix this like it was fixed before . . ."

Alan nodded and downed his drink. He looked at James with skepticism. "After that, it's done. Correct?"

"If there's a discrepancy, people will want the margins of investment changed—which I'm sure Donny won't have a problem doing. *Then,* it's done," James said quietly, his eyes never leaving Alan's.

"All right. But you be sure to tell those people that Donny had *nothing* to do with any of it. His mother is an evil bitch—Namenda? If it was slipped into Haines's brandy, then I'm sure it was because he didn't need it." Alan Moyer turned in his chair, almost toppling his glass as he tried to retrieve his camel hair Chesterfield coat off the back of it. Hot tears stood in his eyes as he fumbled to pull on his coat while still seated, making a jumble of his tailored, charcoal wool suit.

"Here, let me help you with that," Steve said, but his attempt was swatted away.

"Don't touch me, or patronize me, gentlemen. You do your part not to bungle this effort, and I'll do mine." Alan straightened his spine and the lines of his clothing. "For all this indulgence, I'd like to see what the new will contains to be sure that whatever has to be manipulated away, Donny will have something to live on—he deserves that much, after all he's been through at the hands of his ill-begotten parents."

"Ain't our call," James said, unfazed. "But, we'll see what we can do."

Alan stopped flustering in his seat and leaned in toward James. "You *make* it happen. Do some real damned detective work for once in your worthless lives and make sure the real bad guys go down for this, not some innocent bystander." He sat back and smoothed his immaculately trimmed brunette hair and drew his mouth into a tight line. "I know Donny wasn't aware that his father had been slipped Namenda . . . you tell the concerned parties to quietly review Elizabeth's hand in this, as well as her doctor accomplice—those two have probably cut Donny out of everything."

The sleuth partners said nothing as Alan Moyer stood, snatched up his briefcase, and left the tavern with the strides of a man being chased.

"Think we struck a nerve?" Steve said, blithely, hailing the barmaid for another beer.

James turned up his rocks glass and set it down hard. "Ya think?"

"Git the fuck outta here," Jamal said, shaking his head, as he pulled hard on a blunt. He held the smoke in, sipping in more air to keep the get-high from filtering out of his nose and then blew it out hard. He was just glad that it had stopped raining and it had warmed up so people would be out in the streets. "Man, that's some mad-crazy shit."

"I know," his boy said, taking the roach of weed from

Jamal. "The bitch betta share her extra side tips, too. Five grand to make some tea and fuck some old butler. Sheeit. For that much money, I mighta did his ass myself."

Jamal laughed and glanced back at Najira, who was standing with the huddle of women leaning against the basketball court fence. "That's all she had to do—make some tea with the nasty ass flower water, and give the butler some booty? C'mon, man, stop playing."

His friend laughed and slapped his back. "You need to come into the business with me, man. I'm expanding my enterprises, and them Main Line motherfuckers is all closet freaks."

Jamal's contact dragged hard on the weed until the ember blazed between his pinched fingertips, and then after a moment he let the smoke curl up from his mouth to meet the steady stream wafting out of his nose. He passed the nearly gone reefer to Jamal for a last puff.

"Maaan, what I care if they wanna play a sick trick on some old bastard who was giving them the blues. The job was a cakewalk. All my girl had to do was go in, pour out the old tea and nuke some new tea in the same cup before the old buzzard ate lunch. Was kinda fucked-up thing to do, but it ain't my family. Shit was stoopid, though—'cause he was so old he prob'ly ain't know the difference—but five grand is five grand, that's why my business is tight. Give the customers what they want."

"I feel you, man," Jamal said, taking a toke and then handing it off to his buddy.

"J, all she had to do was hide, and lay low till old Harry was by himself and act like she'd missed her ride. Fine-azz Shaquira went in with the ones cleaning," he said, motioning toward a shapely girl standing by the gate. "The girl backed old Harry up in his room, and it was all over wit da shoutin'."

Jamal nodded and sent his gaze up and down the tall curvy form across the court. Shaquira was all that . . . big ass, juicy breasts, tiny waist, cute butterfly tattoo peeking out of her low-slung jeans . . . pretty color—like light toast, hazel eyes, and that long hair that wasn't no weave. "She's definitely fine, man. Was a waste of good ass, if you ask me."

"Half black, half Puerto Rican, brother. *Fy-ine*. But, money is money, and since you ain't got none, keep on dreamin'."

"No doubt." Jamal shrugged, pivoted, and jumped up to make a quick imitation basketball shot in Shaquira's direction. "But I'd be all net, man."

They both laughed and pounded fists. His friend stamped out the done butt and continued looking downcourt. "No doubt. But when you gonna introduce me to your sister proper? She won't even gimme the time of day."

Jamal waved at Najira dismissively. "She ain't worth it, man. Is a pain in the ass. Fights every man she gits with." He laughed it off and changed the subject, trying to keep his sister out of harm's way.

"Yeah, I can fight, though," his buddy said, his eyes fixed on Najira's behind as he spoke.

"Later, man. But what I wanna know is, how you fall into a gig so sweet? Who gave you the hookup?"

"Man, go 'head wit dat shit. I ain't giving you my source so you can end-run me and try to move in on my gigs. Be serious. Business is business."

"It ain't like that between us, man, never was." Jamal began to walk away, seeming offended.

"Aw'ight, aw'ight. Hey, we go back . . . and on account of the fact that your pop was in there working, too—man, the situation is fucked up."

Jamal walked back toward the fence and leaned against it, but kept his gaze on the horizon as though still offended. His friend was dying to tell who put him down with a sweet deal, so it was only a matter of time and patience until his dawg told. Half of the glory of it all was coming back to Southwest with bragging rights. Jamal waited.

"Aw'ight. You want me to really tell you?"

Jamal shrugged. "Naw, that's cool, if you don't trus' me, man, you don't trus' me."

"It ain't like that," his friend said, looking around and coming in closer. "You know me and Howard go way back."

"Git the fuck outta here. Punk ass Scooter? Howard Scott?"

"He a punk, but he cool," his friend argued. "Always had my pockets right from back in the day. Got my start with his ass, my girls serviced his squad up in Mount Airy when they'd have their parties and shit—kept 'em in weed, rock, blow, whateva, and they kep' a brother paid."

Jamal exchanged a fist-pound with his buddy, his mind racing a mile a minute. "Then when he got the food services business."

"Right, man, you know, all of us worked up at Scott Foods and Beverages, then dude got that phat airport contract, and a piece of the stadium concessions—right?"

Jamal nodded. "Took a lot of us in out the rain when we couldn't get nothin' after doing a bid."

"That's who I'm talking about. Well, I watched him open up and expand shit, handle his business, and I always told him that's what I wanted to do, feel me?"

Again, Jamal nodded, a sick feeling creeping into his gut. He watched his boy from 'round the way explain how it was one and the same; it was, but it wasn't. Howard Scott had talked a buncha shit, rhetoric about a black man being in business to brothers who didn't have a chance, while his privileged ass wouldn't dream of doing what they had to do to survive. Suddenly he felt used, and knew that five thousand dollars wasn't jack shit but chump change. As he looked at the excitement in his friend's eyes, he felt violated for him. This was exactly what his father had been trying to tell him for years. *Now* he got it.

"Yeah, man," Jamal finally said, his tone sullen. "He opened up Philly Foods, Inc. when he moved into the airport. I remember."

"Right," his friend proudly replied, as though he owned Howard Scott's enterprise himself. "As his pop moved up and got to be a big time senator, the cash he dropped on us for a little service got mo' betta, feel me?"

"Yeah, I feel you, man."

"Den, see, what had happened was, he reached back, didn't forget those who'd been wit him all-a long. Asked me to hook up a friend of his with this whack shit, and I was like, cool. Who was I to question? Money is green. So, I sent my best girl up there, she did the damned thing, and she was supposed to get a cab and be out—but some unplanned shit went down."

"Sho' you right. The shit wasn't supposed to go down like that, I know." Jamal could feel the neighborhood closing in on him. It was time to go. But his boy had been honest and had helped him bring solid info that Laura needed.

"Girlfriend heard gunshots, and was ghost," his friend said, laughing loudly. "Aw, man . . . She ain't wait for no cab, but ran her fine ass out the house and down them dark streets until she could find a cross street with some lights and make a cell call. I had to drive all-a way up there and go git her, can you believe it? That was bullshit, 'cause I ain't know she was a setup 'cause your pop had beef up there with the sick old man, or a paid job. Howard and his crew be ridiculous sometimes—but that ain't my business. For real. If I'da known, though, I'da sent her in another day so everything stayed smooth."

Jamal's friend shook his head and rubbed his jaw. "Man, don' worry, though. Your pops is old, probably had cause or some shit, and can say it was self-defense, or somethin'. Ain't your cousin set wit dough? She'll get a good lawyer on it, like she did for you, and den your old man might wind up with a case himself—and git *paid*."

"Yeah, man. It's all good," Jamal said, pounding his friend's fist and beginning to walk toward his sister. "I ain't worried. Laura's on it."

Chapter
15

Laura picked at her salad, her mind a million miles away as she waited for the others to rendezvous with her at the TGI Fridays on City Line Avenue. What had become of her life, now that all these bizarre events had been set into motion? Najira and Jamal needed transportation, needed viable career options. Her sisters needed reduced anxiety. Her uncle needed to heal and be cleared. James and Steve needed medical and dental, and the other accoutrements of running a solid business beyond the survival level to make it thrive. There were so many loose ends, and she hated dangling threads. She just hoped that Najira had looked in on Akhan today.

But it was definitely time to move again. They needed to be at another hotel. Sure as rain, Donald Haines would be buried within the week. She also knew for sure that Liz would insist on doing that before the big November elections. Which also meant that any fires that she'd just fanned would most assuredly begin to rage . . . which meant no going back to their houses, but also no cops, until everything was tied into a neat little bow. At least it had stopped raining.

The thing that didn't add up for her was the pillow. That was troublesome. She'd listened carefully to what Jamal had told her, knew about the girl left behind. However, Donald Haines was in good shape—squash, golf, a virtual fitness buff. Even if the medication had rendered him a tad confused, he was still as strong as an ox, just like Akhan was. Unless what he had ingested earlier had begun to kick in, no average female should have been able to put a pillow over his face and hold him down long enough to smother him. Without the poison, it didn't jibe. The bad part was that, at the moment, the cops were going with the theory that only her uncle would have had that much upper body strength to do the job.

She chased away doubt with a swig of iced tea, but the mouthful of salad went down rough and burned in the pit of her stomach like acid. Screw the rendezvous point. It was time for them all to go deep undercover. Laura flipped open her telephone and delivered instructions.

"'Jira. Take Jamal with you to 30th Street Station and pick up a car rental under the names I'll give you in about an hour. I'm gonna give you a guy's name, you ask for the licenses and whatnot, and roll—he'll already be paid. Then go to the Men's Warehouse, get J a couple of suits with the works, go to the barber, hook him up corporate—even if he fusses. You breeze through Lord and Taylor while you're down there and come out strictly Chanel. Two to three pieces, and something real staid for a funeral. You roll like a couple, and check in at the Sheraton Society Hill as tourists. I'll explain later."

She clicked off that call, and got James en route. She was glad that he didn't argue or make a big stink about her instructions to ditch his and Steve's cars and to pick up two rentals at the airport under the names she'd leave, once they'd scored the phony IDs. He didn't even balk at her request to hit Boyd's and pick up outfits that would be prepaid under the new names for him and Steve.

Philly was hot. The department had to have a leak, and people—to her way of thinking—were moving just a little too slowly to act upon known data about Haines's real cause of death. No one was making inquiries to all the poisons and additional medication in his system. No one was really trying to find out about the girl on the tape who'd stayed awhile. And how did she get out without being on tape? Uh-uh. Her fingers flew across the keyboard of her wireless laptop. After chronicling all she knew, she pushed send—one copy to Rick, her media contact, the other to her attorney, Andrea McPherson. She utilized the number that her uncle had always told her was safe for the people to use when it was time to disappear.

Laura stood and folded the newspaper under her arm and paid the bill. It was time to go to the bank.

She rounded the corner of 7th and Market twice, to be sure who might or might not see her, and then went back to Arch to park in the lot behind the African American Museum. She made short work of crossing the streets and heading toward her destination: cash and a safety deposit box.

When she emerged, she had updated her will—sending instructions to her attorney via E-mail while stashing Haines's will. While it wasn't a signed, notarized document, it was indeed sent under duress, therefore if anything happened to her while all of this was sorted out, at least she'd thwart any immediate efforts to jack her holdings. A sister had to handle her business. A cool wire transfer of twelve thousand to the account that had been given over the cell would insure the new IDs. All her people had to do was follow instructions to the letter. Hotel reservations made on-line was easy, all they had to do was check in—same with the car rentals. She found the lot downtown closest to the Avis rental car center, and came out with a nondescript four-door sedan. Now it was time to really play.

She sat across from the Sheraton at Bookbinder's Seafood Restaurant that was situated near the Ritz movie complex, looking out at the historic cobblestone street. Shame of it all was the level of intrigue and drama hadn't changed since the days of Ben Franklin. Politics and money definitely made for strange bedfellows. Maybe one day James would understand.

"Is anyone joining you, ma'am, or are you ready to order?"

Laura stared up at the waiter and then checked her watch. "I'm waiting on a friend," she said in a calm voice, her gaze going past the series of old world wooden tables and chairs in the dimly lit establishment. "He should be here soon."

The waiter nodded and refilled her cup of tea, and then left her side.

Within twenty minutes, the man she was looking for entered the restaurant. He wore an expression of a tortured conscience that seemed to make his fine business attire seem much less formidable. She simply nodded and watched him nervously approach her. She stood and extended her hand. Civilities were always in order.

"Donald, thank you for meeting me on such short notice," she said, and then sat. "I know you and your family have been through a lot, and appreciate your secretary taking my call at your office, and then routing it to you."

He didn't respond but calmly folded his coat over his arm and then sat, seeming unsure what to do with it in juxtaposition to his unwieldy briefcase, until Laura indicated that he might consider draping it over an empty chair while setting the briefcase down on the floor. "My mother said you stopped by, and the visit left her shaken. Why?"

"Because there are irregularities with this whole business of your father's death that have everyone concerned."

He stared at her, seeming totally bewildered. "I didn't hurt my father," he whispered. "She alluded that people might be thinking I have."

There was a level of pain in his eyes that drew Laura in. His features were an elegant combination of Elizabeth's severe porcelain dignity, and Donald Sr.'s refined, intense Anglo-Saxon. Her eyes searched his for authenticity and quietly found it. She hadn't expected that at all.

"No matter what our differences were, or whatever he decided to do in his final days of madness, I would have never put a pillow over his face or have tried to poison him." Donald Haines Jr. let out an exhausted sigh. His face showed the signs of strain that should have been evident in a man twice his age. He shrugged as two large tears pooled in his eyes. "Frankly, I don't care any longer. If they don't believe me and kill me, that would be a most merciful conclusion after all of this, don't you think?"

For a moment, Laura wasn't sure how to respond. She'd expected arrogance, a fight, not a willing defeat. But it was what she needed to know to cross Donny off her suspect list. They'd been leaning on the wrong guy. She was many things, but cold-blooded enough to send an innocent person to his grave wasn't one of them.

In an odd display of compassion, something made her reach her hand across the table to cover Donny's. There was so much she wanted to say but wasn't sure where to begin. She knew his sense of bewilderment; she'd been there a long time ago, and that was something one couldn't fake. The eyes always told the truth.

He looked down at her hand, but didn't draw away from her. Instead he clasped it, peering up at her for understanding. "My mother . . ." he said, faltering as he spoke, "has been through a lot. Things between her and my father that no one could begin to fathom. Terrible years of quiet, brutal conflict." He sucked in a huge breath and then let it out in a controlled stream through his nose. "I wanted her safe, just like I wanted Father safe. But I don't know what she's done."

"Did she tell you about the medication she'd been giving your father?"

Donny held Laura's stare within his own. True confusion spread across his face as though it were dawn. "No," he whispered. "She only said that these mobster types may have been in business with Father, and somehow he was poisoned at home before the whole horrid incident with the nurse. But she never mentioned . . ."

"Did she tell you how he was poisoned?"

Donny clasped Laura's hand more tightly. "Please, dear God," he said, closing his eyes. "Just tell me so at least I can sleep at night."

Laura took her time, gently laying out what she knew, but with calculated edits. Somehow it seemed futile to go on hiding what so many others behind the scenes were aware of. She remembered being stricken by the horrors of her own father's demise. The layer upon layer of onionskin that she'd had to peel away in order to get to the truth had nearly taken her sanity. As a friend of Donald Haines Sr., she felt she at least owed his son peace of mind. Even if he'd been remotely involved in the murder of his father, there was a certain code of honor amongst thieves.

Without resistance, he listened on the edge of his chair, his expression so intent that no waiters approached their table. Quiet tears coursed down his pale face, making his blue eyes glitter, but he didn't bother wiping them away.

"Father ordered this to happen, I'm sure of it," he whispered when she was done. "The man who came was a friend, and even though those two detectives felt confident that he was there for security, in my heart, I knew." Donny looked at her, his eyes filled with empathy. "I'm so sorry that your uncle was that friend for my father, even though I understand why he probably did it. This is as hard for you as it is for me, so that is a tie that binds."

Denial obviously had Donald Haines Jr. in a death grip. She couldn't break it, and gave up trying to go that route. She could tell by the resigned tone of his voice that was beyond confrontation or defensive reaction. The man simply believed what he believed, had built rational walls around his theory to protect it, and had emotionally drifted away from the horror of it.

"I don't know what actually transpired over the years between your father and my uncle, all I do know is that they kept each other's secrets and respected each other immensely. Both had power—informal and formal, within their own circles. I guess it's important to have at least one confidant." It was the truth, what more could she say? Her attempt to rattle Donny hadn't worked; it had backfired and made him retrench. He wasn't a target, in any event. So the only dignified thing to do was to fold her hand and bow out of the interaction with grace, salvaging the tenuous alliance.

"Laura, I tried to tell my mother that her behavior toward you since the whole Paxton travesty made no sense. You'd been a victim, and her refusal to acknowledge that wore on me—but then, so many of her ideologies did, why would that be any different. I hope you won't equate her behavior with mine, and think of me as I'm sure you do her." He looked away, shame staining his cheeks. "I'm so disappointed with them both. I have been for years."

"You're not them, just as I'm not my parents or my uncle's keeper. We can only do our best to live our lives and try to stay clear of all the unfinished business they've left behind."

Donny smiled and sighed. "So true. And you're right. It is important to have at least one confidant. That much my father and I have in common." He looked away from Laura, and glanced at his side. "Alan kept this for me," he finally said, leaning over to reach into his briefcase. He extracted his hand from Laura's with care, and retrieved a large manila envelope. "Alan said never to show this to anyone, and no matter what, especially not to do so now. He's playing with fire, having meetings with very sketchy characters—he's so jumpy and worried about how this will pan out. I tried to tell him that I didn't care and we had a major fight about it. But I'm tired of games, Laura. Does that make sense?"

She nodded as he pushed the envelope across the table toward her, staring at the big blue eyes that had seen too much and, yet, probably not enough, as a child.

"One day, I made a copy of it while Alan was out, just to sit with at my office so I could truly study it without anyone else around. I kept my copy locked in my desk . . . but when he called ranting about how some thugs demanded to see it, and then Mother said you'd stopped by with wild allegations, I was hoping that, somehow, if I gave this to you, since it is the only truth as I know it . . . maybe the right people could understand." He looked at her with unblinking eyes. "Laura, I don't want anyone hurt over something as ephemeral as money. Life is worth more than that."

Laura accepted the envelope, and quietly tucked it away in her purse without breaking eye contact with Donny. "If you think I'm the enemy, why would you give this to me?" Her voice was low and gentle as she tried to make sense of his gesture.

"Because no matter what my mother may think of you now, my father always respected you," he said, slightly lifting his chin. "As do I." He stared into her eyes and his hand now covered hers. "We're so much alike, you and I," he murmured. "I've watched how you made sure all those people got the monies they'd been denied for years. You even played my father," he added with a sad smile. "Made him do things with his money that none of my arguing had ever achieved.

You were probably the son he wished he had, metaphorically speaking, and I really don't care if he's changed his will." Donny chuckled softly. "Laura, I never wanted to be an attorney. And I've seen what money can do to people. Besides, what would I look like managing casino contracts and the like? His politics and business gave me the hives. If it weren't for Alan, I'd be penniless and an artist . . . but Alan always saw after me, even when we were at Harvard together."

The confession was so profound that it nearly brought tears to her eyes. Heaven help her, she'd set the mob on this man, and didn't know how to right that wrong.

"Don," she said quietly, the wheels in her mind spinning as she spoke. "I'm going to ask you to do something that is going to seem to go against every natural instinct you may have."

He smiled, and looked at her wistfully. "What, trust you?"

She smiled. "Yes. Please don't tell Alan or your mother that we had this chat. Do me a favor and give it a couple of days . . . at least until after your father's funeral."

"I can understand not telling Mother, but—"

"Alan, and your mother, should stay as far away from all this as possible," she said, thinking fast. "If he knew you gave me this old will, he might do something or call the wrong person, inadvertently. Your mother, I pray, is not involved in any way, either. She could make the same mistake, and then dangerous balls would be set in motion."

Donny sat back and relaxed. "Okay. I understand. I wouldn't want that to happen, either. But, Laura, what do you think is going wrong? Why is all of this happening?"

"I don't know. That's what frightens me." She let her breath out hard and sat back. "Do you want something to eat . . . maybe something to drink?"

He shook his head no. "A glass of chardonnay is all I can

stomach. I haven't been able to keep a thing down without indigestion since this all began. Alan gives me tea every night to help calm my nerves and settle my stomach, but in a couple of hours, it's back again and I feel even worse."

Laura stared at him. "All right," she said, hailing the waiter and placing his order for him. "But can I ask you a question?"

"Sure," he said with a weary sigh, "why not?"

"What made you go to private investigators in the first place?"

"Oh, that," he said, his eyes filling again. "I could see Father was not himself, his mind was slipping and that worried me. And then there was something he said one day about the wrong people knowing he was not himself being dangerous. I knew he had his hands in a lot of, shall we say, *speculative ventures*, and I wanted him watched to be sure nothing like what happened, did. I told Alan everything, and he agreed. He asked me how Father was doing, daily . . . and I even explained how they would be setting up cameras outside the house to be sure no shady characters got in there while Mother and Father were unaware."

Donny drew a shaky breath and looked up at the waiter who brought his wine, thanking him in a soft murmur and then took a liberal sip from his stem glass. "The detectives told me that he'd hired an old friend as a nurse, and I know my father . . . knew him," Donny corrected and sniffed. "If Father thought he was losing control, he'd even beat death by delivering the final blow by his own hand. Just like he told me I should do—clean, not messy, and very dignified to save scandal and shame."

"I don't understand." Laura sat forward. Something was making her pulse quicken with new alarm.

"I'm dying," Donny said plainly. "It's only a matter of time. Father said to die of that disease was a travesty. It would bleed out my finances, create undue burden, and at the end of the day, I had to handle my affairs in an orderly fashion."

"Oh, Don . . ." She leaned in farther and gathered his hands within hers. Now it made sense why Haines Sr. had only left his son the little that he did. It wasn't an indictment of their relationship, but that fixed, insanely inflexible, Puritan ethic. Die with dignity, by your own hand if you must, but in no way allow even disease to make a mockery of who you were. Instantly she *knew* Haines Sr. would never leave a penny more than was necessary, just to keep Alan from spending a dime of what he'd left his son. Laura closed her eyes. It was a cultural thing she couldn't understand. And that he'd told his son something so harsh . . . there were no words.

Cool hands squeezed hers tightly. "It's all right, Laura. I've made my peace with that, too. I've done as he'd asked, have all my affairs in order, and Alan is the only family that I have . . . the only one who ever truly loved me for who I am, save Mother, and she's already well established . . . so, there we have it. The Mafia, or whomever, can't really do more to me than they already have—unless they hurt my loved ones."

She nodded and looked at him, compassion making it difficult for her to breathe. She understood his position well. "While I've not experienced the things you have," she said in all candor, "I have lived on the edge, and have willed everything to organizations that would not only benefit those less fortunate, but also to organizations that would take extreme and defiant exception if I had a so-called untimely death. Of course, I've also taken care of my loved ones. So, I guess I do understand a little of this, in an odd way. But, know this, I am very sorry that this has happened to you."

"Thank you for saying that," he whispered, and then sipped his drink.

As she stared at him, warning bells went off in her head. "Who's your doctor, Don . . . if I may ask?"

"Dr. Sutherland. He's been our family physician for years, even though my father changed doctors recently due to some rift. Probably because he didn't like being told the truth about having Alzheimer's. But Sutherland is a very dear family friend, nonetheless. Why?"

Laura hesitated. Suspicion clawed at her brain until it bled. "He was also your father's physician, but fired?"

"Yes, of course he was Dad's physician, but my father was as stubborn as a goat. Once he got it in his mind that he wouldn't succumb to the disease, I'm sure he became unmanageable. So, I can only assume that he, knowing Father the way he did, gave Mother the pills to help calm my Father, even if he'd decided to keep going to different doctors until one told him what he wanted to hear. He wouldn't have submitted to any Alzheimer's medications from any of them, however." Donny smiled. "You had to really understand the great Donald Haines Sr. to appreciate Mother's dilemma. That wasn't foul play, just the ongoing games they had between them."

"Your will," she said carefully, now taking up her cool tea and sipping it slowly. "Alan is your sole beneficiary, correct? He'll see after everything for you?"

"Yes," Donny said, sipping his chardonnay and watching the lights dance within the glass. "He's all I have. Not even a pet. Sad, isn't it?"

"No," Laura said calmly. "It's not sad, just your reality. No judgment."

"That's perhaps the nicest thing anyone has said in regards to this," he murmured with a sad smile. "I see why Father liked you. You made him feel, got under his skin, and maybe gave him a little bit of a heart."

"I think you should get a second opinion on your illness. Soon," she said, worry lacing her tone. "The older doctors may not be as up on the newer treatments." She tried to measure her response. But something kept picking at the wound his confession opened in her mind. While all of it was plausible, something didn't sit right.

"When I first learned the diagnosis, I was beyond hope. I was a mess. I was angry. I was afraid. I wanted to fly to the most experimental facilities, fight this thing tooth and nail. I can appreciate where my father was, upon learning of his own personal battle. But Alan advised me to just look at my father's futile behavior—and I'd never wanted to be like him." Donny chuckled sadly and sipped his wine. "Guess I'm more like him than I care to admit, but Alan was so calm and reassuring. He said he'd be with me till the end, and has helped me see the wisdom in embracing the quality of life, versus wasting precious time seeking miracle cures that don't exist."

Tension settled in Laura's shoulders. "He goes to all your appointments with you, and is there for you, then . . . even at Dr. Sutherland's?"

"Every step of the way," Donny said with pride. "He means more to me than you can know. You hear so many terrible stories about partners leaving, or running scared. Not him."

"That's good to know," Laura whispered. "That is so good to know."

Everyone checked into the hotel at staggered intervals, solo. Each had a temporary new identity, a rental car, and a gun. They ordered their meals sent to their rooms, and ate alone. Then one by one, meals were abandoned and the rendezvous point was Steve's room.

"I want you to take a look at these docs," Laura said, her eyes blazing. "Donald had to know something wasn't right. Look at this," she said through her teeth, flipping the pages as her team sat spellbound. "He cuts off his wife from virtually everything—but why? They'd been in combat for years, knew about each other's infidelities and didn't really care about them. So all of a sudden he leaves her without a dime?"

"Maybe he finally got wind of the doctor's angle? Knowing a long-time friend is doing your wife will make a man more than cut her off." Steve shook his head and leaned forward on the edge of the bed.

"Yes. But the Haineses had had affairs on each other for years. Had to be more than that. He changes his will to make it impossible for his son to inherit much more than a pittance?"

"What if the old man knew something wasn't right, wasn't sure, or couldn't prove it, much less get his son to believe it, so was making sure that if something was foul and Donny passed, one Alan Moyer wouldn't inherit jack shit? And if he thought the doctor was messing with his son—doing his wife was one thing, hurting his kid was something else. That would be enough to make him cut her off without a dime, knowing she was sleeping with somebody who had screwed his kid. Especially if he couldn't get Donny to believe him, and if the mother helped keep Donny in denial." James stood and walked toward the window.

"But, damn. The boy's own mother?" Jamal shook his head.

"What if she was blind to the doctor's aim and really believed the hype?" Najira offered. "Wouldn't be the first time a woman went into cahoots with a man behind her husband's back, only to get burned."

"No lie," Steve said. "Happens every day. Maybe that's what pissed old Haines off so bad—and I'd like to find out when he got the scripts." Steve riffled his fingers through his hair. "Wonder if young Donny's diagnosis coincides with when Haines switched doctors, but was still getting scripts dropped in his drink by the wife?"

Laura nodded. "And interestingly enough, check out the link between the casino contracts and the food provider." She motioned with her head toward her laptop. "Scott Foods and Beverages, Inc., just like Jamal had discussed with his contact, had gotten a huge chunk of concession business at the airport expansion. So, Senator Scott's son got a windfall. I started looking into Atlanta start-ups, mergers, and acquisition records, and lo and behold, Philly Foods, Inc., opened a holding company called Charter Foods, Inc. Wanna bet they have a casino food contract worth a mint? Get it? Charter— new casino charters? Look at how they have to have some minority inclusion, and got a non-Philly based firm to fill that gap."

James turned and his eyes met Laura's. "Oh, shit . . ."

"Yeah, oh, shit," Jamal said, standing and beginning to pace. "My boy told me about the girl, and it still doesn't make sense. If she was in there, she wouldn't have been strong enough to smother the old dude, feel me?"

"She would have been if he were nearly paralyzed from the poisons."

Everyone stared at Laura.

"You know what," Najira said, slowly, her voice so quiet everyone gave her their full attention. "Girlfriend was flossing just a little too much ice. Was real loose and real cocky like she had a secret. Was talking shit, too, about her man not getting all her tips. What if she cut a side deal?"

"Like, went in, did the tea thing and gave up the draws," Laura said in a murmur, her gaze roving the group, "but was assured if she did one little extra thing, she'd get a side knot that even her manager didn't have to know about."

"Yeah," Najira said, nodding. "Something real treacherous like that. I know her. She's capable. Would do her own momma for money."

"So," Laura said, standing. "We lay low, do the funeral.

See who Howard Scott talks to. If he and Alan get together, we drop a little science in his ear."

"Meanwhile, we shake the doctor. I'm placing money on it that he's got a two-way happening," James said. "He thinks he's in Mom's pocket through Haines's death, but was getting a little extra somethin' somethin' by doing some skullduggery for Alan—two Haineses, Junior and Senior, in one prescription. Phony diagnoses."

"The whole poison, tea, prescription thing seems a little too sophisticated for Jamal's boy, no offense," Steve muttered.

"Ain't no offense taken," Jamal said. "That's my boy and all, but that's a dumb motherfucker."

"Poisons and meds, that's up a doctor's alley, wouldn't you say?" Najira looked at Laura.

"Yeah, I'd say." Laura gathered up the documents. "And I also know the senator was scared shitless, enough to tell me to look into the wife. What father wouldn't try to protect his son?" She stared at them all. "Get some rest, tomorrow we watch the news, and James and Steve make contact with Alan to rattle his cage and see if he'll bring you the docs."

"He ain't gonna bring those papers," James said. "He can't."

"I know. But what if you all deliver some to him, ones that are real close to the real thing, with a bit of graphic enhancement?" She smiled. "It'll make him wet his drawers."

Steve smiled and walked to the door. "Sounds like a plan. Make him see that killing Donny wasn't worth it, if that's what's going on—and killing Haines prematurely wasn't worth it."

"And make it look like the mob got cut out and they will be really upset. Let's put everything in Elizabeth's name, as though old Haines had a last minute bout of contrition for all his ways." She chuckled. "I'll even include a memo section, a letter, that says he's so sorry for abusing his wife with affairs, and then let's see how the chips fall."

"You're signing her death warrant." James looked at Laura hard.

"And?" She folded her arms over her chest. "She set him up, made him try to take his own life. I can sleep at night if her lover, her son's lover, or a senator's son comes for her."

James smiled a half smile and shook his head. "That ain't Christian, Laura. But, uh . . . I do see your point."

"I should try to wheedle info out of Shaquira," Najira said. "She was feeling me out to work solo on the side with her for some bigger jobs than her man could provide. Want me to go exploring?"

"Half of me does, the other half of me doesn't," Laura said honestly. "Baby, if the people who set this in motion get nervous, they could try to clean up behind themselves." She shared a quick glance with James and Steve, who nodded.

"Your boy is a sitting duck, and so is his woman," James said to Jamal. "You might want to hit his cell phone and tell him to stay alert. Howard Scott is running scared and dangerous, if he's linked to Moyer—which means they have to tie up any loose ends."

"Been thinking about that all day," Jamal said, his voice and gaze distant. "I'ma call him, but not sure what to say to make him see. The brother is blinded by chump change." He looked at his sister. "'Jira, this is one time I'ma ask you not to get in it. Just keep visiting Pops like you did today. Keep telling him we love him and got his back."

"I've got a man on him," Laura said quietly. "I don't even trust the cops, and definitely don't trust the doctors, right through here. And now that we know your boy Howard probably made the call, not Donny, to order the tainted food through his food services business . . . uh-uh. Plus, the only way he would have known who to call to get the right poison in it was through his father or Alan. That links them."

"I wish I could get back into our office, though," Steve muttered. "If Alan knew about the camera placement, then he also could have rigged a move. Just a slight enough tilt to allow someone in or out who had a key."

"Donny would have had a key," James said, staring at his partner. "An easy thing to slip off a ring when you live with someone, and then slip it right back into place—if the girl didn't do the job."

"My point exactly," Laura said, looking at her young cousins. "I know this is your father, but stay out of harm's way, understood?"

They grumbled their acceptance. Everyone stood to leave, except Steve. Laura grabbed her laptop, but she noticed that James hovered nearby as they left.

"Can I talk to you for a minute?" he said as they stepped into the elevator.

She glanced at her cousins and stepped out on James's floor. "Yeah. Shoot."

Chapter 16

Najira glanced at her brother as the elevator doors closed James and Laura away from them. "Whatchu think that's all about?"

Jamal smiled. "You know what that's about, sis. C'mon, girl."

"Yeah . . . he's crazy about her, just like she is about him." Najira stared at the numbers as they lit their floor. "You like Steve?"

Jamal held the door for a second and looked at his sister sideways. "Steve?"

Najira brushed past him into the hallway. "Yeah, Steve."

Jamal loped forward, trying to catch up to her short but angry strides. "He cool, I guess—for a white boy."

"Damn, Jamal. Why it gotta be all that? I just asked you if you liked Steve."

"Like I said, he cool and all. So why you sweatin' me?" Jamal leaned against the wall as Najira fumbled for their room key. "Why? You like him, or somethin'?"

"He's all right," she said, appearing unfazed as she produced the key and sauntered into the room ahead of him. She didn't turn around and began rummaging in her purse. "He's nice . . . you know, in a white boy sorta way. Almost got his ass kicked for me, though, when they grabbed us. Have to give him that. First thing he did was try to get his body between me and the asshole who grabbed me—"

"He used to be a cop," Jamal said, clearly unimpressed.

She jerked her attention up from her bag and shot him an evil grit. "Last time I checked I wasn't the president, and he ain't no Secret Service man supposed to take no bullet."

Jamal laughed and flopped down on the bed. "Aw'ight, aw'ight. I feel you."

She sucked her teeth and rolled her eyes at him. "He's good people, J. A real friend to James and is trying to help us get Dad out of a setup. Last I checked, too, he wasn't gettin' a dime out of all of this, but is going along for the ride with his partner, just 'cause it's right—so why you gotta call him a white boy?"

Jamal pushed himself up on one elbow and gave his sister a sly smile. "Because I don't want Pop to have a heart attack while he's in the hospital, yo. How long he been in the trenches fighting da man? If the gunshot don't take him out, his baby girl messing wit—"

"He was real tight with Haines. He was white." She folded her arms over her chest.

"Still is, even dead, last I checked. But that was business," Jamal said, laughing and rolling over on his back. He slung his arm over his face. "Aw . . . maaan. 'Jira, why you always gotta come up with drama, girl?"

"It ain't drama, J. I'm tired of being treated like a hoochie by your boys, and a lotta men, who just don't appreciate how to treat a woman. Ain't none of them really been nice, unless they just wanted some ass, much less been ready to take a bullet without getting any—and even then, they wouldn't. And while we're out, he treats me real nice, real respectful, is cool . . . and is tight with our family, and—oh, boy, shut up. Forget you." She turned back to her abandoned purse on the dresser and began pulling out her hand lotion and lipstick with jerky, angry motions.

"Okay. He's cool," Jamal finally said on a heavy sigh.

She stopped moving but didn't turn around. "For real?"

"Didn't I just say that?"

She smiled, but still didn't turn, and began touching up her lipstick, and then applied some hand lotion. "You ain't mad that I like him?" she asked after a moment.

"'Jira, you grown, he grown. I ain't mad. I'm just tired."

She turned and stared at him, watching him intently until he slid his forearm off his face and looked at her. She glanced at the door and then down at the floor.

"Aw, girl," Jamal muttered. "See now, you wrong."

"How am I wrong?" She'd asked the question with a smile and without looking at him.

"He ask you to come up there?"

Najira picked up her purse but didn't answer the charge. "Maybe. But like you said, we grown."

"Fine," Jamal said, and rolled over, presenting her his back. "Your ass just betta be back here before Laura calls in the morning."

Najira kissed his cheek, and giggled when her brother shrugged away. "I will. Thank you, J."

"Leave me alone. I'm sleep."

She slipped out the door and walked so fast she was nearly running. Najira depressed the elevator button and tapped her foot as she waited for it to come. She had to get out of the hotel and get to Shaquira. To hell with what Laura said, it was her father who was going to take a fall if things didn't work out right.

As soon as the elevator came, she was on it, and she quickly went down to the lobby and crossed over to the parking garage elevator, rode down a level and collected her car. Driving with one hand and punching in the number Shaquira had given her on the basketball court, she prayed with all her might that voice mail wouldn't come on.

"Yeah," Shaquira said, her tone icy. "Who dis?"

"'Jira, girl. Been thinking about what you said earlier, and I want in."

Shaquira laughed. "I knew money would pull a sistah. This is a sweet deal."

"You really gonna break away from Moon? You ain't just playing?"

"How you gonna play with fifteen thousand dollars, boo?" Shaquira sucked her teeth. "Like I said, what a man don't know won't hurt him."

"Where y'all gonna be tonight?"

"We're going over Tosha's to pick her up, then going down to Club Beyond."

"Maybe I can meet y'all up there?" Najira offered.

"Yeah, girl. That works. Meet us up there, and I'll buy you an Alize," Shaquira said, bragging.

"But, uh . . . I don't know how to do it," Najira said, her mind racing as she drove toward the club.

"I'll fill you in on all-a that when we get together."

"But what if Moon is all up in our business?"

"Don't worry about him," Shaquira said, chuckling deep in her throat. "You ain't neva heard of a meetin' in the ladies' room?"

Najira laughed. "Yeah. I hear you. Thanks, girl . . . 'cause I need some extra ends."

"You wanted to talk," Laura said calmly, closing the hotel room door behind James.

"Yeah, I did," he said slowly. "There's a lot . . . Can we just be real?"

"Yeah," she said, walking over to the small table that hosted two chairs. She put her laptop down and dropped her purse on the dresser, and waited for James to sit down.

She watched him sit on the edge of the bed and lean forward with his forearms on his legs, studying the floor. He breathed slowly, his back expanding and contracting with each breath as though it were laboring with the weight of his thoughts. She sat down and waited for him to gather the words.

He took a long time before speaking, as though not sure where to begin. "Laura, listen . . . what happened down in the islands. I'm so sorry you went through that alone. I should have been there, and would have been, if I'd known."

She nodded and her voice caught in her throat, coming out as a whisper. "I know. But you couldn't be. It was probably better that way."

"No, it wasn't better that way," he said, looking at her now. His eyes held hers without anger, just deep remorse residing in them. "We're a team . . . partners. Should stand together and deal with whatever happens. At least that's how I see it, unless you tell me different."

He waited. She could feel the tension in him and wondered if he were holding his breath.

"I see it that way," she said quietly, and then allowed her gaze to leave his intense eyes.

"I just had to get that off my chest," he said, his stare so burning that it forced her to look at him again. "No matter what, if anything were to happen to you . . ."

"I know," she said quietly. "That's why I didn't want you near this—or me."

He nodded and turned his hands up to beckon her to him. She stared at his palms for a moment, half afraid to go to them. The tenderness that they could deliver would open things in her that would make it impossible to go back to being alone. That frightened her more than the prospect of waging war against unknown assassins. She knew how to deal with cutthroats and the ruthless, but to love a man with all her heart and soul would be foreign territory too vast to consider.

But his stare and his open hands were like a magnet that lifted her slowly to her feet and made her move forward. She stood between his legs and cradled his head as his arms surrounded her waist and he nuzzled his face against her stomach.

"Laura, I'm so sorry you lost the baby."

She petted his shoulders and bent to kiss the crown of his head. "So am I."

He hugged her tighter and they stayed that way for a long time, holding each other. No words were necessary as the quiet mourning circled them. When he looked up at her, his face was wet, and she bent so he could wipe away the dampness from her cheeks. Their kiss was thick and salty. Trembling fingers traced the course of tears. Gentle hands caressed once-hardened jaw lines. Eyes met with understanding.

"I love you," he whispered, his thumbs following her eyebrows until his fingers became tangled in her hair.

She sat on his lap and stroked his soft beard . . . her giant teddy bear could be so fearsome, yet had the soul of a lamb. It was that innocence within him that she'd never wanted to destroy. That belief that there could be such a thing as blind trust in anyone or anything. For so long she'd been poison, and he'd ingested that from her in small doses. She just hoped that instead of quietly dying from it, he was becoming immune.

"I love you, too," she whispered, closing her eyes at the admission. "I didn't work Haines to get you put on the charters. I didn't orchestrate his death, I swear to you . . . and I never meant for anyone to be killed."

He pressed his finger to her lips and then replaced it with his mouth. The tenderness that he sent against her lips made her shudder from the inner warmth it created. Total trust opened her and permeated the soft tissue that surrounded her tongue . . . and it danced with his in a lazy, slow acceptance. Her mind pried open along with her heart, and she sent back a subtle message that she trusted him, too . . . her hands said it as they splayed against his shoulders with care. His repeated it, as they ran up and down her back in patient strokes, summoning away the hurt, chasing away the pain, banishing loneliness as though it were a disease.

And when he pulled her to lie with him, she felt like she was falling from the edge of the earth, going over a chasm into a blanketing warmth that offered only peace.

"Hey, gurl!" Shaquira hollered, walking over to Najira when she spotted her.

"Since when y'all tight?" Moon said skeptically, but eyed Najira with a smile. "I ain't know you knew her."

"I didn't. We got cool out there while you and J was talking. Her brother might be slow, but girlfriend knows what time it is." Shaquira threw her long tresses over her shoulder and adjusted her red halter top.

"You know Tosha?" Moon asked, looking at Najira.

Najira shook her head, waved hi by wiggling her fingers and smiling at the girl she didn't know.

"Hi," Tosha said, sending a nasty grit in Shaquira's direction. "I'm Moon's first woman, she's new." She looked Najira up and down. "Don't get it twisted. I run shit, okay. Not her."

Najira offered a look of respect toward the dark chocolate sister with an awesome, sculpted body. Everything on her was tight and righteous, even her short, sculpture-curled hair, and her S-shaped figure strained in the black ripped mini she wore. But girlfriend seemed like she could definitely fight, long gold nails and black stiletto pumps, regardless.

"Yeah, right," Shaquira said, going between Tosha and

Najira. "But my ass gets the bulk of the work." She smoothed her hands down her body to denote having the better figure and assets, and then flung her hair over her shoulder. "I keep the money flowing."

Tosha sucked her teeth and held up a hand in Shaquira's face. "Whateva."

"My boy cool wit you being down wit us?" Moon moved in toward Najira and looked her over, licking his lips. He stood positioned to separate the women and to stop a potential catfight.

"I'm grown," Najira said with a smile, sipping her Alize. She could only hope that her father's name wouldn't come up now. "What Jamal don't know won't hurt him. A sistah gotta git paid, though."

"Aw'ight," Moon said, laughing. "I feel you."

Najira breathed a sigh of relief, but made it come out in a sexy rush in Moon's direction. If she played her cards right, some things were standard: the girl's manager didn't discuss clients or names. Her dad was in the newspaper as doing the job, but his name hadn't been linked to her, yet—courtesy Laura's calls to her media pals. Maybe Shaquira hadn't put two and two together and would give up the tapes.

"Girl, walk me to the bathroom," Shaquira finally said, pulling on Najira's arm.

"Damn," Moon fussed. "Why you gotta be going to the bathroom all the time in twos and threes and shit? Let the woman finish her drink."

"Let that high bitch go," Tosha muttered, and rolled her eyes. She took a deep sip of her apple martini and draped a possessive arm over Moon's shoulder.

"Whateva," Shaquira said in a huff, and tugged on Najira's arm again. "C'mon, girl. Forget her."

"I do hafta pee," Najira said, laughing. "Watch my drink, Moon?" She batted her eyes at him and slid off the bar stool, pushing her way through the crowd as his stare lingered behind her. She walked with extra emphasis, making sure her butt swayed to the thumping beat of the music to help hypnotize him.

Shaquira dragged her along like a woman on a mission. As soon as they got into the tiny, black and red enclosure, they both slipped into one of the two empty stalls and Shaquira locked it. She opened her purse, making sure it wasn't over the toilet. "Want some blow?"

"Naw, I'm cool," Najira said as Shaquira dipped a small scoop of coke out of a tiny plastic bag with her pinky, allowing it to balance in her red, acrylic talon for a second, before sniffing it hard and then swallowing.

"Damn, that's righteous," Shaquira said, dabbing her nose with a knuckle, and then repeating the process with the other nostril. "Moon got some Ecstasy, too—make that stingy motherfucker give you some so you can get your freak on tonight." She smiled and leaned into Najira. "I ain't know you was cool like that, but glad you called." She moved a little closer, her huge breasts almost brushing Najira's in the tight confines. "Always saw you around when we was younger, but didn't know you was down. Neva can tell, can you?"

"Neva can," Najira said, forcing herself to smile, and trying to avoid Shaquira's hardened nipples. A millimeter closer and Shaquira would be dry-humping her in the rank environment. "But it sounded so . . . exciting," Najira added, baiting her for information. "How'd you do it, gurl, without being scared?"

"Oh, I was scared as shit," Shaquira said, snorting more blow as she spoke. Then she tucked it away, pushed her long Louis Vuitton purse strap up on her shoulder, and got closer to Najira again. Her hazel irises seemed to swallow her dilated pupils as she brought her face in toward Najira's to whisper. This time her nipples brushed against Najira's and she seemed to hesitate to see if Najira would shrink away. When Najira didn't move, she spoke with quiet urgency, swaying her hard pebbles against Najira's blouse in a sensual, back and forth motion. "Moon and that fucking Tosha get on my goddamned nerves, but he, right now, has the hook up for the jobs. I don't have Howard's number, but the white boy that was with him to look me over to okay me for the job, asked to talk to me solo while they was working out the price." Shaquira shivered and moved her pelvis tight against Najira's thigh. "Damn, this shit makes your ass horny."

It took everything within Najira to smile and not freak out. She glanced down at Shaquira's cleavage, watching her breasts push up in the skimpy fabric as her nipples came to the top of it. Shaquira licked her thumbs and began to flick them quickly, her buttocks clenching as she began to slowly pump against Najira's thigh.

"You want to, girl?" Shaquira murmured.

Najira glanced around inside the cramped stall, panicked. "I ain't never done it before . . . and never did it somewhere somebody could bust in."

"Ain't nobody coming in here, and if they do, they know the deal." Shaquira's eyes had gone to slits as she began rolling her tight coffee beans between her forefingers and thumbs. "Just suck 'em the way you like it done. Girl, I've gotta get off soon or I'll die."

When she heard the outer bathroom door open, Najira froze. But it was the perfect opportunity to stall for time. She dropped her voice real low and backed up for a bit as they listened to an unseen woman urinate, flush, and go on about her business.

"Tell me about the money, first," Najira hedged after the other woman went to the sink and finally left the bathroom. If that high bitch, Shaquira, didn't get out of her face . . .

"Okay, yeah, I know—business first," Shaquira breathed, pulling her halter down enough to fully expose her breasts. She cupped them and moved them up and down against Najira's. "Tell me that don't feel good."

"Yeah, but, what did the white boy want you to do for fifteen?"

"He gave me his number on the QT," Shaquira said, opening her jeans and sliding her hand down into them. She planted a wet kiss along Najira's neck and spoke into her ear with an alcohol stained whisper. "Said all I had to do was wait a few hours, do the butler, and then go upstairs and put a pillow over the old white man's face when he hit the lights. But it got crazy. There was this other old dude up there when I went into the dark room. Couldn't see shit but the old white dude, 'cause of the way the outside lights was coming through the window. I ain't know there was two of 'em in there!"

"Oh, shit," Najira whispered, fondling Shaquira's exposed tits to keep her talking. "What'd you do, girl?"

Shaquira threw her head back and had begun breathing through her mouth as Najira's hands moved in gentle circles. "Yeah, like that . . . but, baby, suck 'em for me."

"It's so exciting, I like hearing about it while I work," Najira said. "You think I can do it, next time you get a job?"

"Oh, you got a kinky side, huh?" Shaquira said, chuckling through a gasp. "Your ass is all pro, you gonna make a mint."

"What happened?" Najira hissed, returning the grind of Shaquira's pelvis.

"He hit the other old motherfucker in the head and shot him, while I did what I was paid to do. Then I was out. Got the rest of my money that night and he took me 'round the corner and dropped me off. I called Moon's dumb ass and he picked me up. He got five, I got fifteen—you do the math. Me and you could work this thing until we don't need his ass anymore. Fuck that Tosha. She don't run shit, and is so stupid, she gives him half of everything she makes, like a fool. But I'm a businesswoman, okay. Me and you could be phatpaid, if we work it right."

"Yeah, we could," Najira said, feeling sick. She needed to

get out of there now that she knew all there was to know. "You said Moon had some Ecstasy on him?"

Shaquira looked down at Najira. "C'mon, girl—ain't you wet yet?"

"I'm all fucked up in this bathroom," Najira said, not needing to lie about that. "I want to be able to lie down, not be standing on my toes where it stinks."

"Girl, get over it. A lot of clients like public places fast and easy."

"Give me a hit of E, and let me get some air, then. This is my first time out, girl," Najira whined, playing with Shaquira's long hair.

"I'll eat yours, if you eat mine," Shaquira teased.

"Why don't we get a room?" Najira kissed the tops of her breasts, but bypassed her nipples. "I'll pay."

"Ohhh . . . shit," Shaquira said with a wince. "Fuck that, I'll pay . . . but then Moon's ass will wanna come, too. Then we'll have to fight with Tosha's ghetto ass."

"Let him," Najira said, smiling. "I don't have a problem with a private audience. Maybe if he watches with Tosha sitting on his lap, she won't be mad, and won't be worried about me coming into the business with y'all—if she knows I'm with you, she won't have to worry about Moon tapping your shit from time to time . . . which will maybe make him leave you alone."

Shaquira's eyes widened and she stepped back to look at Najira good. "For real? You'd be down for that?"

"Get my ass on enough, and it won't matter."

They both laughed.

"I'm not sure if I wanna share you with him, though. He'll be hogging your cha cha, once he sees how good I'll eat it, and Tosha's gonna wanna fight your ass, after that," Shaquira said, laughing, her gaze filled with lust as she began to straighten her top. "I want first taste, though—no matter what happens."

"Then let his ass watch," Najira murmured, "then he'll bust a nut fast and we can get back to what we about. The shit we do is gonna make Tosha's ass so hot, she ain't gonna wanna fight. All she'll be worried about is getting some dick. C'mon, girl, get me out this nasty-assed bathroom."

Shaquira nodded and backed away from Najira, her eyes alight with desire as she opened the stall door. "I'ma get you fucked up good, girl. I promise. Damn, I can't wait."

Steve sat in his room watching the late night news. Everything was always the same. Some kids sitting in a club parking lot blown away by a drive by. Two young women and a guy, shot. Over what?

He let his breath out hard, needing a beer. The walls of the hotel room were closing in on him. The bar in the lobby was calling his name. He already knew where James would be. Maybe Jamal might be down for a brewski . . . maybe his sister would join them? Crazy as she was, she was pretty . . . and funny . . . and fine as shit. But her brother didn't play that, nor did her dad. It wasn't his fault he was white. Fuck it. But Najira had always been cool about that . . . and she was fine as shit.

Steve looked at the telephone, and went to it slowly. If Jamal answered, then he'd ask him if he wanted a beer. That was simple enough. But why was it so hard to dial that number? He closed his eyes and took a deep breath, and punched in the digits quickly. Jamal answered on the second ring.

"Yo. It's Steve. Wanna grab a beer in the lobby?"

Jamal hesitated. "Najira down?"

"I don't know, man." Steve paused, hoping she would be. "Ask her. That's cool for her to tag along."

"Whatchu mean, ask her?" Jamal said quickly, his tone escalating.

Steve sighed and sat down on the edge of the bed. He'd

expected the reaction, but had hoped Jamal would be cooler than that. "I can dig it," Steve said quietly. "Some other time."

"Naw, man. Why don't *you* ask her?"

Steve stood up slowly and stared at the phone. Was this some kinda crazy test, or what? "All right. Put her on the telephone."

"Stop playing, man," Jamal shot back. "I'm tired."

"No. I'll ask her," Steve said, finding sudden confidence. He was many things, but a punk wasn't one of them. "Put her on the phone."

"Put her on the phone? She's grown and don't have to ask me what to do. Yo, y'all need to stop trippin' over there and handle your bizness, but keep me out of it."

For a moment Steve didn't say a word. "She's not with you?"

"I'm hanging up," Jamal said. "Stop—"

"She's not with you?" Steve repeated louder, dragging the telephone off the nightstand to get his coat and gun.

"Naw, man. She ain't with you?"

"Meet me in the lobby in two minutes," Steve said, and slammed down the receiver.

Chapter
17

His cell phone was vibrating across the nightstand at the same time Laura's room phone was ringing. Within moments, someone was pounding on the door, just as he was hopping on one foot to pull on his jeans. Laura had snatched her clothes and was in the bathroom, quickly robing, to address the 911. James flung open the door after seeing Steve and Jamal's faces distorted through the peephole.

They barreled through it, just as Laura rushed out of the bathroom.

"She lied to me," Jamal said, breathing hard. "I thought she went up to Steve's room, but she's gone."

"Jamal said she was supposed to be with me, but Najira ain't nowhere to be found. At first we went to the lobby bar, hoping she got cold feet, went there for a drink to work up her nerve to knock on my door, but she ain't down there," Steve said, his words coming between huffs of sudden breath.

"She ain't answering her cell, neither," Jamal said, walking in a circle as James snatched on his sweater and shoes.

Laura raked her hair. "You think she went to the hospital—I mean, no offense, but if she was contemplating going to Steve's room, maybe she got really nervous and went to see her dad, first . . . maybe get the old man's blessing, maybe—oh, I don't know what that crazy girl could have done."

"Maybe she went digging for information, Laura." James's quiet assessment stilled the group.

Laura's hand went to her chest as she closed her eyes. "Pray to God she didn't."

"Well, we just can't stand around here and wring our fucking hands!" Steve shouted, flipping his cell open. "I'm calling Luis. See if we can—"

"No," James said. "No leaks. Even our boy could inadvertently say something to let the wrong departmental sources know we're underground. We do this the old-fashioned way."

Jamal and Steve stared at James as Laura paced to the window.

"Man, we've gotta find my sister. She can't go looking for Moon at night alone."

"Where does Moon hang?" James went to Jamal and placed a hand on his shoulder.

"A lot at Club Beyond, but, his ass goes all over. Delaware Avenue, up the way, wherever he's got a client."

"Club Beyond?" Steve said in a near whisper. His question made Laura turn to look at him. "Three kids just got shot up there. A guy and two women."

"Aw shit, aw shit," Jamal said, walking to the door and back to the center of the room. "You get names?"

"No. No names given yet until families are notified."

"Now you call Luis," James said. "Don't tell him where we are, or who we're looking for—just get three names."

Steve nodded; the others fell silent as he placed the call. Within moments he'd flipped his cell phone closed. "A Monroe Jackson, Shaquira Melendez, and a Tosha Johnson—ring a bell?"

Steve leaned against the dresser in relief and closed his

eyes as Jamal slumped against the wall. Laura sat on the bed slowly and wrapped her arms around herself. But James's line of vision never left Jamal's body.

"You ain't lookin' right, brother. Talk to me."

Jamal glanced up at James with tears in his eyes. "You've gotta find 'Jira—fast," he croaked. "They mighta kidnapped her from the lobby, or some shit. Moon was my boy, Shaquira and Tosha worked for him . . . 'Quira did the job at Haines's house."

She tried not to cringe as the side of her rental car scraped a cement post. Getting the sedan back into the Sheraton garage was harder than getting it out. A hit of Ecstasy was zooming her system, making her sweat. All she needed was a little air. The lie she'd told to escape the club wasn't no lie, she did need air—lots of it, and felt like she was about to throw up.

Staggering out of the car, she dug into her purse searching for her cell phone but found the Glock Steve gave her instead. "Now, see, that's what I'm talking about," she said, giggling and wobbling as she walked. "A practical man." She fell against a parked car as quickly approaching headlights made her squint. She raised her arm to cover her face, and noted the car slowed down. Ooops, the gun. Najira laughed and fell as little popping noises made her ears ring. The sound of wheels screeching pissed her off, and she stood up with attitude.

"Dumb motherfuckers!" she hollered, rubbing the burn on her arm. "Damn."

She teetered and then leaned against another car to put away her gun and find her room key. Her phone was vibrating again, what did people want from her? She wasn't *even* eating no pussy—not in this lifetime. She laughed and grabbed her cell phone as she walked, trying to come up with a suitable lie for why she'd duffed and had left Shaquira hanging.

Laura's number came up, and she began running, giggling, covering her mouth and pounding on the elevator button.

"Go get her, she's in the parking lot!" Laura said fast, moving to the door before the men in the room could even jerk their bodies. "Oh, shit, she's high, laughing, and I don't know what!"

Four bodies tried to cram through the door at once. They bypassed the elevators and headed for the stairs. But laughter stopped everyone dead in their tracks.

"Hey, y'all," Najira hollered down the corridor. "Where's the fire?"

Laura hugged Najira in the backseat of a sedan. Clothes had been rush-packed. Checkout would be electronic or by phone. Najira's car had been abandoned in the lot. Steve and James eyed the shell casing that had missed Najira by a margin. Their brethren would be on the way soon. Sirens were heard in the distance. The team's new destination, the Hilton on Delaware Avenue. One ID was placed down, Laura's. Five to a room would have to work for the night. After Laura transacted business at the front desk, she coolly handed off the key to the others outside.

Najira was hustled upstairs by way of an exit stairwell, and then the elevator on a non-lobby floor. James swept the room with Jamal, while Steve held Najira upright. Everything went like clockwork, until the room door slammed.

James inspected Najira's arm. "Grazed, but she'll live. Gotta put something on it soon, and it'll leave a scar."

"Damn," Najira muttered. "First my knees, now my dag-gone arm when I fell."

"You're lucky to be alive," Steve said, shaking her. "What was on your fucking mind!"

Everybody stared at him, and he let Najira go. Najira smiled.

"That didn't come from a fall, it was from a fucking bullet, 'Jira," Laura said, getting in her cousin's face. "Throw her high ass in the shower and sober her up. *Now*."

Najira covered her mouth. "I'm all right, but, y'all, it was *live* up in there." She glanced around, still half dazed. "They was shooting at the club? When!"

"In the parking lot, darlin'," Steve said through his teeth and turned away. "I need a damned drink."

"Moon, Shaquira, and Tosha are dead, 'Jira," Jamal said quietly, stemming her mirth.

"What!" Najira spun around in circles until she nearly fell.

"Keep your voice down," Laura commanded, and then dragged her cousin in the bathroom and slammed the door.

Najira sat on the edge of the bed nursing the black coffee that Laura repeatedly refilled. She related the story in halting bits of memory until she finally got it all told, and then vomited in a wastebasket.

Laura laid her back in the bed and covered her up, stroking her hair as she spoke to the group. "The girl is crazy," she said, looking down at her young cousin, "but God knows, she got the missing link."

"And they're on the move as we speak," James said, his nerves not allowing him to sit. "Somebody with a young male voice made the call, possibly played it like he was Donny, and got the poison in—and since he'd set up the deal with Jamal's boy, we know Howard sponsored the diversion to keep the butler busy and to mess with Haines's tea—whether the girl understood the implications of that, or not. Although Shaquira smothered Haines, a white male who had access to the house had the key and knew how to avoid our cameras."

"No way to find out now if it was an old man—the doctor, or a young brunette, Moyer, who pulled the trigger to shoot Akhan," Steve said with disgust, his eyes never leaving Najira's prone form. "All of what she was told wouldn't be credible in front of a judge. They'd say she was making wild allegations to protect her father, which, if we didn't know better, would be plausible. A jury would never believe her over the son of a senator and a young, rising-star attorney, not to mention a renowned area doctor and the sterling Mrs. Haines. If anything, the way the new will is structured, and given Laura's recent visit to Haines just before he died, would make it look like she and her family did the jobs." He stared at James. "You being her man and named in Haines's will don't look good, either, partner."

Steve's gaze went to Jamal. "And since you were just recently spotted talking to your boy, Monroe Jackson, and his chicks, given your rap sheet from the old gang days, it could be made to look like you were the triggerman who just conveniently wiped out an old grudge and some people your sister was using as your father's alibi." Steve raked his hair with frustration and sat down hard on the edge of the dresser.

"Shit . . ." Jamal said, hanging his head until it rested on Najira's side. "That's beyond fucked up, man. But I ain't mad at you for jus' being real . . . but, damn." He sighed and closed his eyes. "A brother from 'round the way can't catch a break, ever. That's how the system works—foul, if you ain't plugged in."

James shoved his hands into his pockets. Fury consumed him as he thought about how they'd been boxed into a corner, and how Jamal's defeat may as well have been his own. He understood why the young brothers took what they thought was the easy way out—they'd seen it done ever since they were babies. Only problem was that, the loopholes were open for everybody but them. For them, the loophole was a noose.

"The main culprits are dead, and there's no way to link them to the actual crime in any way that could hold up in court. The people who ordered the job are so tucked away by layers of insulation that the boys downtown will never unravel this shit." Laura exhaled hard and stood.

James wiped his face with both hands and nodded. Suddenly he felt very old. "I know," he said after a moment. All eyes were on him, except Najira's; she was either fast asleep or unconscious. It didn't matter. Right now, he was glad that there was one less pair of eyes staring at him, seeking answers he didn't have. "Only way to do this is to keep those who are nervous on the move, keep them trying to tidy up loose ends. If they slip, they go down."

Jamal knelt by his sister again and touched her hair. "I don't want her near this anymore. She's already in too deep."

"That's why we do this with paper," Laura said. "Tonight, I do the phony docs so you guys can slip them to Moyer, just like we planned. Let's see if he or the doctor flinches, first, in this game of chicken."

"How about if you get a second set drawn up," James said, "and make it look like Moyer gets everything—like the wife was totally disinherited, but the son got the lion's share . . . drop that on the doctor, and see how he reacts."

"Will do," Laura said. "I'll tell him that Haines asked me to deliver the papers, if anything shady happened to him . . . because I was his mistress, and can't stand his fucking wife—but my man said he wanted to have the last laugh."

"Oh, yeah," James said. "The bastard will take your call and do coffee, too."

* * *

Daylight was their beacon. Jamal and Najira were ordered to stay put. Kinko's was convenient, and in less than an hour, she'd printed off the docs from her disk, had affixed a notary's seal on it, backdated it, and had scanned in phony signatures. The art of technology was grand.

She set off in one direction; the fellas went the other way. The doctor's secretary screened her, until she mentioned she was on an errand for the late Donald Haines.

From there, it was easy. His Montgomery County office was a mere whistle-stop on her campaign trail. She breezed into his plush, well-appointed inner sanctum, and sat down with a flourish, allowing her sable coat to fall open just so.

"Thank you for your time," she said, whipping out the phony documents and dropping them on his desk.

"What's this all about?" Dr. Sutherland demanded. "I have patients to see and a schedule to keep. I don't even *know* you."

"Then let's be brief," Laura snapped, her chin held high. She stared at a tall, distinguished, brown-eyed version of Haines. Dr. Sutherland certainly seemed athletic enough to pull off a quick run down a back kitchen flight of stairs into the night after shooting a man, but she wasn't sure and needed to be. "Read it and weep. Elizabeth didn't get a dime after Haines passed. Her son gets everything she would have gotten, and if he dies, he's leaving it to Alan. Casino charters, the house, virtually everything."

Laura watched panic flicker in Sutherland's eyes as he straightened his tweed jacket and sat down behind his wide mahogany desk slowly.

"Young woman, while I'm sure this is all very upsetting to whatever grasping schemes you may have had, I fail to see what this has to do with me. Donald and I were very close friends for years, but I never expected any inheritance."

Dr. Sutherland let out a false chortle of disgust and looked down the bridge of his long nose over his half glasses. He made a face as though he smelled something putrid and shook his head, his eyes dancing toward the papers.

Laura reached for the documents, but he snatched up the paperwork, as though annoyed with it, and perused it in angry flips of paper. That's when Laura allowed a sly smile.

"She's assed out, and so are you."

"Pardon me? What are you implying?"

She stood and snatched the papers from his hands. "Donald was aware of the affair and told me as much, but it pissed him off that y'all tried to rush him to his grave with bogus medication and poisons." When Sutherland opened his mouth to protest, she held up her hand. "I don't want the police in it any more than you do, because that would slow down things in probate, and I don't give a shit—since he left me a substantial trust fund—as you saw. A sister is paid. My uncle is a distant relative, who I can send cigarettes to in prison from a nice little island . . . say, Belize? But you, by way of Liz, ain't paid . . . just wanted you to know. Don made me promise that if he died from foul play, I'd let you know. Just fulfilled my part of the bargain." She shoved the docs into her bag, batted her eyes, and spun on her spiked heels. She held onto the door and glanced over her shoulder at his drained expression. "You have a nice day."

Steve yanked the documents out of Alan Moyer's hands and shoved them toward James, who coolly tucked them away. "See what I mean," he said, shaking his head. "The old man screwed our casino clients with this syrupy, last minute bout of conscience. Donny don't get shit, neither do the boys down in AC. They're really pissed off, because old Lizzy Borden gets everything. They even fucked the good senator and his son out of their share. So, whoever jumped the gun and iced the old man before he was due to go, sorta upset the apple cart. *Capice?"*

"That will can be contested," Alan said quickly. "It'll never hold, because Haines was out of his mind and not competent when it was drawn."

James sighed. "You check the date on it? He made the move before he was diagnosed—which means if this one isn't valid, the first one ain't either . . . since there's not that much time from his last update and the one he did right after it. *Feel* me?"

"Seems like old Donny, or whomever did this bullshit, has their *cojones* in a tight sling—'cause the boys in AC ain't gonna wait for years of legal wrangling to take place before they start breaking ground on construction." Steve shrugged and stood, giving James a nod that it was time to go. "I don't know what to tell you, dude. Maybe you could leave the country, or some shit?"

Alan was on his feet in seconds, his hand holding onto Steve's arm like it was a life raft. "Wait. Donny and I didn't have anything to do with rushing the hands of fate. That dumb bastard Howard was greedy. He didn't want to let things play out."

Steve and James looked at each other and calmly sat back down.

"So, uh . . . we should maybe go have a conversation with Howie?" Steve smiled a sinister smile and glanced at James, who nodded.

"Yes. You should exert your energies investigating him, not me or Donny," Alan said quickly, a sheen of perspiration covering his forehead. He glanced around and leaned in. "He may be the senator's son, but he's a thug. He made the call for the poisoned food, not me."

"Cool," James said, and stood, this time beckoning Steve with a sharp glance. "You lucky, then."

*   *   *

James and Steve sat in their car outside the tavern and watched Alan walk quickly, then jog, and finally flat-out run toward his silver Beamer. Once he'd pulled off, they pounded fists and chuckled.

"Thought he didn't know nothing about poison?" Steve covered his chest with his palm, mimicking a damsel in distress.

"Poison seems a little too subtle for a thug who deals with around the way boys and drive-bys, don't you think?" James smiled and turned on his engine.

Steve nodded. "Ya think?"

James stood on the corner, deep in murmurs and side glances. The brothers 'round the way were suspicious of Steve, so Steve remained in the car with the motor running. But nobody liked the fact that some brothers from North Philly had moved on one of their own from Southwest. It was on, like hot buttered popcorn—and a few thousand dollars casually slid into empty pockets helped produce a name.

Only problem was the police had beaten them to the boy's mother's door. Seemed the drive-by shooter had had a little accident all his own. The people were out on stoops and standing in the street when Steve and James rolled up on the scene.

James glanced at Steve. "Just lost another witness. Wanna go lean on the senator's son, or go back to the hotel?"

"Aw, it's a nice day," Steve said, as James backed his sedan out of the street that was impassable.

"Yeah. Just what I was thinking," James said. "The leaves are pretty up in Chestnut Hill this time of year."

*   *   *

A beautiful woman opened the door. Her caramel complexion looked ashen, though. Her large hazel eyes told of unseen strain. Her smile was tight and her voice very quiet. But her winter white wool slacks and matching cashmere sweater looked freshly pressed, just like her golden-brown bob. Waning sunlight danced off her one-carat diamond studs and thick herringbone gold necklace as she stood in the door and tried to keep her children behind it.

"May I help you?" she asked, her voice so brittle that it cracked.

"Looking for Howard Scott," James said, his tone even and direct.

"He's not home," she said, glancing around quickly and stepping out onto the porch.

"Got any idea when he might come back," Steve said, studying his fingernails. "Would hate to have to come back and bother you over and over again." He looked up at her and then at the tricycle in the driveway. "Especially since you have children, and you ain't in this."

She glanced at James, her eyes pleading. "Wait. Let me see if he came in while I was out with the children."

"Thanks, honey," Steve said, allowing his voice to became theatrically sinister. "You do that for us."

Within moments Howard Scott's wife was behind the huge, oak double doors that held beveled, leaded glass. Her voice was shrill, and a small child began to cry as her screeches to her husband reached glass-shattering decibels.

"Howard! Howard!"

They could hear her footsteps running across hardwood floors and then vanishing into carpet. A man's voice bellowed at her wanting to know what the fuck she wanted. Then all went silent in the house, and male footsteps ran through the house as though wearing storm trooper boots. James and Steve smiled.

"Think there's a little heat in the system?"

Steve smiled. "Ya think?"

Howard Scott flung open the door and slammed it behind him. "Who the fuck are you, and what the fuck are you doing at my house fucking with my wife and threatening my kids!"

"Relax," James said coolly.

"Some people in Atlantic City have concerns and asked us to give you a heads up."

James and Steve watched as all the bluster went out of Howard's voice. He was instantly cowed. Steve whipped out the phony papers and thrust them toward Howard.

"You dumb bastards jumped the gun," he said, turning to the appropriate page in the documents. "Elizabeth Haines gets everything. Donny gets nothing, so your boy Alan gets nothing. Problem is, when old Hainesy redid his will, he also gave her the casino portion to control, as well as his holding company that was supposed to go to them."

"Now," James said, shaking his head, "y'all are running around the city, kicking up dust, leaving bodies and shit—and it looks bad. All this nonsense is drawing attention. The boys in AC want this shit quietly squashed." He stared at the senator's son and watched his almond complexion become pale. "They want it done quick. Need a name, so the right person can take the weight."

"I don't know what you're talking about," Howard stammered, and raked his fingers across his scalp.

"That's cool," James said without emotion. "I'll tell them that, and let them figure it out. Might wanna tell your wife and kids to go stay with her mother for a few days, though." James looked at the house. "Shame, too, they little, she's fine—it don't have to be all-a that."

"My wife and kids ain't got nothin' to do with this shit, man—you *know* that." Sudden tears filled Howard's eyes as Steve slung an arm over his shoulder.

"We know," Steve said, hugging Howard to him like a friend. "Just give us a name and we're out."

"That fucking Alan Moyer got this all twisted," he said in a garbled tone, swallowing hard, his gaze darting between James and Steve like a caught rabbit. "It was supposed to be simple. Poison. That's it. Not a shooter. No pillow. None of that shit—ya gotta believe me."

Steve dropped his arm away from Howard and looked at James. "You believe him?"

Howard's eyes held a plea as he held his breath.

"Yeah, maybe . . . but the part I can't figure out is, what happened to Moon and his babes?" James cocked his head to the side. "Enlighten a brother."

Howard's mouth trembled as he glanced back at the house, and then he waved his wife away from the window and turned back toward James. "Alan said to make a call and order the quail lunch and told me to have some people I knew send a girl in. I did that. Then the shit got out of hand. The whole thing with a nurse being there, and gunshots. He got nervous and figured the people I was in touch with might start talking, might get nervous."

"Shit happens like that," James said.

"But he said the will was a lock, even showed it to me. He said that he'd be sure I got the food concessions when the new casinos were built. Charter Foods, Inc., would be the primary provider . . . me and my dad would be set. Donny has always been under his spell and didn't do business at all—so, he'd be running Donny's share. But now that things were getting messy, I needed to be sure there were no leaks—so, I had to make another call to clean that up. You understand, right?"

James and Steve remained mute.

Tears now coursed down Howard Scott's face. He stifled a sob and swallowed thickly. "I didn't tell that girl to smother Haines, honest to God, man. I also didn't shoot that old man, or anybody else."

"Not directly, anyway," James muttered and looked toward their sedan.

Howard's eyes held such terror that the whites bulged as he spoke and he looked from Steve to James and back toward his house, his motions twitching like a junky. "Alan did this shit, and not me," Howard argued. "They can't prove in court that I made that call or had anything to do with this. Fuck it. Let 'em bring it. I ain't scared of the police."

"The people who are concerned don't give a rat's ass about court." James let his breath out hard and began walking toward the car.

Steve whistled and shook his head. "They want this shit fixed and the man who did this to go down to send a message to Elizabeth Haines. They wanna be sure she'll play nice on paper and get their contracts and investments back in order once the dust settles," Steve said with a sigh. "If you deliver Alan, they'll leave you alone, as well as your cut in place." He patted Howard's cheek and smiled when he flinched away. "If you weren't the mastermind, then you ain't got no troubles."

It was time to do the media drop. Laura sat in her car in the Chart House restaurant parking lot, staring out into the Delaware River. She mentally spread out her hand of cards before her, holding a straight flush. Before people could begin really talking to each other, or there could be any additional diplomatic courtesies of information suppression extended, it was time to create the piranha effect. Let them all feed so furiously that they bit themselves.

Rick pulled up next to her in his ragged Aires K car. Laura smiled and hit her automatic locks to open the door for him. Within minutes he slid into the seat beside her, his eyes alight and readied for the scoop.

"I promised you that if you held on to what I sent you that I'd give you a story of a lifetime."

He kissed her cheek and sat back. "You have always been my favorite girl."

She patted his hand and leaned back in the vehicle and shut her eyes. "I need enough heat on this so that a senator cannot make a call into the department to squash it—enough drama that has the Main Line medical community gasping; and enough allegations into potential organized crime ties that the casino boys get nervous and begin leaning on people who could take years to indict."

He chuckled and shook his head. "That's vicious, lady. But seems like all these dirty hands need to get slapped."

Laura sat forward and gripped the steering wheel. "Evidence has probably been botched, key witnesses are dead— but if it gets tried in the people's court, the press, then reputations will be ruined and perhaps an innocent old man won't go to jail."

"Laura, it's gotta be solid," he said carefully. "These are not the kind of people you can jack around with and only have a single, shaky source."

"Multiple sources, multiple trails. Print it." She offered him a sly smile. "Or I can give it to the eleven o'clock news teams, if—"

"Done." He laughed and shook his head. "I don't know if my managing editor is gonna have a heart attack because it's so good, or because he'll be ready to pee his pants because it's a career breaker. Not my call."

She handed Rick an envelope. He accepted it with a brief kiss and climbed out of her car.

"What's the drop time on this, lady?"

"Twenty-four hours."

* * *

She hadn't even pulled onto Delaware Avenue good before her cell phone was ringing. Laura picked it up off the seat beside her and glanced at the display. A number came up that she didn't recognize and she immediately answered.

"Hello?"

There was a pause.

"Laura Caldwell," a tight female voice said.

"Yes. And you are?"

"It's Elizabeth."

It was Laura's turn to hesitate. "How can I help you?"

"We need to meet."

"All right," Laura said slowly.

"Immediately."

Laura smiled. "Where?"

The caller didn't respond for a moment. "I don't want people to see me out here . . . and I *cannot* go to Center City. I . . . I just want to get some things sorted out with you, and . . . we *must* meet."

"How about on City Line Avenue?" Laura said, growing anxious. There was something very vulnerable in the tone of Elizabeth's voice that she'd never heard.

"No. Oh, no, not there—Channel Ten and Channel Six have offices—"

"Yes, yes, my apologies," Laura said quickly. "I can come to your house?"

"No, it's not safe here. In fact, I've already left."

"Where are you now?" Laura's grip tightened on her steering wheel.

"I don't know," Elizabeth wailed.

"Okay, okay, tell you what—come down Lancaster Avenue to the Barnes & Noble Bookseller in Bryn Mawr. We can stroll the aisles, casually bump into each other, have a latte, if you want, and talk in a well lit, safe, public place."

After a moment, she heard Elizabeth sniff.

"All right," Elizabeth said. "Twenty minutes."

* * *

Laura took a position on the second floor, quietly cruising the shelves near the wide windows that overlooked the lot. At that time of the afternoon, there was only a sparse gathering of book lovers, and she chatted a bit with the store's friendly manager.

"Can I help you? I'm Kathy, and if you need anything, just let me know."

"Thank you, Kathy," Laura said, her eyes scanning a shelf without reading a word. "I'm not sure what I want—just hunting and pecking."

The short blonde who was close to her age and who seemed to have a perpetually happy expression smiled and gave her a wink. "I have those days, too. Enjoy."

Laura watched her walk away, wondering what it must be like to truly love one's profession, and to be happy and seemingly carefree. How did one find the elusive thing called peace of mind? The woman's sunny disposition was no act, and the moment she spotted Elizabeth Haines nervously getting out of her car, she knew that money wasn't the key.

She decided to allow Elizabeth to enter the establishment and roam around on the first floor for a bit. Liz was a smart woman; she'd figure out sooner or later, that she was upstairs. So Laura made her way to a stack near the escalator and waited.

Sure enough, after ten frantic minutes and a curt exchange with Kathy, Elizabeth was on the escalator headed for the second level. Laura gave her a glance and walked deeper into the stacks away from the window. But that Elizabeth hadn't removed her sunglasses was interesting.

Finally on the same row, Elizabeth glanced around and came closer to Laura, only offering her a profile as she poorly pretended to be hunting for something to read.

"Do you have children?" Elizabeth asked, then immediately answered her own question. "Of course not, or you would understand."

Laura bristled but held her response. Elizabeth spun on her and came in close and whipped off her dark glasses. Laura gaped at the bruise that was forming under her eye and badly concealed by makeup.

"My son was never supposed to be involved in any of this."

Laura simply stared as tears shone in Elizabeth's eyes.

"I was to control everything, so that Donny's hands would never be dirtied by his father's affairs." She drew in a very controlled breath that made her body shudder beneath her tawny, lamb's wool shearling. Her hands trembled as she extracted a tissue from her Coach purse, and she dabbed her eyes with care, and then her nose, balling the crumpled tissue into her fist. "Yes, I gave Donald medications to make him think he was going mad with dementia. And, yes, Peter helped that process by giving him a false diagnosis and the prescriptions. From there, we would let Donald handle his own demise. None of this other business was supposed to happen."

Laura couldn't tear her eyes away from Elizabeth's cheek. Beneath her perfect skin was a slight greenish-purplish tinge that told of a sudden, hard strike. "Who hit you?"

Elizabeth turned away, her spine straightening. "Peter. That bastard."

"Dr. Sutherland hit you?" Laura's voice was calm, bordering on gentle, and just above a whisper.

"Yes."

She stared at Liz's profile. "Why?"

"Because after you and I talked, I became concerned and began making calls. I did a little research of my own, and there are several people heavily invested in Charter Foods,

Inc. I asked Peter's secretary who my son came to his regular visit with. She told me how devoted my attorney's son, Alan Moyer, had been—always there."

Elizabeth looked at Laura, her eyes boring into Laura's from the depths of her being. "Then I questioned Peter's diagnosis of my son, and he struck me." She drew in another shaky breath. "That's when I knew."

Speechless, Laura could only stare at the woman.

"I'm a mother first . . . before the bitch that you think I am, before the financial maven you purport me to be, I am *a mother*." She leaned into Laura with such ferocity that Laura was inclined to draw back, but didn't. "My son is my world. No man, not even his father, comes or came, before Donny. Do *you* understand?"

"Yes," Laura said quietly. "I do."

"Good," Elizabeth snapped. "Then you'll understand that, if this should become a media travesty or a criminal case, I will do the time myself before I allow my child to ever be affected."

"I don't think there's a need for that, Liz," Laura said, forging an odd alliance. "We know Donny didn't do this."

She watched tension begin to ebb from Elizabeth's expression.

"He didn't," Elizabeth said quietly, her tone holding so much remorse that it seemed it was hard for her to speak. "After the Paxton fiasco," she murmured, her gaze going to the floor, "I went to Peter overwrought . . . he gave me Valium and a listening ear, which begat something that should have never happened."

For a moment, guilt sliced at Laura's conscience. She could understand how the War of the Roses between the Haines combatants had gotten out of hand, and how things that aren't supposed to happen, do. But she held her counsel, her eyes offering no judgment as she looked at Liz. Somewhere in the exchange, Elizabeth relaxed even more, as though reading the quiet truce in Laura's eyes.

"Michael Paxton Jr. was not a nice man," Laura offered. "He'd killed a friend's father, had helped to set up mine. I had to cut his throat."

Elizabeth nodded. "I was so angry at Donald that I couldn't see it. Any true ally of his was an enemy of mine."

"So, we both erred," Laura said. "But I'm not about to see an innocent person take the weight, or be totally disinherited."

Elizabeth came closer to her. "Are you saying what I think you are?"

Laura nodded. "Give me the bastards who did it, and whatever is in the will going to me, I'll gladly make sure Donny is reinstated. But I do want justice."

Elizabeth closed her eyes and let out her breath in a quiet stream. "As do I."

"Work with me on this, Liz."

She nodded with her eyes closed. "Done."

Chapter
18

When Laura glanced at her cell phone, she held it for a moment before taking the call. Why would the temp at Rainmaker's Inc. be calling her, and not Najira? Potential family emergencies made her hold her breath. She'd left her sisters' well-timed messages on their answering machines while she knew they'd be at work and their children would be at school . . . the messages had all been the same: "I'm fine, Najira is fine, we're going to make sure that Uncle Akhan is all right—he's improving daily. Please don't worry, I have a lot to do in short order, sit tight. I'll call as soon as I can."

What else was there to say? What else could she tell them to make them relax and let her work? Her mind raced as the temp secretary's voice filled the receiver.

"Laura Caldwell, here," she said, her voice tight with worry. "Is everything all right?"

"I'm not sure, Ms. Caldwell," the temp said quickly. "There's a Howard Scott here in my office, insistent that he meet with you this afternoon—but I told him that he needed an appointment. However, he said he was the senator's son, and is very, very agitated. He's in our outer lobby, now, and I'm concerned. Should I call security, if he refuses to leave?"

Laura smiled and leaned back against the leather upholstery in her Jag. "No. Tell him you've contacted me, and that I can meet him down the block at the Omni Hotel for a brief coffee . . . in say, fifteen to twenty minutes."

"Yes, ma'am," the temp said. "I'm sorry to have disturbed you."

Laura's smile widened. "No bother at all."

He was waiting for her in the bar area when she walked into the main lobby. He stood fast, but she held up her hand as she took her time to approach the inimitable Howard Scott. Upon first glance, he looked like a handsome, junior replica of his father—medium height and build, ruddy brown skin, hazel eyes, and wavy, dark brown hair. If he'd been more savvy and less of an entitled brat hoodlum, he could have run for public office, just like dear old dad.

However, his intense stare said it all, fear framed in the lush backdrop of the marble and gold chrome appointed lobby. It amazed her that, for all his education, notoriety, and pedigree, now dressed in his baggy designer sweat suit and Timberlands, he could have passed for a regulation corner boy.

"Howard," she said as pleasantly as possible, giving him an air kiss and intently watching his reaction.

"Hey, Laura," he said, kissing her cheek harder than was necessary. "We need to talk."

Laura nodded and went back to a remote table, noting he'd already begun the evening with hard liquor. She wondered how the wives of such men stood it. "Then, shall we?"

"C'mon, lady," he said, seeming annoyed with her playful formality. "It's me and you, now. Let's be real—no games."

She willed herself not to smile wider or laugh, and readjusted her approach to make him comfortable, lapsing into the around-the-way lingo that he seemed to prefer. "Cool." She sat down and dropped her purse on the burgundy leather sofa they shared, noting that he hadn't even offered to buy her a drink. Cheap bastard. No class. She waved away the server with disgust. No need to order a drink, this would be a short conversation.

Howard let his breath out hard and ran his palm across his jaw. "The shit is getting intense, again," he said, picking up his glass. "I thought all the madness was behind us, ya know?"

"What's going on, now? I mean, a key suspect is already implicated in some pretty foul mess, but you all don't have anything to worry about, right? You should be cool?" She kept a steady gaze on him, monitoring his nervous energy as a barometer of just how and when to yank his chain.

"Yeah, yeah, that's what we thought, too. But some people have the wrong idea about things . . . and you've always had Haines's ear . . ."

"Haines is dead, baby. I don't have his ear anymore." Laura batted her lashes, this time unable to control a sly smile.

Howard closed his eyes. "I know, but people who he was tight with might listen to you, if nobody else."

Somewhere between shock and rage, she'd found her voice. It was amazing to her that he could sit there, look her in the eyes, know that an innocent man and his daughter were caught up in the drama, and not even give a damn—yet want some form of amnesty for his own family. And what about the people who'd just been blown away? Didn't they or their families matter? She wondered how people like Howard Scott Jr. slept at night, and then banished the question. She knew how they did; they just didn't see so-called commoners as human. No sense in being appalled. She had to hand it to him; at least he was honest.

"Doubtful," she finally hedged, "but I can try."

"That's all I'm asking for, baby," he said upon an urgent release of his breath. "I've got kids, and . . ." He looked up at her with a plea in his eyes. "If you could put in a good word."

Oh, so now she was *baby*? Interesting shift from Laura, to lady, to baby. His instant familiarity made her want to gag, especially since he'd been instrumental in setting up her uncle. Had even taken a potshot at Najira. Brass balls. Correction—no balls. Punk. She smiled her nicest, most sincere smile. "Baby, what do you want me to tell them?"

He edged closer to her. "Tell them to check out Alan—he's the one who ordered the poison job . . . I made the call for him, but he knew all the ins and outs. I just took care of some 'round the way boys, understand? I cleaned up *behind* Alan, but would *never* jack with their contracts. I just wanted a little piece, wasn't greedy. I know he's made a side deal somewhere. That's what they need to check out. You've gotta believe me and make sure they do."

Laura watched him grip her hand as she nodded, committing to nothing. "I'll see what I can do."

"Girl, we shoulda hooked up a long time ago," he said with a strained chuckle. "I see why Darien and Paxton had a thing for you."

My, my, my . . . this was desperation at its best, or worst, as the case might be. An offer of tired, married dick to seal an alliance, like she was born yesterday, and like *that* would be even worth her time, much less money. So, she responded in kind, making idle promises.

"Yeah, baby," she said on a husky breath filled with possibilities. "We should have had a drink to come to a better understanding a long time ago."

Rick clicked off his cell phone and made the necessary edits.

* * *

Joey Scapolini sat down slowly and waited for the new paperwork to begin vomiting from his fax machine, and smiled.

Luis sat with Steve and James in the cafeteria of Lankenau Hospital. His gaze went to Jamal and Najira.

"You two are going to fall out in the lobby, give the reporters a real photo op of 'round the way grieving when we pull your uncle out under the tarp," Luis said, his gaze going to each player in the ruse. "My inside squad will relo him to University of Pennsylvania as a key witness, and he'll be under 'round-the-clock surveillance as Mr. Robert Jones."

Najira and Jamal nodded, stood and left the table, as had been instructed. Luis looked at Steve and James hard.

"You guys better be right. This thing has tentacles all the way up the food chain."

"Your lead in Kensington panned out, didn't it?" James said, looking at Luis hard.

"Yeah. The Melendez girl had bills stashed at her mother's house under her mattress, of all places. Captain Bennett is nervous, saying it could have been drug money, given everything girlfriend was into, though."

"But the wife's testimony helps." Steve looked at Luis without blinking.

"Yeah, it does. So did the doctor's tennis shoes. All the boys in forensics need is one drop of Akhan's blood splatter to nail his ass." Luis smiled. "Elizabeth must have really taken exception to the shiner he gave her. Can you see her rooting through the trash looking for those?"

"Not at all," Steve said with a half grin. "Funny how the thought of prison is the great equalizer."

"It wasn't prison, man," James muttered. "It was all about saving her kid." He pushed the papers Laura had given him across the table. "Alan, Howard, Sutherland, and the senator are all heavily invested in Charter Foods, Inc., which is allegedly out of Atlanta. Put that with what they thought was their percentages of the construction investment firm, and the charters that never materialized for them, we're talking millions—which is motive enough."

"The wife had a score to settle, was gonna let Haines do himself, and could be patient. Doc had the know-how, but it seems none of his other partners wanted to wait. So, the young bucks went to work beyond the doctor's meds and added a wrinkle in what would have otherwise been a smooth equation." Steve shook his head. "Ironic, ain't it? For once, the mob ain't the ones to do the hit."

"Insane," James muttered, his gaze going to the large picture window. "Howard had the brute muscle on the street. He had the contacts to drop the food and tea poisons—but we already know that something that subtle had to be orchestrated by a better brain. Alan, who was there when Howard selected the jobbers, and who also had access to the will, via Donny's mind, also apparently got impatient. Waiting on the tea didn't seem fast enough or sure enough, so he cuts a side deal around Howard's oblivious ass to be sure old Haines is smothered. And the senator held the strings to keep a lid on everything."

James sat back and stared at the two men before him. "So, if Alan had Haines smothered to make it look like Akhan did it, then why would there be a shooter upstairs. That's what doesn't gel."

"Two theories," Luis said, holding Steve and James in a tight, confidential tone. "If Donny got a fucked-up diagnosis, and was receiving meds that would make him sick, even if he wasn't—while his lover patted his hand at every visit—

then I'd say the doctor and Moyer had something else going as a side-side deal. But from what you're saying, it seems like there wasn't much love or trust lost between those two, either. Because if one ordered the smother job and the other was the shooter, they tripped over each other doing the hit on the same night."

"Yep," Steve said, leaning on his forearms on the table to come in closer. "Check it out. Alan had already ordered the smother job, and then picked up the Melendez girl, paid her, and dropped her off. The shooting was a wild card. What if the doctor went in, knocked Akhan over the head, and shot him somewhere he knew wouldn't kill him . . . it was a precision shot, one that only a doctor could do—somebody who really knew what he was doing. Both Moyer and Sutherland had access to house keys, by way of their lovers. But what would make the doctor risk everything when he already knew Haines was a goner from the poison? That's what's eatin' at me."

"No fingerprints, equals rubber, surgical gloves . . . true, anybody can buy those, but all of the facts add up to the doctor," Luis said, his worried gaze rounding the table. "We now know Akhan was shot while on the floor. Not as Haines struggled, because of the trajectory of the bullet, which went right through the floor. If it went down like we originally thought . . . Akhan putting a pillow over his face, Haines somehow getting the gun off his waistband during the struggle, firing blindly, hitting Akhan, but dying as Akhan squeezed his last breath out as he began falling backward to hit his head . . . then the bullet should have been in the wall."

"Glad to see you're on your toes, man," James said without emotion.

"Hey, look, we'd been given orders to wrap this thing up fast, brother. It's been less than a week. Don't go there, all right," Luis said defensively. "I went out on a limb to get the forensics done on the food and bloodwork and shit, and in record time. Woulda made my job easier just to follow orders, but I called in some markers, just like you did, man."

James nodded and offered Luis a begrudging fist-pound. "No beef."

"Good," Luis muttered, pushing his Styrofoam cup of coffee away from him. "Peace."

Steve glanced between them. "Peace. All right? You two kiss and make up. The widow is giving us access to the house and the after funeral coffee hour. We do this thing by the numbers. None of the suspects get picked up until after the funeral, because we need to see who's gonna make a false move. Somebody, like possibly the doctor, needed something in Haines's room that was valuable enough for him to go in after he thought the old dude was smothered, only to get surprised."

"No," James said. "Correction. Sutherland might not have known Moyer had ordered the smother job. His poison should have worked by then. Dude went in there to get something that even Moyer didn't know about and got a double surprise, if you ask me."

James rubbed his jaw as Luis and Steve stared at him. "Lights go out in that section of the house, courtesy Moyer, who knows the lay of the land. The girl is upstairs, waiting— and in the moments of confusion, Haines is supposed to be sick in bed, but isn't. Akhan should have already left, but hasn't. Now you've got two older, but able-bodied men, standing in a dark room. There's a struggle in the dark. The girl, at first, assumes the other impossible-to-see male is her contact, so she attempts to do what she's told, then realizes something's wrong, and is outta there. She thinks maybe the butler got in the room, or whatever, but is too panicked to worry about it, since this is her first job like that."

"Yeah," Steve said, picking up on James's logic trail.

"Haines goes down as somebody struggles with him bedside, the girl runs out of the house and lies to get her money cut when she sees Alan waiting in a parked car. Meanwhile, Akhan ain't standing around, but he wants to be sure to hit the right target—so he doesn't immediately fire . . . however, as soon as he can see a little bit from the moonlight, he does, misses . . . but, it's too late. His boy is dead, he's hit in the skull from behind, and someone has to think quickly. Akhan is shot on the floor. The butler hears the commotion and calls the cops—omitting the part about having an early evening tryst with a tardy maid."

"Ask dude again about the shots he heard, one or two," James commanded in a low mutter. "If two men were struggling in the dark, the first shot shoulda went high."

"Damn," Luis said. "This is some shit. Our boys from ballistics will get the bullet outta the trees, if it's there . . . but that's why we missed it—no glass shattered, and it's October. The windows should have been shut, especially in a sick old man's bedroom." He glanced around, an apology in his eyes.

"Then somebody closed the window before they left. Think about it. If a guy is feeling the effects of poison in his system, body temp is changing, feels like he needs air, and if you run a close check on the damned weapon you'd see—"

"Yeah, yeah," Luis said, his eyes unable to keep contact with James's disgusted expression. "I hear ya. We'll check the angle of the bullet in the floor, again, too. At first, we assumed that Haines was standing bedside, was taller than Akhan, made the shot as he was going down onto the bed, and it went into the floor."

"That's why we've gotta bait the room, and keep our only living witness to what happened in that room on the down low," Steve said and stood with effort. "Hopefully, in a few days, he'll be strong enough to talk. Just pray that old man doesn't take a turn for the worse."

"Ya know . . . instead of the mortuary wagon, we could put a decoy wearing a wire in the bed and just move Akhan in an ambulance to another facility, quiet like." Luis studied James for a reaction.

"Yeah, brother," James muttered and stood. "Like Laura said. Then we step back and watch the piranha effect."

Chapter
19

She had to hand it to Elizabeth Haines; the old broad was cool. She stood there with a stiff upper lip as a wire went under her black bra and camisole. She never even flinched as the officers adhered the contraptions to her body, and she did it all without her attorney at her side.

Laura watched her put on her dress with dignity in the back of the church office, and submitted to the same inconvenience, keeping her eyes dead ahead on the wall.

"Okay, you ladies know your parts?" Steve said with a smile.

They nodded.

"You sure Sutherland will attend, now that all hell has broken loose in the press?" James eyed Elizabeth Haines with suspicion, but kept his tone professional and civil.

"I made up with him before it all happened, and ran into his arms horrified by the media odyssey . . . and allowed him to comfort me," she said, her voice tight as she lowered her short black veil. "He'll be here."

"All right," Luis said, focusing on Laura. "You go out the back, have my man drop you off at your car on Germantown

Pike, then you come in late, sit in the back near Sutherland, and work whatever magic you've got, sister. By the time they drop a rose on Haines's coffin and reconvene back at the house for the close family repast, I want his ass so shook that he'll do something crazy."

"I don't," Elizabeth snapped, her gaze penetrating the men in the room. "My son is at risk; they all think he's inherited everything, and ever since the media got wind of it, my son has been inconsolable." She straightened her wide-brim black felt hat, and neatly buttoned her black and white houndstooth Chanel jacket and positioned her pearls. "He refuses to stay at the house with me. He won't leave Alan's side. If they give him something in his food, or—"

"They won't," Laura reassured her. "He's too hot right now, it would be too obvious. Within the next few weeks, then I'd worry. But not today."

She and Elizabeth shared a strained glance of acceptance, and finally Elizabeth nodded.

"Today, then, you're the grieving widow," James said, slipping off his perch on the edge of the rector's mahogany desk.

Elizabeth Haines lifted her chin and glared at him. "Today, Mr. Carter, oddly, I am."

Traffic on Germantown Pike had bottlednecked with funeral-goers, media vans, police, and onlookers. Haines's funeral was a public spectacle, if not a travesty—everything that, in life, he'd abhorred. But then there was this thing called karma, she mused, steadily winding her way toward the hundred-year-old Episcopal sanctuary.

She stepped out of her black Jaguar, glad to have it back and swept for safety. She quietly spotted the unmarked police cruisers in the lot, but didn't acknowledge them. However, just knowing that her ride wouldn't explode when she got back in it made her feel slightly better. But the thought of enduring the service that would surely be bogged down by political fanfare and pontificating speeches, and then the long solo trip to the cemetery, gnawed at her. Despite all that had transpired, Donald Haines had been her friend.

Without much choice, she walked across the wide, gray gravel lot that had been reserved for limousines, family, and VIP guests, ignoring the media that had been kept back a hundred respectful yards behind police barricades. Hundred-year-old, Wissahickon schist stone loomed before her, framing ornately detailed stained glass. It took her a moment, however, to force herself to go up the wide slate steps of a house of worship. She had to wonder how many rules in the Good Book she'd broken, and if there'd be a lightning bolt of wrath for all her deeds. Then, again, she was in good company. The Man Upstairs would have to send a meteor shower to get every liar, thief, and sinner in the congregation on this crisp, sunny day—so she kept walking, spine straight, head held high.

The pews were packed, as had been expected. Her gaze traveled the inside of the church, looking for her mark and found it. Sutherland was seated discreetly on the left in the back. She calmly accepted a funeral program, neglected the sign-in book, and wedged herself into the pew behind him. He straightened, noting her presence without turning. Emboldened by her purpose, she laid a hand on his shoulder, daring him with a firm squeeze to start any public display of unpleasantness.

"I'm glad you came," she said, leaning forward enough to allow her hat to brush his ear.

He didn't answer but simply nodded. Laura swallowed a smile.

* * *

The procession by Haines's open grave was interminable, but she stood in the line and waited her turn, her peripheral vision watching all, as she remained appropriately somber and mute. Donny had nearly collapsed against Alan, who ultimately handed him off to his mother. Elizabeth would have done Jacqueline Kennedy Onassis proud. A single tear, a calm, dignified demeanor, and a kiss on the rose before she dropped it, and a graceful pivot to collect her destroyed son to spirit him away in a black stretch. Alan hovered near Sutherland for a moment. A tense exchange, by her observation. Howard being thoroughly ignored, even his own father distant. Interesting. Mob boys stood close like a line of well-groomed oak trees, soberly glad-handing with real estate developers and politicos, but at an appropriate distance from the open grave. A few nods of recognition coming her way, subtly, and with honor.

Oh, yeah, all the players were at the table, big bucks and heavy chips weighing it down. James and Steve's presence seemed to make Howard pet his children's hair harder and leave quickly. She wondered if he'd visit the house. Not.

But she also wondered if old Liz was as exhausted as she was. Harold, her butler, appeared to have aged ten years within the last week. She knew he'd be at the house, but probably in a very weakened condition, almost too overwrought to answer the door. So if a subset of mourners showed up at the house, then what? The Haines family tree was extremely small; most of the people there would be business associates and hangers-on.

Laura returned to her car after glancing at James to receive a nod. It was good to have someone have her back. At this juncture, there was enough heat in the system to make anything possible now.

On the long return drive to the Haines residence, she continued to work on the puzzle. A girl enters the room, sees a man standing, and then notices another in the room. She thinks it's her contact and goes for the one she can see closest to the bed to smother him. Akhan, initially confused by the female's entrance, hesitates, may think it's Elizabeth. Then Akhan realizes something is wrong, moves in as the girl picks up the pillow. But another man comes in, Akhan goes into the shadows—hearing the intruder—the girl flees and tells a lie to get paid. Now there are three men in the room. Soon two are struggling at the bed with the pillow between them, one standing with the gun—her uncle. A warning shot is fired. Chaos in the darkness, voices escalate. Akhan turns to go toward the door for help. Her uncle is struck on the head by a blunt object that has yet to be found. Akhan is down, then shot. Laura stopped at a light as a dawning awareness overcame her. *Then*, Haines was smothered. The evidence of two athletic men fighting had to be Haines and whoever had entered the room.

Someone wanted him dead, but not before something was done. Something was coming in, not out. If Akhan had been shot while still smothering Haines, blood should have been all over the bed and the offending pillow. If it had gone down like she imagined, then the offending pillow also should still have the same gunpowder residue on it that would have been on the surgical glove.

Laura flipped open her cell phone as the traffic light changed. "Ask the hospital to take a skin sample from the back of my uncle's head," she said, her tone distant. "If the skin wasn't broken so the wound site didn't have to be stitched, it had to be a hard, flat object—metal or wood . . . like a lock box. They've only X-rayed him, and done triage surgery, but haven't cleaned him up because of his critical condition. Scour the doctor's house and his office, see if there's a lock box anywhere in there with a dent and/or Ahkan's blood, skin, or hair."

* * *

Harold greeted her at the door, but never made eye contact. Elizabeth sat in the parlor in quiet repose, bristling for Peter Sutherland's sake, and then stood to go make herself a cup of tea. Hushed voices floated through the home, making it seem eerily vacant, although it was filled to capacity with what were supposed to be close family ties.

Donny had modestly recovered, and he came to her first.

"I know this is a strange cadre of guests, but no matter how Mother behaves, I'm glad you're here."

"Thank you for allowing me to cross your threshold," Laura said. "I just came to tell you that, everything will be all right."

"By and by," he said sadly. "Odd how much I miss him, but we couldn't see even the sky and agree on its color while he was alive."

She squeezed Donny's hands, but was sure not to hug him wearing a wire. She wondered how Elizabeth had managed, but her thick corsets beneath her suit probably had shielded her from suspicion . . . her friends were only giving air kisses, anyway.

"Where's Alan?" she asked gently.

Donny sighed. "He and Mother have been at odds . . . well, you can understand. He said we'd get together later, after all of this was over."

Laura nodded and squeezed his hands again. "Be well," she said and allowed him to waft away from her as two family friends approached. Discreetly talking under her breath, she crossed the room. "Alan is on the move."

Spotting Dr. Sutherland by the bar, Laura declined a canapé offered by a server, and made her way to the liquor near the men.

"We meet again," she said under her breath, opting for a random glass of wine as a tray quietly passed by.

"Don't you think you've upset Elizabeth enough? You really should do the right thing and leave."

She smiled, stepped closer to him, and dropped her voice. "We both should, especially since they've found the lock box with a dent in it. Ain't the marvels of DNA testing grand?"

Laura watched the color drain from his face. "Share, and I have connections that can make this go away, neatly. Like I said, earlier, my uncle is a very old and distant relative. No need for him to testify, or for . . ."

"Why don't we walk and talk," Sutherland said, his gaze on the amber liquid in his glass. "It's a beautiful day outside, no matter the circumstances."

"I agree."

Sutherland left her side, mingling with the small clusters of guests who graced the Haines home as he made his way outside. The media was across the street in front of the house, waiting like vultures for anything that could be seized upon. Sutherland intelligently chose to exit onto the back patio from the side, versus the front door. Senator Scott smiled at her tensely as she passed him, pecked her cheek, but thereafter kept his distance. She found Sutherland standing beneath a tree not far off from the patio guests, but out of earshot from everyone, except those monitoring her wire.

"So," she said brightly. "He needed to sign something, but never got the chance to. Shame."

Sutherland sipped his drink and smiled over the lip of his glass. "You think you've got this all figured out, don't you?"

"Maybe." Laura shrugged and glanced at the sunlight dappling the ground through the leaves.

"A hospital is a dangerous place to be . . . for someone without adequate health insurance, or protection. Nurses, doctors, orderlies . . ." Sutherland shook his head. "We're not concerned about testimony."

"Good." She lifted her glass to him. "Neither am I. Don't need it."

"Really?" he said, seeming unmoved. But worry flickered behind his cool, brown-eyed stare.

"Really."

In a deadlock, she wasn't sure which way to go with her query. This was one ruthless bastard, and very smart, which made him extremely dangerous.

"What did you need from him, when Alan surprised you?" She smiled and sipped her wine.

Sutherland chuckled. "I don't know what you mean."

"Alan is going to jail, you know—and will sing like a canary."

"Oh, Alan wouldn't hurt a fly. That's very unlikely."

She went out on a limb, testing to see if it would hold her. "If he went to the hospital, they've moved my uncle. He's smothering a cop, or attempting to. Bad move. High-strung."

Sutherland blanched. She'd gotten a reaction. Laura laughed and shook her head. "Deal me in, Peter. Pretty please. Alan could have an accident on his way to prison, thrown in with rough street characters . . . you know how that could work, or he could be cloistered like a precious jewel." She leveled her gaze and lowered her wine. "Cut me in."

"There's nothing to cut you in on, *now*," Sutherland said in a hissing whisper through his teeth. "I cannot believe Alan would be so stupid—then again, I can. Donny was heir to everything, just as Liz had been." He walked away from Laura, flinging the last of his liquor on the ground as he clenched his glass, forcing her to take quick paces to keep up with his angry strides.

"You said, *'now,'*" Laura said as she got close enough to touch his arm. She didn't like the fact that she was temporarily out of sight in a dense line of trees.

He stared at her hand with disdain, but she refused to let his elbow go until he shrugged away.

"What *was* it?" she repeated, not backing down or backing away.

"Alan was supposed to *wait*," Sutherland said, raking his hair and glancing back toward the patio. "But that was when he thought Liz was the primary beneficiary. What had been administered would work slowly to give me time to talk to Donald and reason with him. Apparently, Alan found out that Donny was the primary heir before I did, and decided to be the one to control it all. Fool," Sutherland said, nearly spitting with quiet rage. "This is what happens when greed makes one sloppy." He let out an exasperated breath. "Let him rot in prison. I have deniability."

"I don't understand," she said, baiting him as he began to walk farther into the foliage. "What could you possibly tell Donald, after having an affair with his wife and poisoning him with unnecessary meds and whatever else, that would make him sign anything over to you?" She laughed and stopped walking. "That's crazy."

"Is it?" Sutherland said, not amused in the least. "Knowing for sure that his son wasn't going to die . . . knowing that I could produce enough evidence on Alan that would make Donny turn away from him forever—*that's* power. Donald didn't care about my affair with Liz, and was never the wiser about what he'd ingested. But he was in a fragile, confused state of mind and ready to sign a significant portion of the charters over to me as a quid pro quo. *That* was something I wouldn't have to go through Liz for, or stomach Alan to have."

"Uhmph, humph, humph," Laura said. "I guess there is this thing called pride."

"Always," Sutherland said. "No one was to be in that bedroom but Donald and I so we could talk."

"And he could sign."

"Yes," Sutherland said, sighing hard and allowing his arms to drop to his sides in defeat. "So, there you have it. Nothing." He chuckled. "Seems you went to all this trouble to attend a funeral and skulk around behind me for *nothing*.

You saw the will. These were transfers that would have never gone through the inheritance process! There's no money to be had for any of us but you and Alan, if he can wheedle out of being in your uncle's hospital room. He would have had it all. And he can keep it all, all of the motive and mob interest—fool. Going after a witness that saw the girl is a desperation attempt to reclaim what's left of his life. Nothing. I pray the Mafia sees him in hell. You, too, I might add—you got a substantial chunk."

She watched Sutherland reach into his pocket with the hypnotic charm of an adder. Instinct made her begin to back away and glance around, but a strong male hand quickly grasped her arm.

"And to think I was saving this for Elizabeth," he said coolly, brandishing a needle. His eyes contained trapped madness as he yanked her in closer with his thumb over the plunger. "You seem so stressed."

"I'm wired," she said, catching the poised hypodermic within her glass.

Chardonnay washed his arm and both of his hands instantly went to her throat. "Then there's no need for insulin, you bitch!"

"Be very, very cool," a deep male voice said simultaneously with a gun hammer click. James stepped out of the thicket with Steve leveling a weapon. "I've already shot one motherfucker for her. Try me."

"You've got *nothing*," Sutherland shouted, backing away from Laura. "This is entrapment, you have nothing!"

"You're right," Laura said, looking at her spilled drink and the empty needle lying on the manicured grass. Suddenly her faith was restored. There were forces beyond her comprehension at work. "I've got *nothing* worth all this. See you in court."

* * *

The headlines printed it all in bold type:

The son of a prominent Philadelphia attorney was arrested trying to smother a would-be witness.

A prominent Main Line doctor was indicted on numerous charges, including murder and attempted murder.

A notable widow was hauled off for questioning just after her dearly departed husband was laid to rest, but given a lesser charge under a plea bargain arrangement for cooperation with authorities.

A senator is currently under investigation for his role in racketeering, collusion, and a cover-up, while his son is being charged for multiple first-degree murders.

Casino construction is underway while a grieving son silently weeps.

Chapter
20

"You coming back to Rainmakers?" Najira asked, snuggling against Steve in the hammock they shared.

Laura shook her head no, and sipped her pina colada, watching the sunset beyond the deck as she sprawled against James in a wide chaise lounge. The constant rush of waves, the warmth of James's body, and the balmy temperatures mixed with the fourth drink was lulling her to sleep. The last thing on her mind was work. "I'm giving it up, all of it."

"Stop lying." Jamal chuckled and sipped a strawberry daiquiri. "You know you're coming into the biz with us. You da woman."

"I'll go into the PI business the day Akhan goes down to the casinos to play the slots. Get serious." Laura laughed and closed her eyes.

Steve laughed with her and raised his beer. "Yo, J, what's this 'us' stuff?"

"Oh, like I'm not an ace sleuth, too? Don't even go there." Jamal smiled and leaned forward in the huge Adirondack chair that practically swallowed him. "I cracked a big section of that case, and can't wait for the next job."

"Brother, you need to chill," James said with a yawn, his hand making lazy strokes up and down Laura's arm. "We all got lucky and will have enough residuals coming in from even half of the charters Haines left us to keep us out of any business dealings for a long time. Learn to pace yourself."

"That was pretty cool of you to give Donny some of his father's money back," Najira said, suddenly serious. "Family shouldn't fight like that over money . . . I'm just glad Dad is all right and your sisters were all right, once you called them. Ya know. All the kids are fine and provided for. . . . We've had hardships, but we never hated each other, never did each other so dirty as all of that mess up there. We're blessed."

Steve slung his forearm over his eyes and simply shook his head. "It still blows my mind that old Haines named Jim as a will beneficiary because he knew that if my man, Carter, was in the will he'd thoroughly investigate why, any inconsistencies, and watch Laura's back. That was crazy like a fox, guys. Then for him to name his old butler's niece in it, because he trusted Ahkan's family more than his own and knew Laura would worry the situation to death like a dog worries a bone, was profound."

Jamal chuckled. "So, in a way, the butler did do it . . . his original one, our pops, affectionately known as Brother Ahkan to everybody else."

"Yeah," Steve said with a wide grin. "The butler did it, not old Harold, but your dad, by extension of his family working as allies . . . 'cause your people certainly did the Haines family and anybody who screwed over him, righteous. Your pop and old Haines are real crafty old buzzards, no offense. Then our man, Jim, here, gets to walk with enough loot to make him independently wealthy and able to set up a business off shore to employ Akhan's kids, if he wants?

Sheesh. Some retainer, huh? Man-oh-man. That was the most expensive five thousand dollar stiff Donald Haines Jr. and Alan Moyer ever paid, and I bet Moyer is sitting in the federal pen wishing like hell he'd gone ahead and just given us the rest of our money that he and Donny Jr. owed us—but I ain't mad. Gotta love it."

"I say we merge firms," Najira offered. "Work the grant development agency side by side with the PI operation—but not from Philly. Call me suspicious, but maybe we'd all better chill and lay low for a while. The Carribean is cool. We have money. No need to stir the pot."

"I will drink to that," James said, reaching for his glass and lifting it from the deck floor in salute.

Jamal nodded. "I don't even wanna go near any of that construction holding company mess. Scapolini can have it all. It ain't worth it. Peace of mind is priceless. So is family."

Jamal and Steve nodded and fell mute.

A moment of silence quelled the discussion as Laura lifted her glass. "We came out holding—I'm talking about us, not the money. We've got enough . . . and a little something to make that even sweeter. So, in Akhan's words, the universe is efficient. And so it is. Ashé."

Want more Leslie Esdaile Banks?

Turn the page for a preview of
BETRAYAL OF THE TRUST,
SHATTERED TRUST, and
NO TRUST

Available now wherever books are sold!

Betrayal of the Trust

The Four Seasons Hotel
Center City, Philadelphia
Present day

"Yeah . . . baby, like that," Darien moaned, his eyes now slits as he watched the top of Najira's head.

She peered up at him as she slowly dragged her tongue the length of his shaft. "You coulda fed a sister first, though," she teased with a devilish grin. "Dag. I thought we were at least gonna get some breakfast in this swank joint."

"I don't have time this morning. Stop playing with it and do it for real. I'll take you somewhere nice later. I promise."

Najira sucked her teeth and offered him a scowl. She couldn't believe how stupid this arrogant bastard was to be getting his swerve on, especially with everything that was blowing up around him. *This* was who was running the major education programs in the city?

"Oh, so I'm not gonna get mine done, *plus* you ain't feeding me? Now, how that sound? My cha-cha needs a little attention; kitty's purring, too, ya know," she said in a huff.

"Baby, come on. I've gotta go meet my attorney and—"

"And I have to go to work, *on time,* or I'll lose my temp agency slot—"

"I promise I'll hook you up. Don't I always? Didn't I get this room for you and your girls last night, and pick up the room service tab—?"

"But you didn't come last night like you said you was. . . ." Najira sat back, pouted, and folded her arms over her chest. "I coulda paid for my own room, but I wanted something more special to show you you ain't playing me, and—"

"I'll see if Mike Paxton can take you over at his office on a filing job or something, baby. . . . Now stop playing this morning. I'm already stressed. For real. You're special."

She stared at him hard but loved hearing him beg. Big-money family, phat-paid job, to-die-for house, the car of life, and here this brother was begging to get his dick sucked first thing in the morning by some sister he'd just met a few weeks ago in a club. Pitiful.

"Promises, promises. I ain't playing witchu, Negro," she finally said, her voice going soft as her fingers traced the oozing tip of his member. "But you are kinda fine, and all. Hazel-green eyes, curly hair, tight body, pretty color skin . . . Need to teach your wife how to hit it and quit it in the morning instead of messing with my gig, since she don't have to meet da man. That's the least that spoiled bitch could do."

"Yeah . . . but you know she and I don't roll like that." His voice held a blend of annoyance and a plea. "I told you we don't go there anymore."

"Guess that's why you like me, right?"

"Yeah, 'Jira . . . you're all that."

She smiled and watched his eyes close again as her mouth replaced her hand. He had some nerve trying to talk street to coax her, like she was stupid. She wasn't one of his social program chickenheads. He was the fool. Three weeks and he was jonesing like a crack addict. Men were so easy to work, especially the ones with everything to lose.

Najira glimpsed his camera cell phone from the corner of her eye as her head bobbed to the task. Getting him to go to sleep for a few moments might pose a problem, though, she worried. Feeling him shudder, she stopped and kissed his lower belly. She had to be careful, this small-dicked son of a bitch was a lousy shooter—quick on the draw—and could mess up her plan by cumming too fast. Shit.

"You know this sister don't swallow, right?"

"Jesus, Najira . . ."

"Chill, baby. I brought some latex."

He felt her warmth leave him, enjoying how she sashayed over to the dresser with sexy attitude in her stride. Najira Holmes had a nice ass. All ghetto sisters had them—high, round, polished, firm, with thick thighs, tiny waist, and that pretty walnut brown sheen. Yeah. A definite stress reliever. Much better than the athletically slim, high-yellow, high-strung wife that went with his station in life . . . but he hated that dreadlock crap Najira had done with her hair. Mike was never going to go for having *that* in his office, even in the back as a filing clerk. Fuck it, he'd tell Najira whatever and take her to Red Lobster. Why waste another high-priced dinner on around-the-way tail?

But damn, that little skeezer was so slow. All he needed was to get done and get out of there. This trumped-up media bullshit about him taking program money was fucking with his image, and with his head—but with his main man, Mike Paxton, on the case, he was good. Having Paxton on his side was like having Johnny Cochran in his hip pocket. Darien tried to settle back and relax. Yeah. He was cool. That advantage, with all the other serious political favors owed to him in the network, assured this shit would blow over soon. It had to. Najira could suck his dick and relieve some tension before he had to meet up with Mike. No reason to worry.

Najira smiled, watching Darien watch her. "You won't mind if I get a li'l somethin'-somethin', too?" She took her time climbing back on the bed and opening the foil wrapper.

"No," he said, smiling back at her as she swathed him with the barrier and mounted him. "I love the way you get yours."

"Uhmmm, hmmm," she murmured, beginning a slow, pumping, sultry circle with her hips. "I know you do."

It took everything in her not to roll her eyes and say, "Pullease, Negro." But the objective was to rock his world enough to make him doze. His upthrusts were coming faster and harder than she'd expected, and difficult for her to control . . . he was so anxious . . . However, an occasional, seemingly accidental slip-out layered with her vocal drama helped keep him working at his singular goal. Ultimately, it was all good. The harder he worked, the more tired he'd be.

When beads of sweat formed on his brow, she swallowed away a chuckle of satisfaction. She used her voice to give him deeper theater and increased her tempo to harmonize with his moans. Stupid bastard, didn't he know he was only one camera click away from having his whole life blown and not just having his world rocked?

This time when he shuddered, she pulled out all the stops, thrusting her full weight against him and grinding down hard till he cried out. Then she watched him from a very remote place in her mind. He was breathing hard, had his eyes closed, and had slung his arm over his forehead. Very carefully, she climbed down, sure to hold the edge of the condom before removing it from him.

"I'll throw this out for you, baby," she whispered.

His reply was a mere grunt. Perfect.

Slipping from the bed, she leaned down and kissed the tip of his nose, took a tissue and simultaneously palmed his cell phone from the nightstand, then collected her Louis Vuitton purse, and quietly made her way to the bathroom. For effect, she flushed the toilet.

"Hey, girl, you will NOT believe who I did this morning. Darien Price. Will do his best friend, too, soon. Watch me. His wife would have a cow if she thought I did them both. She might even have to do Paxton herself to make her husband crazy jealous. LOL! I'm out. Will try to send pic of him in bed. TTFN."

Najira stifled a giggle as she entered Darien's wife's telephone number and hit the SEND button. This was too smooth. The wife would get the so-called accidental message, thinking it was intended for her husband's lover's girlfriend, all calls would trace back to the husband's cellie, and all hell would break loose. New technology was da bomb! At this rate, every wrongdoing brother in Anytown, U.S.A., oughta be afraid. Najira shook her head. But revenge didn't require slammin' gadgets, just a sistah on a mission. Laura Caldwell, her mentor, had taught her that.

Najira folded the used condom into a tissue, then stashed it in her purse in a Zip-Loc bag. Might come in handy later. A girl could never be overprepared. *Shooot,* after that white girl from Jersey got crazy-paid for doing a president and keeping a stained blue dress in a dry cleaner's bag . . . whateva.

Using the faucet as a sound cover, Najira peeked out the bathroom door to see Darien snoozing. Like clockwork, every man needed a few moments of shut-eye after screwing. She positioned the camera through the cracked door and snapped his picture, then quickly retreated into the bathroom again, clicking the lock. Now all she had to do was send the photo, erase the memory, wash her ass, slip the phone back on the nightstand, and go to work. He would never know what hit him, and his wife would be *off the chain.*

Yeah, like Laura said, to the victor go the spoils. Served

his bourgeois ass right for having her father and the rest of her family locked out of all program funding and black-balled in the city behind bullshit. Somebody like Darien was too arrogant to know who she knew, or what last names down the way were connected. . . . Many times it was the same fathers, different mommas, different last names—it was *on*. That oversight was deadly. A brother should never assume and shoulda checked. Darien Price and his crew didn't stand a chance.

Near The Bourse Building
Center City, Philadelphia
Same morning

The blare of KYW news on the car radio sent an electric current of satisfaction through Laura J. Caldwell. Vindicated. For once, justice had been served. Information about the imminent fall of Darien Price III ricocheted through Laura's sleek black Jag XK-3 and entered her nervous system. Behind the drone of the news commentator's monotonous voice, the distinguishable station trademark sound effect—an AP newswire machine—ticked like a time bomb. Yeah, this mutha was gonna blow. She loved it.

Executive director of the prominent Educate America program, Darien Price, is being sought for questioning by police after extreme inconsistencies were found in his educational nonprofit program accounts. Allegedly, Price used seventy-five thousand dollars of program funds, earmarked for community education, for personal credit card expenses, his car note, and other personal expenses. Price has declined comment, pending the investigation. When asked—

She snapped off the radio, pulled her car into her reserved spot in the Bourse Building lot, and got out quickly. Twenty years plus, and that bastard was still trying to wiggle out of the noose. But this time Price was going down. It was personal, not business, especially after what he and his family had done to her father. Ruined a man's life and credibility because her father had started digging . . . all because her father had done what any father had the right to do—protect his daughter's honor. And her mother had died from the stress. Oh, yeah. She'd deliver Darien's head to the media on a silver platter.

New fury shot through Laura with every footfall. Her feet couldn't move fast enough to get her across the concrete divide to the elevators. Adrenaline rushed through her as she impatiently waited for the garage elevator to come. When it finally did arrive, she got in fast and punched the number panel hard, as though slamming the keypad would make the lumbering contraption move faster. The moment the doors opened to the Bourse lobby, she swept past the vendors, who were just opening, and found another set of elevators that would take her to her firm. Pure frustration at having to wait for the laboriously slow elevator to collect her was driving Laura nuts. There was so much to do, and so little time to do it. But, for once, things were working out in her favor.

A phenomenal power shift was in the offing. She could feel it. Laura tightened her grip on her briefcase as she stepped out of the elevator and stared ahead toward the double mahogany doors that led to her consulting firm. Fluorescent light glinted off the large brass name plate. It was good to be the queen.

Her low-heel pumps clicked out a cadence of sheer authority against marble as she crossed the hall. Every single battle she'd waged to ensure Rainmakers, Inc. became one of the top grant fund-raising outfits in Philadelphia had been worth it—from public school to an Ivy League university, to Wall Street, to coming home holding aces. Damned right. She'd worked her ass off and had followed all the rules of the game. Two decades of blood, sweat, and tears, and now only the white males on the affluent Main Line had the edge on her, and not by much.

As she walked, Laura's mind worked on the power grid of wealth she'd have to deal with tonight at yet another fund-raiser event. They were all the same—but were also interestingly unique.

She always tried to tell Najira that the way money was distributed was like a pebble dropped into a seemingly still pond. That was the so-called trickle-down effect. One could almost see the invisible lines as they rippled through every major project and significant piece of legislation in the city.

Laura hesitated, allowing her hand to rest on the door handle as she summoned a relaxed countenance. She had to distance her emotions from the fact that this game was all orchestrated undercover in private little alliances and secret pacts; the uninitiated never stood a chance. The community was always shit out of luck. It was time to even those odds.

"Respect," Laura whispered as she finally opened her office door.

"G'morning, Ms. Caldwell. You see the papers yet?" Laura's personal assistant asked in a rush, hopping up from her chair and entering the inner office behind Laura.

"Absolutely. Good morning, Najira."

Both women exchanged a sheepish grin. What the hell had Najira been up to that she had to call her by her formal name so loudly? Her cousin was a trip, and she only hoped that Najira wouldn't inadvertently give away their relationship to the other members of the staff one day. Some things were better left unsaid. Especially since the child had bulldozed her way into Laura's covert plan. But it was safer to clue Najira in and keep her close than to allow that kid to do something crazy to jeopardize the bigger picture. Laura studied Najira hard, trying to figure out what new drama the girl had injected into the equation. It was all over Najira's face. What had homegirl done this morning? Hmmm.

Casting her khaki-colored London Fog raincoat on the sofa along with her black Coach barrel purse, Laura never broke her stride. She shook her head at the trappings she had to maintain just to be in the game. One day she'd get out. But she had a lot to accomplish before then: black Rome had to fall.

Deep in thought and not looking at Najira as she'd answered, Laura made her way across the large Oriental rug, collected a stack of incoming mail, glanced at her Movado watch, and dropped her alligator briefcase next to her desk. Seven-thirty a.m., and the whole town was about to go nuts. Excellent. Laura sat down, hit a button on the telephone system console, and punched in her voice-mail code, riffling through her in-box as she multitasked, trying to avoid Najira's wide smile. Oh, yeah, girlfriend had been up to tricks and games. Laura chuckled despite her resolve to remain stoic.

Without waiting for a more engaging response, Najira quickly went to the coffee bar and brought over a fresh-brewed pot. Voice-mail messages droned on as white noise in the background. Offering a coffee fill-up as Laura settled into a sumptuous black leather chair, the young woman pointed to several local rags that she'd laid out in order of circulation dominance for her boss to review, and poured herself a cup.

"Front page, everywhere. This is gonna shake up Philly for serious." Najira adjusted a stray Nubian-twist lock behind her ear, her line of vision fastened on the newspapers, glass coffeepot suspended in midair, as she read along with Laura over her shoulder. "What would make somebody like him take nonprofit program funds to pay credit card bills, his car note, and stupid stuff like that, I wonder?" Her tone was singsong sarcastic, and she fanned her face in mock despair.

Again both women stared at each other, their smiles belying the formal office ruse. Laura cut Najira a warning look that said, *Not here, the office could have ears.* Offices always did.

"I almost can't believe it," Laura replied with false disgust as another staffer passed her office and nodded good morning. Carefully picking up one of the newspapers with one hand, Laura furrowed her brow as though she'd just been clued in, and motioned with her head for Najira to see that they weren't totally free to talk privately yet.

Catching the hint, Najira nodded, feigning the total subordinate-boss role-play as Laura held up her empty porcelain cup for Najira and motioned for her to take a seat in front of her desk. She waited until Najira was settled and had put the pot down on the edge of her desk before saying another word. Both women took a slow, steady sip of coffee, eyeing each other the whole time.

"I have to agree—I can't believe it, either. Then again, yes, I can," Laura added with a wink. "Truth is always stranger than fiction."

"I hear you, but this is absolutely wild." Najira popped up, sloshing the coffee in her mug, hustled past the door to her desk, and snatched up her handbag. When she returned, she shut the door quietly, glancing around first to be sure none of the other staff saw her, and then raced back to Laura's desk. "This morning was off da hook," Najira whispered in triumph.

Laura nodded, chuckled, and glanced up at the young woman hovering nearby. The assignment given to Najira was a simple one, designed to keep the girl from anything too criminal. It wasn't about allowing her cousin to do something that could land that nineteen-year-old kid in jail. Najira

was only supposed to keep tabs on Darien's whereabouts—
that was it. But concern lurched in Laura's stomach as she
watched her cousin's eyes sparkle.

"I did him."

"What?" Laura was incredulous.

"You said to keep tabs on him, and I did," Najira said with
a chuckle. "Pissed his wife off, too, but that ain't my problem . . . but it does add a little spice."

Laura sighed. Screwing some jerk was not a felony, nor
was creating enough static between him and his wife to
cause distrust a crime punishable by law. It was done every
day—domestic. But no matter what Najira said, Laura wasn't
going to let her in on the real action as a potential accessory.
She could tell that Najira wanted to get closer to the sting.
Laura sipped the dark brew in her cup slowly and then fixed
her gaze on the article. "You are so right," she said after a
moment. "Must have been all the way live." What else was
there to say? Now she had to figure out how to work with
this new information and make it work for her. She just
hoped that Najira's father, her uncle, wouldn't find out about
any of this. . . . Akhan would have a stroke. Laura shook her
head.

"Girl . . ."

"Not here," Laura warned with a smile.

"But, boss lady—look." Before Laura could protest, Najira had set down her mug on the edge of Laura's desk and
had thrust her hand into her Louis Vuitton, extracting a plastic bag.

"What *the hell* is that?" Laura asked, leaning forward and
wrinkling her nose.

"It's DNA evidence, just in case—"

"Don't even begin to tell me about it."

Both women dissolved into hushed laughter behind their
hands, straining to keep their voices in check.

"Oh, my God, girl . . ."

"Ya never know when it could come in handy, chile."

"Don't even think about putting it on my desk!" Laura hissed through hearty giggles. "Just stop!"

"And you thought I was an amateur." Najira sucked her teeth and flung the nasty little bag of goo back into her purse with flair.

"My bad," Laura whispered, wiping her eyes. "But that is sooo foul."

"I bet this Darien indictment will be the hush-hush convo of the evening when you go to that Scott-Edward Foundation fund-raiser at the Hyatt. Everybody who is anybody in Philly will be there, along with the media, and I know the who's who will be buzzing about *this* Darien mess. Girl, you're the real pro. I'm just trying to study, okaaay?"

Najira gave Laura a mischievous grin, waiting for a response, and, when she didn't immediately answer, pressed on. "So, how we gonna play this?" Najira laughed hard. "Don't look at me like, *'Moi?'* I know you did it. I just wanna learn how."

"The who's who are my prospects—that's the only reason I'm going to the event tonight. Remember, I have a fund-raising business to run, too. So their speculative conversations are inconsequential, but their money is not," Laura hedged, tempering her emotions and not answering Najira's primary question. "I don't care what they talk about. This guy and his partners are really pissing me off, Jira."

"If it's like that, then why do we have to go through all this slow, double-O-soul shit to bring him down? Why not just have their asses seen?" Najira sighed. "The family tried it the other, legal way, and—"

"It didn't work," Laura replied, her voice tight. This was precisely why she didn't want Najira involved, but she had to keep her cousin close. The last thing she needed was a loose cannon in the family doing something street to upset the apple-cart. This had to go down smooth to be a total and permanent win.

The two women stared at each other, one formulating a response while the other squirmed in her seat like an excited child. Laura focused on the issues before saying a word. Darien's crew was not her real concern, nor was his attorney. The goal was simply to create enough friction in their camp that they'd begin to tell on each other.

"All right. Sore subject," Najira finally conceded. "We both have that in common, so chill." Najira's shoulders slumped. "What's the politically correct way I'm supposed to respond when people ask me have I heard about this yang?"

"Sorry . . . listen," Laura said slowly, then relaxed. "A lot of times when our people are in power, they become unfair media targets." She winked at Najira and forced another chuckle. "Shame, too, because a physical injury heals, a death leaves a man a martyr, but a media smear with a financial wipe-out will leave a man in pain and bleeding forever."

"I can respect that," Najira murmured, taking a sip from her mug and never losing eye contact with Laura. "Which is why you're the boss."

The kid reminded Laura so much of herself: an around-the-way girl trying to make a better life for herself. As the thought crossed her mind, Laura mellowed and smiled at her protégé. "So, we aren't going to talk bad about people without the full story, even though tongues are wagging." Laura motioned with her chin toward the outer office; her meaning directed at Najira was clear: seem shocked and appalled. Play it to the bone around anyone else.

"I hear you. But still . . ." Seeming disappointed that Laura wasn't going to spend a few moments reveling in the latest scoop, Najira finally let out a sigh and nodded in reluctant agreement.

Under the circumstances, Laura didn't want to hear the

blow-by-blow details of what Jira had done to get a used condom into her purse. It was up to Najira how far she went in monitoring Darien's movements. But *nooooo,* Najira went in for high drama. Laura almost laughed.

Nervous energy had a stranglehold on her, though. The remaining parts of the plan had to go down without a hitch. Now it was time to go to the ball and work the serious-money angle. All contracts Darien had promised his cronies had to be derailed, and those funds rerouted. His life would be ruined, with no way to rebuild . . . just as her father's life had been trashed.

"You sure you're up to this?" Laura whispered.

"I know what to do—create a diversion so you can work the room before his main money man gets there." Najira shrugged.

"I need to have a clear shot to convince Haines to let me manage who gets those funds, before his attorney, Michael Paxton, blocks my free throw. Understand?"

"All right, all right," Najira agreed, growing testy.

"Be smooth, stay out of sight, and no more drama." Laura looked at Najira hard to be sure the underlying message took root.

"Why not?"

Quiet fell between them for a moment as Najira's eyes continued to sparkle with excitement.

"Because it's too dangerous."

"Like I'm scared of them soft punks." Indignant, Najira sat back in her chair and folded her arms over her chest.

Laura laughed out loud. "I know you're not, and neither am I. But trust me on this. Okay?" She stood and walked to the window.

"All right," Najira said in a weary tone. "Whatever." Najira's face had gone stone serious in the exchange. "Now, I did my part, so while I've got your back, you'll have fifteen minutes to verbally crack that old white boy's safe. You got a small window, sis, to pick his pocket clean—feel me? Got my mind on the money, and several million on my mind."

Laura let her nod silently answer Najira's challenge. In this faltering economy, every rainmaker in the nation knew that so-called philanthropic campaign giving was at risk. Every firm's clients were on financial life support, and she had a slew of clients to generate substantial funds for, to keep them alive.

What could she say to Najira? Out of the mouths of babes came words of wisdom. Laura went back to her desk and sipped her coffee as she chose her own words carefully, trying to help Najira understand the bigger picture while also fully appreciating where her younger cousin was coming from. But the girl needed to learn how to be strategic in her thinking. All women did. Especially one as bright and altruistic as Najira. This young sister had a chance to make something of herself, if she didn't get wrapped up in the political madness—or in some dumb shit that could land her in prison. At nineteen years old, Najira deserved to have a life. It was not about divulging information that could put Najira in harm's way.

"Let's not lose focus," Laura said after a moment. "Since nine-eleven, all contribution money has been tight. The donors have either diverted funds to where they can recoup their investment with Homeland Security contracts or have lost so much in their Wall Street portfolios that they just don't have it to give. The Price family was always good for an annual fifty thousand in contributions to buy favors around the region—not much, when you really think about it. Their leverage was with the contracts they could influence . . . No doubt Darien has laid out a laundry list of security and education contract favors—I just need to find out who's slated to get them. That's why I have to do the wine-and-cheese circuit to find out. But it looks like the Price family will be spending their grease-the-skids money on legal fees this year."

That was all she could give Najira to go on, and she hoped it would satisfy her cousin's thirst for information at this point.

"Embezzlement was brilliant," Najira said fast, appearing revived. "I'll give you that. I just want to know how you pinned it on him." She stood and leaned on the edge of Laura's desk. "They might indict him. Can you believe it? Darien Price? With all the money *they* have?" She laughed, but the sound of it was hollow and brittle. "What would make him do something that crazy as to steal from the city program coffers like that, when his people have all the money in the world? It was a glory position anyway, and he got paid a mint for a salary. I'm loving watching him and his fancy attorney try to scam their way out of that shit."

Najira was talking with her hands now, becoming more animated as the weight of what could befall her enemies took root in her soul. "For chrissakes, Laura, he was only in that job, because his big-time family got him appointed to it, for less than a year!"

"Tragic," Laura said, her tone wry and dismissive. "Money . . . and how much is enough is all relative," Laura added, smiling gently at Najira, although her patience was wearing thin. She'd been up all night, had things to do, and as much as she shared her cousin's savor of comeuppance— as well as her disdain for the rich and foolish—it was time for them both to get to work.

There was a stack of client requests with deadlines in every one of her secretaries' in-bins. Plus, there would be a shift in power, and she needed to devote her mental energy to dissecting where the chips might fall—her goal to grab as much of the realigned contract and grant moneys for organizations that did real work in the community, as opposed to allowing the pretenders to gobble it up before it hit the ground. Then there was the not so small matter of vengeance. Laura scanned the headlines again, mentally checking every variable. But no matter how much Najira cajoled her for a confession, she wasn't telling the girl what she did, or how she'd pulled it off.

Najira shook her head, still in disbelief, lingering despite Laura's growing distraction. "Fine. If you still don't wanna tell me how you did it—because I know you did something—then you *have to* tell me what the insiders are talking about, boss lady, even though I'll be in the hotel, out of sight. I mean, I know you'll hear some real dirt between all the chi-chi discussion and the wine-and-cheese event tonight. I just want to know, just want to see them twist."

"It'll just be idle gossip, but I'll clue you in if I hear anything really juicy. However, I don't expect to." Laura set down the newspaper and flipped open her Palm Pilot. "My main objective for going to that event tonight is to get to a few well-heeled insiders, to make some more rain for our largest-paying clients, with some spillover for the little guys. At the fundraiser I can also find some scraps for the clients we have who simply can't pay our full freight. Balance, Najira. Balance. We take ours off the bottom, not the top, and that keeps the heat off our butts."

Laura sighed and pushed back in her chair. "It's what keeps the lights on in here, too, all of this drama notwithstanding." She studied the young woman with compassion for her point of view. "Remember, even though the Kennedys started with bootleg liquor and mob ties, eventually they had to go legit to keep things smooth. Balance is imperative. Always."

"Yeah," Najira protested, one hand going to her hip, "but it is sure nice to see that sometimes folks like J. Darien Price get theirs."

"No argument here, sis," Laura murmured, and then focused her attention on the appointments in her electronic calendar as she synched up the handheld device to her desk system Outlook software. "It is pretty bizarre, all things said and done. Cosmic justice."

"You ain't said a word."

"Uhmmm hmmm . . . That's why, this morning, I've got to figure out who'll be left standing when the dust settles, kiddo." Laura peered at the flat, black LCD screen and let out a weary sigh. Mondays were always intense. She never got used to the onslaught that the top of the week insisted on, but she had a grant-developers' meeting and a team that would require close direction in order to pull down a couple hundred thou this morning. By noon, and if the trains held to schedule, she'd be up at the state capitol, in Harrisburg, lobbying with politicians to get her portion of the practically nonexistent state-funded contracts within the Department of Community and Economic Development. This shake-up meant that a few struggling grassroots organizations finally had a shot at some significant resources, that is, if she could use the diffusion of power to her advantage. Shame that Darien had crossed her; his empire would crumble, and he'd never know what hit him. Again Laura glanced at her watch.

Najira pulled away from Laura's desk slowly, catching the hint. Seeing the young woman withdraw with such a dejected look on her face gave Laura a twinge of regret. If she'd had more time, she would have given in to Najira's unspoken request for a little more female coaching interaction—but this morning she couldn't take her cousin under her wing. Her nerves couldn't withstand the "delicious details," as Najira often referred to them, and the full plan was too fragile to give Najira the total play-by-play. As volatile as the girl was, Laura knew that Najira had already risked her entire life by peripherally colluding with her. But, hey, family was family.

The more things changed, the more things stayed the same. The kid just wanted to learn while also serving old-school justice, and she could appreciate that. One day. Laura studied her cousin from a sidelong glance as she walked out of the office, shaking her head in psychic agreement with their private assessment of Philadelphia's black elite.

Laura paused, staring at the attractive young woman, briefly considering the way the deep rust tones on Najira's mud-cloth skirt and matching silk blouse matched her hair, which matched her skin and her suede boots, and the leather on her cowry shell earrings, which matched her bracelet. Everything that Najira wore closely complemented the natural woods, fibers, tastefully understated furnishings, and African art of Laura's well-appointed, historic Fifth Street, Bourse Building office.

She just wondered how J. Darien Price III would blend into the penal system's basic color of gray.

Laura raked her fingers through her short, naturally curly hair, a new strategy simmering inside her head, her focus returning to how she would approach the targets at the gala later that night. She brushed an invisible fleck of lint off her black and khaki-colored herringbone Chanel jacket sleeve, adjusted her pearls, and made a mental note of each VIP phone call that she needed to return personally.

Needing something in her hands, she reached forward for the red Mont Blanc pen suspended in the crystal ball that sat next to an etched-glass vase of fresh-cut sunflowers, and began jotting down a short list of whom she would approach, and then crumpled up the note in her fist before tossing it in a waste basket. Her mind allowed in a shadow of doubt before she banished it. Her nerves were drawn taut as a wire, making her reach for her briefcase to extract a cell phone, then absently punch in numbers. Irony of ironies, huh.

Laura peered at the newspapers strewn across her wide mahogany desk. God was good.

Not bad for somebody once called a ghetto bitch.

* * *

Fury collided with sadness and gave way to the hot tears of defeat. Monica Price sat in the driveway of the Montessori School and held her cell phone, staring at it as though it were some foreign object. How could he? She always knew Darien had a slew of little bitches out in the streets, had known for years. Theirs was an uneasy truce and a marriage totally of convenience. But seeing it was so much different from knowing it. They had children, for God's sake! Little children. Beautiful children. Their children.

A new flood of tears threatened her composure as she brought her hand to her mouth and swallowed away a sob. This time her husband would pay. The lesson would be visceral and cut his wayward ass to the bone. Her fingers trembled as she punched the number she knew by heart into the cell phone and pressed SEND. Michael Paxton could fix this.

He felt the vibration on his hip and almost ignored it. But at this early hour, and with everything blowing up around Darien's bullshit, instinct made him take the call.

"Give me a minute," Paxton said to Darien. "Could have a bearing on our conversation." He spun around in his chair, gazing out of his Liberty Plaza office window and giving Darien the high back leather to watch instead of his expression.

"Paxton here," he said, thoroughly intrigued that Monica Price's cell number had flashed with a "9-1-1" on his digital display. Obviously, she knew he was in a meeting with her husband—but why wouldn't she have come through his secretary? Anne would have patched her through.

For a moment there was no voice response, just a long sniff. Very interesting. He pressed his ear closer to the small device in his hand.

"Mike . . . can we talk for a moment?" A fragile female voice finally replied. "It's important."

"I'm in a meeting right now, but—"

"Is Darien with you?" Monica immediately shot back.

"Yes." A slow smile dawned on Paxton's face. "But that's all right."

"I know you said to come to you, if ever . . . well . . . I want to send you something that I just received this morning, and I need this to be between you and me until I can figure out what to do about it."

"All right," Paxton said carefully.

"Please, under no circumstances are you to show this to Darien. I've been trying to call that son of a bitch all morning, and he won't return my calls. And I know this puts you in an awkward position, but . . ."

"I understand," Paxton said in a controlled tone. "Go ahead."

"It's awful."

Sobs entered the cell phone, and Paxton glanced at his watch. "It will be all right. Send it."

He waited and stared at his color display and shook his head, bringing the telephone to his ear again after clearing the image. "I understand. I'll deal with it."

Renewed sobs filled his ear, and he waited until they abated. "We should meet about this—this isn't something to deal with on the telephone . . . and as I said, I'm in a meeting right now."

"Okay. Thank you, Mike. Where?"

Paxton spun around and looked at Darien, giving him hand signals to infer that he was trying to get a nuisance client off his phone. When Darien relaxed and nodded, Paxton closed his eyes and leaned his head back. "I have to go to a charity fund-raiser tonight at the Hyatt. After that, perhaps we could meet for a drink?"

"Give me the room number later, okay?" the female voice whispered.

"Will do. I'll leave it on your cell."

"I can't thank you enough, Mike. He's looking at you, isn't he? Staring right down your throat."

"Yeah. That works," Paxton said, doodling on his blotter.

"Good," Monica said crisply. "I'll make the meeting worth your while, as I know your time is valuable."

"Most appreciated," Paxton said, dismissing the call and hanging up without a good-bye. He hooked the cell phone back on his belt and sighed, shaking his head as he picked up the thread of conversation with Darien.

"Guess everybody wants a piece of you today, man," Darien said in a weary voice. "Can't say I blame them—you're the man."

"A pain-in-the-ass corporate client," Paxton replied in a blasé tone. "Had to take that. Sorry. Now, where were we?"

No Trust

Maui, Hawaii

Jamal dropped the keys to his Hummer on the dresser, pulled his cell phone out of his pocket, and clicked it off. It was amazing what a couple million dollars could do for a brother. God bless his cousin Laura! If this was how the other half lived, then he better understood his cousin's philosophy: get rich or die trying. Membership most definitely had its privileges. If he had it his way, except for a few quick annual visits to see his father, he'd never go home to North Central Philly again. It was cold, nothing but concrete jungle and hassle. This was paradise.

Jamal looked at Safia and the way she sprawled out on the bed for him. *Damn,* she was fine. He didn't care that she felt more comfortable at her house rather than at the plush environs of the hotel. Whatever she wanted was cool, as long as it made her get nasty like this. So what that her joint had just a few pieces of rented furniture.

This female was *all that* . . . Hawaiian, she had gorgeous, silky, chocolate brown hair hanging way down her back and dusting her ass, skin like caramel, a pretty face, man-made tits, legs longer than his, and a cute little belly ring. Yeah, a brother could get used to this. Even though the rap career never took off and he'd gotten caught up doing a short bid for possession, he was now living the life—and it was all about the now.

Watching her watch him, anticipation added to the throb that was making his stomach clench. Jamal yanked his white Phat Farm T-shirt over his head, pleased with Safia's reaction. That's right, he wasn't the skinny, lanky kid anymore. A personal trainer, eating properly with time to work on his build had changed that, too. The correct bank digits in the seven figures could definitely change a man's life, just like it put two rocks of ice in his earlobes.

He kicked off his Air Force 1 sneakers, stripped off his white walking shorts and boxers, and smiled. He couldn't believe it—she'd actually licked her lips and closed her eyes and then slid her hand between her legs. *For him.*

He walked forward, balls aching. It had been so long since he'd gotten any, given all the bullshit that was always going down in the family—always on the run, always somebody shooting at 'em, and he didn't have any real cash before.

Safia pulled herself up to kneel in front of him, as he approached the edge of the bed, and looked up with a sultry smile. He was trying to act cool, as though females did this to him every day, but it was something that he'd experienced only once. Sad but true, it was in the backseat of his boy's ride, performed by some fat chickenhead with a bad weave who was trying to get some product for free. But it definitely wasn't anything he'd ever had done by a female so fine that she looked like she'd stepped out of a Luda video.

Her intention was clear, though, as she kissed each newly created brick in his abdomen on her way down. Just knowing what she was about to do made his dick jump and begin to leak pre-cum.

His palms roved over the butter-soft lobes that he'd been craving to touch since he first saw her in the club . . . the way they jiggled in her halter, and now they were in his hands, their tiny brown nipples biting into his palms as she pressed them hard against his touch and moaned. He could see her round, luscious ass beginning to tighten and release in a promised dance. Feeling like he was about to pass out, he closed his eyes for a moment and held his breath, determined to chill. But when she pulled the head of his rod into her wet, lovely mouth, the sensation made his body buckle.

"Oh, shit . . ."

His voice had come out in a strangled rush as she drew him in slowly all the way to the hilt, then caressed the lobes of his ass with satin palms. He looked down, breathing hard; she didn't even gag, just took it all like a pro. Dazed for a second, he wasn't sure what to do with his hands, and definitely didn't want to interrupt her flow by trying to touch her awe-inspiring breasts while she worked.

Eventually, his hands found her hair and his fingers reveled in the silky texture. It was real; there was no glue to snag his fingers. She was real, not an image on cable to beat off to at night. Her big, beautiful eyes held his as her tongue worked in a swirl each time she pulled back, and then she finally gripped his base with both hands in a way that let him know she was about to get serious.

They shared a still glance for a moment, both breathing hard. She smiled a sexy half smile and lowered her head to his body again. This time there was no way to be cool, no way to fight against the rhythm she set. He was panting, sweating, and thrusting out of control. Then she suddenly stopped, threatening to give him an aneurysm.

The immediate loss of contact with her warm, tight, sucking motion made it seem like all the air collapsed out of his lungs, pulling his stomach and nuts up into his chest. For a few futile seconds he couldn't stop moving and was thrusting nothing but air.

"Don't you want to finish off inside me?" she murmured against his stomach.

Truthfully, at this point, it really didn't matter, but he told her what she wanted to hear. "Yeah, baby," he croaked. "Find the latex."

He'd just have to make it up to her next round. In his heart he knew that in a few hard strokes he'd be finished. He watched her lean over, get a condom off the nightstand, and open it. The moment she began to sheath him he winced from the needles of pleasure that were stabbing his shaft. He couldn't help it. When she sprawled back against the bed, he instantly blanketed her, clumsily finding her opening and entering her hard. She cried out and her nails dug into his shoulders. He didn't care; he was practically swooning from the sensation of being inside her, feeling her heavy breasts cushioning his chest, feeling her satin-smooth legs wrap around his waist, her ass in his hands putting a hump in his back.

Oh, *shit*, he was gonna get it and get it good—would make it up to her later at the mall. She smelled so damned good, and her tight pussy was putting starlights behind his lids, the harder he pumped. Her soft hands were caressing his cornrows, gliding over his scalp. She was thrashing and murmuring to him in a language he didn't know, and he didn't care as long as she kept swirling her hips in that snap-jerk motion that put tears in his eyes.

He came so hard and so fast that he almost swallowed his tongue. She was still moving beneath him, trying to get hers, but he couldn't help it, he was too far gone.

"It's still hard, baby," he said after a moment, gasping. Sweat was rolling down his sides and back and he kissed her forehead as she held him tighter. "Let me put a new one on so we don't have no accident, feel me?" He kissed her slowly and then traced her pout with the pad of his thumb. "You just so fine I couldn't help it . . . but trust me, I'ma make sure you get yours, too. Aw'ight?"

She nodded and closed her eyes, brushing his mouth with a kiss. He really felt bad when he held the rim of the condom and pulled out and she gasped, her expression agonized like she had been right there but just missed busting a nut. Although he'd initially had no intention of going downtown on a babe he technically just met . . . this one was fine enough and definitely sweet enough to make him forget all his self-imposed rules of booty chasing.

Jamal rolled over and stood with effort. "I'll be right back." He watched her roll over and offer him a sad smile as he crossed the room to head for the bathroom.

Yeah, this one stood a very good chance of being *the one*. She was sweet, didn't argue, didn't ask for much, was off da meter in bed. She could dance and liked to party, but wasn't a bona fide hoochie. He could get used to having a quality woman like that on his arm on a permanent tip, no doubt. When he got back to bed, he was gonna do her right. Then, maybe he'd take her somewhere real nice when he got back from Philly, like take her shopping, treat her to a real expensive dinner, maybe they could check out a flick.

He dropped the used condom in the toilet and flushed it, and then grabbed a towel to clean up any semen residue that could get her pregnant.

But a loud noise made him freeze and stare in the mirror, too paralyzed for a second to even turn around. It sounded like the front door had come off the hinges, and the heavy footsteps running down the hall were worse than a raid by po-po. Then, all of a sudden, the biggest, burliest, blackest, dreadlock wearing motherfucker he'd ever seen in his life crossed by the half-cracked open bathroom door as a spooky flash in the mirror, and headed for the bedroom bellowing Safia's name in a Jamaican accent.

"Wha' you tink, I'm crazy? You wif 'im in me house and expect wha, woman? Where 'im at! I'll blow him ass away gulley, you fuck 'im den, hear!"

"I don't know what you're talking about!" Safia shrieked. "Just because you helped me with rent a few times doesn't mean you live here, Terrence! I was getting dressed for work and, and—"

"Bitch, you got an open box of condoms on de dresser! You ass is wet, and you smell like sex! You tink—"

"'Cause I missed you, baby . . . I was hoping you'd come over, but you came in here accusing me!"

A closet door banged open. A search was obviously on.

"I told you wasn't nobody here."

"Den whose motherfucking Hummer is in da driveway, and who keys and cell phone is dis, huh? You wear a shirt dis big, love? You now wearing size fourteen Air Force 1's? Don' fuck wit me, Safia! You too gorgeous to hit, but I'll bust a cap in his ass!"

"I don't want you to go back to jail, baby—let him go," she wailed.

Jamal's mind processed everything in hundredths of microseconds—he was naked; a big, crazy-ass Jamaican was gonna cap him for fucking his woman. His car keys, cell phone, wallet, and everything else were in there with a madman. Safia would be all right—this was her man. Chivalry was dead, and he wasn't trying to be. *He was out.*

Towel in hand, Jamal dove through the bungalow window. He hit the ground with a thud and was up in a flash. Neighborhood dogs barked. Driveway gravel cut into his feet. But a hollering Jamaican was now hanging out the bathroom window, too big to get through it as quickly as he had. Gunshot report put every instinct from the old streets of Philly into

Jamal's legs as his Hummer windshield took a 9-millimeter shell. Jamal moved like a zigzag blur, dodging bullets, ducking low, moving forward like greased lightning. God heard his prayers. The crazy Jamaican bastard had left his Jeep running.

"I'll kill you . . . touch me Jeep after touching me woman, bitch, and you a dead mon!"

More gunfire rang out as Jamal jumped into the Jeep's driver's seat and shifted into reverse, burning rubber against blacktop, and jumping as the side-view mirror exploded off the vehicle.

"Where is your brother?" Laura groaned, plopping down on the couch. "If he doesn't come on, he's gonna be late for the airport, and we all promised your father we'd come home together for a visit this time."

"I know," Najira said. "You know how Jamal is." She looked over at Steve. "You think we should just leave the suitcase he packed and all his travel docs here at Laura and James's house, or take them back to his apartment?"

Steve raked his fingers through his blonde buzz cut and began to pace, growing agitated. His face was red and his mouth had become a tight line. "Why does your brother always pull this shit, huh? He brings his bags over here, says he's just gonna make a quick run, and then disappears for two hours."

"It's not my fault, Steve," Najira said, growing peevish. "I've been blowing up his cell all afternoon and he's not answering!"

James leaned against the wall with a thud, folding his arms over his chest. "Why don't we give him a few more minutes? Worst case, since he's not answering his cell, we can leave a voice mail on there and at his apartment. He's got a key to everybody's place, so you can tell him where his gear is and then he can catch the next available flight home. Case closed. No need for us all to get bent."

Grumbles of dissension wafted through the spacious living room of his and Laura's beachside bungalow. James watched Steve sulk away to go find a beer, which wasn't a half bad idea. Najira plopped her short, curvy self down on an over-stuffed portion of the ivory leather sectional and flung her rust-toned dreadlocks over her shoulders with disgust. His wife did what she always did—Laura paced.

For a moment all he could do was watch her smooth her hands down her wheat-colored linen slacks as she stood. When Laura was pissed off she was often at her most sensual; his Scorpio woman had a way of turning quiet outrage into an art form. Her dark, moody eyes smoldered, and her normally lush mouth was set in a kissable pout, resolute. There was a slight tinge of rose hue beginning to creep into her caramel complexion that was very reminiscent of a sexual flush. Then she raked her long, graceful fingers through her short, silky onyx curls, leaving a just-tousled-in-bed look that he adored.

James rubbed his palm over his close-cropped hair, and then his newly clean-shaven jaw. He had to get his mind out of the gutter, but last night and this morning had really put a strain on his libido. All his wife had wanted to do was cuddle and talk.

He stared at her unashamed as she took in slow, cleansing breaths, her full breasts rising and falling beneath the linen shell she wore, and each slow, sauntering stride she took between the door and the window was like watching poetry in motion. Her regal height that made her fit so perfectly against him, her long legs, the mesmerizing sway of her hips, and the distinctive curve of her gorgeous ass. God, he loved that woman, and should have insisted on a little attention before this huge family affair. But how could he? She'd just wanted to be held when her uncle Akhan had called. The old man was cryptic as usual and refused to discuss anything on the telephone, but had insisted that the whole family come home immediately.

James had to admit, as he stared at his wife, that part of him was really pissed off and wanted to just yell to the old neighborhood street warrior that *the man* wasn't behind every goddamned corner. But then again, Akhan didn't get to be almost ninety without knowing something. It was just the brother's timing. Why did the call have to come after he and Steve had been away for almost a week deep-sea fishing?

Glimpsing his old partner from the force, who was guzzling a beer, James was sure that Steve quietly shared the same lack-of-nookie blues. If Laura Caldwell-Carter was concerned, then her young, high-strung cousin, Najira, had to have been a basket case last night—which meant that neither he nor Steve got lucky when they came home.

A whole week, and now they'd be traveling back to Philly not knowing what conditions they'd meet, since Akhan had gone conspiracy-theory-cryptic on them . . . which could mean even more emotional drama that would make his wife disinterested.

James sighed and made a mental note to remind himself to kick Steve's ass the next time he wanted to do some guys-only shit. He didn't care whether it cleared his partner's head so that Steve could decide to pop the question to Najira or not. Before long, Najira was gonna be showing, so it was pretty much a done deal. Akhan would probably try to shoot Steve's crazy ass if he didn't marry Jira. Maybe that's why Akhan had called for a family meeting—to get a clear sense of what was gonna be up. Who knew? But both Steve and Najira were sweating bullets about the visit, so Jamal being late was just plain ole fucked up.

Growing weary and philosophical, James pushed off the wall, needing to get Laura out of his sight. Hankering for what he couldn't have for the foreseeable future was just making him ornery. He headed for the kitchen and opened the fridge. Steve didn't say a word and just handed him a beer. The two nodded. After years of working together on the force before they'd retired, some things were simply done by telepathy.

Still, the disappearance of Jamal didn't sit right. James popped the top off a Heineken and turned it up to his mouth. Everything in his dormant cop senses told him that something was wrong. True, Jamal was prone to get lost in a good card game, might go AWOL smoking weed or chasing tail, but he wouldn't blow off going home to see his father. Those two were tight, and Akhan was getting up there in years.

The old man had suffered and survived World War I, the Great Depression, World War II, Jim Crow, civil rights, marches, water hoses, and dogs; fled lynching states and the system, survived the mean streets of Kingston and then Philly, raised two sets of kids and outlived two different wives; had taken a bullet, had struck the deal of life with old man Donald Haines, and had probably done more in each decade of his life than most folks did in their entire lives. So, no, Jamal wouldn't blow off a flight home, even if Akhan had called a war council meeting. Of that he was sure.

The sound of a vehicle screeching into the driveway confirmed James's suspicions. He relaxed. Yeah, Jamal was running late, got caught up, and had driven like a bat out of hell to get there on time. Now, maybe everyone could relax. James and Steve shared a smirk and gave each other a fist pound. They both watched their women's shoulders drop by two inches and polished off their beers, silently sharing the same thought about Jamal's probable whereabouts.

But when Jamal burst through the unlocked deck screen door, eyes wild, naked except for a towel, hands shaking, nobody moved much less blinked. Jamal was a splash of fast-moving mahogany against the expansive sand-hued interior of the beachfront mansion. The sight was surreal and seemed as though one of their huge African sculptures in the living room had suddenly sprung to life in a disoriented whirl.

"Oh, shit, oh, shit, I ain't have my keys and that big motherfucker was on my ass—but I gotta get him back his Jeep some kinda way 'cause I'm not going down for grand theft auto over no bullshit—honest to God, I ain't know she had a man! Damn, this is fucked up—he shot my Hummer windshield, man. Probably fucked it up—my wallet and shit is at her crib, my cell, my license, my gear—I can't believe this shit! Her ass was too fine to be that fucking crazy, yo! Oh, my God, his ass was as big as James, like six five and shit, but built like he was on the prison yard bench pressing two-fifty for ten years and shit! He shot at my ass with a nine, unloaded what had to be a whole fuckin' clip in broad-ass daylight, yo!"

For a moment no one said a word as Jamal clutched his towel and closed his eyes.

"Damn," he murmured, slowly calming down. "She was sooo fine, too."

Najira was on her feet; Laura sat down slowly in a chair. "You mean to tell me that Daddy called with some important family business and you was getting *your swerve on* and that's why we are all waiting on you?"

"Najira, are you out of your fucking mind!" Jamal shouted, his voice cracking from stress. "Did you hear what I was saying? I was shot at, girl, I was—"

"About to get a mud hole stomped in your narrow ass," James said with a sigh and then couldn't fight the smirk.

Steve glanced at James with a grin. "You got an extra nine-millimeter in the house?"

"You know me, dog," James said, chuckling. "Never leave home without it."

"Shall we get this guy his wallet and keys back, maybe his Hummer in a fair trade for the Jeep?" Steve peered out the window. "Damn, this is just like old times. Bullet holes in the back panel, no side-view mirror—"

"The crazy motherfucker shot it off!" Jamal hollered. "I told you, his ass wasn't playing."

"Y'all ain't going over there!" Najira shrieked. "You heard Jamal. This is some crazy domestic drama with a wild-ass Jamaican."

"Since this guy knows where you live, and your key ring has all of ours on it, I'll have the locks changed on all the doors and push back the flight," Laura said through her teeth, giving Jamal the evil eye. "Then, I will call your *father* and explain *why* we have to be delayed. I cannot believe you sometimes."

"Baby, that's cold," James said, trying to soothe her. "Don't go there . . . just tell your uncle something came up. That's the man's business. Okay?"

Laura glared at James and let out a breath of frustration. "All right, fine. He doesn't need this ghetto mess on his soul anyway, at his age." She then turned her narrowed gaze on Jamal. "But I suggest you plan on breaking your lease, a hefty expense for the lesson, and that you stay out of whatever clubs she frequents with her man, and that you get a new cell phone and find a new place really close to your backup— James and Steve. Serves your short-sighted, booty-dazed behind right."

"She was drop-dead *fine*, Laura," Jamal said quietly, humiliation singeing his voice. "Hawaiian, and shit."

Laura lifted her chin and walked toward the telephone, ignoring him.

"What dat mean?" Najira yelled, looking as though she was about to stomp her feet.

"Jamal, man, I feel you, but lemme get you some sweats and a T-shirt, man," James said, trying hard not to smile and remembering being Jamal's age once. Yeah, in his twenties, maybe even his thirties, he would have taken a bullet for some really exquisite tail.

"It's cool," Jamal said, his voice weary. "I can just take whatever from my suitcase—but, man, I need a shower."

"You *feel* him?" Laura echoed, her hands going to her hips. "Oh, now Hawaiian women are worth a nine-millimeter slug in your ass, huh? Men!"

"Or worth blowing off a trip home to see you elderly father." Najira cocked her head to the side and hotly folded her arms over her petite bosom.

"Baby, I didn't mean it like that."

Laura and Najira sucked their teeth in a unified click.

James let his breath out hard as he glanced at Laura, whose eyes burned with an open threat. The direction of the conversation had the potential to get real ugly real fast. He could feel his wife whipping herself up into what could become a sudden tirade, and Lord knew the woman held a grudge like nobody's business. He glanced at Steve, who shrugged and left him hanging.

Trying to forestall any further issues, James held up his hands in front of his chest and spoke as calmly and as rationally as possible under the circumstances. "I was just saying that I understood that if the brother was saying goodbye to his new lady and it got intense, time has a way of slipping by. We *all* know how that kinda thing can happen, so let's not act like we don't." Satisfied that both Najira and Laura looked away, and that Steve was now studying the ceiling, James pressed his point. "And if the woman didn't come clean with Jamal and she got him in a position, you know—hey."

Steve shook his head and chuckled. "How big is this sonofabitch we've gotta do a vehicle trade with?"

"Huge," Jamal said, looking much improved by the male support in the room.

"Now my man and our cousin's husband could go get

shot behind your booty chasing. Just great." Najira flopped back down on the sofa and folded her arms over her bosom again. "You didn't even think about that, did you?"

"Hey, people," Jamal said, looking around the room. "I don't want anybody to get hurt. It's not even worth it. I can just leave off his Jeep somewhere, call her, tell her where it is, you know . . . and—"

"We'll do this the old-fashioned way," James said calmly. "Real smooth. Local cops know we used to be one of them—old school respect, and since we occasionally do some PI work to help them out, we have a few lightweight markers that we can call in."

"Man, Philly never looked so good to me," Jamal said, raking his fingers down the oiled parts in his scalp between his cornrows, remembering how Safia had touched him there. "I can't wait to go home for a few. Fuck all this beach and warm weather and palm trees and shit. I'll take the concrete and frostbite of home any damned day over this madcap bullshit."

"If I'm reading my partner right," Steve said with a grin, "we'll have the boys in blue go by your lady's joint, if they haven't already from the gunshots, give the chick and her man the Jeep keys, and go in with the cops to get yours, plus get your wallet, cell, and clothes. Whatever's missing, you're just gonna have to suck it up and call your credit card companies to reissue."

"Right," James agreed. "No doubt all your cash will be gone, too, not to mention whatever was of value in your Hummer—"

"Oh, maaaan . . . all my CDs . . ."

"Yeah, but you're alive," James said, shaking his head, "and it's a good thing you never took off your Rolex. But this doesn't need to make it to an episode of *Cops.*"

"No doubt," Jamal said with a sigh. "No fucking doubt."

Shattered Trust

Villa on Grand Cayman, Present day

James Carter's skin was like dark, bittersweet chocolate. Smooth, a confection that had slowly melted in her mouth all night long, a flavor that she could still savor hours later on the back of her tongue.

Laura stood in the kitchen of their newly rebuilt house, her hands besotted with mango nectar, as she meticulously peeled the skin away from the fruit and watched dawn burn the dew from the hibiscus that nearly covered her kitchen windows with their bright-hued wash of color. Heaven on earth.

After the terrible storms that had decimated the property over a year ago, only her battered memory of the disaster remained. There was no physical evidence left of the destruction. So why were their souls restless after more than a year of hiatus from the hectic, insane urban reality of Philly? she wondered. All those who'd hunted them had been either imprisoned or permanently neutralized by death. Her family was no longer at risk, nor was she in peril. The money was righteous; she'd come out holding financial aces worth millions once she was done. Therefore, the quiet, nagging feeling of unrest made no sense.

Her wild and crazy cousin, Najira, was safe and sound and living not far from their house on the island with James's partner, Steve, and her brother Jamal. Their father, her Uncle Akhan, had healed nicely, and was back in his old home in North Philly, safe. Her sisters and their children were stateside, well provided for, and going on about their normal lives without interruption. So why the case of nerves?

The only thing she could chalk it up to was memories . . . gruesome, visceral memories of treacherous games, dangerous liaisons, and heavy losses. Like the angry storms that had swept through Florida and the Caribbean, she'd swept through Philadelphia's black elite and had served a harsh blow of justice like a force of nature. Yet, by all accounts, it seemed as though the landscape had healed over, things had gone back to normal, and all evidence of her wrath was invisible to the naked eye.

But that didn't mean it hadn't happened. It had. Infrastructure had been rebuilt, just like it had been in paradise. Power, literally and figuratively, had been restored. Roads, water sources, homes, and buildings had been newly constructed and replaced. However, no one forgot what had taken place not so long ago. Every time it rained hard, people were wary. Human nature. Every time folks probably heard her name in Philly, she was also aware that they most likely whispered about Hurricane Laura in hushed, reverent tones. So be it.

What was there to do? She and Najira finally accepted the reality that her fund-raising business was dead from it all; it had died on the vine from foundations, politicians, and grant sources too wary of her capacity to inflict destruction to accept proposals. Thus, like some of the facilities in the Caribbean that would never come back after the storms, she'd ultimately shut down Rainmakers, Inc., and had given all loyal employees a hefty severance with glowing recommendations. Rest in peace. She and her small inner circle could live off the residuals of millions. Whatever. Maybe it was finally just time to meld into the obscure and become a private citizen again.

Laura rinsed her hands and reached up into the cabinet for the coffee to begin a fresh pot. Carefully opening the vacuum-sealed mason jar of fresh beans, she breathed in deeply before dumping some into the small grinder. Her new husband was like black coffee, too. . . . James always filled up a room without saying a word and eclipsed all vacancies within it, silently, mysteriously, and lingered in her subconscious with his wonderful aroma. In a very quiet way, he'd filled up her spirit like that as well, a gentle force that created an urge, a hankering that could rarely be ignored.

He poured over her senses still, hours later. The pungent scent of their lovemaking clung to her skin beneath her dampened robe. Remnants of his sticky essence made the flesh of her thighs fuse together as she made coffee and a small plate of fruit. She stared at the huge diamond on her hand, allowing the natural sunlight to bathe it and sparkle in the facets. More than a year of rapture, and her soul was now restless. Why?

For all his slow, calm delivery of words and actions, she could feel something palpable constantly roiling just beneath the surface of James's skin. He seemed to be at peace, but wasn't . . . like her. In fact, as she turned the dilemma over and over in her mind, Najira and Steve also had a quiet desperation in their eyes when they all got together. The only one who was being honest was Jamal. He'd flat out admitted that for all the glory of paradise, he was bored.

Laura pressed the top of the Cuisinart grinder and the aroma of freshly ground coffee entered her nose. The slight hum in the kitchen connected to her spinal column and she lifted her hand; the noise seemed out of place in the early morning silence. This hour required reverence, stillness. The atrocities of the world seemed so far away, yet she knew they were also close enough to breathe against her ear until the hair at the nape of her neck stood up.

"Hey," a quiet male voice whispered from the kitchen doorway.

She didn't turn around or start. "Hey," she said calmly. "I was making coffee and some fruit. You want some?"

Laura glanced over her shoulder. James leaned against the doorframe and raked his hair, but didn't sit down.

They both just looked at each other for a moment.

"I know," she said quietly, and then went back to the task of finding a filter for the pot.

He nodded. "You feeling it, too?"

"Yeah," she said just above a whisper and added water to the coffeemaker. "How long have you?"

"Couple of months," he admitted and entered the kitchen. "Something's nagging my gut."

"It isn't over, is it?" She stopped making coffee and stared at him. "Your gut is never wrong, James. Neither is mine."

He slowly sat down in a chair, closed his eyes, and leaned his head back against the wall. "I know, baby. I know."

James let his breath out in an audible sigh. She turned on the coffeemaker and came to the table to sit across from him.

"You first," she said with a half smile.

He opened his eyes and ran his palms down his face and gave her a sheepish grin. "That's not what you said last night."

She chuckled. "Yeah, I know. But you're avoiding the subject. So, since I got mine multiple times last night—you first, this morning."

He nodded and chuckled with her, leaning on his forearms on the table as he sat forward to stare at her. "I'm not trying to blow the groove, Laura, but I've got this weird feeling like . . . like it's too quiet. I keep telling myself that it's just because I'm not used to a life without drama that I'm feeling like the other shoe is about to drop. Does that make sense?"

She leaned forward and clasped his hands within hers. "Yeah, I know exactly how you feel. I've been reading the newspapers from back home online."

He chuckled, squeezed her hands gently, and then sat back. "I thought we were gonna banish the States for a while?"

She smiled and stood. "How about that coffee?"

He watched her move to the counter, loving the way her shapely body flowed beneath the peach silk of her robe. Her cinnamon brown skin looked like it sucked up the color of the fabric and reflected it back out through her pores. Her short, dark, velvety hair was a mussed profusion of curls on top of her head, evidence of the torrid night before. "Coffee, huh?" he said, trying to keep his nature at bay as he watched her fix their morning brew. "Isn't that how this all got started a long time ago?"

She laughed and glimpsed him over her shoulder. He loved the way her dark, smoldering eyes glistened with mischief in the privacy of their kitchen . . . and the way her lush mouth pouted as she devised a comeback line. He waited patiently for her and the coffee, wondering why he was trying to ruin paradise. It made no sense.

He had all that any man could want. Screw the fledgling detective agency. He and Steve could open a small water sports business by the resorts and live out the rest of their lives in peace. What better way for two ex-cops to retire? They had both made it out alive, whatever gunshot wounds they'd sustained had earned them citations, they'd healed, had gotten out of the system with a solid pension, and they'd even scored a nice profit from their one and only job. There was no need to stir the pot with unfounded worries. But his gut was never wrong.

Laura brought two mugs of coffee to the table with a fruit plate and slid into a padded wicker chair. "Your coffee," she announced, and then sipped her java with a sly smile.

"And the Internet says what?" he said, taking a slow sip and then picking up a piece of mango from the plate, his eyes never leaving hers.

"The good senator resigned office and got off with a spurious plea bargain. He's been acquitted. All charges against him have been focused on the doctor, Senator Scott's errant son, and dead people."

James nodded and put the piece of mango in his mouth, half chewing, half sucking the flavor of the sweetness, and allowing his tongue to enjoy it before answering her. "Figured as much," he said, casually sucking the juice off his fingers. "If he went down, a lot of other very high-ranking politicians all the way to D.C. would have also gone down, baby. You know how this goes."

She sighed and took a piece of fruit up from the plate, stared at it for a moment, and then popped it into her mouth. "Uhmm, hmmm," she mumbled, chewing. "It's a viper's nest all the way to the top. That's why I shut down Rainmakers."

He smiled and slurped his coffee. "So, if you're out of the grant-making and political fund-raising business, then why are you following the stateside news like a hawk?

"I'm not, really." Her gaze slid away from his with a smile.

"My Scorpio wife is such a gorgeous liar," he said, leaning his head back and dangling another piece of fruit above his mouth, and then allowing it to drop in.

She laughed. "It's not a lie. It's—"

"An evasion. Talk to me, Laura." He smiled and leaned forward, taking up his coffee again. "What are you up to?"

"Nothing," she said sheepishly, sipping her brew and staring at him over the rim of her mug. She set it down with precision. "I'm just watching our backs."

He slurped his brew with a half smile. "You've got serious trust issues, baby." He set his mug down calmly. "But I can't talk too bad about you, because so do I."

"You've been online, too, I take it?"

He chuckled. "You know me well."

"You're worried, too?"

His smile faded. "We did a lot of damage. People with an axe to grind are out in the world again—temporarily gone, but not forgotten."

Her grip tightened around her mug, although her facial expression remained serene. "You think I need to get Akhan out of Philly?"

"Might not hurt to bring him in close with the family down here for a while, until our guts ain't in a knot."

They both stared at each other for a moment.

"You know my uncle loves his community and won't leave Philly."

"I know," James said quietly. "He's one of those old-school warriors that will be there until the bitter end with a shotgun at his door, talkin' about ain't no revenuers coming on his property."

Laura sighed and smiled. "You've talked to him."

James smiled and nodded. "So have Najira and Jamal. Repeatedly."

"I see," Laura said, taking up her coffee again. "Glad to know I'm not the only one with secrets."

He laughed and shook his head, his hand sliding under the table to stroke her thigh. "Nope. But it was all with good intent."

The heat of his hand there made her relax, just as much as his words had. It was oddly comforting to know that he was also on alert and that she was not alone in her wariness.

"Now that I'm fully awake," he said in a low murmur, "and I've had some Joe . . . I have other intentions that are *real* good, too."

"Hmmm . . . sounds like an attempt to distract me."

"No, more like an attempt to relax you and to get that big brain of yours to let go of what we can't do anything about until it happens."

"I like to be prepared for the worst-case scenario," she said, closing her eyes as his hand stroked warmth into the flesh of her leg.

"Me, too," he said quietly, still caressing her thigh. "We'll get Akhan to visit, for an extended stay. I can beef up security here and I know Steve is on the same page."

She opened her eyes. "You're not worried about an actual physical hit, are you? I was more thinking in terms of some financial attack, something to screw us business-wise, or to shut down our contacts to entrepreneurial ventures back home."

James pulled back his hand and leaned forward to clasp hers. This was exactly what he didn't want her to think about. Truthfully, it was exactly what he didn't want to consider, but had to, especially now that the subject had been broached.

"Laura, listen to me. The man's son will be behind bars until the end of time. His niece was killed, shot by her own husband—whom I'm sure they all know by now that you had a hand in bringing down, even if they'll never be sure how. All his cronies and contracts were fucked. The man's reputation was so badly damaged that he can't even get a job in a 7-Eleven back home. All his allies have distanced themselves from him. The casino boys won't even jeopardize their construction contracts to help him out, given that the big eye in the sky, the media, has been all over this thing like white on rice. To my mind that leaves an old man with nothing to lose, a lot of time and energy to focus on vengeance . . . which you and I both know can fuel the craziest of things in a person for years, baby."

She squeezed his hands tightly and let her gaze drift out of the window toward the horizon. James slipped his hands out of her grasp and stood, rounding the table to stand behind her and caress her shoulders.

"I didn't want to worry you," he murmured, bending to land a kiss on the top of her head.

"I'm all right. Just thinking."

His hands slid down her shoulders in a slow, comforting rub back and forth. "No you're not. But that's OK. I got this, baby. Maybe that's why you married a cop."

She forced herself to smile. "You still have your Peace-keeper?"

He leaned down and nuzzled her neck. "Yep, plus a shotgun, a rifle, two nines, and plenty of shells."

He felt her body tense and gently pulled her up from the chair to embrace her. "I told Mr. and Mrs. Melville the situation a few weeks ago. The man is coming this week to install a security alarm system in here that should have been a part of the rebuild while construction was going on, anyway. Plus security cameras . . . and I've alerted the island authorities of any potential issues. Steve's getting his house wired, too, with a monitor in his office that links to ours—plus panic buttons."

Laura laid her head on his shoulder, her hands caressing his back. "You're really worried, aren't you?"

His answer was a tender kiss. "No . . . I just have trust issues." He forced himself to smile for her sake, and knew she had done the same for him.

She looked into her new husband's intense, dark eyes and saw an old fear flicker within them. She understood it well, and knew the same was frozen within hers.

Without more conversation, she surrendered to his method of banishing reality as his hands untied the sash of her robe. Yes, she understood his need to touch skin, to keep himself rooted in the present. That had also become her need.

His mouth took hers in a slow opening of lips, a gentle duet of tongues, and she understood that their minds no longer had amnesty from the past, now that the dread had been admitted and named. Paradise had been compromised, but coffee-sweetened mango still tasted so good first thing in the morning. Their hiatus had been a placebo; they knew that. Caresses and passionate days and nights were just anesthesia . . . an endorphin rush, like morphine, to chase away the adrenaline tension of bad nerves. That didn't matter right now.

She helped him shed his burgundy silk boxers, and allowed him to lead her back to the kitchen chair. She totally understood James's way of saying, "Baby, I'm worried." That was her way of banishing fear, too.

It was all in his eyes, the way he took her mouth again ever so gently as she carefully straddled his lap. It was all in his touch, the way it grazed over the surface of her skin like she was fragile glass. It had been so obvious in his newfound interest in opening a small sporting goods shop with Steve . . . the way they'd both talked in rapid-fire sentences about the most mundane of things; serving burgers and light fare, frozen drinks, Najira doing the books, Jamal working the registers, her marketing the concept to the resorts.

She understood that James's way was an easy slide into the present that kept him anchored, the same way he'd just slid into her. His motions were steady, not rushed, like his planning. Methodical to the point of crazy-making was his trademark, unraveling her resistance to let go of the past and the tension, one slow stroke at a time . . . his unspoken signature making her keep her eyes on him, her eyes on the present not the past, a gentling of her spirit, the way one would calm a frightened thoroughbred. *Just don't look down and come to me,* his touch beckoned, hands gliding over the now too-sensitive tips of her breasts, causing her soft gasp, which he swallowed.

"I got this," he whispered into her mouth.

She swallowed his promise with a slight shudder. "I

know," she murmured against his neck, allowing her fingers to revel in his short-cropped hair, the slight waves within it teasing her fingertips. Her husband knew her very, very well, just like she knew him and could tell that he needed her to stay in the here and now.

Releasing the threat of tomorrow, she bore down on him harder, gently rotating her hips in a slow, undulating circle that finally drew a quiet gasp from him and made him close his eyes.

God yes, his wife knew him so very, very well, and the disturbing conversation began to ebb and flow like her hips, pushing itself into the far recesses of his mind. His hands found her tight, fleshy backside as her hands rested gently against his shoulders. Thoughts of possible hit men embedded in their future seemed so remote as he became more deeply embedded within her, their thigh muscles working in unison, in partnership to keep their slow, steady rhythm, the flow of agonizing movements unbroken.

He loved the way coffee and mango lingered in her sweet kiss . . . the way her tongue explored the inside of his mouth, pulling a moan up from his lungs as her tempo increased ever so slightly. Yeah . . . right now, nothing else mattered, and that was just the way he liked it—easy. Nothing too profound. Her body heating until he could feel a light sheen of perspiration beginning to claim it. Her voice a muffled whimper grazing the soft tissue of his palate, something to savor and allow to hold him hostage, just like her natural scent.

She threw her head back and gave him access to kiss her windpipe, and down to the soft cleft at the base of her throat, her full, pendulous breasts swaying slightly to every rise and fall of her voluptuous body against his—easy. Coffee with her in the morning, have mercy. A slow sip of hard, java-hued nipples between his lips; his most favorite of ways to begin the day.

"Laura." One strangled word, her name, brought her back

to him hard, and fast, and hot—scalding . . . making him meet her where she was, close to the edge, as the burn ran down his shaft and imploded in his sac.

She moved against him like a sudden island rain, pelting his groin with intense pleasure, no longer a slow dissolve of his sanity. This morning wasn't a light shower, but had opened up to an unexpected, torrential downpour—an event that would now happen quickly before the clouds parted and allowed in the sun of her smile again.

Humid, wet, she contracted against him, consuming worry, washing it away with a steady beat against his hard ground until he almost lifted them both out of the chair with each upward thrust. The steady sound of the wicker's groan was no comparison to his, her breaths now a chant of urgent compliance—easy was gone, heat surreal. His hands in her hair, not long, needing the feel of her fleshy backside, her hips to anchor and gain leverage until he could barely breathe.

The sound of his voice thundering throughout the kitchen had done her in. *Slow*, what was that? *Tender*, the word had lost meaning. Patience was an impossible concept when she could feel his definition sliding within her . . . the head, the groove of it pulling against her agony-fired canal, lodged so tightly inside her that she could feel the vein pulsing down his engorged shaft to the wide berth of his base each time he drew out again.

Then he'd found that spot like he always did. His tight, muscular legs were pushing them both up and half-out of the chair till she nearly shrieked it felt so good. Every bulge of six-packed abdominal sinew worked like a hard, fast sit-up, his arms steel cable wrapped around her waist—her hands ached to hold his fantastic stone-carved ass, but his massive shoulders were all she had access to.

His touch was now a severe, aggressive sweep of pleasure against every aching place on her skin, leaving her unable to take enough of him into her fast enough, hard enough. Forget about tomorrow, when his name became a non sequitur fused with the Almighty's, "OhmigodJames!"

Head thrown back, mouth open for air, he felt the first lightning strike arch her, and then it immediately sent a crack-whip of motion down her spine that opened him up to a pure holler. Nails in his shoulders, he didn't care, just don't stop the electric current; let it flow. Jags of pleasure sent a convulsing wave through his scrotum that he couldn't hold back if his life depended on it. Her body froze like her gasp had for a second as though she'd been hit with another sudden jolt of lightning, then she released in repeated, jerking shudders that ruined him to thunder her name one more time.

And just as quickly as it had begun, the storm was over. Damp forehead to forehead they stayed in the chair for a long while, breathing hard, clinging to each other, dazed.

When he could finally focus and open his eyes, she peered down at him with a brilliant smile like the island sun had just come out again.

He wiped his brow with the back of his forearm and let out a deep exhale. She dabbed at her cleavage with the heel of her palm, chasing a tiny trickle of sweat that rolled down between her breasts. He watched the perspiration, his eyes following the path of it until she'd blotted it dry, his mouth also going dry in the process. Lord, his woman was fine.

"Good morning to you, too," she said with a soft chuckle and then kissed the bridge of his nose. "Want another cup of coffee?"

"Maybe in an hour," he said, smiling, and dropped his head to her shoulder, beat. "Coffee like this every morning might kill me, woman."

GREAT BOOKS,
GREAT SAVINGS!

When You Visit Our Website:
www.kensingtonbooks.com

You Can Save Money Off The Retail Price
Of Any Book You Purchase!

- **All Your Favorite Kensington Authors**
- **New Releases & Timeless Classics**
- **Overnight Shipping Available**
- **eBooks Available For Many Titles**
- **All Major Credit Cards Accepted**

Visit Us Today To Start Saving!
www.kensingtonbooks.com

All Orders Are Subject To Availability.
Shipping and Handling Charges Apply.
Offers and Prices Subject To Change Without Notice.

Look For These Other
Dafina Novels

If I Could   by Donna Hill
0-7582-0131-1   **$6.99**US/**$9.99**CAN

Thunderland   by Brandon Massey
0-7582-0247-4   **$6.99**US/**$9.99**CAN

June In Winter   by Pat Phillips
0-7582-0375-6   **$6.99**US/**$9.99**CAN

Yo Yo Love   by Daaimah S. Poole
0-7582-0239-3   **$6.99**US/**$9.99**CAN

When Twilight Comes   by Gwynne Forster
0-7582-0033-1   **$6.99**US/**$9.99**CAN

It's A Thin Line   by Kimberla Lawson Roby
0-7582-0354-3   **$6.99**US/**$9.99**CAN

Perfect Timing   by Brenda Jackson
0-7582-0029-3   **$6.99**US/**$9.99**CAN

Never Again Once More   by Mary B. Morrison
0-7582-0021-8   **$6.99**US/**$8.99**CAN

Available Wherever Books Are Sold!

Check out our website at www.kensingtonbooks.com.

Grab These Dafina Thrillers

From

Brandon Massey

__Twisted Tales
0-7582-1353-0   **$6.99**US/**$9.99**CAN

__The Other Brother
0-7582-1072-8   **$6.99**US/**$9.99**CAN

__Within The Shadows
0-7582-1070-1   **$6.99**US/**$9.99**CAN

__Dark Corner
0-7582-0250-4   **$6.99**US/**$9.99**CAN

__Thunderland
0-7582-0247-4   **$6.99**US/**$9.99**CAN

Available Wherever Books Are Sold!

Visit our website at **www.kensingtonbooks.com**.

More of the Hottest
African-American Fiction from
Dafina Books

Come With Me   0-7582-1935-0 $6.99/$9.99
J.S. Hawley

Golden Night   0-7582-1977-6 $6.99/$9.99
Candice Poarch

No More Lies   0-7582-1601-7 $6.99/$9.99
Rachel Skerritt

Perfect For You   0-7582-1979-2 $6.99/$9.99
Sylvia Lett

Risk   0-7582-1434-0 $6.99/$9.99
Ann Christopher

Available Wherever Books Are Sold!

Visit our website at **www.kensingtonbooks.com**.